JENNY

G000069804

IN THREE PARTS

BY

Ivan A Peartree

To Joe every good wish
+ much love Dad.
+
thanks for all you do
for me

An environmentally friendly book printed and bound in England by
www.printondemand-worldwide.com

Mixed Sources
Product group from well-managed
forests, and other controlled sources
www.fsc.org Cert no. TT-COC-002641
© 1996 Forest Stewardship Council

FSC

PEFC
PEFC/16-33-415

PEFC Certified
This product is
from sustainably
managed forests
and controlled
sources
www.pefc.org

This book is made entirely of chain-of-custody materials

Ivan A Peartree

www.fast-print.net/store.php

Jenny – In three parts
Copyright © Ivan A Peartree 2013

A catalogue record for this book is available from the British Library

ISBN 978-178035-591-7

First published 2013 by
FASTPRINT PUBLISHING
Peterborough, England.

FOR CLARK

EXPRESSIONS OF LONELINESS

Loneliness is oft a mournful place in which to be ensnared. It is a place where timorous people go to flee the crowded streets of man so that for the while they may be installed in worthy peacefulness and thereby gain assurance of their complete and utter self.

It is a place where desolate people go to seek a fond connection and to gather world approval as the mother of the young. Then to nurture that loving friendship which others deem unreal, until the falseness fades away and love alone remain.

It is a place to hide away from fear that harms the undefended, when cowering is the only means to pass that dread away.

It is where all manner of orphans go, no matter what their age, and so consent to a surrogate's care whilst eagerness remain.

It is a place where learning seeks to reinforce the skills of youth and so to add to that already learned from life's abounding depths.

It is a place to hide when all around is mixed and muddled up, when worthlessness appears one's only friend in all of life's depressing gloom. A place to go, as well, to sort the strife that life can throw at times, and so persuade a troubled mind to seek tranquillity.

It is a place where a torn in sunder heart seeks tender healing refuge till long lost love is eventually restored; but for the while, in that warming solitude, be soothed from heartfelt grief.

It is a place where the sick and dying go to await decision's hour, perchance to gain a respite or go where angels lead.

PART ONE

CHAPTER ONE

It was a dank and dreary early morning that swathed the southern area of Dorset's county in the early part of April, nineteen hundred and fifty three.

The hazy sun, being vaguely seen through small breaks in the passing rain clouds, which had already served their purpose overnight, attempted to fulfil its original intention, as the morning of the day changed its mind and attempted to be more charitable and well behaved.

A pretty girl, fast approaching the twelfth year of her young life and who had spent the biggest part of that uneasy time fully friendless, walked tentatively through the rain drenched grassy mead next to the dark, broad-leaved forest that had stood for centuries close to her home in the heart of Dorset's scenic lands.

Suddenly, she stopped her saunter and stood awhile as she listened to an unfamiliar and far carrying tapping sound. A greater spotted woodpecker was revealing its presence by drumming away at the thick, crinkly-barked trunk of an oak tree that had stood for nigh on two hundred years next to the mother that had seeded it.

She stole a little closer in order to catch sight of the industrious bird intermittently employed at its tapping display; and with her eyes sparkling and looking upward and her close attention focused solely on the drumming sound and not on where she was going, she stumbled as she caught her foot in a rabbit's burrow close to the wire netting fence that bordered the forest; and pitching forward, she sprawled headlong onto the dirty, rain drenched, grassy ground.

As she raised herself her little face became distorted in mental anguish and disbelief. She opened wide her eyes and lips to scream in terror but no sound was heard to come from that grief stricken, gaping mouth, not straight away, for fear had taken control enough to prevent a single sound escaping.

She had come face to face with the most horrific scene imaginable to a small child of tender years; one that none alive would ever care to see. Her only feline friend had been caught by his hind legs in an evil gin trap that had been deliberately placed to catch any reckless passer-by that dared to chance its luck. And in a hopeless attempt to free himself from those steely jaws, the blue-grey cat had further added to its misery.

Wicked wounds, caused by the slashing of those devilish jaws, through which the broken bones of both hind legs protruded, were stained by dried, brown blood. Stretched bare skin that once had been covered with fine fur was alive with maggots, while the vilest of foul flies flitted and buzzed around. And the mouth, opened by its agony, showed the tiny gaps between the white front teeth to be infiltrated by the same brown, dried up blood as other fly-blown, pus producing maggots slithered in and out.

Its festering neck and rapidly rotting body had been greedily gorged and then abandoned by the fearless carrion crows and after all this agony had been completed the remains had been left desolately disarranged. The finale was the leaving of the now vile carcass to its inevitable grizzly fate that in its turn would be the cause of many a tear to flow.

***

This little girl, who lived with her wealthy parents, was watched over and sternly schooled by a formidable governess. And the small family, including staff, shared the many spacious rooms of a huge Victorian mansion set in the tiny village of Hyde in the midst of a vast setting of scenic grounds; although a show of appreciation for what was habitually theirs was nowhere to be seen.

No pleasure was gained by the child living in such an influential home as this either, how could there have been, since the whole place was devoid of love. And so it was that this particular little girl was steeped in loneliness - a loneliness that seemed to heed no bounds.

And with no siblings to share her tedium and help pass each dreary day away; her self reliance was increased beyond all measure as her dependence on other people's care diminished to non-existence.

But for little Jennifer Kent one saviour, from this unpleasant situation, had been Bluey. Bluey had entered the scene, and then her life, just two years previously; the day after Jenny had reached her tenth birthday, in actual fact, and at a time when she was experiencing one of her lowest ebbs of loneliness.

The larger than life, fluffy haired, Blue Persian cat, with its broad round head and its rather stocky body, had suddenly appeared as a total stranger - from nowhere as it were - and from the very beginning he made it clear that he was to be seen and not handled in any way. He had spat and hissed at the little girl for days, whenever she'd gone too close to him, but he had never thought for a single moment to escape from the loving attention that Jenny offered him.

A full four days had passed before the child was able to befriend the cat with any degree of confidence. But on that final day, Bluey succumbed to all the affection that was on offer; at last she had convinced him that not the entire human race was evil and devoid of kindness and that even a little girl such as Jenny could be trusted like no other.

And so the couple, the little girl of ten and the cat of no known age, became close friends, the one loving and trusting the other implicitly, and without any of the usual misgivings resulting that are often associated with relations of this sort.

Never and on no account, of course, was the cat allowed in or near the big house; far too mangy and flea ridden for such a privilege; she'd had no need to ask.

Because Bluey's food was not included in the household budget, Jenny would help herself to tasty morsels of meat and fish, or whatever else she could lay her hands on from the table or from the kitchen too: that is, when cook had had her back turned.

She would then take the titbits to the rear of the house close to the old tool shed where Bluey constantly passed the day and night away. And it was there the now inseparable twosome would play and purr away together in contented harmony.

Two years had silently passed away and the same routine was still in place; and so it continued both summer and winter with the cat finding himself a hidey-hole in the old tool shed to shield him from the winter's chill.

On one particular morning when Jenny, with her discreetly hidden paper bag, turned up at the usual place, Bluey was nowhere to be seen. Jenny searched the shrubbery, every nook and corner of the garden, way out into the fields she went and into the surrounding woods as well but nowhere could she find her devoted friend.

Two very long weeks passed slowly by with Jenny still intent on searching the whole place whenever the opportunity presented itself but her friend failed to show himself at his usual place of hiding - or anywhere else, for that matter.

Eventually, feeling heartbroken and devastated, little Jennifer Kent surrendered all belief in ever finding her only friend again, although the habit in searching continued; and she turned in on herself once more in disheartened hope and loneliness.

"For loneliness is oft a mournful place in which to be

ensnared. It is a place where a torn in sunder heart seeks tender healing refuge till long lost love is eventually restored; but for the while, in that warming solitude, be soothed from heartfelt grief."

***

Sir Angus and Lady Margaret Kent made a striking pair and although not overly thoughtful or attentive in the usual manner befitting that of parenthood, they did in fact recognise their child's birthday - and every Christmas was celebrated as well; not with their small daughter in mind perhaps - but it was celebrated for all that. By mentioning this, one might well assume the Kents to be rather selfish people - well they were - selfish to the core, in fact, for although they always exchanged time and pleasantries with everyone else in their limited world they had found precious little time to share with Jenny.

In spite of this, they would tell you they were kindly enough toward their only child and willingly referred to her as 'Jenny' when a happy occasion warranted it, or 'Jennifer' when the need arose, quite as if this was the be-all and end-all of loving parenting; but it was mostly Jennifer when they referred to their daughter and hardly ever Jenny, even though the little girl much preferred the latter name.

Sir Angus was a tall, upright, distinguished looking man for the age of forty-two; with brown, swept back hair that was sparingly greased and vaguely greying at the sides with a slightly waved appearance that added to its attractiveness - but which was in nowise curling.

His large hazel eyes were always actively directing their attention to everything that was going on around, forever seeking the main chance, one might assume. And at each and every opportunity he would closely scrutinise all that was in his easy reach with the sole purpose of gaining control; for gaining control of everyone and everything was his sole purpose in life.

His generous mouth, set above the squarest jaw, was lined on either side with well defined lines of discontent and aggravation and his high forehead repeated the same imprinted frustration furrows there. But all of this gave the gentleman a distinguished countenance, a deservedly distinguished countenance, he would argue, which he cherished above all else.

Although he possessed a vanity that was obvious to everyone who came in contact with him, he was totally unaware of the fact himself. He considered his humility to be beyond reproach for in his own eyes he portrayed a fine gentleman of longstanding who had

7

achieved the pinnacle of modesty, and only noticed vanity or any other human inadequacies in everybody else.

He enjoyed all the pomposity his station in life afforded; and the continuous and unconditional respect and admiration that other people seemed so keen to heap upon him only served to heighten his already inflated ego.

Sir Angus mostly dressed conservatively in sombre colours, and in order to symbolize his Scottish ancestry he wore a plaid bow tie at every hour of the day; except of course when riding, which seemed less and less often these days, oh, and of course in the evenings when he always dressed for dinner.

His long tapering fingers possessed a spotlessly clean appearance with perfectly manicured, almond shaped nails filed neatly short. And his brown brogue footwear was always immaculately clean and shining: probably dating back to his former army days in India where Jenny was born - or by the shoe shiner's assertive efforts.

Jenny's mother, the former Margaret Wood, had been married to Sir Angus Kent exactly two years to the day before their only child was born. She was a tall slender woman with an attractive countenance and a striking figure that set her apart from other women of her age. But all these fine features were beginning to desert her by this time owing to her feelings of almost total despondency. Self imposed despondency, as everyone knows, can have an adverse affect on ones facial appearance, which, in her case was brought about by her horrifying daughter's unruly temperament; well of course - what else?

And to cap it all, it seems that Jenny had a liking for her own company rather than seeking the company of others and especially as far as her own mother's company was concerned. The child had developed this infuriating inclination toward self reliance slowly over the years but which had nothing whatsoever to do with the mother - or so Margaret had convinced herself.

So, all in all, the bond between mother and daughter was not a healthy one; at least, not as healthy as the bonding a more normal mother would have enjoyed with her only child.

This disjointed mother and daughter relationship, coupled with her husband's appalling infidelity, which Margaret had discovered during the immediate period prior to her giving birth to her daughter, seemed to have provided her with seasoned comfort within a state of laziness, a laziness she had developed for herself over the years. This, coupled with a condition of self-obsession, made Margaret what she was today: an idle, self-centred woman who had little time for others - least of all for her lovely daughter.

Both of these circumstances, that is, the situation with her daughter and that of her husband, were solely responsible for her so called 'unremitting misery' and she dwelt upon both difficulties incessantly. Of course, this only served to exacerbate the constant 'thinking about herself' disorder and instead of seeking remedies for the plight, which, a more normal persons might be tempted to do, she tolerated them and wallowed in their existence and in her own self-pity.

The birth of her daughter had not, by any stretch of the imagination, been an easy one for Margaret: her extremely low pain threshold had seen to that, and of course, the degrading condition of being pregnant in the first place; and so she had allowed this incredibly painful birthing incident, together with her husband's infidelity, to remain in her mind and to provide her with this favoured but unsavoury excuse to set herself apart from her daughter; she concluding that all would have been well with the marital home and the situation as a whole had Jennifer never been born at all.

Not that Margaret was continuously at enmity with her child in an obvious way, not outwardly - or so she would have you believe - for Margaret never possessed an enemy in the entire world; she thought that was abundantly clear to everyone. Why, even her husband's extramarital behaviour had been continually ignored and she had never allowed herself to betray the fact of the knowledge she possessed for all those years, to anyone; not to a living soul. She didn't wish harm to her own flesh and blood either, that is to say her daughter, not deep down; except on the odd occasion when a bout of extreme selfishness took control of her spirit - which seemed to be more often these days than ever before.

Margaret Kent did, however, in her own self-righteous way, try to bring about a state of sociability to her daughter's life, within the confines of her own capabilities that is - but just the once. A personal friend from her distant childhood who resided close by and who was blessed with a daughter of Jenny's age was approached by Margaret and with a lukewarm attempt she had futilely introduced the two girls together. But it hadn't worked out for little Jennifer Kent and so she stayed as she was, quiet and alone. But then, Jenny did seem to have this strange, built-in covering shell about her, an almost impenetrable cocoon it seemed, which would only be broken when the child was good and ready.

9

....

Eventually a cry for help did break forth from those terrified lips. Not a loud scream as others might screech at such a fright as this: for Jenny was not in the habit of betraying her own feelings, even to herself, but a cry loud enough to express her own fear of hopelessness at the finding of her Bluey in this state of wretchedness.

She tried, with many desperate efforts, to pull back the evil jaws of the trap that so firmly and maliciously latched on to those tender legs; the legs he had used so effectively to leap into her arms but through lack of bodily strength coupled with nervous panic she was unable to shift the rusting metal.

Tears of alarm, now streaming down her pretty face, fell gently on her furry friend as she continually plied her feeble force and in this mindless effort she tore the flesh on her own hands until the child's blood mingled with Bluey's upon the red stained, sodden ground.

'What in hell's name are you trying to do?' asked a stern enquiring voice, from the forest side of the barbed wire fencing.

Jenny looked up instantly and her eyes narrowed as she temporarily ceased her labour of love.

'What does it look like I'm doing, you stupid man?' replied Jenny, still beside herself in painful grief and answering one question with another,

'I'm trying to undo the evil jaws of this wretched trap in which you have so cruelly caught my cat.'

The weather worn lad of eighteen or thereabouts, with long, straight, jet-black hair and a pleasant enough look attending him, carried a bold earthiness and displayed the widest grin that would instil confidence in everyone he met.

He slung a short handled, narrow bladed spade over the fence, which was quickly followed by a string net and a wicker basket. He then straddled the fence before positioning himself beside the little girl and studied the unhappy scene closely.

'Here, give that to me young 'un... let me take a look,' he instructed, and taking the devise and cat from Jenny's hands he commenced to ease the jaws of the gin thereby freeing Bluey's mangled body and shook all the filthy maggots to the ground.

'Thank you,' said Jenny, trembling, and with a single tear stealing from the corner of her eye once again, she looked into the stranger's face as he placed the cat on the ground at her feet.

'What are you howling for young 'un? It's not you who was caught in the gin y'know, only a silly cat,' said the youth, still smiling.

'I'm crying because you killed my Bluey and he meant the world to me,' answered Jenny, wiping her face with the sleeve of her dress.

'For a start, he's not your cat anyway... he's mine,' stated the youth, his smile levelling out. 'See the split in his left ear; he got that from scrapping with my other tom. I lost him a couple of years back, haven't seen him since but I'd know that old cat of mine anywhere. And besides... that's not one of my traps; don't use the wicked things, must belong to some poacher or other or one of the gamekeepers they probably keep up at the big house yonder. That's where you come from I shouldn't wonder... well, am I right?'

'Yes, if you must know, I do live there... with my parents,' Jenny replied, now cheering up a little. 'But if you don't catch rabbits then what is that spade and net for?'

'I didn't say I didn't catch rabbits I said I never use gin traps, there's a big difference you know,' said the youth, his broad grin now returning. 'Come and take a look.'

And grasping Jenny firmly by the arm he led her over to where the wicker basket lay firmly closed on the wet grass. After carefully removing a wooden peg that held the lid tightly in position, he lifted the top to reveal three ferrets: two were albinos and one was brown.

He took one of the pink-eyed white furry ferrets by the scruff of its neck to show Jenny and allowed her to stroke the animal gently. Then he replaced the ferret in the basket, closed the lid again and applied the wooden peg firmly in position as before. And then, after lifting the wicker basket and with its slender leather strap being firmly placed about his broad shoulders, he commenced his return to the woods.

'Just a moment,' Jenny called, 'why do you carry a spade and a string net with you? Not stealing potatoes I hope.'

The young man laughed loudly as he returned to Jenny's side.

'No not potatoes miss. You see, I do catch rabbits alright but with the help of these little fellows, not traps,' he said, patting the basket as he spoke. 'I peg the net over the rabbit's bolt hole and then send one of my mates here down the other end. Any rabbits below run out 'cause they're mighty scared of ferrets and they get themselves entangled in the net for me to bob over the head and take home for my supper. And the spade, well, sometimes these little beggars are a mite reluctant to follow the rabbit out; you see, they much prefer to play all day with the other rabbits that are still in the burrow or torment them, or maybe eat them alive, so I have to dig the ferrets out as soon as I can... or risk losing them altogether... hence the spade. Got it?'

And with that he once again moved toward the forest. Hesitating yet again, he returned; and placing the basket and net once more onto the wet ground, he commenced digging a sizeable hole close to where Jenny had tripped.

'I suppose we had better bury the little rascal and maybe say a few words over his grave... if you want to, that is,' he said.

Jenny nodded. And taking the remains of Bluey's body in his hands he placed them gently into the grave.

'Perhaps you might like to do the honours,' he added.

The little girl hesitated quite a while in not knowing what to say and so the young man recited the unexpurgated version of the Lords Prayer for her. He then filled in the grave and patted it firmly and after pulling up some tufts of grass, he planted them into the muddy soil and disguised the whole burial place with some small dead branches, bracken and partly decomposed leaves.

'Don't want no scavengers digging him up again now we've planted him, do we?' he said, as he gently caressed her cheek with the back of his strong fingers.

At last, he finally made his way to the barbed wire fence and clambering over with the basket attached to his broad shoulders, and with the spade being held securely under his arm he completely disappeared from Jenny's view.

'What's your name?' he called back from the depths of the forest. 'Mine's Tom.'

Jenny hesitated again and then shouted at the top of her small voice:

'Jenny,' she returned, 'its Jenny.'

'Bye then young Jenny.' His call was loud and clear as the voice reverberated widely through the tops of the lofty trees. 'See you again sometime I expect,' it said.

CHAPTER TWO

It was a strange release to know that Bluey was dead and it was stranger still to learn that he had once belonged to someone else. But at least Jenny knew that the young man, who had first owned her friend, would have behaved kindly towards him and that it was another cat who had been responsible for sending Bluey to her - not some cruel human. And she felt calmer too, now that she knew the spot where Bluey had found his resting place; at least she would be able to visit with him every now and then, when the need to resolve her loneliness arose.

But at the moment, the little girl had another problem which she had to contend with, a problem that was not beyond her understanding - but a trying one all the same.

Jenny had not applied for a leave of absence when first she decided to walk the fields in some forlorn hope of finding Bluey that day. As already stated, the night clouds had brought about a cascade of rain and had Jenny asked for permission to be about, then the request would most assuredly have been refused. *'The ground is far too wet and the weather most unreliable'*, would have been the answer. And so she had spent the morning break of a quarter of one hour, which had almost trebled in scale by the time she returned, once again scouring the meadow down by the forest edging; when she should have been spending the time resting and reading.

***

Sarah Wood was Lady Margaret Kent's elderly maiden aunt. The formidable, short, corpulent woman with her grey-white hair being dragged to the far reaches of her head to form a chignon there was completely frigid in every sense of the word. She had never experienced the lusts of the flesh in any way shape or form, or so it was assumed, and she was unfortunately cold, stiff and formal - thereby exemplifying all other meanings of the frigid word.

Miss Wood had been invited to Hyde Hall five years earlier, after she had retired from her head mistress post at a high school for girls in East London and when Jenny was in her seventh year.

Although she was a fairly close relative of Jenny's, Miss Wood had never met the child; in fact she had never met the father of the child either, for that matter. And as far her niece, Margaret, was concerned, well, they had only met on two occasions: the once when Margaret was christened at the age of three and the second time when Margaret's father, Sarah's only brother, was buried in an Oxford cemetery, just two years later, where he had resided at the time of his demise; (resided in Oxford, that is, not the cemetery).

So, to say that this was a most peculiar state of affairs within the structure of this peculiar household, with no one seemingly knowing anyone else, would be an understatement it might easily be supposed; in fact, an understatement to surpass all understatements would be a more accurate description of the relationship that existed within the boundaries of the Kent, Wood, establishment.

Be that as it may, it was because she had nowhere else left to go and no one else in the family directory left to turn to that Sarah Wood had willingly consented to the position of employment as Jenny's governess - a full month after her retirement - almost to the day.

Although the arrangement lacked much in the way of job satisfaction, it promised even less. But Miss Wood didn't seem to mind - not at the time; she had battled with far worse positions than this and so she would roll up her sleeves, (figuratively speaking) get on with the job in hand and be content with that which was on offer - what else could she do at her time of life anyway?

The task of permanently fixing the 'correctness of behaviour' in a difficult daughter belonging to her niece and who was proving far too tricky for that niece to deal with on her own had been an unanticipated problem. The played down 'difficulty clause', which seemed to have been added to the contract when Miss Wood wasn't looking, or it was carelessly overlooked at the time of consideration - or something of the sort - ought to have been a matter of some concern for the lady. But she hadn't been aware and so she would have to suffer the results of her oversight without complaint; or indeed, look for a suitable alternative position to fill a dwindling existence - but, at her time of life, there was nothing else and so she had to silently bear the consequences.

As plainly alluded to above, the facts of the matter surrounding this request had been somewhat ambiguous to Miss Wood - at the time of her acceptance, anyway, but after being situated within the family unit for only a very short time she had, not surprisingly, formed the opinion that the parents, themselves, were more to blame for the child's behavioural patterns than the girl herself. She, it seemed to Miss Wood, was innocent of all charges that had been set against her.

The fact that the child did need a firm hand, with which to control her conduct, was beyond all reasonable doubt; after all, what child didn't; however, it was something the new governess would be more than capable to contend with in the future. Firmness coupled with fairness had always been Sarah Wood's watchwords; although firmness did take precedence over fairness from time to time; as scores of her ex-pupils would be delighted to affirm.

It might also be added at this juncture and before we leave the whys and wherefores pertaining to Sarah Wood's engagement as governess at Hyde Hall, that Margaret Kent, not having the precise information to hand referring the correct address of her aunt's residence, had, after continuous searching through many family documents, contacted the new head of the girls school where she knew her maiden aunt had been employed for the past umpteen years. Margaret, in her investigations within the family archives, had also, rather inadvertently it seems, learned her aunt's age and so it was a considered deduction on her part as to the time of her aunt's retirement but one that proved to be most accurate.

It may likewise be assumed the degree of shocked surprise that the elderly lady received to her aging system when the invitation eventually arrived at her door from out of the blue and from a source as yet unknown to her.

***

After her meeting with Tom, Jenny walked over the meadow on her return to the big house. Not in a rushed sort of way but in an unhurried manner as if she hadn't a care in the world and cared for no one in the world either, come to that; which was probably germane to both parts.

A physical discomfort in her tummy, however, did cause the little girl some concern which she desperately tried to ignore but which had begun bothering her with a degree of suddenness; and so she continued on her way at intermittent intervals and progressed with difficulty.

Jenny ambled to the rear of the house and entered the back hallway, and then, finding the narrow stairway that the servants used, she climbed it until she reached the room that was being utilised as her own classroom - and walked in.

She was seen to be clutching at her lower tummy region as she entered and was bent at the waist by this time, quite as if she was in considerable discomfort.

'What's the matter with you? And why are you late back... yet again?' asked the stern looking governess.

'I went for a walk to stretch my legs Miss Wood and unfortunately went altogether further than I intended and I overlooked the time,' answered Jenny, staring straight into her governess' eyes. 'And on the way back I developed a cramp-like pain in my tummy which slowed me down rather. I think that what you explained to me, a week or so ago, has started; at least I feel as though it has,' she added, in all truthfulness.

'I suppose you haven't experienced any bleeding down there yet?' asked Sarah Wood, uncaringly and curling the index finger of her left hand over her lower lip as if she really did care and at the same time pointing to Jenny's pelvic region with the index finger of her right.

'I don't know,' replied Jenny, as meekly as she knew how, 'I haven't examined myself yet but I do feel that this might be the case.'

'Well it's nothing to be concerned about. It is quite the most natural thing in the world to happen to a girl of your age, so get used to it. I'll give you a pad and bandage later; you can examine yourself and apply them if it's necessary, when you finish your work. In any case these matters are private, Jennifer, and you must deal with them discretely in future... do I make myself clear?' said her tutor, in a most abrupt manner.

Rather insufficient compassion was being used by the stern Miss Wood at the moment, which didn't sit at all well with Jenny; this was to be expected, to a certain extent, from an untouched lady. But the tutor, it seems, was feeling incredibly embarrassed by the subject being brought forward in the first place, or so Jenny thought; for the look on her face said it all.

So, what did all this mean to Jenny? Probably a hundred lines or more for being late back and a further hundred for being so inconsiderate; but what did she care about that? Not a fig.

Although the stern lady had been headmistress at a girls school for many years, rarely, if ever, had she contended with matters of this nature. That sort of thing was always dealt with by the matron, teachers, or the individual parents concerned and so a person of Sarah Wood's calibre had always been spared the awkwardness of such offensive and objectionable intimacy.

The afternoon's algebra lesson was new to Jenny and baffled the little girl considerably as she failed to grasp the fundamental principle of letters and other basic symbols being used to represent unknown numbers in algebra. But she battled on slowly, as did the afternoon, and looked, if nothing else, as though she was vaguely interested.

At last, as if a week had passed, the afternoon's lessons were over for another day; now she had an hour of homework to face up to and lines to scribble but all of that would certainly wait until the evening; if she decided to do it at all.

Jenny cleaned the boring blackboard and tidied the dreary room ready for the next day's learning to commence, then she put away all of the mind numbing books in their appropriate places. When all of this had been completed, she hobbled down to the drawing room where she thought her mother might be waiting for her.

Jenny stood in the open doorway of the drawing room leaning untidily against its inner support and gazed at the figure of her mother as she reclined full length on the elegantly stylish chaise longue, just browsing a heap of magazines and flipping their pages with no real interest.

She held a tortoiseshell cigarette holder containing a full strength, lighted cigarette in the same hand that she held the glossy magazine, with its curling smoke drifting aimlessly in the direction of the wide open window. In addition to this, a cut glass tumbler containing the dregs of an amber fluid of sorts stood on the small table next to her.

Lady Margaret failed to look up or even desist from browsing as her daughter silently presented herself; she felt her daughter's presence all the same, in a tedious, tiresome kind of way, as she almost always did.

'What is it Jennifer?' she asked irritably, as if not wishing to be interrupted from some exhausting and exacting exercise. 'Did you need me for anything in particular or have you just popped in to exchange the time of day and be a hindrance to me?' she added, querulously.

'Neither as a matter of fact,' said Jenny, in a low voice and without furthering another word on the matter, she hastened away to her bedroom.

This was a typical reception the mother would bestow upon her daughter, a daughter whom she hadn't spoken to or even seen since the previous evening's dinner. The rude ritual, unaltered in any way from one day to the next, had been thus installed for as long as Jenny could possibly remember.

The sameness in rhythmic patterns of parental inattention, even neglect, was ever present at their meetings and not unlike the boring educational lessons she had just undertaken, it was fast becoming intolerable to the little girl.

She quickly examined herself in her bathroom and applied the pad and bandage Miss Wood had given her, and then she pondered for a while.

"I don't care how mummy treats me; I never have anyway, so she can go to hell for all I care. But she cannot spoil today, I won't allow it," she deliberated on these words silently to herself. *"Because today is an extra special day for me, today I have positive evidence that I have at last grown up."*

And so, of course, she had. As soon as she had completed her ablutions, she entered her room and collecting her diary from the draw of her desk, she turned its pages to find the day's date. Then she, smiling with self assuredness, thought deeply, and reflecting upon all that had gone before - all the days she had had to spend alone - and wrote down the fact that today she had at last entered that stage of her life where truly a state of spiritual blessedness existed; now she could positively consider herself to have grown freely, wonderfully and with certainty, into womanhood.

***

Three weeks later Jennifer Kent went walking yet again. May had now arrived and her birthday had passed by unnoticed; well almost unnoticed; on the fifth day of that month she had received a single birthday card containing a ten shilling note and hurriedly written in her father's hand were these frosty words:

"This is from your Mother and Father."

She walked the same walk she'd walked before, when she had discovered her Bluey's body nearly a month ago, only this time no searching of the pasture had snared her thoughts, no unexpected terror to bring her fear, and no demonic monsters laid waiting to pounce out at her.

And so she ambled along, picking a posy of buttercups on the way; and holding them under her chin, she giggled to herself at the thought of the yellow creamy spread; she knew she liked it; she didn't need a buttercup to tell her that.

She skipped for a while holding her arms in the air pretending she was a ballerina; at least she considered that her stance claimed to be the approximate posture of a dancer, she didn't really know, she hadn't seen one, only in books, and mulling it over, she decided she was right; so she continued to pose. She had fashioned a small wooden cross the previous evening and now she carried it with her; the cross in one hand and the buttercups in the other.

Jenny had visited the grave a week or so earlier when the weather, like today, was warm and sunny. She had seen the badly spelled note that had been pinned by a twig to the grave, and had read it smilingly. The note was from Tom asking, no telling her to meet him at Bluey's grave on this very day in May at fifteen minutes past midday. She glanced at her watch, she was five minutes early.

After placing the small wooden cross where she remembered Bluey's dear head had sadly been positioned, she stood back and inclining her own head she smiled with admiration at the simplicity of her handiwork.

The sound of distant whistling broke the relative silence as she dropped the buttercups beside the cross, a tuneful whistle that she had never heard before, and then it stopped, abruptly. She strained her eyes and her ears for a sighting or a sound but no further evidence of Tom's presence came to her, and so she bent over the grave once more and lost herself in the arranging of the buttercups more appropriate to her liking.

'You made it then young Jenny, I thought you might.'

Jenny turned round sharply; it was Tom, the lad she had so willingly befriended after discovering her Bluey's body that dreadful day. He wore the same clothes he had worn the first time they'd met only now he wore a piece of red paisley cloth carefully folded and knotted around his neck. This gave him the air of an adult and presented him as being the man of the road he truly was; Jenny's approval was wholehearted.

He carried the same wicker basket he had carried before but minus spade and net. He walked over and placed the basket gently onto the grass, close to where the young girl stood.

'Hello Tom,' said Jenny, offering him her hand, formally.

He took the dainty hand in his strong rough one and bending down he kissed it gently.

Jenny blushed.

'Afternoon Miss Jenny,' he said, 'and how are you this glorious day?'

'I am well thank you Tom, how are the ferrets?' she asked, coyly with an uneasy look upon her face.

'They're good thanks Miss Jenny. 'Haps you'd care to take a look,' he said, as he crouched down to free the lid.

She hesitated for awhile and stepped two paces back, not feeling obliged to handle the killer animals again no matter how furry and attractive they were or how kindly she may have regarded them the other time.

"They are still killers," she thought, to herself *"and they will always be killers."*

Tom, noticing Jenny's reluctance, went to her and reached for her hand; Jenny took it away.

'What are you afeared of?' he said, smiling broadly. 'You were OK with them the other day, so what's happened in between times?'

'N - Nothing,' she said, stumbling a little over her words. 'It's just that... I've had time to think and I now consider them to be rabbit killers no matter how fondly you may think of them, and... well I don't really care for animals that harm other animals... that's all.'

'Come on... don't be silly,' he said. And then, taking her hand and elbow he almost frogmarched her over to the wicker basket and opened up the lid.

A tiny blue kitten, half asleep, lay curled up on a woollen blanket. Opening its eyes it stood, arched its back and stretched its front legs, then sitting up it raised its tiny head to look up into Jenny's wide eyes.

'She's yours; if you want her that is,' said Tom, as he bent down and picked the kitten up by the scruff of the neck. 'I can't keep her you see, too many dogs and tom cats at my place so she's now looking for a good home. Do you think you could provide her with one of those, young Jenny?' he asked, temptingly.

Jenny took the tiny kitten into her arms and kissing its head she laughed and cried at the same time.

'I should so much love to have her,' she said, as she caressed the kitten tenderly. 'But there is nowhere I could possibly keep her. Bluey, well, he was a big cat and could fend for himself out of doors, both summer and winter; but as for this little creature, well, she's far too small to survive on her own. You see, everyone at the Hall... they are all against cats I'm afraid and consider them to be full of fleas and riddled with the mange; that's why Bluey was never allowed to follow me inside. I'm so very sorry, I wish with all my heart that I could take her home with me... but I'm afraid the answer has to be no.'

Jenny placed the kitten back into the basket and closed the lid herself and with no further conversation, no goodbyes or anything at all, she walked back the way she had come but now with her head bowed low as her cheerfulness had deserted her completely. Twice she wiped away a tear from her cheek - maybe more - who knows, but one thing was very certain, Jennifer Kent was a most unhappy little girl.

Tom had called out after her, telling her not to worry and that he would sort something out for the kitten, but she pretended not to hear and kept plodding on up the hill towards the Hall.

With sudden impetuosity an unexpected idea leapt into her mind, a stupid irresponsible idea that she ought to have known better than to harbour. She stopped, and looking back to where she saw Tom climbing the barbed wire fence she watched as he entered the broadleaf forest with the wicker basket over his shoulder.

CHAPTER THREE

It was a few minutes past the hour of nine o'clock on the following morning when a somewhat timid tapping was heard on the bedroom door belonging that of Sir Angus Kent.

As indicated above, the tapping was quite gentle at first but little by little it increased in volume until it became more persistent. Apparently the urgency of this appeal was growing by the minute.

The unexpected storm that had started late afternoon on the previous day had centred itself over the local area where it raged continuously for most of the long hours of darkness; thereby disturbing the gentleman's night-time repose. And so it was with a high degree of annoyance that he handed out his frosty greeting to the individual stubbornly tapping on his door - so early in the day:

'Yes? Who the hell is it that is making such a fuss at this unearthly hour?' he asked. The hushed, drowsy voice of Sir Angus sounded rather angry though it failed to reach the ears of the person who was causing the din. And so, the knocking continued until it finally gained a considerable increase to its loudness.

After the fatigued gentleman had donned his black, silk, kimono styled dressing gown to make himself more presentable, he moved across the room, inch by inch, to investigate the rumpus; mumbling continuously under his breath as he went.

It was the robust figure of Sarah Wood that stood in the passageway outside her master's bedroom door that morning and who was found to be guilty of the continued penetrative knocking; and with some considerable force at the present moment, it seems. She had an apparent nervous energy firmly installed in her customary sluggish body which seemed to cause an unusual twitchiness to persist on the left side of her cheek.

The gentleman half opened the door unhurriedly and wedged his head and shoulders within its available space; holding on tightly to the revere of his dressing gown with his right hand, to lessen his embarrassment, and the door with his left.

'Yes Sarah, what the bloody hell is going on? The ruddy house burning down around our ears is it?' he asked, with meanness to his voice that did a significant injustice to the gentleman's usual temperament.

'No Sir Angus, its Jennifer. I haven't seen her since yesterday, just before lunch time to be more precise, and as she failed to turn up for her schooling in the afternoon and again this morning I thought the matter should be brought to your immediate attention,' answered the tutor, with a high degree of apprehension still showing on her features.

'Well why on earth didn't you bring the matter to my notice yesterday?' he asked, leaving go of the door briefly and combing his hair with his fingers then scratching the back of his head with those same appendages.

'Because it is indeed not the first time that she has failed to turn up for the afternoon lessons,' she explained. 'You see, she has always arrived for the following day's class, frustrating me with some feeble excuse or other for her previous absence. Usually she spends the time in her own bedroom, apparently reading, or just feeling sorry for herself.'

'Well there you are then. You have just provided yourself with the obvious answer to a problem which really isn't a problem at all. The inconsiderate young madam is probably in her bedroom reading a book or playing some silly game, probably doing a jigsaw puzzle, if the truth be known,' he said, brusquely.

'You fail to understand my meaning Sir Angus. That is not actually the case; you see I have already checked her room she certainly isn't there and her bed hasn't been slept in and what with that terrible storm last night, well, you will no doubt understand my anxiety.

'I have questioned the servants but it seems no one has seen the girl. Would you advise me to wake her mother? Perhaps Jennifer spent the night with her; she, most probably had been frightened by the storm and may have gone to her mother for some sanctuary,' said the governess fast running out of ideas.

'No, don't do that.' The answer was abrupt. 'I am quite sure Margaret would not appreciate being disturbed with such a trivial matter as this. Why not leave it until this afternoon; let us see how the little madam responds after having to exist in her own company for a few hours longer. Yes that's it, leave the matter until this afternoon; we will much better be able to reassess the situation then,' said Sir Angus, revealing the hint of a smile for the first time that morning. Not that he should have felt he had anything to smile about, but the said gentleman was not one to panic in an emergency and certainly not one so trivial as this.

He closed the door quietly and stripping himself of his robe he discarded it on an adjacent chair. He then repositioned himself upon his bed, pulled the silken sheet and covers over his head and fell fast asleep again.

The day advanced to half an hour after midday before Sarah Wood took the decision to make further contact with the master of the house, in order to express her continued concern about the disappearance of his daughter; and she did so just as he was stealthily descending the wide staircase: probably on his way to escape the boring governess with her infernal badgering and her interfering ways - it might be supposed.

He firmly believed that his wayward daughter was up to some sort of mischief or other and that she would show herself when she was good and ready - and not before.

Sir Angus assumed, quite wrongly, that it was Jennifer's way of heaping vengeance upon her relentless tutor for some irritation or disproportionate harshness she had most likely dealt the girl at some time or other:

"Good for you Jennifer," he thought, *"probably most deserving anyway."*

'I don't suppose the little madam has returned?' said he, expressing a feigned interest in the feeble question when he realised there was no escape from this woman's harassment.

'No Sir Angus, she most certainly has not,' was the reply to the half hearted inquiry. 'So what do you propose we should do about it?' asked Sarah Wood, more than a little disturbed about her charge's disappearance than she would otherwise have cared to admit.

'Well, I would be inclined to give the matter a little longer, let's say until late this evening,' he answered impassively. 'I have spoken to Margaret briefly and thankfully she is in complete agreement with me. The longer the wretched girl is away the more likely she is to feel a yearning for her home comforts again.

'It may take a little awhile you know, Sarah, but she has to be taught a strict lesson in correct behaviour; she has to learn here and now what I am prepared to accept as being tolerable and what I am not. After all, I am her father and so I must have some say in how she behaves... don't you agree?'

Sarah Wood didn't agree. The more she talked to this contrary man the more he seemed to show a total disregard for his daughter's welfare or indeed her freedom from any risk of harm; turning a blind eye to a situation of these proportions was, to her mind, indefensible to say the least; and she wondered how much of what he was saying was in fact the expressed opinion of her own niece being foisted upon him.

'I wish I could share your opinion Sir Angus but to my way

of thinking the sooner we consider contacting the proper authorities the better I should like it,' she said; but nervously thinking she may have overstepped the mark in her estimation of the situation.

'What! Involve the police d'you mean?' he asked rather abruptly. Sarah equalled his abruptness by nodding in the affirmative. 'Nonsense Sarah, no need for steps in that direction; I can assure you of that.'

Sarah's proposition, he believed, would lead to a humiliating situation, and so his measured answer was made in profound earnestness and as if to underline his opposition, he continued, almost angrily. 'Having the police marauding about the place, would be tantamount to admitting that I run an easy going, undisciplined ship here and that would never do. No Sarah, out of the question, definitely not the police.'

'But don't you see Sir Angus, Jennifer might easily have been abducted for whatever reason and the sooner the police are involved the greater the chances would be in bringing her home safely. Who knows what might have happened to the little girl. Oh, I know she can be a worry at times, but then, so can most girls of her age; I should know I've had enough dealings with the little rascals before this. But the last thing you need right now is to receive some anonymous phone call making all sorts of demands on your estate, Sir Angus, I can assure you of that,' said Sarah, with a forced smile to indicate her earnestness.

Her argument was convincing and slowly she could see the sense of it being clearly revealed in Sir Angus' face. She fidgeted about, distributing her unbecoming weight from one leg to the other whilst waiting for the penny to drop completely. A tense silence then rested on the two of them until Sir Angus opened his mouth to speak.

'Sound thinking Sarah,' he said, thoughtfully at long last and stroking his chin, 'I hadn't considered that angle.'

Just then Margaret was seen at the top of the stairs and as she began her descent she offered her contribution to the already existing conversation.

'Sound thinking, what do you mean? What's going on Angus?' she asked, without proper care or interest. 'You still pondering over Jennifer are you? I thought we had made our joint decision with regard to her absence; let the little beast stew, that is all I have to say about the matter, I don't really care if she never returns.'

This unbecoming declaration from a so called caring mother not only rankled in the hearts and minds of the heretofore debaters but was found to be undignified and totally unhelpful.

Sir Angus and Sarah both failed miserably in their minds to justify such a statement as this and surveyed each other obliquely, each hoping the other would correct Margaret or at least make clear to her the dangers of such an attitude. It wasn't until her husband had explained to his cantankerous wife the vague possibilities of Jenny's disappearance and all the potential implications that might surround such a situation as this that she retraced her thoughts and fully agreed that all should now be done to bring about the safe return of her darling child.

***

Tom had smiled inwardly to himself as he listened to the breaking of twigs and the scrunching of dried leaves beneath Jenny's fatigued feet and he tried to understand what it was that had driven the girl to such lengths. But he didn't lessen his stride in any way or stop to enquire her reasons for following him, or advise her of the significant dangers of such a stupid action.

"She must have set her mind on something that is pretty important to her or she wouldn't have followed me in the first place," he thought to himself; and so he continued the half mile long, dense forest, striding calmly and with no clear urgency in his step. *"Anyway I shall certainly have to make sure she is safely returned to her home later... after she has realized her little adventure has been completely foolhardy and for nothing; and when she has got the silly escapade well and truly out of her system she'll realise how childish she has been, I'm sure of that,"* he thought.

On more than one occasion he heard her slip as the darkness within the woodland became intensified and with each trip he glanced over his shoulder in Jenny's direction to be assured of her immediate safety - and then he continued as before.

At last, on the further side of the forest, where the undulating verdant pastures claimed precedence over the trees and where cattle grazing became more important to the farmer than that of lumber, there, in a shrubby recess at the forest's edge and being perfectly hidden from any casual onlooker who might pass along the road a mere two hundred yards away, he found his bow topped caravan centred on a well worn area where other homes had recently levelled the grass.

The dully decorated vardo stood alone now; and a couple of moth-eaten mutts were chained securely to its two front wheels in such a way as to allow them the opportunity to wander around the full length and breadth of Tom's home; one now situated on the right side, the other on the left, both looking languid and indifferent to their master's return.

A large blue grey cat, curled up fast asleep on the step by the padlocked door, seemed to have one eye half open. And a lean, highly feathered skewbald horse, tethered to a stake driven deep in the ground close by, grazed continuously on the long, sweet grass.

Other than these, the place was deserted; the rest of his friends had left hours ago: he knew they would have gone by now. But this didn't bother the young man in the slightest, it wouldn't take him long to catch up with the others; even if he failed to leave until next morning he'd find them to be not too far away - he always preferred travelling by himself anyway.

After he had deposited the kitten next to its mother he climbed the five narrow steps to his home, unlocked the door and waited inside for Jenny to arrive.

"It will be fun to have some young female company around the place for a change, even if it should only be for the shortest of short stays," he thought to himself, smiling broadly. *"It will be much better than the weary women folk that pester me all day long and badger me in doing jobs for them, like they do!"*

Tom was lounging on his bed at the back of the van with the door to his home wide open when Jennifer Kent arrived looking sheepish and rather guilty. And she displayed her complete embarrassment as she peered round the doorway - not knowing what to expect from Tom.

'Well now, what do we have here? Young Miss Jenny doing a spot of intruding eh?' said Tom, with a wide grin, occupying the full width of his face which he mostly always carried. 'Followed me all the way to my home, I reckon. So what made you do it Jenny?' he asked, in a concerned but kind-hearted fashion. 'What made you do a stupid and dangerous thing like that?' A brief pause followed the summarized version of a pertinent question while his countenance altered to take on a look of sternness. 'Couldn't you see what sort of position you would be placing me in if your mum and dad came looking and found you here with me, *and* bringing the police with them as well, I shouldn't wonder? Wouldn't look too good for me, now would it?'

Jenny was still loitering in the open doorway as Tom spoke and she lowered her pretty head in embarrassment. In fact she was looking even more shamefaced whilst being questioned than when she'd first arrived.

'I'm sorry Tom,' she said, 'I truly didn't think. I needed to get away from my home quickly you see; I am so dreadfully unhappy there and I just can't take any more of my parents treating me as if I don't exist all the time. I sort of guessed you lived in a caravan and moved about the country sometimes so I followed you, hoping you would take me with you.'

'Well, did you now!' Tom spoke the four words more as an exclamation than as a question, although he probably meant it to sound logical from both angles. 'Did you now!' he repeated, more quietly and looking more intensely into Jenny's dark brown eyes than he'd done before.

'Please don't look at me like that Tom, you don't mean to frighten me, do you?' she said, lowering her head still further.

'Don't be silly, of course I don't, why would I want to do that?

'How old are you Jenny?' he asked, still with a serious tone to his voice.

'I was fourteen just two weeks ago,' she answered, with a definite look of uncertainty at the deliberate falsehood she had uttered.

'Surely you don't expect me to believe that now, do you Jenny? You're more likely to be a late ten year old or by stretching my imagination a bit, I might go along with… well, maybe eleven, but certainly not fourteen.'

The little girl coloured up considerably at Tom's supposition and she felt awkward with herself, wishing deep within she had told the whole truth in the first place and thought awhile as she considered rectifying the blatant falsehood.

Tom remained patient; he surely knew the truth would eventually come to the surface - if he waited long enough.

'I'm sorry Tom, I haven't been entirely honest with you,' she said, eventually; twisting her narrow fingers together and looking pensive and sad. 'The plain truth is I was twelve on the fifth of this month, I don't know what made me pretend I was older, maybe I thought you would allow me to stay with you if you thought I was fourteen.'

Tom didn't much care to being lied to in that fashion or any fashion at all for that matter.

'Well now, what's to be done with you then, young Jenny?' he asked, and he sighed deeply as he considered the alternatives. 'You certainly can't travel the country roads with me… that, young Jenny would be completely out of the question; so I guess I must return you to your home without further delay, don't you agree? I can't for the life of me think what else I can do with you.'

Unbeknown to the unlikely couple, dark, stormy clouds had unexpectedly been gathering from the west, just beyond the forest. A sudden clap of the loudest thunder immediately following a streak of the fiercest forked lightening interrupted their decision making, as heavy rain, mixed with hail stones the size of glass alleys, fell straight down from out of a totally filled in, black sky.

Without hesitation, Jenny, quickly followed by the blue-grey cat with its kitten in tow, entered the caravan completely and closed the door behind her as torrential rain blotted out the surrounding scene.

She sat down upon the, cushioned bench-like seat at the side of the narrow van nursing the kitten and staring anxiously out of the small window as the rain and hail stones beat aggressively upon the rounded roof.

'What about your dogs Tom, shouldn't they be in here with us? They'll get absolutely drenched out there,' said Jenny, displaying an air of concern.

'Oh, they'll be OK, they'll hide themselves under the van to keep themselves dry so there's no need for you to worry yourself about them,' said Tom calmly, 'What concerns me more is what I should do about you. Obviously I can't return you home in this goddamned awful weather so you better hope it stops pretty soon otherwise you'll be here for the duration and that is not going to look too good for me... or for you either, come to that, young Jenny.'

But the storm didn't stop or even look like stopping and so the young girl and the much older young man were trapped within a situation about which they had no control and as night time fell Tom found himself with no alternative but to offer to share his exceedingly narrow bed with his recently found companion.

Jenny had never felt the comforting arms of another human being before as Tom clung tightly to her in an earnest attempt at preventing himself from falling to the floor and she had never felt the security of being held so warmly as this either so that all the worries and all the discomforts in her lonely little life simply melted away in an instant.

Neither her selfish mother nor her self opinionated father, had ever offered her comfort such as this, or anything close to it; all they had ever been capable of was the protection of their own wellbeing and the high regard others ladled on them; there could never be anything approaching love or tenderness left over for her, why should there be - when they didn't give a damn about their daughter anyway. Not that they would have known how to bestow comfort or affection even if they had wanted to - she knew that to be patently true.

Very quickly, the little girl, amid all the raging of the mighty storm outside, fell asleep. She fell asleep in the tender arms of innocence, in the tender arms of a man of whom she knew nothing, nor yet cared to know.

Tom continued to cradle his small, half naked companion exceedingly close even though he had felt her relax into the world of sweet slumber and it wasn't long before he gently withdrew his arm and rolled over onto the floor; and wrapping himself in the floor's matting for renewed warmth, he also fell fast asleep.

For six and thirty weeks I'll wait for you, in moistened warmth I'll grow until we meet, sent from the portals of concern not angrily but in unplanned tenderness, until at last all loneliness will be forever gone.

***

Tom had started a fire and was busily preparing breakfast when Jenny awoke the following morning. Time was getting on and the enraged storm had moved itself to a further location by this time and left in its place a day of the freshest sunshine.

He hadn't noticed her standing in the open doorway watching him as he held the small frying pan over the hot embers of the recently lit fire. The bacon and eggs sizzling, and the recently plucked small mushrooms' spluttering, produced an aroma that wafted about the place, filling the whole area with a wonderful homeliness that the child could never have known before but which she would remember for the rest her days.

Looking beyond Tom, Jenny become aware of the pulchritudinous pinkness of the blend of red and white campions as they grew in clusters just a few yards away; most of them had been broken by the force of the storm so intense its power had proved to be.

With no word of greeting she idled past the young man and after picking a small posy she returned to the caravan and delicately arranged them in an empty vase she'd found on the small window sill. Then she returned to the top of the steps to continue her gaze on Tom.

'It's no good you thinking to make yourself at home here young Jenny, as soon as we've eaten breakfast we have to make tracks. Your folk will be worried sick, I'm sure, not knowing where you are; and won't be too pleased when they find out you've spent the night with me. So look sharp and eat this breakfast I've prepared for us both. It has been good having you around young Jenny, but as you must realise by now, all good things must come to an end sooner or later.'

Jenny nodded her head solemnly; as much as she hated the idea she knew Tom was right, she had to return to face the consequences of her silly actions, no matter how painful she considered them to be - not that she agreed with Tom about her parents concern though, *"he doesn't know them as I do and so he is in no position to form an opinion,"* she thought.

CHAPTER FOUR

Sir Angus stormed across the great hall and into his study with provocation plainly written all over his face, and closed the door none too delicately behind him.

The slamming of his study door was not only an indication of the foul mood the man was in; it was also a precautionary measure to assure his privacy. Having said that, he might just as easily have left the door wide open, for no one in their right mind would have considered eavesdropping on any private conversation Sir Angus Kent may wish to have - not today - and not in the foul mood he was in either - they wouldn't dare.

Despite all the inconvenience that had occurred to him that morning he still considered his daughter's absence to be a private matter and so having a chat with the local constabulary may well prove to be somewhat awkward. But as the idea had been forced on him by Sarah Wood, he had no alternative but to go through with it.

Nevertheless, such a matter as this was bound to result in an amount of psychological discomfort for the gentleman, brazen as he was - it was bound to - but he didn't wish to display any private humiliation to any member of the household staff, now did he?

He picked up the receiver and dialled the number of the local police station carefully but not wishing to disclose his identity in a forthright manner, for reasons best known to him, he used a vague and rather garbled - practically muted voice to reveal his personal identity.

Sir Angus then went over the details of the matter as he saw them; as the officer at the other end smiled to himself with contempt; at least, that was how it felt to the humiliated gentleman, that he was being ridiculed in some way or other.

At a snails pace then, to begin with, before he ventured into the heart of the matter with all the information that he considered supported his fears.

'... and so I need to report, what would appear to be, a most heinous crime. To make everything perfectly clear to you so you are best able to grasp what I am saying, I shall speak slowly... it is the abduction of my daughter by some ruthless individual and who is about to make demands for ransom upon my estate that is causing me all this needless anxiety.

'The kidnapper is endeavouring to get in touch with me at this very minute... as we speak... more likely than not, so if you don't mind I will make this as brief as I possibly can. I'm sure he will have already estimated what his demands from me will be... there can be little doubt of that. So I need a team of your chaps round here pretty damn quick to work out precisely what is going on and what they intend doing about it.'

'I see sir; you seem to have worked out everything rather neatly, don't you, sir?' said the voice, at the other end, rather doubtfully. And his voice had about it a hint of sarcasm which gave the distinct impression he was already reaching his limits in so far as this particular caller's attitude and demands were concerned. The officer suddenly became irritated when he heard Sir Angus' final demands - and he didn't mind stating the fact.

'You have clearly indicated, sir, that this so called kidnapper hasn't contacted you yet and so you appear to be jumping the gun a little... if you don't mind me saying so, sir... only I always consider one should be a little more certain of the facts than you appear to be at this point sir... that is to say: certain before you go around making assumptions of this sort... best not to shout before we're hurt, sir... if you get my meaning.'

Sir Angus Kent totally ignored the advice he'd been offered, and after he had presented his statement in a reasonably shortened form, he sensed a wry grin issuing from the police officer's mouth coming to his own mind via the telephone's wiring. In spite of this, he did manage to control his nerve and failed to take the officer to task for such insolence; even so, the incident did cause him to feel annoyed, to a certain extent anyway.

The sluggish telephone conversation dragged on for a further few minutes before it was brought to a timely end; however, this did not happen before Sir Angus had been asked to state his views on how he considered the crisis might finally resolve itself, if indeed an ill-fated scenario did eventually occur; meaning, of course, did Sir Angus fear for his daughter's safety in any way. In addition to all this, the police officer needed to know what Sir Angus expected from the police or what their likely roll might be in this situation as nothing untoward had occurred, as yet.

Sir Angus managed to end the conversation by stating those views and expectations very succinctly indeed. He thought, and quite rightly so, that the longer this conversation dragged on the more likely it was to turn into a complete fiasco - probably with Sir Angus losing his dignity altogether.

This whole shambles and especially the police officer's manner had caused considerable doubt to dwell in the gentleman's mind. Surely, he was being mocked beyond all reason here, and he adjudged the final part of the conversation to have not been taken seriously - so much so that he felt he should consider lodging a complaint to the officer's superiors - but then again, after serious thought, he resigned himself to the notion that it would harm his fine reputation far more than a complaint of that nature would be worth.

At the end of the farcical debate, Sir Angus restated his full title, name, address and the telephone number of Hyde Hall - very clearly indeed, in fact, with emphasis this time. Not only was he going over the personal details he had already given at the beginning of his statement he was also making much clearer who it was who the officer had been speaking to, thereby stressing his own importance. All of his details had been civilly requested by the recipient of the call at the very beginning but it seems that the interpretation of these had been lost in transit, either that, or the officer had an acute memory problem and so Sir Angus had no alternative but to oblige the officer by restating his details more clearly.

After Sir Angus had been kindly informed that a small delegation would be on his doorstep within the half hour, he returned the gesture by assuring the officer that a welcoming committee would be on hand at the said doorstep to attend the minimalist representation likely - if they were not too late! If they were not too late, meaning - didn't the police realise he had a hundred and one other things of far more importance to attend to that afternoon and he wasn't prepared to waste valuable time over such a matter as this.

Sir Angus replaced the receiver abruptly and then returned to the large front door leading to the wide portico.

It was from this focal point he saw the two ladies as they edgily waited for him at the foot of the wide open steps. And after joining them there, they waited together as an unfortunate falling-out occurred thereby engulfing the three of them in moodiness and bad humour, though it must be said, Sarah did attempt to refrain taking part in the argument as best she could.

Twenty-five lengthy minutes came and went, with not a hint of a policeman to be seen anywhere but with the self same, silly tetchiness persisting.

It was during this unfortunate waiting period that the dispute between the husband and his wife raged to a state of name-calling and it wasn't long before Sarah Wood was also dragged into the arena - no matter how unwittingly. Luckily for Sir Angus it was at this point that he was surprisingly dropped from the altercation altogether so that only Margaret and her aunt occupied the central rolls of the dispute.

The disagreement between the two ladies, that was as unattractive to the eyes as it was to the ears, gathered momentum, with Margaret placing the total blame for Jennifer's disappearance firmly at the feet of her corpulent aunt. Of course Sir Angus made every effort to restrain all the unpleasantness as best he could by attempting to reduce the argument to a simple family debate. Unfortunately for him he was only successful in making matters a good deal worse than they already were - and he did this without too much difficulty - by taking Sarah's part in the row.

And so, the unbearable wife, taking immediate umbrage at her husband's stance, decided to re-enter the marital home in a mood of rage; and not wishing to discuss the matter any further until 'the little witch' had returned, she commenced to climb the stairs to her room.

She hadn't long to wait though, for as soon as she had reached her bedroom door, Jenny was seen crossing the large lawn which led down to the broad leafed forest and being escorted by someone who Sir Angus could only describe to himself as being: "*a filthy Romany Gypsy fellow.*"

An embarrassing situation immediately took place, for as soon as the little girl and her companion drew level with Sir Angus and the governess, an unmarked police car arrived with, what turned out to be, two plain clothed policemen sitting on its two front seats - gravely surveying the scene.

The motorcar drew to an abrupt halt.

With no sense of urgency about them, the two men exited the maroon car simultaneously and commenced to walk over to the waiting group with frowned looks of suspicion immediately occupying their already serious faces.

'Good afternoon Sir Angus,' said the older of the two, while they were still a few yards off; 'I take it that you *are* Sir Angus Kent?' he hastily added,

Sir Angus, with a flush of crimson hiding his vexed complexion, moved forward to meet the two policemen halfway but without there being any formality in the way he greeted them.

'Look, I'm sorry to have bothered you people, but it would appear that my daughter has decided to exhibit herself this afternoon after all; as a matter of fact, she managed to perform this illusionary act the very moment you people arrived... quite extraordinary really; and so I have been unable to save you a wasted journey,' said Sir Angus, before either of the policemen had taken the occasion to introduce themselves.

'That's alright sir,' said the more senior of the two, 'so long as you are perfectly happy with the situation as it has turned out and as it appears at the moment. But I think it might be helpful if I have a quick word with the young lady's companion before we leave you altogether.'

Then turning his attention to Tom, the detective asked the young man for his account of events since yesterday afternoon - the answer to this was supported by Jenny. Being perfectly satisfied with Tom's response to the pointed inquiry, they decided to drop the matter.

Sir Angus had clearly heard all that had been said, and decided to adopt a magnanimous view of what the young man had so kindly done in sheltering his missing daughter from a most fearful storm. After reaching for his wallet from the inside pocket of his Harris Tweed jacket, he slowly withdrew a twenty pound note and offered it to the young man for his trouble, thus displaying his own generosity in front of the two detectives.

'No thank you sir, I don't want your money. I offered shelter to your daughter when she was in need and was lost. She is safe now, and you have her returned to you for you to cherish. I compliment you on having such a fine young lady for your daughter sir, she makes a very pleasant companion, you should try it sometime,' said Tom, as his wide smile melted away; and as he turned to Jenny he stroked her cheek with the back of his fingers as he had before stroked it.

With moistness in her eyes, Jenny walked after Tom as he deserted the group in favour of the leafy forest.

'Thank you Tom, for everything, I shall never forget you, you must know that,' she said, as she caught hold of the hand that had provided her with such tender closeness - and she clutched it tightly to her young bosom.

'I shall remember you as well young Jenny. You are much older than your years and wiser too despite everything, so don't let anyone tell you different; but don't grow up too quickly, will you. See you again when I'm around these parts perhaps,' he said, as he walked away from her and back again towards the dense growth of the green trees.

Sir Angus had been anything but pleased with Tom's directness in offering him advice in the art of parenting or indeed with his attitude in the refusal of recompense for his kindness, which must have been a substantial sum indeed for the young man to have snubbed; both of these humiliating gestures had left the mind of the father in a slight dilemma.

Nobody had denied him his open generosity before, not in matters of the wallet anyway, and so, not wishing to be outdone, he offered the money to the older of the two policemen:

'For the police ball... or whatever you people call it these days,' he said, with frankness and trying hard to produce the hint of a smile as he spoke.

'Thank you Sir Angus... but no thank you,' said the older of the two policemen. 'I'm not prepared to accept gifts while on duty sir. Now if you were to drop the money in at the police station when passing; well, that would be a different matter altogether.'

Sir Angus Kent was absolutely seething at yet another blatant rejection of his generosity and so he turned his attention to Sarah thereby upsetting her with his spite.

'I shall leave you in charge of the situation now Sarah, after all, you are supposed to be the child's governess; perhaps you will attempt to act the part in the future... if you please,' said he; and without expressing recognition to anyone in the assembly, including his own child, he stormed off in the direction of the garages while the small group stood aimlessly around looking at one another with vexed concern.

***

Sir Angus was still enraged as he drove his big silver Mk v 3.5 litre Jaguar away from Hyde Hall that afternoon. And the narrow twisting road that led to Basham Killington situated ten or so miles north of Hyde and where he now sought refuge, was proving incredibly difficult to manage.

The rivulets that poured out of the steep, sandy banks onto the already dampened lanes, formed slippery mud patches with long, deep gullies, which were not easily negotiable and all these problems, added together, didn't help the gentleman's temper in the slightest.

Even the small amount of concentration that Sir Angus was able to lay claim to, kept slipping away just when he required all the dexterity he could muster to keep his car on the road and he cursed the night's stormy deluge for its determination in creating chaos out of calmness, particularly in this merry month of May when everything, everywhere, should have been unhurried and tranquil.

Although he was livid with his daughter for bringing the

problem to his door in the first place and of course with her lack of consideration for his concern, his lividity didn't finish there, for he also bore malice toward Sarah for what he considered to be the distinct lack of regulatory instruction on her part, and also to Margaret, his alienated spouse, for never providing a reliable and homely environment at the Hall, both for his daughter and more especially - for himself.

Why, Margaret's bedroom door was always firmly closed to Sir Angus these days even though there were times when he was particularly enamoured of her; which, he had to admit, were extremely infrequent in recent times. He wasn't too happy at the way the police had handled matters either.

'Both of them were particularly unfriendly,' he said aloud, to himself, 'and as for that gypsy fellow, well, who in hell's name did he think he was, refusing my favours in that offhand way and offering me his irritating advice in parenting.'

These aggravations, it seems, found no necessity to leave him - not yet awhile anyway - and so they continued to beleaguer the gentlemen for the whole of the journey.

So, all things considered, Sir Angus was suffering a spate of defeat for a change; his feelings suggested he had been ruthlessly outflanked on all sides and by enemies that had neither wit nor wisdom - or so he thought.

Nevertheless, he now considered he was in need of a hasty restorative to help him through this current flurry of difficulties; although it should be clearly understood that the gentleman would never admit to the need of such emotional support or, indeed, any other support for that matter.

In the whole of the county of Dorset and in many of its bordering and surrounding regions, the Kent family was held to be an important part of that English social class, known as the landed gentry; ranked below that of the aristocracy of course: they not being of noble birth, but importantly landed enough to warrant a coat of arms to signify the ancestry they shared, together with all of the rigmarole that their station in life dictated.

As already mentioned, Sir Angus was clearly a distinguished looking gentleman; and he, being very well presented at all times, was highly favoured by members of the opposite gender. In brief, the ignoble gentleman was a philanderer, a flirtatious man of sorts, and one who was rarely short of propositions from ladies of a certain reputation. Not that he indulged in too much flippancy - no, that would never do, he was always most serious about the woman in his extramarital life: there being but one at this moment in time.

In any case, his reputation as a ladies man was a closely guarded confidentiality which was never likely to be talked about: favours owed had seen to that.

Most, if not all of his tenant farmers, from whom he obtained the greater portion of his substantial income, held him in high regard and considered him to be honest and fair, which indeed he was - well fair at any rate. And so his charismatic standing was as clean and bright as the finest crystal, in everyone's eyes - that is with the possible exception of the eyes of his cold wife Margaret. In her brown eyes he was the most loathsome creature imaginable; she had held this judgment of her husband for a very long time and she could envisage no reason in changing her opinion of him now.

She had had no hesitation in predicting precisely where her husband was destined when he left Hyde Hall in such a hurry that afternoon as she attentively watched his hasty departure from the seclusion of her bedroom window, a station where she mostly positioned herself these days contemplating the world and all its shortcomings. And she was right.

Half of one hour to the minute after the big silver Jaguar had left Hyde Hall, it endured the usual potholed lane that preceded its ultimate end, and drew up outside pretty Bramble Bush Cottage on the far side of the tiny hamlet of Basham Killington; where Sir Angus' mistress lived.

The immaculate white cottage was neatly thatched and had the straw effigy of a pheasant occupying the centre of its roof's ridge; and the herbaceous garden that had been carefully tended was filled with old-fashioned varieties of everything that could possibly be imagined, all growing in colourful profusion and looking beautiful.

After being precisely parked, the Jaguar's door was duly secured and Sir Angus walked hastily to the porch covered doorway and tried the handle without first ringing the doorbell.

To his further irritation he found the door to be firmly locked and so he tried ringing the bell and hammering loudly at the same time with his patience frayed and almost lost.

'Angus, what on earth are you doing here?' said a genteel, womanly voice belonging that of a pretty lady of about twenty and five years, possessing particular sophistication and who had shown herself to be slowly walking round the side of the cottage.

Jane Howe was pleasantly dressed in a lengthy, fully flared, pink floral frock but with no make up at all covering her face; in fact the lady's face didn't need any further enhancement: her features and her light brown hair were attractive enough without.

'I hadn't anticipated your visit today Angus, not until tomorrow darling, surely! I do hope nothing is wrong,' she further added - suspecting that there was.

'Might we go inside Jane,' answered Sir Angus eagerly, 'I'm in need of a large drink; if you would be so kind.'

'Yes of course, darling, but do you mind if we use the side door, the front door's latch is none too secure at the moment so I have kept it locked for the past couple of days until I can get it fixed,' she answered, looking at Sir Angus affectionately and taking his arm as she spoke.

As soon as the couple had entered the tiny lounge with its chintzy curtains and its matching chintzy covered small settee and armchair, Jane went directly to the cocktail cabinet and poured two very large whiskies, and handed one to her devoted, sexual partner. They both occupied the small settee and faced one another, casually holding hands, but with no other, more obvious, indications of their affection showing.

'So what is it that brings you knocking at my door so unexpectedly, Angus?' asked the lady of the house, looking away from her visitor and not at him.

'Nothing of any real importance Jane,' he answered, his countenance not revealing the intended contradiction to his words. 'I just thought I might surprise you with a fleeting visit, that's all.'

It was not difficult for Jane to recognize from Sir Angus' face that that, most certainly, was not the sole reason for his visit with her that afternoon and that there had to be some underlying motive. She knew her lover well enough to realise he did nothing just for the hell of it; he didn't possess enough quality of character for any on the spur of the moment decisions and so it was pretty obvious something abhorrent was inconveniencing him deep within.

'It's not like you to turn up unannounced, I must say; but none the less pleasurable for all that. Is all well back at Hyde, both Jennifer and Margaret agreeable are they?' she probed.

'Well no, since you ask, all is not well, not well at all,' announced Sir Angus, firmly; hiding no self-control to his sentence whatsoever. 'It's that wretched daughter of mine, assuming she is mine of course.' He continued, after the briefest of brief pauses. 'She spent the whole of last night in the company of a Gypsy fellow, the two of them, together, and alone, in his caravan; can you believe it? Well I ask you, what child in her right mind would allow herself to be placed in such a potentially compromising situation as that.

'Of course, Sarah persuaded me to involve the police when the wretched girl failed to turn up this morning for her schooling; well it did seem the right course of action to take at the time; theoretically she could have been abducted I suppose; but now, in the cold light of day, how the hell do I look in the eyes of the whole of the local community? It's bound to get out of course, these irritating and belittling incidents have a habit of showing themselves sooner or later you know, and so I repeat, how do you think I will look when they do?

'The situation is ludicrous, Jane; quite ludicrous I tell you. And as for Margaret, well, she is of little help to me, no help at all actually, not in times like these; she just retires to her room and pretends nothing is happening, nothing is happening,' he raised his voice quite appreciably at the second 'nothing is happening'.

'I ask you what in the world are things coming to when even ones wife will offer no support or interest. I tell you Jane, I am at the limit of my patience with that awful girl and with her mother too... I surely am.'

Sir Angus took a long heavy draught of his single malt at this juncture and felt and looked all the better for it; and the reddening in his features slowly diminished by the second as Jane now focused her eyes on his and expressed her uneasy concern without speaking; but with her tender touch and her sincere affectionate gaze she gave her lover sufficient solace for the moment.

Eventually, Sir Angus, feeling trapped within the confines of his domestic situation or in need of the stretching of his aching limbs, (he wasn't at all sure which), stood up and walked the tiny chintzy room. His brain, now all but numb with its constant ponderings didn't give up its obligation but continued to seek the hard to pin down solution to the dilemma he had so burdened it with; while Jane, still seated where he had left her, likewise ruminated over the quandary her man had set before her.

It was Jane who broke the stubborn silence with what she considered to be a promising answer to their now mutual but difficult situation. She suddenly sat bolt upright as she raised her lovely head.

'Darling, why don't you send Jennifer away from Hyde Hall?' She had made the suggestion off the cuff, as it were, with looks and smiles of complete composure upon her attractive face. 'Perhaps your brother Hamish would look after her for you; after all he is childless and must be very lonely since his wife died. Don't you think that might provide you with the best answer darling?'

'No Jane, that wouldn't do at all. Under no circumstances

would I burden that man with a child of mine, he would never be able to cope and fulfil her educational needs and what is morally right and necessary for a girl of Jennifer's temperament and age,' he answered regretfully. 'Hamish lives alone, and with a girl as silly as Jennifer for company, well, it could lead to all sorts of complications... sorry Jane but it has to be a definite no to that one!'

'Well then,' rejoined Jane, 'why not invest in a modest property close to where he lives and allow both Sarah and Jennifer the freedom to share it together. Sarah would then be able to continue with Jennifer's education and her care and your daughter will be well and truly out of your hair. Of course, I would offer to have the child living here with me, you know that, but it would curtail our relationship considerably if I did that.'

Sir Angus thought intensely for awhile, and then, walking to the window, he scanned the near horizon and the hollyhocks in particular before turning to his lady.

'Jane Howe!' he exclaimed, the broadest of smiles at last rearranging the features on his face. 'You are a positive genius my dear, that is indeed the solution to all my misgivings regarding my daughter's future; how ever did you manage to come up with that little gem? That is wonderful Jane, truly wonderful my dear.'

Sir Angus quickly walked over to where Jane was sitting and taking her hands in his he lifted her up from her seat and kissed her passionately.

CHAPTER FIVE

Ever since her return, Jenny had been extremely anxious about her father's reaction to her temporary absence from Hyde Hall and what he may see fit to offer as retribution.

She was already aware that her father's concern for her own happiness had been discarded long ago, if indeed it existed in the first place; so why all her nervousness? She had no idea; but it was there all the same.

She was also sensitive to the fact that her father's main concern would be how he looked in other peoples eyes; she thinking perhaps that other minds may place the blame for her bad behaviour at her father's feet. She knew, of course, that the world's opinion meant a great deal to him and so her childlike thoughts seemed pretty valid to her now.

For this reason alone, she comforted herself that her father may see little advantage in punishing her at all this time, and that the whole escapade would be forgotten fairly soon.

But she hadn't expected her father's departure to have been quite so spontaneous or instant all the same - not now that she had presented herself once more.

His going from Hyde Hall without the single expression of a greeting, had been afforded her, after she had returned with Tom by her side, or a single word of farewell when he had left so angrily, and his failure to acknowledge her presence while they stood together - yes, all this lack of decency on his part had encouraged the bitter feelings to linger, and made her seem more unwanted and alone than ever.

Sarah noticed her charge's reaction to her father's hasty departure at once.

After hesitating for awhile, but with a level of warmth about her, she took a most strange and impulsive initiative by walking over to Jenny to place a kindly hand upon her slender shoulder.

'Jennifer, I should consider it a polite gesture for you to apologise to the two police officers for your behaviour today; now... at once... if you please, before they actually leave. Do you think you could cope with that?

'No matter how inappropriate and unnecessary you may consider such an apology to be, in my view it is always advisable to stay on the right side of people in authority... and especially the police... it may hold you in good stead for the future, in their eyes anyway, who can tell.'

Her words were uttered as kindly as she knew how, although they did contain a certain emphasis of precision about them, in an informal sort of way, the like of which, despite her seemingly changed attitude, hadn't deserted the governess altogether.

The tutor and her young charge approached the policemen as they were entering their motor and not only did Jenny offer her own words of regret but Sarah also stated clearly that it was her own inspired idea to involve the authorities regarding Jenny's disappearance in the first place, and not that of Sir Angus'.

At the time she had mistakenly thought the position warranted positive action but she now regretted pre-empting the situation by rashly soliciting the concern of the police.

The two policemen merely nodded their acceptance of the apologies from both parties but failed to support their acceptance with any reciprocal words and after entering the motor vehicle they were seen to be in close conference, the one with the other, and then, with the doors and windows of their motor vehicle firmly closed, they left without a backward glance.

Governess and pupil eventually entered Hyde Hall as one, anxiously awaiting the ultimate return of Sir Angus Kent, with a certain amount of trepidation building up within the minds of the two of them.

They went straight to the classroom, where, at Sarah's insistence, Jenny presented a full verbal account of the events that had led to the existing state of affairs which included both cat and kitten and Tom's caring attitude toward her, the storm and the caravan; in fact everything the little girl considered to be of relevance to her disappearance was included.

Jenny was astonished at receiving Sarah Wood's forthright but sensitive words of understanding; this was indeed a changed governess who stood before her now and one that Jenny was at last beginning to appreciate.

"Did it take all that has gone on in the past, and indeed more recently, to swing this stodgy dumpling of a governess into becoming a more reasonable human being?" wondered Jenny, with probably not those exact words being used by her mind but the gist of her thinking was almost certainly in line with them.

Jenny continued with the day's lessons lethargically, since her mind was persistent in being weighed down with anxious thoughts of her father's return. Her teacher also seemed to have her mind set firmly in the clouds with thought provoking problems;

concerned, no doubt, that her earlier debate with Sir Angus may have been misconstrued as being dictatorial and not at all compliant with the master's arrogant wishes.

"His wishes," she thought, *"ah yes! Well they were plain enough for me to see and understand, so why on earth didn't I carry them out at once without considering the doubts that may have plagued my mind at the time. I can remember an instance when I would have raised the roof had my wishes been debated in that way, but there was I, questioning the ins and outs of his opinion with no regard at all as to my own position. That would have been a dischargeable offence in my day, most assuredly so, and without hesitation either; perhaps it will be this time, who knows? I shall have to wait and see."*

***

It was early evening before a greatly changed Sir Angus Kent at last returned to Hyde Hall; five forty five to be exact, as he, inclining his head, acknowledged and admired the accuracy of his timepiece with a smile of satisfaction. Then, tossing the car keys to Jenson the handyman to put the car away, he climbed the wide front steps to the portal of his home.

A reformed character he most certainly seemed to be and even though the change was withheld from his outer façade he certainly felt improved within.

His temper had now levelled and the resentment he felt toward his wife and daughter in the immediate past was not so bitter now; not in his own view anyway.

In spite of this, Sir Angus had no intention of disclosing these amicable heart warming changes to Sarah or to Jennifer, not yet anyway; he felt the need to approach his estranged wife first in order to gain her reaction to this his most recent of proposals.

Margaret, of course, had noticed her husband's arrival and had instantly turned away from the window in total disgust and had repositioned herself upon her bed achieving much the same position she had abandoned before she'd heard the sound of her husband's car.

She anticipated the tediously long debate Sir Angus would now be seeking, and regardless of any carefully planned proposals he may have in mind to offer as an answer to their daughter's bitterness toward her parents, she would certainly oppose them rigorously, and from the outset.

'No deviously scheming and pushy mistress of his is going to dictate to me how to bring up a daughter of mine no matter how wayward I may consider that daughter to be,' said she, audibly to herself as she rehearsed her opposition with a raised voice that exaggerated her innermost feelings - despite the fact she had no idea what proposals were going to be offered to her - if indeed any at all. However, anything Angus cared to say regarding their daughter at the moment, even if it was of little or no consequence at all, would still be opposed by Margaret in no uncertain terms, she was in that sort of mood.

The awaited tapping on her door was unanswered at first but eventually after more persistent knocking she rose from her bed to feebly respond.

'Oh, it's you is it,' she said, abruptly, as if taken by surprise. She then opened the door slightly wider and greeted her husband with a coldness that would have frozen the ears off even the warmest kangaroo. She then turned, unsmiling and seated herself on a nursing chair conveniently situated next to the open window. Her husband remained standing: he not being invited to relax his weary limbs.

'Margaret, we need to discuss Jennifer's future,' said Sir Angus, forcefully. His opening to the debate was immediate with no frills or niceties, but evenly spoken, and more importantly, without a hint of the raising of his voice. 'I don't think either of us could tolerate another episode like the one we experienced today and so I propose sending her away until she is much older so that both you and I can get on with our lives in peace.'

Margaret hadn't expected a proposition of this scale, which, on the surface, seemed an ideal solution as far as she was concerned. But she, most definitely, had no wish for her husband or his mistress to be seen as being instrumental in bringing about this astonishing answer to her unspoken prayers; unspoken to her Creator that is, for often had she wished and had described to others how much she'd wished her daughter out of her life; it wasn't a secret, why, even Jenny was well aware of her mother's need to be rid of her.

'Oh, and whose moment of inspiration was this; yours or that trollop you have the damnable audacity to call a mistress?' she asked, allowing the previous thirteen years to slip away in a single moment and for secret knowledge at last to flow from her lips.

It was with some relief too, it must be said, that she allowed the closet door to open and for her husband's secret to escape, for she was now able to view, with delight, the look of complete surprise as it flashed across her husband's features - and she showed him instantly, by her sarcastic smile, just how much pleasure she was deriving from the disclosure and would continue so to do.

'Don't look so surprised darling,' said she, cynically, 'I've known of your vulgar secret for simply ages; Jane isn't it? I wonder if she is aware of the countless other Janes there has been in your sordid little life over the years before she came along.' She paused for a brief moment, to allow the full extent of her pronouncement to sink in. 'Well, is she aware?' she added, with some vocal force.

'Margaret, I have come to you in order to debate our daughter's future, not to discuss our marital situation, which, since you have brought the subject up, is currently non existent; and as you well know it has been so for some considerable time,' returned Sir Angus, still with total calmness. 'Now shall we abandon all this nonsense in favour of a more civilized discussion or would you prefer to contaminate the debate and yourself with its continuation; which one can only describe as being an uncontrolled fishwife slanging match... on your behalf.'

Margaret didn't answer, she wanted with all her heart to be rid of her daughter but how could she possibly agree to this proposal without totally losing face when negotiating a likely submission. In the end she thought she might possibly skirt round the distasteful allegation she had made; she didn't really care what her husband was capable of doing behind her back anyway, or who he bedded for that matter.

'Well, when do you propose to carry out the unexpected liberation of our daughter? I take it that you are intent on placing her in a haven of pure opulence, and not in a place where she can present me with problems from afar. Or can it be you are going to put the little witch under the earth, in her coffin and sealed up so there can be no escape for her,' said Margaret, with the trace of an evil smirk upon her face, which contorted it's once beautiful features into something black and sinister.

'Please, do you have to be so ridiculous Margaret? All of your fictional and malicious remarks will be taken seriously one day, and then where will you be? Locked up behind iron bars I expect,' he said, as the suggestion of an arrogant smile swept across his now cautious face.

'I warn you Angus,' rejoined the wife, menacingly, 'you are to make uncompromising, watertight provisions for me not to be involved, I repeat, not to be involved, do you hear me, Angus? I am never to be implicated in anything that creature does or is concerned with and that includes her upbringing, and that she is to be as far away from me as she possibly can be so that she causes me no problems, inconvenience or embarrassment; if you do that, then I will agree to your seedy plan. If you do not comply with these terms then your sordid secret will be exposed for the whole of the world to hear, and you and your prostitute will have to suffer all the embarrassing unpleasantness I can possibly muster to heap upon the heads of the pair of you.

'I mean it Angus... it is plain enough so that even you can understand what I am saying, just keep to the terms and your secret is secure, involve me in anything concerning that monstrous child of yours then your secret most certainly is not; in fact it will be quite the opposite... I shall spread the news of your questionable activities like the proverbial plague so that you will be glad to move to the far side of Timbuktu.

'So there you have it; it's up to you now Angus, it's your choice, so get on with it; there is no need for me to know your depressing plans for her; I'd rather not know them anyway.'

A restless silence now existed between them, even though Margaret did consider that she had made a worthwhile point and had swung the debate in her own favour.

And so Margaret amused herself by fixing her eyes on something of no particular interest outside the window of her room while Sir Angus tried his damnedest to put into effect some sympathies for his wife's opinion and her attitude toward their daughter, and quite surprisingly, for her hateful demands as well. But no suitable grounds for amnesty could be found for her, even though he searched every inch of the capacity of his mind.

Being totally aware of his wife's uneasiness about him being unnecessarily present in the privacy of her bedroom, he walked toward the door, and then, with his left hand lightly resting on the levered handle he turned toward her.

'As this matter involves Sarah,' he said, 'I intend having a short meeting with her straight away. If you wish to attend we shall be in my study.'

He opened the door quietly but before he could make his escape his wife turned on him with more of the same.

'Just a moment Angus, what do you mean by saying the matter involves Sarah?' she asked, aghast at the mental imagery of her own thoughts. 'Surely you are not going to ask her to leave Hyde Hall, are you?'

'No, I am certainly not going to ask that of her but as you had no wish to be acquainted with my plans for Jennifer, I see no reason why we should prolong this discussion, do you?' The reply was more than a little condescending but showed enough mockery to spark off Margaret's logical curiosity.

'Anything that involves my Aunt Sarah is of importance to me Angus,' said she, curtly, 'so yes, I certainly do wish to be present in your discussion with her.'

'As you wish Margaret, then perhaps you will be in my study in thirty minutes time,' he answered, as he left the room and the undignified atmosphere behind him.

***

It was six thirty that same evening and Sarah Wood was at her bedroom table busily preparing the morrow's lessons and contemplating, with some nervousness, what might be said by Sir Angus regarding her future at Hyde Hall when they eventually met up; this she anticipated to be very soon indeed.

She went over all of the uncertainties of the limited possibilities in her mind, as she had when she left her last post, desperate in her need to find some alternatives should the need arise for her to leave at once; there were none, none that sprang readily to mind, at any rate.

A gentle tap upon her door interrupted her thinking and then swamped her mind with nervousness as she rose from her seat at the table to answer the call.

It was Lucy one of the housemaids.

'The master's respects Miss Wood, and would you please attend him in his study in thirty minutes time,' she said, in the most minute of voices possible.

***

'Come,' said the stern voice of Sir Angus in response to Sarah's tender tapping.

Sarah Wood opened the oaken door in a state of hidden nervousness but walked boldly in.

The gentleman of the house was seated behind his magnificent mahogany desk and her niece, Margaret, was standing once again surveying the gardens from the window, looking fidgety and tense.

'I was told you wished to see me, Sir Angus,' offered Sarah nervously.

'That's right Sarah,' said Sir Angus, 'but don't look so worried, it's nothing serious. I have a proposition to put to you that's all, and because you are family, as it were, Margaret has decided she would prefer to be present when I place it before you.

'As you know, Jennifer has proved herself to be quite a handful over the years, which indeed is why I invited you to Hyde Hall in the first place. Now the whole of the child's unpleasantness has culminated in today's fiasco; a fiasco which I might add, Margaret is not prepared to tolerate any longer.' He looked sideways at his wife and noticed the disapproving look issuing from her face, at being so accused.

He paid it no heed.

'Now the proposition is this: as you may or may not know I have a brother now living in Lincolnshire whom I have already contacted and who is willing to keep a stern eye on our little bundle of mischief. Now I am not prepared for her to live specifically with my brother, although he is childless; but he lost his wife awhile back which has placed him in an unfortunate and vulnerable situation.

'I am therefore proposing to invest in a modest property, near to where my brother lives, and for both Jennifer and you to occupy a small cottage in order to continue her education to a satisfactory standard and to its ultimate conclusion. Your remuneration will remain much the same as it is at present with the exception that you will be expected to financially support yourself; all of Jennifer's needs, will of course be met by me.'

Margaret's defence of her aunt was clearly expressed by the look on the fierce woman's face as she stood to confront her husband in a most unbecoming and intense manner.

'My aunt is being supported by this estate in her position as governess at this point in time, so I see no reason why her financial situation should not remain the same and that her living expenses should be met by the estate, as they are now,' said she, with an unconvincing tone to her voice, which she appeared not to be able to strengthen.

'Margaret, you kindly expressed your terms a short while ago; and your requirements to be rid of our child were properly noted; now it's my turn.

'These are indeed my terms and they will remain should Sarah decide to accept them or should she not,' said Sir Angus, ruthlessly. 'Well Sarah what do you say? Are you compliant with the agreement which I have outlined, or do you have other proposals you wish to put forward? The decision I might add is yours; you will not be expected to forfeit your residency with us should you decide not to go; I would merely seek some alternative arrangement for Jennifer's education if that be the case and if it is really necessary.'

Sarah looked comforted, at least the appearance on her plump, round face gave that distinct impression and she even affected a smile as she wrung her hands in pleasured relief.

'That sounds a wonderful proposition Sir Angus, thank you very much, I'm sure Jennifer will make great progress once we are completely settled in our new home and with all the excitement that that will bring the two of us. Yes, all in all, I think that to be the best solution for all your problems and I am sure we will soon find our feet once we've moved to Lincolnshire. So yes I shall be extremely pleased to accept your kind offer, no need for further consideration on my part, I can assure you of that. Where exactly is the property positioned Sir Angus?'

'Don't know yet Sarah; my brother lives in a pretty little village called Brenton quite near to Lincoln, or so I believe, I'm hoping something will turn up close by and in the same village. I am indeed hopeful but one cannot be entirely sure how things will turn out; but there is usually something on the market at this time of the year.

'I shall leave you to break the news to Jennifer, if you have no objections, I'm sure she will be equally as excited about the prospects of the move as you appear to be.

'You might also instil upon the young madam's mind, while you are together, the vital importance of involving herself with other people's company. I most certainly expect her to get out of the stupid habit of spending endless days on her own, very quickly; it remains, after all is said and done, a most unhealthy habit and there is most certainly no need for it, no need at all; besides, it might be the making of her to involve herself with other more common people's society. But there, I shall leave all that sort of nonsense in your most capable hands Sarah.'

After a few incidental remarks had been made by the master of the house, amid Margaret's deafening silence, the meeting was closed and a contented Sarah walked hurriedly back along the narrow corridors to the resumption of her preparatory work in the confines of her cosy room.

Jenny arrived in her classroom well ahead of the recognised time the following morning, considering she had a good deal of making up to do if she wished for her tutor to remain harmoniously disposed toward her.

But it was with complete surprise that she found Miss Wood already in the classroom with a happy, smiling disposition and was seen to be carefully writing on the blackboard a few words in the form of a declaration to her pupil.

Jenny seated herself at her desk without being able to remove her eyes from the wording which was simple enough to read and to understand-

JENNIFER, BOTH YOU AND I ARE LEAVING HYDE HALL
TOGETHER, VERY SHORTLY.

PART TWO

CHAPTER ONE

Two long months passed lazily by, indifferent in their attitude as to whether they hurried themselves along or whether they didn't.

And it was during this drawn out period that little Jennifer Kent, in an effort to discard all hopeless thoughts and to replace them with expectations of hopefulness, worked single-mindedly at her tedious lessons both during the daytime and in the evenings - still friendless and alone.

"Loneliness is a place where learning seeks to reinforce the skills of youth and so it adds to that already learned from life's abounding depths."

Jenny smiled openly at the sentence she had taken so much pride and time in composing and had written so carefully in the front of her diary. But she kept all these endeavours to herself without discussing or sharing them with her tutor even though her governess had been more pleasant towards her of late than she had ever been before the episode of absenteeism had taken place. But did a close and harmonious amity exist? No, that was still nowhere to be seen in spite of everything that had taken place.

Jenny had visited her dear Bluey's grave on several occasions during the two, long months and had chatted to him with some relief about her solitude.

She had even ventured to the far side of the dense forest, desperate in her longing for an indication of her friend, Tom's, whereabouts and although the scorched earth betrayed the remnants of a campfire in a couple of distinct places, not a single caravan was to be seen.

Finally the lost and dejected little girl had had to retrace her weary steps back to Hyde Hall once again, where disappointment and loneliness were to be found in abundance and where every dreary day followed the previous dreary day, until excitement in the form of her relocation to Lincolnshire would ultimately replace them.

It happened all at once and with no prior warning being offered. Her despair suddenly turned to joy after she had been told by Sarah Wood that it would be early the following morning that they were to leave Hyde Hall together, and for good.

Jenny, in her excitement, packed all of the bits and pieces

she'd decided to take with her into the large tea chests on that newly arrived morning: two large plywood boxes with their razor-sharp metal corners had been unceremoniously dumped in her room the previous evening for that result.

It was while she was packing her things away that she allowed her imagination to drift a bit from her chore as she wondered thoughtfully if she would ever see her gypsy friend again or be allowed a kitten after they had settled awhile within their new home. These were the only two events that had meant anything at all to Jenny in the past years, yes, these alone had exceeded all other events at Hyde Hall, and looking back it wasn't much to show in the way of satisfaction for twelve long years of living.

On the morning of her departure and with a feeling of perfect happiness in her heart, Jenny had stood at her window looking out and wondering if she would ever see Hyde Hall in her future years - she hoped she wouldn't.

As she gazed her attention was drawn to the two removal men as they slowly loaded the chests onto the undersized cream and brown removal van that had waited beside the marbled entrance since the early hours. It looked to Jenny as if one of the men was finding some difficulty and he slipped a little, thereby allowing some items spill to the ground. Looking around himself with a degree of embarrassment he retrieved the two objects of her clothing from the gravelled ground before he was successful in completing his task.

Parked behind the truck and looking shiny and new she noticed the small, black Morris Minor motorcar belonging that of her austere governess but which had never been used: as far as Jenny was aware.

But there it now stood; regimentally waiting to take her and her governess to Lincolnshire's county where Jenny hoped to spend the rest of her life in bliss, just learning from her governess and finding out what life is like in the more northern parts of England.

No one was available to witness the departure of the little group that morning. Both Jenny's mother and her father were away at separate locations, either busying themselves or being amused, it didn't matter which, but certainly with alternative arrangements occupying their time and feeding their pleasure - that much was clear.

Not a single parting word of good fortune or wish for their daughter's wellbeing was being offered; no penned words were left behind, not even a message of regret for the parent's absence was relayed to their child or to her governess.

55

To Sarah, the express obligation upon her niece, and her niece's husband too, was for them both to be present at the start of this particular journey and to bid their girl a fond farewell in a right and proper manner; this would have been of supreme importance, to Sarah's way of thinking - though seemingly not to theirs.

And not only for the child's benefit would this gesture have been appropriate but for the family as a whole - for it would have illustrated the quality of their skills in basic parenting which the two of them seem not to have grasped and would have dispelled Sarah Wood's now rancid opinion of the them both.

It was plain to see by the frown on her face that the parent's non-attendance had affected Sarah in a most objectionable way and that this alone was dwelling heavily on her mind; and so with a feeling of considerable disillusionment taking root in her heart she walked very slowly from the house all the while glancing around her for the sight of any latecomer - but no one came forward to present a farewell of any form.

As she positioned herself behind the wheel of her car she offered a diluted smile of acceptance of the situation to her little charge who was impatiently seated beside her and ready for the off.

But why should parents act like this? Sarah had no idea and for the first time in her long life a feeling of pity went out to someone, namely to a little girl, who had done nothing recklessly wrong, nothing for anyone to have a fit about anyway, for Jennifer was no worse than any other girl of twelve, who had been treated so shabbily, and a good deal better than most, she decided.

Merciless thoughts of her malevolent niece's selfish attitude, on the other hand, was destined to play heavily on Sarah's mind in an excessive manner; this would be inescapable, and for some considerable time to come at that.

Jenny, in contrast, couldn't care less whether her parents were present or not when the party left; at least she wouldn't admit she was fretful in any way. In fact she had told herself earlier, as soon as she awoke, that they wouldn't be available to offer their goodbyes to her, so what difference did it make? Nothing at all; not so far as Jenny was concerned.

As stated many times before, Jenny had always considered her parents to be selfish, unfeeling people and it really hadn't occurred to her young mind that anything differing from the norm would present itself anyway; she was estimated as being worth less than nothing by her parents, you see; an irritation of little consequence that wouldn't go away.

For these reasons alone, as they left Hyde Hall that morning, Jenny deliberately encouraged an expression of pure delight to shine from her now freed countenance instead of gloom. And when turning her head to take a last lingering look at the house where she had spent the previous twelve years and as the two vehicles moved cautiously along the lengthy, slightly curving driveway, she instantly saw three of the younger household staff waving frantically with handkerchiefs, dusters and towels in their hands.

After Jenny, had screamed for Sarah to stop the car they both got out and returned the eager waving with some considerable return, at least Jenny did; Sarah, having a tendency to emotional restraint, appeared somewhat reticent and offered only a modest indication of a wave.

Then once again they entered the car to recommence the long journey ahead and to all that awaited them in far off Lincolnshire.

***

The best part of nine hours had been taken up by means of weary travel, with Sarah following the removal van closely; in fact she didn't lose contact with the slow moving van for all that time.

Following three brief pauses for their convenience and passing through as many rumbling, turbulent thunder storms, the little party eventually arrived at their new Lincolnshire home in a state of physical and mental exhaustion.

Despite all these unwelcome feelings hanging over them, and with a deficiency in energy, caused by hunger, thrown in for good measure, they rallied round and shored each other up with displays of cheerful optimism; particularly Jenny, who, despite her age and size, proved herself to be of a confident temperament with immense durability accompanied by a determined and lively spirit.

'The Cottage', so called, it was considered, because of its thatched roof and characterful appearance, proved to be the unlikely couple's new home.

It seemed a delightfully modest place, from what they could see of it: for the day's light was fading fast. Even so, it was vaguely seen to be remotely situated next to a pleasant rural lane and opposite fields of growing grain.

But, as already mentioned, the daylight hours were fast becoming shortened by this time thereby preventing the couple from viewing their new home with any degree of close observance; and with no key with which to unlock the small cottage door, they were stuck and had to wait, patient in the certain knowledge that they were to be expected at an undetermined hour by Hamish Kent, brother to Sir Angus, who's own home was believed to be close by.

For almost a full hour they waited and with the removal van leaving as soon as it had deposited its load of tea chests, bags, suitcases and classroom clutter inconveniently close to the small sheltered entrance and by using the chests as seats upon which to park their exhausted bodies - they waited still.

No one conveniently passed along the lane that evening; no one to whom they might call for assistance or information and no lights were seen to show the presence of near neighbours. To Sarah, who was now feeling some concern about the difficult role she was expected to play in the future as surrogate mother, teacher and companion to a problematic child, the wait seemed never ending.

By using her over active imaginings and her recall, Sarah Wood, amid troubled feelings of considerable magnitude, began silently to question how it was she had allowed such a commission to have been imposed upon her or why she had even considered such an assignment as this in the first place.

She had been hindered, at the time, by her own insecurity at Hyde Hall, that much was easy to see and she would have been heavily reliant on others' opinions that may have differed from her own, had she taken time for careful thought or had had the nerve to speak to her niece about her worries; that much was clear as well. And with the obvious expectation of a problem or two beleaguering her, as the passing years would undoubtedly increase at their usual pace, she wondered whether she was in fact up to such an undertaking as this, especially at her time of life. And as she sat and ruminated about all her newly found problems her legs became uneasy and fidgety.

Despite the fact that all of these concerns would most assuredly revisit her from time to time, her anxieties for the moment were cut short by the almost inaudible 'hullo' from a quasi-mannish voice coming from the far side of the gate that was bordered by the passing, narrow lane.

The voice seemed to drift clumsily over the evening air and was immediately followed by the appearance of the silhouetted, shortish figure of a male person as he slowly approached the cottage via the front garden path.

He closed the gate, none too silently behind him, as he extended his greeting.

'Hope you haven't been waiting there for too long,' said he, cynically, and coming across as being not overly concerned whether they had or whether they hadn't.

He continued edgily, as up 'til now he had received no response from his first hullo. 'I'm expecting to find a Sarah Wood here, from Hyde in Dorset; could either of you possibly be she?' he asked, with little expectancy in his voice.

'I am Miss Sarah Wood,' said the owner of that name, displaying a feeling of intense irritation. 'I have been waiting here for well over an hour when I thought my arrival would have been met more promptly and at a more appropriate time than this.

'I take it you are the holder of the key to my cottage, if so I shall be glad for you to open the door at once and allow me to enter.'

'Sorry for the regrettable delay Miss Wood but Mr. Kent, he forgot to mention to me the exact time of your arrival and has only a few minutes ago realised his own forgetfulness,' said the short man, with a lack of urgency in his voice as he slowly sauntered up to the cottage door. And after successfully fitting a key into its lock, he turned it, and opened the door to its fullest width.

'Perhaps you would allow me to help you in with these here chests, suit cases and things,' he indifferently offered, with a hint in his voice that a worthwhile gratuity might be forthcoming at the end of the exercise. 'Can't allow you to carry these heavy boxes in on your own now can I? No, course not, that'll never do!' he added.

Within the dim illumination, issuing from a light bulb attached to the end of a double twisted flex arrangement and being suspended from the centre of the small, pretty lounge ceiling, with its plain shade slightly askew, the individual was seen to be a youngish man of about twenty years or so with an acute squint in his left eye that made him look somewhat menacing.

Not being cleverly attired and with a certain tattiness about his person, the youngish man, despite the disturbing squint, carried a carefree expression or rather a careless expression, which failed to betray an attitude of convinced sincerity. Instead he portrayed the distinct manner of someone upon whom one should, most definitely, not place too much reliance, if indeed any at all.

After the tea chests and things had at long last been, placed in their designated rooms, waspishly organised and aided by Sarah Wood and Jenny, the youngish man decided to leave, and with his hand being extended to the elderly lady, by which gesture he intended to indicate the termination of his visit, he stated that his name was Barnabas Bell and that he hoped he had been of service, and if he could be of further assistance in the future he would be very pleased to make himself available.

'You can depend on me,' said he.

Upon hearing this statement of good intention and noticing the extended hand, Sarah Wood fumbled in her handbag and after some confusion produced two twelve sided, brass 'thrupp-nee bits' and offering them to the man Bell for all his trouble, she smiled her assurance of gratitude.

The youngish man looked at the two small coins now resting in the palm of his open hand; in point of fact he gazed at them incessantly and inspected them in a manner of unappreciated astonishment and disbelief, and, after turning them over once or twice with clammy, pliant fingers, he raised his disappointed head to glance at the coin's contributor.

'You sure you can spare all this money,' said he, with an unmistakable hint of sarcasm in his voice that spoke volumes for the youngish man's reason in assisting people in distress with his usefulness.

'Oh yes,' Sarah replied, now smiling happily and with equal cynicism she added, 'you've certainly earned it.'

Jenny, for all this time, had been busying herself by unpacking a few immediate and necessary items in her allotted room, just happily humming a few repeated cords of no known tune; and then, ceasing her discordant humming, she quietly descended the narrow staircase in time to witness Barnabas Bell's unhurried departure.

The disturbed look of discontent in the youngish man's countenance when he received the scant reward for his labour, caused Jenny to smile with a degree of amusement; she, in all probability, and with some calculated suspicion in her mind, did reasonably believe that the youngish man had kept them both waiting at the door quite unnecessarily in order to make the delay seem more worthwhile for himself and that he had been more than adequately compensated for his efforts, all of this was obviously shared by her governess.

Upon being left in relative peace by the mysterious Barnabas Bell and upon a further brief inspection of their new home, both Sarah and Jenny were delighted to find that not only had the cottage been made homely with freshly presented beds in their individual rooms but that the cupboards in the kitchen had also been stocked aplenty with everything necessary to serve them for a full week's living.

With no further delay, Sarah set about preparing them both a supper of good sustenance and upon the consumption of this they climbed the narrow stairway to retire to their respective bedrooms, and slept soundly until daybreak.

***

It was the noisy warble of the birds in the trees outside that decided to act as an alarm clock for Jennifer Kent at six the following morning. Their chattering and singing presented a more favourable start to the day than anyone could possibly have hoped, for never before had she slept close enough to nature so that she might be subjected to such remarkable melodic sounds; or indeed, experience such extraordinary contentment as this. Why, even in Tom's small caravan she had missed the bird's chirpy palaver and only awoke when the fiasco had finished; and in the hugeness of Hyde Hall she was situated too far away and too high up to appreciate such rapture.

Now she lay for a moment or two with her small hands and fingers entwined behind her head, her mind wrapped in wonder at her new situation and with the smuggest of smiles stirring her pretty face, she welcomed her deliverance.

For the first time in her young life, she no longer felt the loneliness that the last twelve and a bit year had dealt her; instead, she looked forward in eagerness to the next twelve and far beyond.

For a further hour and thirty-five minutes the little girl lay within the pure white coverlets of her new bed in blissful repose; and once the awakening sweet dawn chorus had been completed and the light of the new day had been sufficient for their feathered flight, there she stayed. And she allowed her mind to busy itself in the pondering of the past day and in the excited anticipation of the immediate morn.

Soon she would have to busy herself in preparation for the first day of her new young life; the first day's learning would be upon her soon enough, yanking her mind in all directions and bringing with it all sorts of bewilderment and dismay, but for the while, she would snugly savour each blessed second of this, her new delight.

The gentle tapping on the door of her room brought Jenny slowly back to the reality of the moment as Sarah Wood's familiar voice instilled the necessity for her reply.

'Jennifer, are you awake?' she asked, in a low voice. 'It's time for you to move yourself!'

'Thank you Miss Wood, I am awake and am getting out of bed straight away,' was the immediate response. And with that,

Jenny hopped out of bed and made for the bathroom.

When she had completed her customary wash and brush up to the required and necessary standard and dressed herself appropriately, she hurried down to the small kitchen where her governess was patiently waiting for her charge. And an appetising, savoury smell of a freshly cooked breakfast hovered about the place and greeted the little girl's hungriness as she idled her way into the room. This heady smell of sizzling bacon reminded her of the wondrously happy time she had breakfasted with Tom which she would always remember each and every time the smell of bacon wafted her face.

After they both had had their fill of their first day's meal, Sarah turned to her charge and unexpectedly produced a smile that was both broad and slow, even though her face had been unaccustomed to such a gruelling exercise as this in the past; but it lingered still while she impatiently hovered about the kitchen.

'You'll be pleased to know I have no lessons planned for today Jennifer,' said she, with this her unusual smile continuing to awkwardly play upon her round, plump, old-fashioned face. 'So I thought we might familiarise ourselves with Brenton village and possibly explore its surrounding area, if we have time; and then, later on, we shall call upon your uncle at The Old House to introduce ourselves and to inform him of our arrival.'

At the happy receiving of the 'no lessons today' communiqué, a look of complete and utter joy promptly erupted upon Jenny's face and a feeling of absolute delight swelled in the very heart of the young girl.

"*If only every day would turn out to be as wonderful as I am sure today is going to become, then I am certain to be the happiest girl alive,*" she thought to herself, contentedly, and she smiled broadly with the mouth that had hitherto been set in a mode of hopelessness and gloom.

The couple were already reasonably acquainted with the layout of their new home, for it was a sparse and simple cottage, but the portly governess and her happy little charge both agreed to increase the previous late evening's scant viewing, and to further familiarise themselves with a more concentrated study of the limited interior, before venturing out into the garden for a similar explorative venture there.

Each room was small but well proportioned and quite the opposite to that which they had been used to back in Dorset.

There was no hallway; the front door entered immediately

onto the cosy little front room, which was spotlessly clean and with a small settee and a single armchair providing the only seating arrangement.

An open inglenook fireplace dominated the largest of the four walls and on its red bricked breast the usual old fashioned horse brasses were seen to be hanging in irregular formation. And to the side of the brasses an antiquated set of blackened bellows hung over a brass coal scuttle, which sat upon a stone hearth in a convenient position, complete with a stash of shiny black coal inside.

With each wall's dimensions appearing to be at variance with the other three the quirky quality of this phenomenon was found to be a most curious one, but appealing to the eye for all that.

The ceiling had been freshly whitewashed between the supporting heavy beams that had had their oldness disguised by a newly stained black matt effect, thereby leaving the beetle bored holes, alone, to provide the evidence of character and aging.

All of the windows in the tiny cottage were modest in size but none more so than the upstairs apertures, where the thatched roof overhung their upper regions by a good twelve inches or so. Although this feature of the cottage presented an air of olde worlde attraction, the brightness of the light, entering the windows through their leaded glass, was plainly inadequate and created an unacceptable degree of intensity for reading or for any other close concentration. For that reason a subsidy, by way of candlelight or some other form of artificial lighting, was needed at all times of the day and night, both in wintertime and in summertime as well.

Adding to the excitement each neat and tidy room provided, a degree of satisfaction was seen to radiate from Jenny's pretty face and although Miss Wood expressed a more reserved appearance of contentment, they were, indeed, both at a loss for words so pleased were they with this choice of home provided by Sir Angus Kent and chosen by his brother.

After filling their visual appetite with approved fondness for their newly presented and pleasant cottage, they wandered the winding pathway to the bottom of the bright, colourfully filled, herbaceous borders - to a patch in the garden that contained rows of ripening vegetables and soft fruits, all growing beneath a net covering in order to keep the dawn chorus at bay.

Then quite unexpectedly and with no apparent reason the rotund figure of the governess with the plump, old fashioned face, took hold of her little charge's hand and with the kindest of smiles and looking directly into Jenny's eyes she offered words of reassurance:

'You know Jennifer; I think both you and I are going to be very happy living in this place. The cottage is all we could ever have hoped for and the garden so beautiful that we would be foolish not to seek it's consoling tranquillity at all times; and from now on I would be most happy for you to address me and regard me as your Great-Aunt Sarah. I now wish for the two of us to fashion a new relationship; a bond should exist between us to last me through to the remainder of my days. I have never, in the whole of my life, experienced closeness with any other human before, including that of my parents; I would never have allowed such a relationship to exist in any event, let alone encourage it. But now, just walking through the beautiful cottage and wandering this lovely garden with you, I realise that for the whole of my time I have been a foolish old woman and quite wrong in my attitude to life and to others. So, now I wish... no need, desperately, to make amends and change all the nonsense that has gone on before and become as much part of your young life as I need for you to be part of mine.'

Jennifer Kent was dumbstruck. Never in a million years would she have expected such a declaration of familiarity, not from her stern governess, and with so much sentiment and feeling of affection accompanying it too.

She returned her governess's gaze solemnly - standing silently for awhile in contemplation. And then, with her arms hanging lifelessly at her side she stepped closer to the great-aunt she had never known and gathering her little arms together to form a prayerful attitude on her chest, then spreading them wide, she fastened them round the rotund figure standing before her and with her head resting on the huge shapeless bosom she wept with tears of sheer delight.

'Thank you auntie,' she said, as unrestrained tears of joy rolled down her pretty face. 'Thank you so very, very much.'

CHAPTER TWO

'The Old House', this being the name of the home of Hamish Kent, was located without much difficulty. It was situated a mere three hundred of the smallest yards, as measured by Jenny's stretched strides, along the lane that bordered 'The Cottage' where great-aunt and niece now lived; and although the name implies an ancient house of former years, this most certainly was not the immediate impression presented to the casual passer by.

An immense wall, some twelve feet in height, sturdily built and durable, surrounded the grounds belonging that of the house and a pair of large, classically ornamented, black wrought iron gates, being supported by two rock-bricked pillars with a lion couchant atop each, were set in from the narrow lane by some yards and provided the introduction to an orderly gravelled driveway.

All of this introductory assemblage looked overly superior and therefore rather forbidding to the unsuspecting visitor, a focal determent even, which, in truth, was the object of its existence in the first instance.

The orderly driveway, of some fifty full yards or so, led to an orderly house of some proportions and although constructed of similar rocky brickwork to that of the pillars and the immense wall that surrounded the estate it presented an image of considerable contrast to the aforementioned.

Only a welcoming freshness could satisfactorily describe the orderly house on this sunny day; quite as if it had been scrubbed clean for this particular occasion.

A clinging Virginia creeper, already changing its colour from green to orange in places, occupied an adequate proportion of the building's frontage and stood out against the paleness of its rocky brickwork with an appealing difference.

The Old House was a sturdy place, more like an extended Georgian period house than anything else; not being ultra modern in appearance, or indeed ancient either and with its lines being clean and sharply angled it indicated a house where the elements had had little or no effect on its wearing over the years; and, all in all, did not appear to be more than an estimated one hundred years in age.

The house had nine upper windows looking to the front, four being presented on either side of the extensive landing window and from this, it might be assumed to have a similar amount of windows installed at the rear, and so a superior house of sixteen bedrooms might have been expected. Of course, each room might easily have possessed two windows, that being so, a mere eight rooms would be likely on the uppermost floor of the house or indeed a mathematical permutation of any amount of windows per room, in which case the sum total of rooms would have to be a reasonable deduction; and without some internal inspections, an architectural conundrum of certain proportions might be anticipated. Nevertheless, suffice it to say that the house was more than reasonable in size but not nearly proportionate to that of Hyde Hall, the home of Hamish Kent's brother, Sir Angus, in the heart of Dorset.

The party of two walked tentatively in the direction of the two large steps that preceded the roofed entrance to the single mounted doorway of The Old House; not actually hand in hand, it might be observed, howbeit close enough together for there to have been a quiet conversation existing between the two of them, had one been in progress. But in this instance the conversation, quiet or otherwise, was being omitted and the party of two ambled up to the front door in total silence.

The robust great-aunt Sarah Wood rang the bell and the two of them listened to its monotonous droning as it resounded throughout the whole of the house; the sound of which was not dissimilar to the introductory bell tone of Big Ben within the confines of its lofty tower when it strikes the longest hour but somewhat faster, more continuous and a little higher in tone.

They waited awhile and exchanged uneasy glances, as nervous smiles settled on their faces.

Soon a slightly built lady with pure white, waving hair arrived at the door and she opened it wide with a welcoming gesture. She seemed of an age with Sarah Wood but much more sprightly and with energy radiating from her motherly face, a face that spoke of kindness, sympathy and compassion. She was clothed in a smart uniformed dress of navy blue together with dark stockings and plain, black shiny shoes. All of this was set off by starched, white collar and cuffs.

'Ah, Miss Wood and the lovely wee Jennifer I do believe,' said she, in the softest, most kindly voice imaginable and with a slight Scottish brogue that must have perfumed the highlands bluebells in springtime's eventide. 'How lovely to see you both, we have been expecting you're visit for the whole of the morning, especially Mr Kent.' she added, still smiling gently.

The kindly greeting was as unexpected as it was gracious and the smile as motherly as Mother Teresa's most calming smiles upon a nursery of needy, newly born Calcutta babes.

'My name is Janet Nunn and I'm housekeeper here at The Old House for Mr Hamish Kent,' she continued, without the necessity of an introduction or a single word passing from her visitor's mouths. 'Please, won't you step inside the pair of you?' she said, after which, the smallest of pauses existed. 'I do hope you approve of the wee cottage I chose for you both; it has been on the market for some considerable time just now but without there being too much curiosity for it, I have to say; fortunately, property doesn't move very quickly in these parts, not at the moment anyway, or you might well have been unlucky.

'Mr Kent has two other similar cottages for sale at the moment, one has been on the market for well over nine months; and without too much interest being shown in that one either at the present time; so you can see how slow the market really is at the moment; but as your cottage is so close to The Old House, almost next door, you might say, I decided to choose that one for you.

'So... we are indeed neighbours, and very close ones I do hope we'll prove to be; these doors are always open to you both, you may rely on that.'

The couple, Sarah and Jenny and being preceded by Janet, stepped into the brightly illuminated square hall with its tall walls intermittently hung with pictures of Scottish country scenes; and large oil paintings of a variety of expressionless dignitaries lining the walls of the generous stairway.

The black and white tiled floor was partly covered by a pleasing square of carpet; soft to the tread and calm red in colour with an indiscernible pattern woven in relief.

It wasn't difficult to feel relaxed in this place or in this company and by the returning of smiles and by the entering into the most casual exchanges of good natured remarks, the task was made even easier.

Usually, when strangers meet for the first time, conversation may be slightly inhibited at the onset and almost disjointed every now and then, but not so on this occasion, for with the progression of a short period only, the dialogue developed into a most congenial exchange.

Sarah and Jenny were immediately shown into the large drawing room and were offered seats of startling comfort while the conversation between Sarah and Janet instantly developed into words of triviality; but none the less interesting and free from contradiction.

After a full fifteen minute period had elapsed, the conversation was interrupted by the entrance of Sir Angus Kent's double. The alikeness was so incredible that both Jenny and Sarah were taken aback by the absurdity of it. And Jenny, in puzzled surprise, all but asked what her father was doing here in Lincolnshire.

'So you have found us at last have you?' asked Hamish Kent, amused by their reaction but with a confident and gentle smile about his countenance. 'I can see by the looks on both your faces that the resemblance between my brother and me hasn't escaped your notice; but I hope that is where the similarity ends,' he further added, with his smile becoming even more pronounced.

He greeted his two visitors cordially by shaking Sarah's hand and kissing Jenny gently on both cheeks. And after some preliminary and light hearted repartee he turned his attention to his pretty niece.

'If you two ladies would excuse us I should very much like to speak to my niece privately for awhile,' he said. Then, looking Jenny fully in the eyes he added, 'Jennifer, I wonder if you would be so kind as to follow me and for us to leave these two charming ladies and allow them to get fully acquainted with one another; I'm sure they will find a great deal to talk about and I think that we also should have a quiet chat together, so that we too might, at last, become acquainted... without there being too much fuss,' said Hamish, extending his hand for the little girl to hold. 'I promise not to keep you long from your great-aunt; all I ask is for a little of your time... that's all.'

With eagerness the little girl rose from her comfortable chair and, with no awareness of concern in her mind but rather a feeling of well-being spreading the depth of her mind, she took hold of her uncle's hand and walked with him from the room.

It was Sarah who opened the chatting as her niece left the room with Hamish Kent. She turned to Janet, as she sipped the tea that had been brought to them, with an expression of enthusiasm in the need to make the most obvious of comments.

'The resemblance between the two brothers is uncanny, yes, quite remarkable, Janet. Never before have I seen two people so much alike, even in twins.'

'So I believe Sarah, but as I haven't met with Sir Angus for some considerable while it is difficult for me to comment; so I shall just have to take your word for the phenomenon,' returned Janet, her eyes widening in a twinkling indication of uncertainty.

'What do you suppose Mr Kent meant when he said that he hoped that the similarity between the two men ended with their physical resemblance?' asked Sarah, clumsily expressing the question of puzzlement that deep down she already knew the answer to, but in the hopes that her inquisitiveness would not provide any form of embarrassment to Janet.

'Perhaps it might be as well for me to enlighten you a little regarding their family background, Sarah; that way you will fully understand what Mr Hamish intended by his remarks,' said Janet, sitting forward in her chair as she spoke to ensure herself of Sarah's full attention.

'As you will no doubt have worked out for yourself by this time Sarah, Hamish and Angus are identical twins who were born within minutes of one another,' said Janet, her smile deserting her slightly for the moment, just for a short while, but it soon established itself once more as she continued in the same vein. 'But because Hamish is supposed to have been the last of the twins to enter this world, by a few minutes; although nothing, regrettably, can really be proven one way or the other, Angus has always taken advantage of his own opinion upon the matter. You must remember that at this particular time in childbed history, it was difficult to keep tabs on issues of this nature, even though it was most certainly of great importance to do so.

'Anyway, when the laddies' father, Sir William Kent, died, the grand hereditary title, dating from way back, passed to the elder of the two boys as claimed by Angus and he also inherited his father's estates in Dorset. Angus shouted the loudest so Angus got; he being the more dominant male of the two, d'you see.

'Anyway, their mother, she being of Scottish decent and very wealthy in her own right, favoured Hamish as being the first-born, not that her nationality or her resources had any bearing on the matter, of course; but she knew about these things, as mothers often do.

'Nevertheless, Sir William, who wasn't the most pleasant of gentleman at the best of times, and who most certainly was not present at the birth, favoured Angus as being the eldest, simply by claiming he was the first of the two bairns he had held in his arms soon after the birthing had taken place.

'To be quite honest with you, Sarah, I don't believe the business of who came first matters to Mr Hamish one way or the other, not really; but I think Angus is a more insecure person and is ever fearful that Hamish might someday prove that the title is rightfully his after all; and so he keeps his distance from Hamish, unless he needs a favour from his brother, of course, as he does at this very minute.

'Anyway, it was Hamish who had always been his mother's favourite son; not that mothers should have favourites, I know that, but he was the ever caring and considerate one; the only one of the two boys who was kind to everyone he met: he follows his mother's nature d'you see. He always displayed such wonderful traits of affection, right from his early days, in contrast to his brother; I certainly know that to be true. Anyway, when she died, not long after her husband's death, six months, no more, it was Hamish's turn to inherit.

'Of course, Angus challenged the will and fought tooth and nail to get a share of the inheritance, and through the courts as well, I might add; but at the end of the day it was their mother Alice's determination that prevailed; I expect the powers that be realised that Angus had enough wealth already,' here Janet's smile became exaggerated with favoured bias. 'And so Hamish was able to continue with the lifestyle he had been used to and he bought this estate when he married his now recently departed and lovely wife Martha. Unfortunately Martha died childless and so it was a blessing that his brother's daughter has visited him this day.

'Of course you both might easily have stayed with him here as there are more than enough rooms. But it seems that, Sir Angus, for reasons best known to himself, was totally against the idea even though I know Mr Hamish did put forward the proposal with all the best intentions; but he insisted on renting the cottage from Hamish instead for you both to occupy, which I suppose, in a way, is much better for the two of you and allows for greater independence.'

After Janet had completed her short narrative she became more relaxed, and took advantage of her restful chair once again as she tentatively awaited Sarah's response.

'I must say that what you have told me of the family history, and in particular that of Sir Angus does not surprise me one little bit Janet but I can't help wondering how you know such intimacies regarding the Kents. I should have thought that only the immediate family would have been allowed to possess confidentialities such as these,' enquired Sarah, with a degree of tactlessness attending her voice.

'Sarah, I am really glad you asked me that question as I was uncertain how I was going to tell you, without sounding utterly conceited,' said Janet, with a look of relief issuing from her still radiant face. 'Well now, first of all Mr Hamish asked me to mention the subject to you myself, in complete confidence you understand, as soon as he was certain you would both be coming to live in Brenton, for I am quite certain he has no intention of relaying any of this to wee Jennifer, not at the moment anyway, if indeed ever.

'You see Sarah; it was I who officiated at the confinement. I was the young midwife who was there from the very beginning of the boy's lives and it was me who caused all the problems to come to pass soon after the twins were born. I messed up Sarah - and in a very big way indeed. So you can see it is I who still bear the responsibility and the indignation of the identity crisis all those years ago; my only excuse is that I was a young probationer at the time who had only just qualified as a midwife and I was still in need of supervision. Oh, I know that is a lame excuse for such a momentous blunder, but it is the only one I can offer. It would have been basic procedure to have tagged those little ones on their arrival I realised that very soon after they had been born... but I failed to do it.

'Anyway, it was but a few days later that I was discreetly contacted by Alice Kent, the laddies' mother, who had seemingly taken a shine to me, or felt sorry for me because of my blunder... I can have no idea which it was, but she asked if I would care to look after the two bairns for her on a permanent basis. Of course, I was delighted to accept the position and so I have been with the family ever since, and here I shall stay, I hope, for a good few years yet.'

Sarah cast her eyes discreetly to the floor in case she inadvertently betrayed any look that may indicate disapproval in any way. She had seen instantly that the mistake Janet had been guilty of making all those years ago could have been attributed to the most attentive of people; and felt every sympathy for a lady who was obviously so totally committed to her consideration and support of others.

***

Jenny was not at all overawed by the opulence of The Old House; indeed Hyde Hall in Dorset contained far more lavishness about it than this - but she tried not to compare the one with the other, although the urge was difficult to contain.

The room where Hamish Kent had taken Jenny was reasonable in size with walls of pastel green, and the pure white ornamentally moulded cornices that bordered the walls were unusually dropped from the ceiling by a good eighteen inches. Below this, could be seen a collection of large, rich oil paintings of Scottish landscapes as seen in sunlight and in cloudiness, in calmness and in turbidity; each being encased in a gilded frame and hanging from lengthy cords all aligned with unique straightness.

In the centre of the farthest wall and set in an even wider, more ornate gilt frame, hung the portrait of a most beautiful, but troubled looking lady; casually seated on an elaborate white marbled seat with tall scrolled arms to either side.

Although the picture as a whole was beautifully painted with hardly a brushstroke visible to the eye, the look upon the lady's face was of prominent importance, for it carried with it an expression of gentle melancholia, quite as if she needed to take the whole world in her arms to bring it cheer.

Jenny stood for some time just gazing appreciatively at the painting, lost in wonderment and searching for an intended reason for the lady's apparent distress.

'That, Jennifer is a painting of my dear mother as she was seen by the artist Gilbert Long soon after losing her husband, Sir William Kent, my father; hence her downcast look I suppose. Well with all the moroseness flying around at the time its little wonder she looks so melancholic. Sad to say she died, just before the painting was completed, in fact' said Hamish, cutting short the thoughts and ponderings of his niece. 'You are a lot like her you know… when she was your age,' he added.

After he had walked over to his mahogany desk he opened the uppermost drawer to produce an unframed photograph and showed it to Jenny. The picture was in varying tones of sepia and revealed the portrait of a girl, about Jenny's age, with her small hand gently resting on the head of a cocker spaniel dog and with a contented smile upon her pretty face.

'Allow me to introduce you to my mother, Jennifer. You see, she's just like you, don't you think?' he said, handing Jenny the picture; and standing behind his niece, he placed his hands upon her narrow shoulders, in a paternal way, while they examined, closely, the aging picture together.

'Yes I suppose we are alike but I can't tell from this the colour of her hair,' she said, turning round and looking up into her uncle's kindly eyes.

'You may take it from me, my dear, the colour of her hair was a dark, brownish black, tinged with olive; in other words it was ebony and identical to that of your own hair,' he assured her.

The uncle reclaimed the photograph and replaced it to its

former position. Then offering Jenny a seat they sat together upon the two chairs that had been purposely arranged.

'Well how are you Jennifer? And more importantly how have the last twelve and a half years been for you down there in deepest Dorset?' He asked both questions in quick succession giving his niece no chance to answer the first before asking the second. But she coped well with the rapidity of the questions by saying that she was well, and happy to be living in her new Lincolnshire home, and totally evaded the historical question.

Her uncle smiled a wry smile appreciating the fact that she was remaining loyal to her parents even though he was fully aware of their domineering characters and overshadowing customs, but he had no intentions in pressing the child for further admissions of their ungraciousness.

'That aside,' he said, 'your father has asked me to keep an eye out for you and I shall certainly be available to help you in any way I possibly can; and so, if you have any real problems or any difficulties at all that you feel your great-aunt cannot deal with, then I urge you not to hesitate to call on me immediately; I will always be here for you in whatever capacity is necessary, so please, try to remember this.

'Your father also informs me that he is making you an allowance of seven pounds each week for the foreseeable future, which you must personally look after; it is for your food and clothing, and which, I might add, is a very generous amount. Your father wanted to pay the money to me and for me to look after your financial arrangements for you.

'But I considered it only right that you and you alone should be in charge of your own finances and when I suggested this arrangement to your father he agreed with me, wholeheartedly.

'You see, Jennifer, I consider this to be a golden opportunity for you to gain the feel and involvement of money, which, I hope, will serve you throughout the rest of your life; we all need that sort of experience you see, so be careful with it and use it wisely.

'You are too young to have a banking account upon which you would be able to draw but I am sure we would be in a position to open a post office savings account for you, into which I shall deposit the allowance and then either you or your Aunt Sarah may draw on it as and when the need arises. In any case I doubt you will find you have very much left over each week so a good sturdy purse or a money box might be the answer; but you shouldn't take the money out of the cottage unless you intend to spend it and then only the approximate amount you require.'

Needless to say, Jennifer Kent was delighted at being given this opportunity to demonstrate her financial responsibilities, especially as she had now entered the first stages of her adulthood and as the interview continued so too grew her confidence in Hamish Kent; and her liking for the man she now knew as her uncle was unexpectedly favourable.

CHAPTER THREE

Brenton village is a peaceful sort of place, with nothing of importance or air of notoriety attached to it; other than the prominence of agricultural activities taking place in the flat fields that surrounds its borders and of course the easygoing country folk that has dwelt here since the world begun - all labouring relentlessly from early morn till late evening, just to earn an honest crust.

Following Jenny and Sarah's introductory visit with the welcoming Hamish Kent at the Old House, the happy twosome wished to add to their already established good opinion of the locality; and so they chose to walk awhile along the dried-up dung and mud splattered lane which passed its front gate by no more than a couple of feet.

Not towards the village did they intend to stroll, for that exploit had been carried out earlier, well before their visit to the Old House had taken place. But the opposite direction attracted their attention instead; away from the centre of Brenton village and out into the evenness of the Lincolnshire countryside where nature is well supplied in all its pleasantness.

It was an agreeable afternoon and feelings of good humour and those of sociability ran high in their veins: undoubtedly left over from their visit to The Old House.

And so it was felt that a country walk would be just the thing to indulge their inquisitive minds; whilst the soaking up of the afternoon summer air would encourage the cosy feelings of homeliness, they each had found in this lovely place, to become a sort of permanence.

At some considerable distance along the lane, a distinct dip in its concrete surface was seen to be still awash with a depth of water; water it was supposed, that had been left from the deluge that had fallen a few days earlier.

Unfortunately, this flood had been churned into a state of muddiness by the rotating wheels of farm vehicles: as their comings and goings along this stretch was thought to be routine. And because of the water's cloudiness, its depth wasn't easily assessed; not by the naked eye at any rate, or without a measuring rod of sorts being used.

It may easily be assumed that any flood of water, large or small, would hang around at this point and for some considerable time, for there was little in the way of drainage to cope with such an extensive pool as this. The fact that an overgrown ditch existed to one side was immaterial as the gullies leading to it were completely blocked.

The murky pool of water stretched for a longish distance too: some twenty yards was guessed to be its length from end to end.

A mix of tall trees and an overgrown hazel thicket had formed a sizeable copse on either side of the lane at this point and by so doing a pretty archway was created above.

Obviously, because of the trees, any gentle breeze of warm air would be hindered on a calm day such as this, thereby curtailing the evaporation of the cloudy water and allowing the dungy stench to stay.

In order to continue with their ramble so that the exploration of the local area could continue, this trying hindrance surely must be overcome, for neither great-aunt nor niece would be put off by an obstacle such as this; no matter how difficult it was deemed to be.

But, gaining the furthest side of this particularly large pungent puddle, which stretched the full width of the lane up to each embankment that paralleled its length on either side, without at least one of them getting their feet wet, seemed an impossible task.

After standing motionless with questioned looks for a minute or two, they considered their options in a more rational manner.

Needless to say, the only way the crossing could be achieved was by skilfully skirting around the depth of water, using one of the muddy banks as a footpath - but with great care, it should be noted - since toxic stinging nettles covered the entirety of both banks - and in abundance.

After further discussion, both Sarah Wood and Jenny applied themselves to the task in hand.

Once they had accustomed themselves to picking their way warily along the newly formed footpath by treading on the firry weeds one by one, and amid nervous laughter from Jenny, they achieved their objective within a relatively short period without meeting the difficulty they had first envisaged.

Naturally, they were both hugely satisfied with the outcome of their spirited effort and congratulated one another in a cheery manner; at least Sarah said, 'Well done,' to Jenny - Jenny merely chuckled.

They had scarcely reached dry land on the furthest side of the muddy water, when the shortish figure of a slight individual of questionable masculinity, both in stance and gait, came into view from around a twist in the lane.

He was seen to be quite away off at first sight; then, as this person drew closer, the couple, both aunt and niece as one, recognised the figure as being that of the inscrutable Barnabas Bell, the youngish man with the unruly squint in his left eye who had assisted them with their luggage and school items the previous evening.

The parties finally converged on an aspect of the open lane a few yards beyond the watery edge of the muddy pool but out of the shadows, where all around was bathed in dazzling sunshine.

The inscrutable fellow briefly shielded his eyes from the sun's glare and then, upon recognising the two females, he threw his arms in the air and proceeded with an immediate greeting of great enthusiasm.

'Hullo, hullo,' he called out, quite loudly.

And after a look of satisfaction had finally occupied his face: caused no doubt by his own skill in recognising the two females at first glance, he extended his greeting even more.

'Well, well, well... bless my soul, if it ain't the overgenerous lady and her little niece,' said he, with a degree of cutting sharpness in the tone of his voice. 'You making yourselves familiar with the local countryside, I shouldn't wonder. That's nice!

'Have the both of you settled into your new home yet?' he further asked. And as his glance settled on Jenny's figure his left eye deserted its central position and wandered further to the left side of its socket than was usual - but with a degree of offensive admiration causing its movement.

'Mr Bell isn't it?' returned Miss Wood. 'How very nice to see you once again; and not working at The Old House today I see; a day off I expect, for good behaviour, is that it?' said the rotund Miss Wood, with equal sharpness of tone.

'Oh no Miss Wood, I've just delivered a letter that was left at The Old House this morning by mistake. You see, there's another big house a mile or so further up the lane... way out into the sticks you might say... called The Old Barn and the postman often makes the same mistake he made this morning by delivering one of their letters at Mr Kent's house. Sometimes he leaves all of 'em there. Now, that's either by accident or because he can't be bothered to bike the extra distance; not sure which, but I suspect its laziness on his part 'cause he don't do it all the time... see? Can't say as how I blame him though, it's a long way to pedal with just a single letter... so I has to do it for him,' said Mr Bell, with the suggestion of irritation altering his features.

Then all at once he perked up and he grinned again as he

further added what he considered may be a helpful proposition, one which he would be able to arrange to his own advantage.

'Have you thought any more about me being able to help you settle in? I'm a dab hand with the old paintbrush y'know and I handle a spade pretty well and all. So, if you want to use my services, don't hesitate to ask me. I pass your cottage twice a day: about nine in the morning and about five at night, so you can keep an eye out for me then; but I can tell you here and now, I should be looking for a whole lot more than six lousy pence for my services.'

'That is indeed a very noble gesture Mr Bell and one well worth remembering,' returned Miss Wood. 'But as my cottage appears to have been recently decorated and as the garden is in fine shape at the moment, it looks as if I am not in the market for your services - not just at the moment. Nevertheless, I may well be looking for a window cleaner in the not too distant future... if cleaning windows falls within the range of your skills,' she added, with a smile.

Jenny, for the whole of this exchange was looking about herself in search of some visual diversion with which to occupy her eyes. Her grim nervousness failed to pass her aunt unnoticed as did Bell's gaping mouth. And Jenny, being very conscious of Barnabas Bell's intense staring and his impolite and blatant ogling, felt extremely embarrassed at such attention.

After she had been intensely concerned by these feelings, Jenny was rather relieved when the inscrutable Barnabas Bell, assuring her aunt of his fundamental skilfulness in window cleaning, decided to continue his journey once again in the direction of The Old House.

He had not walked a great distance, and not looking at all where he was going, since his head was being constantly turned in Jenny's direction so that he may continue to smile so hideously at her, when he realised that both his feet were fast becoming soaked: no doubt, the process of walking ankle deep in the muddy water didn't help his plight; and wishing to avoid the increase of such a filthy soaking, he leapt awkwardly to the muddy verge on his right.

It was a regrettable lapse of concentration on the part of Mr Bell that his effort in gaining an immediate escape from the soaking to his feet was not altogether successful. For, as he landed on the muddy verge, he completely lost his footing and sat down in the murky water in a most ungainly fashion, both wetting and staining the backside of his trouser with an embarrassing muddy greenness. And to cap it all, he stung his hands as he clutched at the noxious stinging nettles, he, overlooking the fact that their general inclination was to administer poison when being handled. But he was hoping to provide himself with a degree of safety by this automatic reflex action rather than to encourage the disaster that in the end befell him.

Obviously, the whole of this unfortunate incident could have been avoided had he paid more heed to where he was going and less to the ogling of the young lady's figure, which he'd found to be so fascinating.

The sight of his unfortunate calamity formed an immediate source of amusement for both great-aunt and niece alike, even though they were prompt in enquiring, with compassion, it should be added, if the inscrutable youngish man had damaged himself beyond that which was quite obvious.

But the mishap failed to accomplish very much for Mr Bell's self-esteem - nothing at all, in fact, for humiliation shone from his face in the form of a purple hue.

The inscrutable Barnabas Bell, after regaining an upright posture once more, continued his journey without there being a backward glance.

***

The three mile walk, or thereabouts, provided both niece and great-aunt with the refreshing exercise Sarah had believed necessary, for she had found herself to be sorely lacking such activities of late. This unrelenting, physical stimulation was just what was needed to restore her mental alertness; furthermore, she had found it to be equally pleasing and inspiring to stroll with Jenny, for since the change in their relationship, she had discovered that the more they were in each others company the stronger the bond of affection between them became.

All of this was conveyed to her charge in a direct manner as they approached the gate and was greeted by Jenny with a silent but approved understanding and a gentle nodding of her head.

Soon after they entered the cottage, Sarah occupied herself with the preparation of a fine evening meal in which her charge was also involved, for, as had been hoped, the exercise had stimulated both their appetites beyond belief.

It was during these preparations Sarah suggested Jenny should occupy the remainder of her day with the writing of a small composition about their nature ramble and which should include any inner feelings the walk may have stimulated; but the episode of

Barnabas Bell's unfortunate mishap was to be excluded; for the sole reason that dwelling on other peoples misfortunes would be totally inappropriate and would most assuredly be construed as being unkind; which wouldn't do at all.

As a result of the instruction, Jenny attended the task with some hesitation and without the fervour she knew she was capable of applying; and all because the unsolicited attentions that had been installed in her mind by Mr Bell still filled her with feelings of unease.

The following day's lessons were considered in a state of dread and panic by Sarah Wood. Not only had a separate room for this particular undertaking been totally overlooked but it was also found that the area in Jennifer's room and indeed every other room in the small cottage, there being but four including the kitchen, was inappropriate for a room of education and the cottagey setting most certainly too homely, and therefore unfit for such a commission.

And so it was with some reservations that Sarah Wood visited The Old House to seek Janet Nunn's advice about the situation.

After some considerable debate over the problem and upon the close inspection of two or three of the more likely rooms available at The Old House, it was finally decided that a small but perfectly adequate space within the confines of the west wing of the uncle's home, could be allocated for this particular purpose.

Consequently, and with the assistance of Barnabas Bell who was elated by his being of service, the small, spare upper room at The Old House was furnished with desks, blackboard and books that had been brought from Dorset and stacked in Sarah's bedroom.

To everyone's delight the small room took on the shape of a classroom of complete acceptability straight away and without there being too much in the way of the ridding of existing furniture either.

But it was on the landing atop the cottage stairway, during the final moving of certain text books that would be in continuous use by tutor and pupil alike and in the absence of Sarah Wood, that Barnabas Bell pinned Jenny to the wall and rudely stroked her shoulder, her arms and other private parts of her body in a most improper manner, just as she was about to take the first step in her descent. He then used his clammy, sinewy fingers to run desirously down the length of her spine with shameless meaning thereby adding to the anxiety he had already caused to the young lady's frame of mind the day before.

Jenny struggled and removed herself instantly from the

situation and continued with the carrying of the books down the stairs with agitated fury.

After she had gained the ground's level she turned to look at the inscrutable fellow, hoping he would falter on the final few steps in order to break his neck or at the very least a digit or two.

It didn't happen.

She held her tongue for the moment though and said nothing more about the incident so that the situation was not enflamed beyond reason.

Instead, she showed her immediate annoyance by handing out a severe look of disapproval to Barnabas Bell: she considering that a severe look would be enough to put him in his place.

But a lewd, hungry smile issuing from the offender's eyes and mouth settled itself about Jenny's body once again and in a most lecherous way, thereby causing her further anxiety and increased in her a heightened and unyielding feeling of resentment which she revealed with an even more contemptuous stare.

'Don't look at me like that,' said he, as his lecherous smile intensified about his hideous face. 'You know you liked it,' he added, insolently, as she walked away.

But neither the unacceptable stroking of her person nor her feelings of anger were ignored or would be forgotten by Jenny; she would keep them to herself, stored up for now but waiting for an appropriate moment to present itself when her fury would be unleashed. It mattered not how long she would have to wait, as long as she was able to bring Bell's offensive misconduct to an end completely.

***

Since the house moving process had taken so long, it was decided that normal lessons would not begin until the late afternoon: three thirty to be precise.

But even when that time arrived no commencement of teaching had been made; for Sarah, during the previous evening, had prepared a most important moral lecture, which she considered would adequately fill the one hour period left in the day.

Despite the fact it wasn't essential that this lecture was delivered before lessons commenced - any fitting time would have done, but Sarah decided that now was as good a time as any, and in any case she was determined to get the thing over and done with as soon as was humanly possible in order to eradicate all the humiliation that may occur, but mainly for herself.

This serious speech, which the rotund governess calculated to be of some considerable worth to Jenny, even though it failed to fall within the guidelines of her concept of the recognised curriculum, began on the half hour precisely.

'Jennifer,' said Sarah, as an unfortunate wobble in her voice illustrated the level of her uncertainty and caused her to incline her head and clear her throat in an uncomfortable way. But being the complete professional she truly was she continued without haste or urgency.

'Jennifer,' she began again, 'you may or you may not be aware of the fact that you are developing into a most attractive young lady; this was indeed emphasised by Mr Bell's attitude towards you yesterday afternoon when he failed to take his eyes off you. You exhibit a stateliness and beauty that is of classical proportions and will be a talking point with many, if not all, of the opposite gender that cross your path in the years to come.'

Sarah felt instantly relieved that the commencing words of her prepared message had at last left her mouth but at the same time she realised that these first two sentences, alone, had caused a considerable flush to mantle the cheeks of the beautiful young girl who sat attentively before her; causing her to put on view, what can only be described as, a display of complete unease.

Jenny's eyes had widened, as this mode of surprised awkwardness took over, and Sarah, herself, shifted her weight from one leg to the other in an ungainly fashion but settled them once again after the unease on both their parts had subsided.

'I can see that my remarks have caused you some feelings of considerable embarrassment thus far, and I am sorry for that, but you now have to face facts, Jennifer; you have for the past twelve and a half years lived within a situation, not of your making I fully appreciate that, but still within a situation where you have had limited contact with the outside world and I consider it my duty to prepare you for what that world may throw at you in the way of ridicule, disrespect and envy; openly coming, I am quite certain, from the intense jealousy of others, but mainly coming from young women of varying ages.

'Also, you will, no doubt, experience the distinct danger of desires of the flesh, namely cravings and lustfulness, being derived from the hearts and minds of certain of the opposite gender. Ignore all of this, Jennifer, for it will be of little consequence and may well hinder your progress through life... if you do not.'

It was Jenny's turn to shuffle about at this point.

"It's already happening" she meditated, as she cast her mind back to both her encounters with Barnabas Bell and she shuddered with intense revulsion at the thought of him touching her; and she struggled to dismiss the disgust and hatred she still felt inside - for she knew that the disgust and the hatred would always be there to unsettle her.

'Now my own personal experiences in such matters are definitely non existent,' Sarah continued, with speed; wanting to gloss over all of this private confession, and was quite successful in doing so, up to a point. 'But I do possess a certain amount of knowledge that I have gained second hand over the years and I also possess a small booklet which I have studied and found to be most enlightening.

'Naturally, it was your mother who should have talked to you about such matters, Jennifer, but in her absence it is I who must prepare you, as best I can, for the pitfalls that will surely lie ahead of you.'

Sarah then went on to explain, in general terms, the differing aspects of the male and female genitalia and the reproductive system in brief with the aid of her acquired booklet, which, she now considered to be well worth its weight in usefulness.

And so, what was intended to be a short parental address, with Sarah not wishing to get bogged down with some lengthy biological lecture - it did, in fact, turn out to be just that.

The afternoon lecture sped along with a rapidity that both surprised and pleased the aging tutor, for never before had she known a pupil demonstrate such aptitude for a subject before. Even during the short break, when they walked through the gardens of The Old House for a few minutes, Jenny's intense enthusiasm was maintained and their minds were only briefly distracted as they watched the sky's reflection in the placid waters of the koi's translucent home.

Eventually, upon their return to the classroom, and despite the fact that Jenny continuously enthused a positive interest in the subject by asking pertinent questions that were both embarrassing at times and extremely awkward at others and all in all showing a quiet and genuine intellectual curiosity, Sarah did manage to sway the debate to the more modest and agreed principles of the accepted standards relating to the aspect of sexual relations, which of course was the intended point of the exercise in the first place.

'Although Doctor Marigold Mason's booklet, 'A Guide to

Unexpected Expectancy' does explain the clinical features of sexual development, pregnancy and all their relative aspects,' continued Sarah, 'it really doesn't cover the moral debate that has always existed.

'Some people consider sex to be a dirty word, and it is almost continuously being brushed under the carpet whenever it raises its head. Some would say it is a subject that shouldn't be discussed at all.' Here Sarah paused awhile with the realisation of her own now altered conviction; but soon continued. 'But as I can now appreciate, the subject should be openly discussed; not for titillation, Jennifer, no that is definitely not the intention God had in mind when he devised the process of reproduction; but for edification so that the young and the uninformed might receive all information regarding God's intended method of our procreation. And although it is, hypothetically, meant to be a pleasurable experience it is undoubtedly not to be used for self-indulgence or for self-gratification, Jennifer; no matter how appealing the thought and intense ones feelings might be.

'No, and that is a definite no, Jennifer; it was designed and must only be used for the procreation of ones offspring when man and woman are happily settled within an assured marital situation; that means a family environment, Jennifer, filled with love and security and with the one you love at your side; no matter what anyone else has to say upon the subject.

'So always remember that, Jennifer, whenever sexual temptation is placed in your path; always be in complete control and protect yourself and your feelings at all times with good sense and wisdom; that, indeed, my dear, is my best advice to you.'

With each and every unfamiliar word being carefully explained to her, this passionate discourse and especially the compassionate advice Sarah Wood had so fervently promoted at its ending, would undoubtedly stay with Jennifer Kent for the rest of her years, she couldn't possibly forget a single word so great and intense was the impression made on her young and innocent intellect. And she made up her mind there and then that she would keep herself for her husband, when and if ever he came along.

***

Janet Nunn was busying herself in the kitchen when Hamish Kent popped his head round the door, displaying a look of concerned curiosity.

It was late evening and dinner had been finished and the dishes cleared leaving the somewhat lonely man deep in thought and it was upon a sudden impulse that he decided to have a few quiet words with his housekeeper.

'Janet,' he said, the hint of a calm smile being displayed upon his manly features. 'I have been trying to come to terms with some troubled thoughts regarding my niece Jennifer. I haven't had the opportunity to speak with you at length before this time but I was wondering what sort of impression you obtained when she first visited us?'

The question was clear enough but the look on his face was one of concerned curiosity, as mentioned above.

'Well now, Mr Hamish,' returned the housekeeper, cheerfully maintaining a happiness that never seemed to desert her. 'I truly found her to be a most delightful young girl.' She rolled the 'r' in the word 'truly' with extreme effectiveness. 'She seemed to me to be happy enough with the cottage and at ease in Sarah's company, most polite and appreciative in every way. Yes, I think her to be an extremely personable young lady, Mr Hamish, very personable indeed, and of course very beautiful to look upon.'

'Thank you Janet,' returned Hamish Kent, 'that is precisely the conclusion I came to. What I fail to understand is why her parents observe her as being unconcerned about her life when I recognised a good deal of fine mental ability and sensitivity about the girl. I mean, she seemed to glean more feelings from the portrait of my dear mother than I have noticed coming from any other person I know who has looked, with any interest at all, upon the remarkable painting. I am certain she would have still been there, gazing at its superb quality, an hour later had I not interrupted her. And her loyalty and devotion toward her parents was beyond belief, bearing in mind what their attitude must have been toward the child and knowing them as I do. And if Jennifer is such a difficult person to live with why on earth didn't they send her away to boarding school?'

Janet thought awhile, and considered carefully the words her employer had spoken.

'It is indeed true, Mr Hamish, we all behave and interact differently when in the company of others. Perhaps her mother is right, perhaps she is a problematic child when at home in her own environment, but I must say I find that most difficult to believe. Perhaps I should ask her Aunt Sarah's opinion; maybe she could throw some light on the matter.

'And as for her schooling away from home is concerned, well, that is a far simpler question to answer. You see sir, boarding schools do tend to have prolonged holiday periods and that wouldn't answer her mother's dilemma. No sooner is the wee girl away from home then she'd be back again producing a most unsettling situation for absolutely everyone concerned; and if her mother is maladjusted or neurotic in any way, then that wouldn't do at all, now would it? No, complete separation would indeed be the only answer in that case.'

'Yes I do understand what you are saying Janet, but I should certainly appreciate a third party's opinion on the situation with Jennifer; only I should hate for her to be branded a problem child especially when the two of us can see no real evidence to support such a claim. So yes, do have a discreet word with Sarah Wood, if you please Janet, and let me know what you find. You see I should prefer my brother not to fabricate stories about his daughter merely to suit his own cause; I have had quite enough of that from him in the past, as you are no doubt aware.'

And so, on the pretext of it being merely a social call the kindly housekeeper paid a visit to the newly situated classroom sharply at eleven o'clock the very next morning. While Jenny was still busying herself with her morning lessons the ladies talked out of earshot of her, with the housekeeper gleaning all the information about Jenny's life and background that had hitherto been a mystery to her.

After discovering, to her dismay, all that had taken place at Hyde Hall since Sarah had first been invited to the place; and the scarcity of affection that had cruelly led to unbelievable heart-breaking loneliness for Jenny, Janet was horror-stricken and greatly appalled.

CHAPTER FOUR

The summer holidays, that had seen the closure of The Old House schoolroom for a month, had been over by a full two weeks and a new routine of learning was now doggedly in place.

Those final two weeks had passed so quickly it seemed as though an hour had furtively slipped by since the holiday had ended and the holiday itself had been more of a brief interval from tedious teaching than the welcomed break from learning it ought to have been.

Its true Sarah had used her Morris Minor car for them both to explore the local area on the odd occasion but other than that not a great deal in the way of pleasurable holidaying had been fulfilled and most of the time had been spent lounging in the cottage garden in laid-back conversation and in puzzle solving.

Despite all of that, the four week interval had been appreciated by Sarah Wood who was beginning to feel her age by now and some of the minor hindrances that beleaguer many people in their latter years attended her too, from time to time; although, it should be stressed, she still enjoyed tolerable physical health.

The exceptional bond between Sarah and her young protégé continued to develop and to such an extent that much warmth existed in Sarah's soul because of it. This was an unfamiliar experience to the aging tutor but one that she held dear and in some curious way, had really longed for.

It also appeared that Jenny was possessed of an eagerness to learn, an eagerness that outshone all Sarah's previous pupils by a mile. Not that Jenny was brighter than most girls of her age but her enthusiasm was considered to be exceptional. She continued in wisdom too, even though she was still so very young.

In spite of all these opinions of approval, Sarah was beginning to wonder if her years of teaching would ever be succeeded by a well deserved retirement and even though the four week break had provided a welcome departure for her, it stirred up desires for a longed-for withdrawal from her obligation to the Kents, which, deep down, she knew would never happen.

As a result of this, the old misgivings regarding her suitability as a responsible teacher, guardian cum child minder, and at her time of life, visited her more often of late, than was acceptable.

The struggle with these doubts had became a difficult burden for the portly lady, so much so, that in the end, as she lay contemplating the morrow's tiresome lessons, a state of alarm and panic would overtake her.

She also reassessed her teaching life, at this point in time, to see if there was any merit left to it; or had her life been worthless and for naught?

Not only was the dread of each new working day becoming a stressful burden it also showed the speeding of those days to be adding to her years at an alarming rate, thereby depressing the aging tutor still further.

Even so, she would never allow herself to display these feelings of despair, not to her wonderful charge; for that, indeed, is what Jenny had become to her and in a very short period of time at that.

But it wasn't the 'dutiful governess' position that was the root cause of Sarah's despondency; for she was delighted in being with Jenny. Neither was Margaret, the child's neurotic and self-obsessed mother, the cause either; although Sarah's own mind was so greatly tried by this particular agony it was little wonder her mental state hadn't become unhinged completely by this time.

In point of fact Sarah's despair had been brought about by an absurd insecurity problem left over from her former years; when being the principle of a girls school wasn't all it was made out to be. These feelings of despair, brought about by moral obligations all those years ago had gradually taken their toll and had so continued with her until they had become a basic part of her personality.

The wonderful change in her interaction with Jenny had done much to settle Sarah's mind, of course, and she was glad they were both out of the clutches of her evil niece, Margaret, at last.

The deep-seated hatred that dominated her niece's personality had always been there for every one to see, and it had been revealed to Jennifer as soon as she was born. Even Margaret, had no way of knowing how evil she truly was, for wickedness was second nature to the woman, from which there was little hope in the way of deliverance.

The realization of Margaret's problems did bother Sarah; though to a lesser extent of late and it bowed her mind low only occasionally. But she wasn't at all surprised to be troubled in this way, for she had been forewarned it would turn out to be like this, even as they'd left Hyde Hall.

Even so, Sarah had no desire to prevent any hopes her little charge may have in establishing a relationship with her despicable mother at some time: if indeed hope existed in Jenny's young mind at all, but she debated, with herself, in her quieter moments, as she hoped she might be able turn the mother, daughter relationship round to become at least something worth the having.

But no matter how confident Sarah may have been with this notion, her best endeavours were unfortunately not amounting to very much; in point of fact Sarah had struggled ever since they'd left Hyde village. For even though she had, on more than one occasion, insisted Jennifer telephone her parents since their arrival in Lincolnshire both during the summer recess and at other times as well in order to bring about a reconciliation of sorts; and she, herself, had also made a significant effort in performing the selfsame exercise - sadly, no positive response had been achieved - for whenever either of them had got through to their erstwhile home the same negative reply was received; *"no one available to receive the call"* And so all future efforts were now abandoned or left on the shelf of no hope - littering Sarah's mind alongside everything else that had proved to be of little use.

So, as neither Jenny nor Sarah were able to make contact with those useless, worthless people, it had to be assumed that all family ties, as far as the two of them were concerned, were in fact now broken, and broken, most assuredly by parents who couldn't give a damn about their only child; for wasn't that the only logical conclusion Sarah, or anyone else for that matter, could come to regarding this depressing situation - that all ties with both Jennifer and Sarah were now deemed severed?

Oh yes, Sarah's monthly salary was secure and Jennifer still received her weekly allowance via her kindly uncle, but as both these payments were made via a standing order routine, under the supervision of the bank, no one at Hyde Hall was seen to be involved in such undertakings. It had been the estate's solicitor, financial advisor and legal dog's body, Colin Tooke, or one of his staff, who had set the thing in motion in the first place, anyway.

Who cared or gave a damn? Certainly no one in Hyde Hall, that much was clear - and so here they were the two of them - stranded; but it was the night-times when Sarah's fading mind did most of its reflecting. The numerous sleepless nights that she'd endured were beyond belief, and the times when she'd lain awake with unrestrained feelings of loneliness all gaining their control - were endless.

"For loneliness is oft a mournful place in which to be ensnared. It is a place to hide when all around is mixed and muddled

up, when worthlessness appears one's only friend in life's depressing gloom; a place to go, as well, to sort the strife that life can throw at times, and so persuade a pensive mind to seek tranquillity."

***

September was proving to be a resplendent month with the sun repeatedly making its serene overtures whenever the fluffy clouds allowed the rays of its brightest light to shine.

The local farmers, praising the days they were able to reap a safe harvest and cursing the days they couldn't, were perfectly delighted with the generous donation that mother nature now bestowed.

The stacking of the sheaves when all the fields were cut and cleared away, and then, after the threshing machine had completed its task, the storing of the grain in the granary, or selling immediately: the wheat, the barley, rye or oats that had taken all the spring and summer months to grow - all of this registered complete satisfaction in the farmers' eyes, for a change.

A heartless tenant farmer, local to the tiny village of Brenton, even now, in these modern days, employed the labour of a first-rate team of powerful Suffolk punch carthorses to perform the thankless task of towing the binder when harvesting the corn.

With their muscle bulked bodies, short, stocky legs and chestnut brown coats, they made a proud, handsome looking pair. And with every movement they showed endless determination in serving their master's needs at any time of day; and it mattered not how laborious or difficult that requirement proved to be.

On this intensely hot, late afternoon in September, when learning had been over for another day, Jennifer Kent, walking dreamily back home from The Old House schoolroom, stopped awhile and stood with excited anticipation as she scanned the sight of wheat harvesting in progress, opposite her home.

Desperately wanting to take a closer look and feeling the need to be part of this rural scene, she felt herself being drawn into a situation that seemed to have a hold over her - a fascination even. And so, slowly at first and then more boldly, Jenny entered the open gateway that led into the field of golden grain that she had noticed growing since she first arrived in Brenton.

From the narrow window of her tiny room set deep in The Cottage's white wall, Jenny had watched every day as the wide mead's darkest green gradually gave way to the golden shade it was now seen to be. She had considered the wheat to have been ready for harvesting at least two weeks ago but it wasn't until today that the farmer's judgement finally submitted to her views.

After cautiously treading the stiff, prickly stubble where the wheat had already been shorn that morning, Jenny stared, with fixed concentration, at the two heavy horses as they painfully struggled with the cumbersome binder.

The steamy sweat that lathered their muscle-bound backs glistened with whiteness and ran imperceptibly down their flanks. White frothy saliva, too, in prolific sticky strings were hanging from their tender curling lips, as they, without justification known to them, save that of doing their master's will, trudged wearily on without complaint, snuffling and champing at the cruel bits that tortured the softness of their gentle mouths.

The ever willing, horses, already worn from a day of heavy toil, trudged unerringly on. Round and round the extensive field they went, always following an anticlockwise path with their huge heads rising and falling again and again with each weary step they took; and their front hooves, being lifted high before them, were planted firmly down once more into the heavy damp clay soil, with laboured tedium - one after the other - over and over.

This farming scene would be viewed as being romantic to some. To others it aroused a sentimental recollection; it called to mind the past awhile; a sight, reminiscent of a bygone age, but with an outrageous callousness about it now that seemed all too barbaric for the cultured eye to see.

With a single horseman atop the curved, sprung metal seat at the rear of the ancient binder, the horses asked no favours nor yet found any in return. And so, with blinkered eyes, whip and reins continuously checking their every movement and a hasty 'whoa' determining the course they took - they laboured on.

The continuous jangling noise of the heavy chains and the monotony of the binder as it chucked out the bound sheaves - one after the other - and the rotating sails as they turned the standing corn onto the cutting knives - and the mind-numbing, incessant rattle of the canvases as they carried the wheat to the binding and rotating sheaf chucker - and the hearing of all of this thunderous mayhem - all but deafening the animals - still they continued in their plight regardless; for they had a job of work to do for a few handfuls of oats a day, and a bed of straw at the end of it all.

Jenny stood silently, her hands clenched in front of her as if in prayer for the heavy horses' deliverance, while she watched aghast at the animal's trudge as they traversed the cornfield in ever decreasing circles.

She noticed a few youths and younger boys closely following the binder, each one heavily armed with long clubbed sticks - just waiting for the kill.

Then all at once she saw a hare type animal as it bounded for safety; leaping the sheaves of corn as they lay waiting to be stood on end, and shrieking in a high-pitched voice of terror.

"*It could have been a hare*," she thought to herself, "*but more than likely a rabbit,*" she considered, as it dived headfirst into one of the hand assembled stooks of wheat - all standing in rows - neatly upright with their ears leaning into one another to dry - all ready to be hauled away.

The small, breathless creature, panting in fear, must have heard the advancement of the gang of boys, as they hollered with bravado their desire to club its life.

"*A final dash might make you safe little rabbit,*" thought Jenny, her pretty face filled with anguish. "*You are already quite close to the hedgerow, so why don't you get away... fast... while you still can?*"

The rabbit must have been thinking along those very lines, for as soon as the first club descended upon the stook of corn it made a bolt for the nearest hedge.

Unbeknown to the rabbit the field had been netted to prevent such dinners escaping the farmers table and so it found itself entangled in the mesh as it writhed and fought to free itself - only to get more entangled and knotted up.

As the rabbit felt the back of its neck give way, crushed in brokenness by a wicked club delivered by the first of the dastardly youths, and as the others arrived, shouting for their share of the fun and slaughter, its tiny life gave a final, pitiful squeal of pain - and was gone.

The biggest of the youths claimed the trophy and with his sharp sheath knife, he paunched it immediately, allowing its entrails to fill the nearest rabbit hole. Then slicing between the two long bones of one of its back legs he tucked the other through the wound and threading his clubbed stick through the gap the hind legs had provided, he resumed his position behind the binder.

The innocence of little Jennifer Kent was heaped in anguish as she witnessed the sickening kill. Then she calmly walked to the hedgerow, leaned over the netted perimeter and vomited profusely.

Suddenly the sickening sound of a gunshot filled the air commanding the young girl's attention once again, and a small fox, probably from this year's set of cubs, was seen to be bounding towards her closely followed by the largest of greyhound dogs that she had ever seen. With the quickest of snatches the young fox was in the dog's mouth and being shaken as if it was a rabbit. Despite a yelp from the dog (the victim had obviously put up a brave battle), the young fox was hurriedly taken back to the dog's owner who tendered the greyhound's bitten mouth with a master's loving care.

Jenny had seen enough of the so called peaceful harvest in rural Lincolnshire for one day - to last her a lifetime she had thought and so she at once repaired to the gateway she had entered but a few moments ago.

'Going so soon?' asked a penetrating voice from the right of her. And stopping, she turned round to see the hideous smirk upon the menacing face of Barnabas Bell.

'Didn't like the gore of harvest time, didn't you?' he added menacingly. 'Perhaps I can cheer you up a little with a friendly hug, if you wants me to that is, and maybe find you a pair of rabbits to take home for your dinner... now that would be a welcome change for you, wouldn't it?'

His provocative suggestion put the fear of God into the little girl as her already ashen face turned even more a ghostly white. And as tiny beads of perspiration spread her pretty, pallid face she felt a misty dizziness overcome her head and a sickening heaviness inside the pit of her stomach.

'I'm not feeling too well Mr Bell, so if you'll excuse me I shall be going home now. Thank you for your concern but Miss Wood is expecting me,' she said feebly, hoping the sinister Barnabas Bell would go away and leave her alone.

'Now don't you take on so,' he disappointingly retorted, his left eye dancing about in its socket as if it wanted to escape, 'I'm sure I can make you feel a whole lot better if you give me half a chance. I should like to give you a bit of my own affection and it won't take me long either. You just come along o' me; you let me give you a caring hand and touch you where no one else has touched afore; you know you wants me to, you've been asking me to do it ever since we met,' he further added desirously, as his sinewy fingers stretched to their fullest extent at the ends of his sweaty palms and reaching out he clutched lustfully at the young girls arm, compelling her to pull away from him in dread and intense fear.

'That will be quite enough of that Bell,' said a sternly spoken voice, which was heard off left of the lane and which belonged to a figure of equal sternness.

The housekeeper of The Old House stood alone with arms folded across her chest - with one eyebrow raised to emphasise her annoyance, and probably for the first time in her entire life not a hint of a smile was to be seen upon that usual face of kindness.

'Didn't mean anything by it... Miss Nunn,' said Barnabas Bell, as his left eye was stilled in an instant and his earlier extended fingers began to tremble. 'Just mucking about that was all; I didn't mean anything by it; course I didn't, come on, you know me by now Miss Nunn; wouldn't hurt a fly, now would I?'

'That's what I used to think Bell but after hearing all I heard a moment ago I've changed my mind; yes, I heard every word you said to the wee girl, every syllable you uttered was quite distinct to my ears and I didn't take kindly to what they heard,' said Janet Nunn, with the harshest of tones to her voice. 'And so if you will kindly remove yourself and any possessions you may have hidden at The Old House, immediately, I shall bid you goodbye Mr Bell; we will not be requiring your services any more. Do I make myself clear?' she further added, with a severity to her words that disturbed Barnabas Bell to the core; so much so, in fact, that he stormed off up the lane ranting and raving and muttering oaths and threats of revenge to his ex-employer and to the 'brainless girl'.

'Are you alright Jennifer my dear,' said the housekeeper, her mode of benevolence at once returning. And after placing a kindly arm around Jenny's shoulders, she walked her home.

Sarah was in the kitchen when Jenny walked in, still cloaked in Janet's arms. And then, looking concerned that something was amiss, she went to her charge and held her comfortingly to her breast. Then looking up enquiringly into Janet's face she asked what had happened.

'Nothing to worry yourself about, Sarah,' said Janet, reassuringly, 'it's just that Jennifer has received some unwelcome attention from one of the lads who used to work at The Old House... but he is now gone. A very unpleasant lad he's shown himself to be but I can assure you it won't happen again.'

Sarah wiped the tear stained face of her charge on her apron, then went to the cupboard, and pouring a lemon drink, she handed it to Jenny.

'Who was it Jennifer, who was it that has upset you so terribly.'

'It's alright auntie, I'm just being silly that's all,' replied

Jenny, cheering up a little, 'I think I must have misunderstood what Barney Bell said to me.'

'You most certainly did nothing of the sort!' exclaimed Janet Nunn, intensely. 'You forget I heard everything that the awful lout spoke; which I might add, will not be forgotten by me, not for a very long time, I can promise you that.

'Jennifer, if I were you I would take a nice warm soak while your aunt and I have a pleasant cup of tea together. No need to hurry dear, take your time: we shall both be here when you return.' The suggestion was made as if Janet Nunn was eager to have Jenny out of the room.

Jenny looked at Sarah without properly turning her head but as if seeking permission to do what had been suggested to her - but hesitantly; for she usually bathed in the morning and rarely in the evening - such was her routine.

Her aunt inclined her head in apt approval and so without furthering another word, Jenny left the room.

As soon as the room was clear of her young ward, Sarah filled the kettle to make a brew of the cup that brings instant relief from all unwanted grief and in less than five minutes the two ladies had made themselves comfortable in the chintzy living room.

'I'm pleased to have this opportunity to talk with you Sarah,' said Janet, in a gentle voice. 'A few days ago I had the opportunity to talk with Jennifer as she was shopping for you in the village.' The change in her voice took on a note of seriousness as she reached this initial point and she moved slightly closer to her host speaking more softly, which both alarmed Sarah and intrigued her at the same time.

'Yes,' she said, 'the wee girl was coming out of the new shop in the village and with a brown paper carrier bag hanging from her arm. At first I failed to notice the difference in her looks but at a second glance I became aware of the change from when we first met on your visit to The Old House. When was it? A couple or so months ago, I suppose. Then, Jennifer appeared to be quite a normal pretty looking girl with nothing untoward about her at all. Since then, and particularly when I saw her coming from the shop, I noticed a dramatic change in her and all in the space of the said two or three months. Her face was now radiantly blooming and her chest had developed a fullness that I certainly would never have expected; and roundness to her tummy too that rarely appears in a girl of her age... unless of course... she is with child.'

Janet's talking had stopped abruptly at this point, as she looked deeply into Sarah's face, and the face that she was speaking to suddenly became alarmed. The tired eyes now opened widely and the wrinkled chin dropped onto her chest.

'Is that what you are telling me Janet,' said she, with an unsteadiness that was filled with instant dread. 'Are you telling me that you think my niece is pregnant?' The state of apprehension that overtook the aging teacher was felt from the top of her head to the tips of her toes.

Janet ignored the questions and instead went on to develop her enquiry.

'Do you know when Jennifer last had her period?' she asked, following the pertinent question with another of equal importance. 'I take it that the wee girl has started her menstrual cycle by now, has she not?'

'Yes a couple of months before we left Hyde Hall,' replied Sarah still in a state of trepidation. 'That was when she started, but since then she has managed to deal with these matters discreetly and privately, upon my persuasion of course, and so I really cannot say what the present situation is with her... for she has never made a fuss that's obvious to me.'

Janet Nunn considered the current situation for quite some time as she inaudibly sipped her tea. She was almost certain that Jennifer was indeed pregnant; superficial signs were there - nothing more - but she had seen enough of those through her shortened career to form an opinion even at this early stage and without examining the girl either.

'Then we shall have to wait for Jennifer to return to us,' she said, at length, 'perhaps, with your permission, I might ask the wee girl a few questions; to which I doubt we will succeed in obtaining the most accurate of answers. I mean, when a wee girl of her age is faced with such an unfortunate dilemma as this, rarely do we manage to get to the bottom of things, not precisely... not at once. A frightening situation for them, you see, and one's inclined to have to read between the lines, as it were, to get the fullest picture. Anyway, we shall try,' she added, as she heaved a sigh, thinking that this kind of happening should have been over and done with, at her time of life.

It took a further half of one hour for Jenny to put in an appearance once again, but when at last she showed herself the paleness had left her complexion and in its place was a radiant beauty of vast proportions and a smiling face that filled the small chintzy room with cheer.

'Ah, there you are Jennifer,' said Sarah Wood, smiling, as

her ward entered the room. 'Come and sit by me dear; Miss Nunn would like a word with you.'

Jenny did as she was asked.

'Please allow me to be quite blunt with you by coming straight to the point, Jennifer,' said Janet Nunn, trying to employ her usual countenance of complete kindliness.

'Can you remember how long ago it was that you last menstruated Jennifer?' A slight pause followed as Jenny looked from Janet to Sarah and then back again. 'You know, when you last had your monthly period?' She added the explanation as an afterthought, to clarify what she had already asked.

Jenny turned to her great-aunt and looked intently into her burdened eyes in shocked dismay, as if she sought her great-aunt's support before she answered the embarrassing question.

Then she turned to Janet and in her innocence she made her soft reply.

'I haven't had anymore, not since I had the first one a few months ago.'

CHAPTER FIVE

September's soft summer breezes performed their role with particular proficiency in the county of Lincolnshire, where the earth meets the sky all-around, and shared its finest fortune with Dorset's varied scene.

This mild cosseting, caused all the menacing clouds, which had covered Dorset a week or so ago, to be swept away and to bring about a gleaming brightness to radiate through the noonday heavens instead.

So intense was this brightness felt that it bestowed the gentlest feelings of optimism on even the meanest of pessimists contained within the populace of the village of Hyde.

Sir Angus Kent was experiencing neither meanness nor pessimism on this bright new morning in the middle of September; on the contrary, his mind was filled with a supply of generosity and optimism, which simply dripped from his mannish visage; and, for a change, he was in harmony with the greater part of humanity too.

In other words the man was feeling cock-a-hoop regardless of all the petty problems encircling his mind at the moment.

Actually, it was true, trivial problems had chased around in his mind more often than he cared to admit these days; although at this point in time, and because he was feeling so perky, he couldn't give a damn.

At the moment, though, he was sure he could take every problem, life could possibly throw at him, in his stride - grasp it firmly by the scruff of the neck and heave it out the window thereby confounding any future hindrances that dare to confront or beleaguer him.

He was sure he could overcome the world as well - solve all of its problems in one fell swoop and dictate to everyone what was needed to be done to keep everything as he wanted it kept, but with added excitement - if his imagination saw fit, that is.

And so, with incredibly chirpy thoughts bolstering his morale, and excitement surging his veins at a rate of knots, he smiled a smile of smugness; the like of which was seen to spread his facial features every once in a while these days, especially when conceit had got the better of him and his arrogance was at its highest peak.

Anyway, top of his list of priorities, at the moment, was the anticipation of his carnal desires being fulfilled by the love of his life, Jane Howe.

He had all but assured himself that matters between the two of them would be resolved today and that their union would be made stronger because of it; goodness only knows he'd waited long enough for this to happen.

And so, it was the thought of this meeting with his beloved Jane that was the sole reason for his excitement now; and with the wild expectancy of an all-embracing intimacy before hand being thrown in for good measure, well, it is little wonder that his imaginings were running riot.

And to add to all this fervour, today's visit was to have taken the beautiful lady completely by surprise; for it was to be an impromptu, unannounced visit that the loving couple would remember for the rest of their lives; or so he had predicted.

He had received no recent hard-hearted or sarcastic comments from Margaret, his now completely estranged and callous wife, not sufficient to cause him feelings of foreboding at any rate; so this aspect of a dying, nay, already lifeless, marriage was added to his joy, for it would give him the freedom to satisfy his carnal wants still further - no guilt to fret him now, you see - not that guilt had ever been a problem in the past for this arrogant gentleman.

Not all that long ago, cutting remarks had seldom been absent from Margaret's once sensuous mouth; for spitefulness had always been Margaret's forte; in fact the one and only strong point the lady possessed, it might, without too much difficulty be assumed.

As with most strained marriages, some unfortunate moments of confrontation had arisen from time to time. Moments that usually ended up with prolonged intervals of silence being observed by both parties. On those unfortunate occasions, Sir Angus had always battled on regardless by ignoring the cause of the quarrel, despite who was at fault, and despite the fact that foundations were being laid for these disagreements to be revived for future debate.

But Sir Angus being Sir Angus had never been one for keeping his mouth closed, not at the easiest of times and not for long, no matter what the circumstance and no matter who the opponent he was battling against might have been.

Because of his temperament, life became more than a little difficult at times for the self-satisfied, sainted Sir, with relations between him and his wife, being strained to the nth degree.

So, in order to avoid conflict and to prolong a peaceful coexistence, he had decided on a more effective way in dealing with the unseemly side to his inappropriate marriage. He had found that by using a newly discovered ability to walk away from strife and to exercise silence in preference to din, and to tolerate his wife's callous mood swings during moments of war rather than battle against her, did the trick rather well. Although, it must be said, it did cause Margaret a certain amount of frustration each time he walked away, which she was quick to express in no uncertain terms and enthusiastically to boot.

But witnessing his wife's frustration only delighted Sir Angus; in a strange sort of way it provided him with boundless satisfaction and caused the wryest of smiles to cover his jubilant face.

Sir Angus, the man, not the dominant male or lover, was often in need of solitude and peace of mind and so he had sought this sanctuary from his wife's nagging ways often - that indeed, was the only way forward. And so, the reward gleaned from the price paid for silence was well worth the absence of the odd hullabaloo or two.

By the time the banishment of their daughter and her tutor to the tiny village of Brenton had taken place, the marriage 'twixt this man and wife had completely lost its reason for existence; not that there had been much purpose to their relationship in the first place but at least they'd always had a wayward child in common to contend with and argue about.

Sir Angus had praised himself continuously for the way he had so ingeniously arranged, with the help of his sensitive but unsuspecting brother, the ridding of the obnoxious girl that he and Margaret had brought up and tolerated for twelve long years; as an unwanted daughter at first and more especially of late, as an aggravation.

That is why it was with some release and kindly thoughts for himself that the good-natured father, of such a loathsome child, had become set free from a life of patched serenity; but best of all he was now able to live a life of perfect bliss; a bliss that was his own, removed from everyone, his bothersome and disruptive wife included.

As a result of this marital disconnection, Sir Angus' relationship with his pleasing mistress, the lovely Jane Howe, had flourished both in the likelihood of sexual passion and in the opportunities of persuasion too - at least in the recent past that had been the case - but now, well, who knows what the situation is.

Their meetings had still continued even though their liaisons had borne precious little in the way of pleasure of late, not for the ignoble Sir at any rate. Not that there had been a major rift, or anything close to it, but relations had become a little stale recently and so something in the way of a revitalizing course of action was needed.

Despite all this, everything was hunky-dory with Sir Angus Kent at the moment - well, as hunky-dory as could reasonably be expected in so far as this out of the ordinary gentleman with his out of the ordinary way of life was concerned.

Strangely enough, though, it was because of his nonexistent home life that Sir Angus had no further use for the 'poor me' attitude he'd formerly portrayed to Jane, that is, in order to gain her sympathy; for he was now a liberated man of great importance and not the puppet of some dissatisfied, undomesticated wife. A wife, whose sole endeavour in life was directed towards the humiliation of the man she willingly married and to the total destruction of his very existence, if that were ever doable; maybe that would be putting things a little too harshly - but then again - maybe not.

It was with a degree of purpose coupled with good humour reigning in his adulterous heart that Sir Angus speedily made his way to Bramble Bush Cottage at the stroke of twelve on this bright, sunny day.

This particular visit, however, would turn out to be an earth-shattering experience of the utmost gravity for a man who was fired with enthusiasm and eagerness. A visit as well with a terrible consequence attached to it and one with more immoral implications being presented than ever a cleric's sternly disapproving homily could conceivably possess.

As already mentioned, this particular visit was to have been a complete surprise for Jane, it being the lady's birthday in two days time; the day when Sir Angus Kent would have to be away in Bournemouth attending to business matters with his solicitor, Colin Tooke, which were far too important to ignore and the date far too difficult to rearrange.

And so he had come fully armed with expensive gifts, a huge card containing a message of love and with his mind fully prepared to make spoken recompense for his unavoidable non-attendance on her special day - and all at a time to suit his own convenience.

As stated before, Bramble Bush Cottage was located at the very bottom of Sandy Lane which in its turn was positioned within walking distance of the outer reaches of the tiny village of Basham Killington. The lane itself had dense undergrowth to right and left of it and served the cottage exclusively.

This charming cottage, being precisely placed and ideally isolated in this way, provided its inhabitant with complete privacy and was, without a doubt, the perfect location for any clandestine liaisons to occur.

Because of the lack of near neighbours, it offered the said privacy at all times of the day and night, which, needless to say, was essential for the two lovers needs and was the sole purpose for its purchase in the first place.

Sandy Lane, being about one hundred yards long and restricted in width to a lesser extent in places, was a brute of a lane to negotiate - but why it hadn't received attention years ago was unknown, for nobody in their right mind would have allowed the frustrating problems that this lane presented to exist longer than was really necessary. Maybe its dire condition was looked on as a deterrent - it certainly acted as one.

It had a surface that was both rock strewn and potholed, with areas so uneven as to prove extremely problematic to even the springiest of sprung cars - as the big silver Jaguar that Sir Angus drove so gingerly at the moment was finding out - and not for the first time either, for it had experienced the ordeal numerous times before this.

But the big car had never found complete answers to this lane's hostile challenge, despite its size; and twice it scraped its chassis on some protruding boulder, only to groan in agony.

All the same, it doggedly journeyed on with both its engine and its suspension crying out as it navigated, with sluggish success, the lane's ungracious surface; and it all but parked itself unaided and sighed with great relief so thankful was it to have arrived at its destination.

The car was a few yards short of the restricted driveway when Sir Angus quietened its almost silent engine - and he sat awhile as his over anxious mind concentrated its over anxious thoughts on what his over anxious eyes saw ahead; but that on which they were now focused was as plain as plain could be; although somewhat unexpected by the uneasy gentleman, to say the least.

A brightly coloured Volkswagen Beetle motorcar was parked in the small gravelly driveway to the front of the equally small garage and was almost completely hidden from the lane by a border of tall, red, bush roses.

Its front wheels were turned awkwardly toward the offside of its body and were acutely positioned in such a way as to fall short of a flowerbed by a mere two inches; quite as if the driver was in some hurry to gain access to the cottage, it might be thought.

Consequently, a puzzled Sir Angus, after silently closing the door of his Jaguar car, walked tentatively past the awkwardly parked Beetle, wondering all the while, in his suspicious mind, just who the owner of the vehicle might be.

Because this particular motor car was alien to the gentleman his brain tried its hardest to lay claim to its identity, but without result. In consequence of this, his inquisitive mind became aroused and his imagination contaminated by its presence; for never before, to Sir Angus' sure and certain knowledge, had a motor of this description ever been parked at Bramble Bush Cottage before, he most certainly had never witnessed it there or anywhere else, for that matter and his lover had never mentioned the existence of such a vehicle.

Normally, Sir Angus wouldn't have hesitated in opening the front door to the cottage unannounced: he would have shown no concern or given the matter a second thought, for he was, undeniably, the owner of the property after all.

But in this instance he refrained from such an intrusion; for he considered the likelihood of Jane having a visitor as being the only reason for the strange car being there. Of course Jane might easily have bought the car herself, which he considered only briefly but as she had not mentioned such a purchase he thought this to be most unlikely.

Once he had settled on the idea that a visitor was in fact at the cottage he decided it would not be in his best interest to admit familiarity with the place, or, with its occupant either for that matter. All the same, ominous feelings did still fill his questioning mind.

Sir Angus rang the doorbell courteously though all the while he wished he had spotted the brightly coloured Beetle earlier, before he had actually committed himself to his driving down the lane, would have been good, but it was far too late for regrets like that.

The doorbell's din wasn't answered straight away, and so he appealed to the instrument's vocalization once again, almost hoping that Jane was out walking with a friend so that he might be able to stealthy creep away without being noticed and thereby avoid any potential embarrassment.

The third time the bell was rung it brought with it complete success; for Angus could vaguely see, through the dimpled glass of the door, the distorted outline of his mistress' figure approaching, and as she did so, she seemed to be adjusting her familiar pink coloured dressing gown nervously, as if it was with some growing exasperation that she walked towards the entrance.

She opened the door narrowly.

'What on earth brings you to my door today Angus? Have you no respect at all for other peoples' privacy?' was the discourteous and startling greeting he received from his beloved. 'You seem to have developed the habit of turning up unannounced lately which I most certainly do not welcome and which I wish you would stop. There are limits you know; and there are times when I am in need of some space of my own, and this happens to be one of them,' said she, as an intense scarlet colouring to her cheeks provided prominence to her most attractive features.

The door was hastily closed in his face.

Because the miserable, adulterer was left standing, just staring at the dimpled door without having said a single word, a bout of awkwardness belittled him.

And so, he simply stood there, bemused, without the flicker of a movement betraying his inner feelings but which, in point of fact, were quite numb at this particular moment in time; for never, in all his years, had he been spoken to in such an insensitive manner. Normally he would not have tolerated such verbal inaptitude, not from anyone, let alone his own darling Jane; well maybe from Margaret, but that was an entirely different matter.

"What on earth can be the matter with the blessed woman?" he thought to himself, worryingly, as he eventually walked from the doorstep slowly and deep in thought.

"I have never seen her in such a state as this before. It would have been no good me remonstrating with her in the doorway: I would certainly have drawn attention to our affair had I done that, especially if a visitor was to overhear our bickering. A visitor - ah yes, of course; a visitor being there would make her unseemly behaviour to be perfectly excusable. She didn't want any visitor to be aware of the fact she had a lover... especially a visitor who might spoil everything for us. Yes, it's perfectly understandable, given the delicate situation... perfectly understandable." He extended his thoughts with these unspoken words excusing his beloved but with a mind so clouded with anxiety he missed his footing and trod carelessly on the neat edging to the flower bed thereby causing his shiny shoe's imprint to be registered in its soil.

Regaining his composure, and quickly smoothing over the imprint, he wandered back to his parked Jaguar, reasonably satisfied with his own conclusions. Nevertheless, an omen of considerable magnitude overtook him as he opened the door, one that urged him, by some inexplicable reason, to be conscious of the fact that at least one pair of eyes was following his every movement; maybe two, he couldn't tell.

As he entered the car, but without lifting his head, he focused his eyes on the upstairs window in the apex of the thatched roof and noticed a slight movement in the lace curtains; two faces, not one, with two sets of eyes, (he was now quite sure of his figures), were examining each steady move he made.

'What the devil are two people doing furtively watching me out of the bedroom window?' He asked himself, aloud, as the excuses for his lover's words and behaviour gradually faded and finally gave way to doubt.

And so, a very suspicious philanderer now drove the big Jaguar car away from the cottage in a state of unavoidable fretfulness, but painstakingly enough so as to gain the further end of Sandy Lane more swiftly than he had arrived.

Here he parked his vehicle discreetly - completely out of sight and sound of the cottage and the lane and here he waited, with the unsure hope of discovering the true identity of Jane's mysterious guest filling his mind.

For a full half hour he remained, as he impatiently drummed his neatly manicured fingers on the steering wheel; without there being so much as a flutter of a bird showing itself from the direction of the Bramble Bush driveway.

His impatient irritation was beginning to get the better of him and more than once he considered storming the cottage for complete assurance of the situation.

Then, glancing at his watch, for the umpteenth time, to secure in his mind his time of waiting; and at the same split second, he repositioned the key into the ignition to start the car. Then, all at once he turned his head, and glancing through the dense bushes he noticed the brightly coloured Volkswagen Beetle motor slowly reversing out of Jane's drive.

It passed Sir Angus Kent's secret refuge with great care, and in so doing he was able to observe it to be a left hand drive model and behind the steering wheel, and sitting next to Jane Howe with one hand on the controls and the other about the shoulders of his beloved mistress, was the plainest faced woman he had ever seen in his life but with a voluptuous upper figure of great proportions.

It wasn't until the Beetle was out of sight that Sir Angus Kent made a speedy exit from Basham Killington; and with the most degrading of thoughts occupying his cluttered mind he put his Jaguar to the test with great and immediate effect.

....

As expected, the answer to Janet's question was not altogether conclusive, for it failed to explain that if Jenny had experienced just a single period why a second hadn't subsequently followed - one month later; unless, of course, the fertilisation of an egg had in fact taken place. If this was the case, then the explanation she was now seeking would have been perfectly obvious.

Janet was well aware that at the onset of such matters a certain delay often occurs between the first and second flow, depending, largely, upon the individual concerned, but for there to have been just the one occurrence of menstruation and then nothing for the last two months, well, this would indeed demand a further investigative examination and one she wasn't at this precise moment in time equipped to perform.

After excusing herself by saying that she would return within the half-hour - she left.

In actual fact, a mere ten minutes had elapsed before Janet entered the cottage once more, carrying with her an aging stethoscope.

Janet examined Jennifer most meticulously by using all the recognised antenatal techniques of the day in order to bring about a satisfactory deduction. The investigation was being carried out within the confines of the young girl's bedroom, and Janet, being satisfied with her own conclusions returned to the chintzy front room where Sarah was apprehensively waiting to receive her report.

As soon as Sarah saw the expression on her friend's face she feared the worst.

'As far as I can make out the wee girl is at least three months pregnant, maybe four, its impossible to give a precise indication with one so young and small and so she must see the local GP for a more accurate opinion,' said Janet, with a smile of reassurance upon a face that failed to illustrate her innermost feelings; feelings that were causing her confusing and questioning thoughts.

Sarah had stood up as her friend stepped carefully down the stairs to enter the room, and was still standing when she received the report.

Now she sat down again, rather heavily, as she digested Janet's words with great sorrow. She hung her grey head in shame, carefully supporting it in cupped hands with her elbows on her knees; as a school child might do in the midst of fervent concentration, and there she brooded; intently searching every inch of her mind for some credible answer to the implausible question.

'How can this be Janet when Jennifer has hardly been out of my sight since my arrival at Hyde Hall and certainly not at all since we arrived here,' said Sarah, as unhappy and dark forebodings filled her mind and a look of disappointment lingered upon her usually sanguine face. 'Can it be that I have misjudged her character in spite of everything, and that the parents' assessment of the child was more accurate than mine all along, more accurate than I was prepared to accept anyway, and that she is, in fact, the most deceitful, the most devious of girls? I can't believe it Janet; and what is more I won't believe it.

'There has to be some other explanation, there really has to be, but until this is put into plain words for me to understand, we have to, or rather I have to, for she is my responsible and not yours, seek measures with which to save Jennifer from this dreadful situation?

'This situation could easily be the ruin of the rest of her life, Janet, and, if I am not at all careful, will be the cause of the saddest regret to everyone concerned; especially to her uncle, who I am sure, thinks the world of his newly found niece.

'But, how on earth can we be discreet about a matter such as this, when, in a very short time, everything will be perfectly obvious to everyone?'

'Well, the first thing is to try not to get too caught up in a fever of emotion or despair,' said Janet, trying to apply the utmost sensitivity to her words. 'And, although you may consider Jennifer to be your own responsibility, I most certainly will be by your side, Sarah, advising and assisting you in every way possible. The thing has been done now and there is no undoing it, so it is up to us to put it into some perspective and evaluate the problem with care.

'But before doing so I should very much like to know how Jennifer came to be in this condition in the first place, if as you say she has rarely been out of your sight for any length of time and not at all since her one and only period. She should be dressed by now so perhaps I might call her down to see if we can get to the root of the matter.'

But the kindly Scottish lady didn't have to move herself very far at all, for as she turned round she caught sight of Jenny sitting halfway down the stairs and not unlike Sarah, her little face, too, was wrapped in total bewilderment and cupped in trembling hands with tear moistened cheeks.

'Ah, there you are my dear,' said the kindly housekeeper, a

benevolent smile broadening her face. 'As you have, no doubt, been carefully listening to our conversation regarding the question of your condition perhaps you would care to join us and maybe enlighten us if you are able.

'But first of all you have to know that no one is thinking badly of you Jennifer or blaming you in anyway, all we need to know is who has done this to you and work out how best we might be able to cope with the situation.'

The look of anxiety that had clouded Jenny's face intensified as she struggled to explain to herself, let alone to the two ladies, how she came to be in this state, but without too much success. She had just this minute heard that she was to have a baby - that much Jenny had taken in - but how it all came about was totally beyond her understanding.

The recent lecture given by her Great-Aunt Sarah upon this very subject lingered and was now uppermost in her mind, but she had at no time been subjected to abuse by anyone, be it man or be it boy and so she was totally at a loss to offer an explanation; she didn't know that many boys anyway.

'Please believe me auntie, no one has touched me in the way you described last term, I wouldn't have allowed it anyway, honestly I wouldn't,' said Jenny, she being filled with indescribable bewilderment; but she managed to keep herself surprisingly composed, given the state she was in.

'I believe you my dear,' said Sarah, unloading her head from her cupped hands at last. 'So it must have happened without you being aware, but how that might have come about, I can have no idea.'

Then all at once a notion entered the governess' mind, a notion she felt she should have considered at the beginning of the dilemma and which now may well prove to be the answer to the conundrum.

'Jennifer,' she said, without a pause, 'no doubt, you will remember staying out all night when that fearsome storm was raging... you know... when that kind gypsy gave you shelter.'

Janet's eyes widened as her attention was alerted to its sharpest, for this was the first time she had been made aware of the saga. But she held her tongue and listened intently as Jennifer nodded her recollection of the event and then seated herself beside her aunt as Sarah Wood continued quietly.

'Did you both share the same bed Jennifer?'

'Yes, I believe so,' returned Jenny, 'but because I fell asleep as soon as my head touched the pillow I'm not really sure. But I did feel his arms cuddling me and holding me very closely, so I suppose we must have shared the same bed. And I can remember thinking that this was the first time I had been held in anyone's arms since I was a baby. But he didn't touch me auntie, not so that he made me pregnant, he didn't.'

Janet's senses were even more attentive at this point and she moved over to where Jenny was now seated beside her aunt and kneeling down beside her, she took the child's hand in hers and looked affectionately into her tear filled eyes.

'Now, don't you fret any more, Jennifer, my dear; there is no need for you to worry your pretty wee head any longer, your auntie and I, between us; we will sort the whole thing out, you can rely on that?'

CHAPTER SIX

It was with a reckless disregard for the safety of others and at a speed so insane as to be beyond belief that Sir Angus Kent drove his Mark V Jaguar through the winding lanes that led from Basham Killington to Hyde Hall that steamy afternoon.

As well as driving like a man deranged he was also wallowing in an abysmal state of uncontrollable temper, which he would never be able to cope with by himself, not without sinking into the depths of some sort of psychological disorder.

This appalling state of mind, which was stirred by emotion and exaggerated by self-pity, was too terrifying to contemplate, or so it appeared.

The foul mood itself couldn't possibly be regarded as being genuine though, even to him; it was more like a fantasy - some sort of romantic drama he was acting out than anything resembling reality. Perhaps it was a kind of safety device, behind which he needed to protect his pride awhile, who could tell!

It was as if he was allowing, nay, encouraging his reasoning to be wildly out of control and with an obvious feeling of despair about it that was fast turning the situation into a nightmare and which, in the end, could easily become far too much for him to handle by himself.

To a more normal person this situation would be estimated on a level slightly higher than insignificance, that's all - one that Sir Angus ought to have brushed aside fairly easily, especially when one considers the man.

After all, this walking talking piece of conceit was the proud possessor of an elevated status in life and held a reputation in society that was the envy of mere mortals; and, of course, one who always felt the need to dominate everyone else; as well as life's little schemes. As a result, he ought to have been practised enough to exercise more composure than this, even if no one but himself was listening - but he didn't.

With his wide eyes blazing and his temper far more flared than it had ever been allowed to flare in the past, and with his confused mind running riot and lacking reasonable thought, he was proving to be a danger not only to himself but also to anything and everything that was unfortunate enough to stand in his way; especially so, because at this moment in time he couldn't give a monkey's cuss what he knocked down or what he killed; the whole world could go to hell and burn there eternally for all he cared.

Not only did he feel a queasy sensation in the pit of his empty stomach at the moment but his whole body was stricken with irrational jealousy. His face was bleached with anger; and it betrayed alien feelings of insecurity and uncertainty as he debated loudly with himself so that the car was filled with the vilest of words issuing from the widest of mouths.

After he had bellowed a final roar of oaths, his tone was quietened to a murmur as the deepest and most bizarre meditations claimed his self respect, or rather what was left of it.

His recently reasoned mind was being haunted by what he considered as being the greatest rift in a loving relationship that the world had ever seen and far greater than any leading author could possibly devise. This desperate situation was not made any easier because of his complete obstinacy, the nature of which permits no good reason for excuses and no room for merciful forgiveness either.

So, who was to blame for this unfortunate rift that was causing the man so much heartache? Well, Sir Angus Kent himself of course, and to a lesser extent his now not so beloved mistress; although it was mainly down to the gentleman's acute imagination, stimulated by suspicion that was the main reason for his behaviour - juvenile reactions to the unexpected also played a largish part - that much was obvious.

Although not altogether unexpected, but catching him suddenly by surprise and during the final part of his frenzied journey home, questioning thoughts of his possible miserliness loomed up before him, which almost certainly added to his mood.

But there was no need for this latest curse to bother him for whatever else he may have been Sir Angus had always been a generous lover - materially speaking.

All of these feelings were as odd as they were foreign to him but over which he evidently had no control; and so they were outwardly spoken or bellowed.

'I shall return the eternity ring I bought for her; that's for sure; and the diamond studded bracelet and the broach as well; she certainly will not be receiving any of those trinkets, not now, not ever, her wretched birthday or not.' He spoke these words with a firmness of intent and openly to himself, not just once but time after time, as if to underline his miserly intentions; and at the final 'her wretched birthday or not' he raised his voice to such a crescendo that it drowned the sound of the Jaguar's continuous drone.

'And that detestable house as well; that hideous hideaway

where she thought she had entertained me with all her blasted fantasies; just romping about the place and exposing herself like the trollop she really is... just as though she was playing a part in some sort of sexual production at some seedy theatre or other and then positively encouraging me to stay the countless nights in her damned bed when I ought to have been home with my family; there will be no use for that any longer; so I shall get rid of the damned house, and everything inside the place will go as well. She had nothing when she arrived so she will have nothing when she leaves, I'll see to that.' His voice dropped to a lower pitch as he uttered the final phrase of his sentence. 'I shall get in touch with the estate agents and put the blasted place on the market this afternoon... sell it over her head, that's what I'll do... if I have to; and then where will she be? Homeless that's where... out on the damn streets where she belongs.'

He continued in this vein for the remainder of the journey, sometimes in anger, sometimes in hatred, but not once did he shed a tear for his apparent loss; not once did a memory tare at his cold heart strings so that he might have had to swallow hard to avoid a distressing moment and not once did he examine an alternative explanation to that which he considered to be the reason for the affair to be at an end; it was as if he really wanted an excuse for the situation to be terminated in this way but didn't want to openly admit it - and so he wallowed in the self-pitying belief that life was being merciless to him - hurtful in every way.

As he entered the long driveway to Hyde Hall his murmuring gave way to contemplations. Thoughts of the immediate past and those of the near future, and his willingness and ability to cope with both now flooded his mind.

"So she has been my mistress since god only knows when... well, what of it? Who cares or gives a damn? But I can positively inform her here and now that the party is over, my dear, over for good... and there will be no worming your way back into my kind affections, I can assure you of that. There are plenty of damsels queuing up out there to take your place... damsels, I might add, who would be eternally grateful for my continuous generosity; and not staying with me just for the money I spend on them either... or for bedroom satisfaction... she was never that good in bed anyway, and now I know why, the woman obviously prefers other women to men. Well good luck to her, that's what I say... I shall certainly tell her so and tell her straight... she can use some other place for her dubious assignations now... that's for sure. I'm not about to allow her to

sully any property of mine with her licentious indiscretions, so she can go and find somewhere else to carry out her damnable whoring."

As soon as he arrived at Hyde Hall he abandoned the Jaguar in the yard, outside one of the garage doors, expecting someone else to put it away; and then made his way up the stairway to his bedroom - climbing the stairs three at a time.

He changed his cloths for something more suitable - his riding garb was selected; and then he urged an outer display of controlled calm to exist about his face - just in case Margaret happened to have witness his return, one might very well suppose.

After that, he retraced his steps along the corridor and sped across the landing; and hurrying down the stairs, he used the same energy in his stride he had used when he had climbed them - and went immediately to the stable block.

Now all of this was incredibly strange; even by Sir Angus Kent's standards these actions would be regarded as being weird. For if he was completely out of control of his senses, what on earth prompted him to change his clothing? Maybe it was force of habit - or conceit - or both. Or quite possibly he considered his present mood to be a dramatic act, as mentioned above, but an act in which he decided to play the leading roll - just for the hell of it - who could tell?

There were half a dozen horses being kept at the stables these days: one belonging to Sir Angus, two belonging to Lady Margaret and the rest, Joe Abrams, the stable lad owned and was allowed to freely stable at Hyde Hall in lieu of wages for looking after the others.

But Sir Angus hadn't ridden for ages; the novelty had worn off over two years ago; soon after he had met up with Jane in actual fact. Oh yes, Margaret was still a keen horsewoman, she helped the stable lad exercise all the horses daily, mostly riding alone but occasionally with Joe. Sir Angus had often speculated, in his suspicious moments, if anything improper was going on between the two of them; for those who cannot be trusted find it difficult to trust.

Not that he would have been overly concerned either way; if Margaret had decided on an affair with Joe, or encouraged an intimate relationship to exist between them when they were out riding together, or at any time at all come to that, then it would have been alright by him, he would have applauded the relief he gained from such a liaison, anyway.

But as for Sir Angus riding horses for pleasure in recent

times, no, not at all - that was totally out of the question. It would have been equally in keeping for him to have ridden a bull as to be seen astride a horse these days; much too grime-ridden and smelly for his liking. Why, even going near a foul-smelling equine creature, which had a stupidity equalling nothing else he cared to know on four legs, usually brought him out in a cold sweat.

But at this particular moment on this particular day Sir Angus hastily entered Pilot's loosebox where he knew the big black stallion would be waiting to mindlessly gallop over the Dorset countryside. So long as someone was astride his back and he was being put through his paces - what cared he if he was being used merely as a diversion in order to cleanse some idiot master's mind of the pollution that had collected there over the past half hour or so?

Sir Angus attempted to bridle the stallion far too hastily; and the extreme difficulty he was having with the bridle straps and bit tended to test his patience beyond reason. This fleeting failure and the clumsiness he was experiencing with his fingers and thumbs were probably due to the gentleman's appalling mood rather than any lack of practice. But eventually he completed the task and threw the loose reigns over the animal's head and positioned the saddle with far less fuss; even though Pilot's belly appeared to have gained a few inches so that the girth failed to tighten to its usual position.

After retrieving his ancient riding crop from the stall's inner wall, he hurried Pilot across the cobbled yard, opened the gate and continued out into the field. Here he mounted the beast by use of the huge, dark grey rock he had had positioned there for that very purpose - simply ages ago.

The afternoon was warm and airless but the slight breeze he felt caressing his angry face quickly turned into a gale as Pilot increased his gallop across the open field.

Soon the breeze became warming in the extreme as his body temperature increased and it seemed to curb Sir Angus' irritation so effectively that he removed his riding hat to encourage the wind to waft his wavy hair.

He threaded his arm through the strap of his hat carelessly and kicked his heals deep into Pilot's flanks in order to get every ounce out of the big horse.

No one knew what happened that day or how the big black stallion, minus its saddle and rider, came to be wandering the cobbled yard alone, aimlessly waiting to be led into the comfort of his secure loose box.

Joe, the stable lad, had wandered into the yard astride his

grey mare and found the over heated stallion dripping with a white, lathery sweat. He quickly dismounted and led Sir Angus' horse into his stall and bolted the door just as Lady Margaret came into view.

'Just found Pilot wandering about the place ma'am,' said he, worriedly. 'Looks as though he's been put through the wringer alright... it seems to me he's been ridden way too hard and for quite a while at that... but his saddle is nowhere to be seen. Do you think Sir Angus has had him out?'

'No idea Joe and what is more, I don't really care,' was the blunt, sniggering reply.

'Perhaps I better take Snowball out again to see if anything has happened to your husband,' he said, as he remounted his grey mare and wandered off into the meadow. 'You couldn't see to Pilot for me could you ma'am?' he called back, 'he's in a bit of a state!'

'OK Joe - leave him to me,' shouted Margaret, who had all the time in the world for horses but not so much for her own kind; all of whom, especially her husband, were of little consequence to her. The exception being Joe; he was considered to be a fine young man by Margaret - good looking too.

***

Because there was no lingering embarrassment or unease persisting at The Cottage between great-aunt and niece, Jenny continued her learning practices as usual the following day with complete assurance. In fact quite the opposite climate existed to that of embarrassment, since the awkward discovery of Jenny's condition; with the dedicated tutor heaping heartfelt warmth on her protégé at every opportunity.

As the light, pouring through an adjacent window, dazzled Jenny's eyes a little; she rose from her seat and pulled a single curtain to shield her face from the sun's persistent glare.

After she had re-seated herself awhile she was startled by the unusual tapping of Janet's hand on the already open classroom door as the kindly housekeeper, seeking an impromptu consultation with Sarah, interrupted the class of one, so that Jenny's mind strayed a little.

"They will probably need to spend more time together now; I expect they are trying to work out what's to be done with me," she thought, although this particular reflection failed to bring about any feelings of anxiety in the young girls mind. She had every confidence in her two mentors in any case, and besides, both of them had

expressly instructed her not to be overly concerned with her dilemma and so she wasn't; everything would quickly fall into place or be worked out for her - she was sure of that.

'I shall be with you directly, Janet,' said the governess, who was wearing the same look of warmth she had worn since the previous day. 'Perhaps if I pop down to see you in say half an hour or so… would that be alright with you?'

Janet waved her hand in acknowledged approval but failed to accompany it with any supporting words: not wishing for her interruption to be felt, it was supposed.

Like most days lately, the weather, being keenly aware of its early autumnal responsibilities allowed subtle warmth to flood the classroom where Jenny sat contentedly writing her sketch on 'autumn and all things to be expected'.

"In the northern hemisphere," she wrote, *"autumn is the time of year when the days become shorter and the temperature begins to get colder, many fruits, apples and the like, to ripen, and for leaves on the tall elm trees and oaks to change their colour and fall to the ground. The season's period starts from the twenty second of September and finishes on the twenty first of December when it finally gives way to the final season of winter."*

She reread the writing in her book and inclined her head with a smile as she mostly did when she was pleased with what she had written.

Then, blotting her page, closing her book with care, and lifting the top of her desk quietly, she put her book away ready for her teacher to mark her work, which was attended to at the end of each challenging day.

As with most lunch hours, Jenny walked back to The Cottage to make a pot of tea for Sarah and herself and to prepare fresh sandwiches for them both to eat.

Janet occasionally accompanied the duo, when she was stuck for something better to do and sometimes she prepared sandwiches for the three of them at The Old House. But, the situation was without routine and on this particular occasion Jenny walked the short distance home alone, skipping along the lane without so much as a care in the whole world; that is, until a grating voice disturbed her cheerfulness.

'Don't know why you're looking so damned pleased with yourself; you got me the sack from my job, you did, and now I've got no way of earning a few bob for my poor, sick old mother,' said Barnabas Bell, petitioning Jenny as he leant against the five barred gate that led to the, as yet, unploughed field of stubble where Jenny had fearfully watched the corn being cut a few weeks earlier.

Jenny nervously watched as the underdeveloped young man's left eye once again agitatedly deserted its central position - as it always did when she was on the scene. And she felt the dreaded sweat of fear sweep over her body at once and with just cause, for the inscrutable Barnabas Bell, not unlike his left eye, also deserted the central situation of the gate he was leaning against.

In an instant he walked over to be by the young girl's side with an obvious threatening action attending his movements. He stood before her now; and with his crossed arms embracing his feeble chest and his face distorting itself into an intimidating expression of aggression, he continued:

'Now I reckon as how you owes me for getting me the sack that day and placing me in the situation I now find myself to be in,' he said, menacingly. 'Yes, I reckon as how you owe me quite a few quid, so you had better get yourself some money so you can pay up; do you understand me? Five quid is the first payment what I reckon you owes me, and that's how it will be 'till you pay up all of the debt you owe; so the next time we meet you had better have it on you to give to me or you will find out that I ain't the nice, kind fellow you once thought me to be. I hope you completely understand what the consequences will be if you don't, Miss La-de-da, it won't be nice for you... I can assure you of that.'

And with that, he scornfully chucked her chin with a crooked finger; and with the smuggest of sneering smirks set on his sallow face, he walked away, turning his head a couple of times to assure himself of his success.

Jenny, shaking in fear, instantly breathed a deep sigh of relief and then ran quickly to the home she had come to love.

Because she had spent half of the one hour lunch break in conversation with Janet Nunn, Sarah Wood was late in getting home that day.

After much discussion and consideration both ladies had agreed that confidentiality or rather secrecy had to be maintained regarding Jenny's condition, for her own sake if for nothing else. It would probably be in Jennifer's best interest for her to give birth to the baby as far away from the village as possible and where she was known to no one of any consequence.

Apparently Janet Nunn had a spinster sister who was younger than she by two years and who lived in a remote part of north-west Scotland. After an in depth telephone conversation between the two sisters had taken place the previous evening and the sister in Scotland had been put in the picture regarding the current situation with Jenny, and after debating the various difficulties involved when giving birth to a little one in a place like talkative Brenton, the sister had sighed deeply before coming up with an admirable solution to the heartfelt dilemma.

No one wished to burden the immediate family both in Dorset or here in Lincolnshire with the untold disgrace that bearing a baby out of wedlock would most certainly cause at this time - of course not. And so the sister went on to suggest that it might be appropriate for the three of them to adjourn to Scotland for the period leading up to and for the duration of the young expectant mother's confinement.

After a further drawn out conversation the contrived reason for the visit was decided upon. The broadening of Jenny's geographic mind regarding the British Isles was deemed to be the reason - or so it seems. It was most necessary for the young lady to gain all of the geographic experience possible at this present time because she was expressing great interest in Janet's scenic homeland, and besides, she was considering an eventual teaching career with a geographical flavour in the long and distant future.

All of this would seem somewhat implausible to most people's ears - but that was how the matter was left - but with a great deal of tongue in cheek existing.

Jenny was not at all alarmed by the proposal put to her when her great-aunt eventually arrived home; she had guessed that something of the sort would happen anyway. But rather, the little girl greeted the idea with an open smile and with an air of keenness that, in Sarah's eyes, illustrated the child's capacity for good sense, and the basic understanding of the moral obligation a young mother must have for an unborn child - and everybody's peace of mind as well.

And so it was arranged.

At an appropriate time before little Jennifer Kent was decidedly showing to be with child, the party of three, together with a quantity of suitcases, boarded the train at Lincoln Railway Station at ten minutes to eleven o'clock on a cold October morning; all heading for what was little more than a cluster of homes on the north-western borders of the Scottish Highlands and to a small village named, Kyle of Lochalsh.

Hamish Kent had taken the little party to the station himself, at a cheerless hour, totally unaware of his niece's condition and quite unsure what it was the company had hoped might be gained by such an illogical venture as this. But having complete faith in the two ladies' judgment he surrendered to their wishes and bade them all a fond farewell, hoping they would soon return in good health to their acknowledged homes.

The journey was long and wearisome and with there being little or no interest with which to occupy herself for most of the passage, little Jennifer Kent slept soundly, resting her head upon the lap of her great-aunt and with her legs doubled up awkwardly beneath her; while the two elderly ladies involved each other in muted conversation.

With much platform waiting between most of the changes the small company had first to change, at York, then Newcastle, then Edinburgh then Perth and then Inverness. The final change came when they reached Dingwall where the small steam train, with but a few passengers left on board by this time, took them across mountainous, snowy countryside to their final end.

It was in the early hours of the following morning when they wearily reached their objective and entered the taxi that had been prearranged for them. And not unlike everything else attributed to Lochalsh the taxi was ancient and rusty and cold; compared, that is, to the comfort of the train they had just left.

But that was the only transport available to take them to the outskirts of the tiny village where a small cottage, not much more than that, was sought amid an almost impenetrable barrier of snow that had drifted over the hills to where it could - and drifted to where it was inconvenient in every way to have drifted.

The Scottish lady, who eventually answered the loud knocking on the door, was homely, robust in stature and not unlike her sister, Janet, in facial appearance.

As soon as the door was firmly closed she busied herself in the preparation of some hot broth and served it with thick crusty bread that was way beyond being appreciated and in which the taxi driver also shared - but obviously not until he had deposited the luggage in the small bedrooms ahead of the cranky stairs.

Jenny was more than a little bewildered with all that was going on around her by this time; she was tired in the extreme too, as indeed they all were; but such a long and arduous journey had also caused the child's mind to be sluggish.

Upon looking out of the tiny window she noticed that where the pitch black of night gave way to the reflected light from the dazzling snow it caused her to be somewhat confused. And so, upon the eating of her delicious broth and upon the routine exchanges of expressed goodnights she climbed the crooked stairs to the warm room that was to be hers for the duration of her visit and which was to be shared with her Great Aunt Sarah.

As both Jenny and Sarah were both sound sleepers, and failed to indulge in fidgeting or snoring that much, the arrangement was considered to be most satisfactory. Janet and her sister would be sharing their sleeping arrangements in any case - so that was that - no complaints; it was the only solution possible, anyway.

The white sheets of the bed were inviting and the towel-wrapped, beige, stone hot water bottle beckoned her to a hoped for slumber of great soundness, so she climbed between the sheets as quickly as she was able, and cuddling the hot-water bottle closely to her tummy, she immediately fell asleep.

***

Sir Angus Kent lay where he had fallen that fateful afternoon. His head was turned in such an odd way, in relation to his body, that it failed to invite speculation.

The man was still breathing, that much Joe could see but the attitude and position of his physical form was far to complex for Joe to examine closely or interfere with. He didn't even bother to dismount his white mare; instead he turned her round and headed back the way they had come as quickly as she could gallop.

Margaret was still attending to Pilot, when Joe reined Snowball to a sudden halt outside the stable door and she raised her head quite unconcerned as the look of anxiety on Joe's perspiring face gave way to words of panic.

'I hate to be the bearer of bad news ma'am, but I've found Sir Angus about two fields away. He's lying on the ground where he must have fallen; the saddle is by his side with its girth snapped clean in two. He must have been riding Pilot at such a terrific force for that to have broken. Can you telephone for an ambulance right away ma'am? He's in a pretty bad way,' said Joe breathlessly, his reddened countenance awash with anguished sweat.

'Yes of course Joe. Please use the house phone, or ask one of the staff to do it for you... Mr Spiller will be able to help you, I'm quite sure,' she said, as a smile flashed across her undisturbed face. 'I shall just finish poor old Pilot here and then I shall be ready to receive the medics when they arrive; I'm almost done.'

The ambulance took over half an hour to arrive at the big house and it reached the side of the unconscious Sir Angus Kent two minutes after that. The doctor, who had accompanied the ambulance, examined the patient extremely gently and oversaw the transference of the all but lifeless man to the cream vehicle with equal care.

Sir Angus, being only slightly conscious but minus his usual faculties was strapped securely to the stretcher. After applying padded bandages carefully, to ensure his twisted neck maintained the same position it had held after the fall, they placed pillows either side to keep his head fixed firmly in position. Then, very slowly and with extreme care the ambulance made its way back across the meadows to Hyde Hall and from there to the hospital whence it came.

CHAPTER SEVEN

Now that the current farming year was drawing to a close, Hamish Kent, found himself being less involved with the day by day running of the Brenton Estate and he had allowed his thoughts to be taken by his Scottish housekeeper and his well-regarded niece during the first few days of their absence and his feelings to dwell upon their wellbeing with a fair amount of concern filling his mind.

Because nothing to the contrary had been reported, Hamish had all but satisfied himself that the party had been installed in the lonely wilds of Scotland, reasonably safely; but because he had not fully come to terms with the reasons that Janet had given for their departure in the first place - his satisfaction wasn't complete.

His mind was slightly relieved, however, after he received a phone call from his sagacious housekeeper a couple of weeks after their departure; although, it did appear that the kindly lady was seeking some sort of reassurance regarding Hamish's own well being, which he found to be a most pleasing thought for her to have considered.

This phone call, then, was more or less sufficient to dispel any doubts his mind may have had on the subject of the questionable Scottish venture; but, as the canny lady failed to become involved in any in-depth dialogue during this extremely short call, certain questions still hovered his fretful mind.

Christmas cards had quite naturally been given and received to express all time honoured wishes so that in the end Hamish was naively content to leave matters much as Janet had deviously left them - and so, without any further worries or cares left to bother him - not in so far as the visitors to bonny Scotland were concerned, anyway, he placed the matter to the back of his mind and allowed his attention to focus on the following farming year instead and on one other matter - a totally domestic issue that had lain dormant in his mind for some considerable time but which now required some considerable thought.

***

In the Scottish village of Kyle of Lochalsh the awaited Christmas period had passed more or less unnoticed and not too much in the way seasonal festivities had been observed. The adults, although on tenterhooks over their ward and the smallest problem that a new born child might bring, hid their fears discreetly - and as for Jenny, well, she was only concerned with the passing of the days.

As the weeks rolled slowly by, Jenny was caused to gain size both in girth and chest. Not in an ungainly, graceless manner, but modestly visible as befits a young expectant mother of delicate years.

Her state of mind was considered to be a contented one by the adults: bearing in mind the backache her condition caused from time to time; and her hopes for the future were optimistic and cheery in every way.

She also expressed confidence in her supervisors' judgment without the slightest opposition being uttered or even left showing upon her lovely face, no matter how slight that expression might have been.

By presenting such respect openly, she unwittingly displayed her own strengths both in courage and in her optimistic attitude - for optimism had always been an asset for Jenny; indeed it would have been a vital necessity for her to have possessed such spiritual endurance for she would never have been able to endure the lengthy years without it.

Never before had she felt such confidence in other people either as she did at this moment. Confidence in others had always been, to Jenny's way of thinking, some sort of prop that feeble people rely on and so she'd never found the need. But now she knew the blessing and the comfort that having confidence in others now brought, and it made her feel secure.

From late autumn and long before the party's arrival in Kyle, this small isolated village scene had been piled with frosty snow, and long pointed icicles too had hung like stalactites from the gutters of the cottage for all that time. Now, both these wintry wonders presented a subject to occupy at least part of the daily chat but neither snow nor icicle were looked on with irritation or loathed in any way and not at all like the coldness itself which always caused complaint.

Whilst the noonday's sun did its best to warm the highland air, the ever thickening clouds cast their doubts on its ability to bring a favourable result. And so, Jenny, still in edgy uncertainty, warmed herself beside a roaring open fire whenever the necessity arose or walked awhile to ease away the pain her condition brought at times.

With tall fur boots protecting her dainty feet and legs from the coldest winter she had ever known, and with long scarves wrapped about her coated body, the now not quite so little girl walked amidst the snowy dunes in idle observation of the January scene; quite as if it was a necessity for her to witness the snowy waste first hand.

Now and again, Jenny gleefully played at throwing chilly balls of snow with her surrogate family, although she threw each missile with only mild intent; but the heartfelt warmth, that both her protectors wrapped the young girl in, meant that great affection, compassion and esteem attended her at every playful minute of every playful day.

Mary Nunn, whenever she found time to join the others, also played or walked with them awhile; and she too grew in fondness of the small expectant mother of the as yet unborn child even though she did from time to time look warily forward to the mission being finished.

But despite all the effort that was being made to protect Jenny from the miserable chills of winter, her body warmth diminished quickly as daytime turned to dusk. It was then that the glow from the evening fire came into its own and rekindled the warmth the day had taken away.

It was late in the afternoon on the seventh day of February nineteen hundred and fifty four when Jennifer Kent bent over and clutched at her lower tummy in abject pain.

Sarah and Janet, both standing by the side of their ward, had been merrily playing snowballs after taking in turns the gentle toboggan rides down the slippery slope that had been formed outside the small stone cot; each one calling with great amusement despite their differing age and size; whilst the corpulent smiling Mary looked from the wood framed kitchen window as she prepared the evening meal.

The sudden cry for help was answered in a moment without there being a hint of delay and the two surrogate mothers, fully alert and with utmost care, helped the child quickly into the front room and to the warmth of a blazing fire. Here Jenny rested awhile before she was taken to her shared bedroom in shocked dismay and with irregular, strength sapping pain tearing at her body.

The emergency plan for the preparation of hot-water and clean towels was instantly installed and within an hour of her waters breaking, little Jennifer Kent, in trembling fear and stressed discomfort, was delivered a baby boy. His ebony hair was straight and long, his slender body flawlessly bowed, and his tiny hands, fingers, feet and toes, were perfectly formed and curled.

With his life dawning breath he displayed his young authority and told the world to clear the way; he had decidedly arrived - he was not prepared to be quietly put aside in embarrassment or shame - so it had better not be tried.

Weeks before the day of his birth, Jenny, in her own mind, had decided on a name for her unborn child, should he be a son: which to her young intelligence was beyond all doubt. She wanted, no needed, a strong name that exemplified both dependability and honesty, a name that her son would be proud to own, a name depicting gentleness, but above all else, a name masculine enough to shelter him from any future unwanted wit; and in her quirkiness of mind, a name to bear the same initial as her own. And so, when asked by her aunt one day if she had decided upon a name for her unborn child, Jenny responded instantly and without hesitation.

'His name is to be Jacob, Jacob Kent.'

The summarised version of the birthing result as calculated by Sarah Wood, Janet and Mary Nunn together, but with the biggest blame for the decision falling to Janet and her sister, was for the new born babe to stay with Mary in Kyle of Lochalsh, and she alone was to bring up the infant as her own grandchild.

The three ladies had talked the matter through on numerous occasions and in the end they had considered that the task in bringing up a child was far too weighty for one as young as Jenny to bear and too restricting in every way. And should anyone request some detailed explanations as to the baby's presence, they were to be told that Mary's own niece had died during childbirth and that the dying mother's last request was for Mary Nunn to bring up the child in a way that she herself had been brought up.

The baby was to have been taken from Jenny as soon as it was born even before it was able to draw its first breath, in actual fact; taken, temporarily, to a near neighbour, who already had a tiny child of her own and that Jennifer was to be told that her own baby had died during the trauma of the delivery.

In theory, the horrendous ruse had seemed quite reasonably conceived, but in reality the deception left much to be desired as little or no thought had been given to the final outcome.

And so, unfortunately for the three adults and much against their feelings of concern, little Jacob Kent, upon his arrival, kindled other ideas in his tiny mind, ideas that both shamed and mortified the three adults. He quietly aired his lungs immediately his head had entered this wonderful world, and Jenny, upon hearing his tiny bleat and amid tears of joy and ecstasy laid claim to her darling lamb before the devious ploy could be achieved.

Accordingly, the shocking objective of such an atrocious scheme was abandoned, with two innocent children winning the day;

the one being the tiny son, the other being the mother.

All the child's healthful needs were purchased in a small general store in Kyle of Lochalsh and more besides; for the three women, taking their changes in the caring of the infant Jacob and arguing with each other as to whose actual turn it was to be absent from the infant's side at any particular time on any particular day, made certain he was well cared for, and with the loving attention any child could ever wish have.

And so the child grew and waxed strong in spirit; as the good book says; but with a greater emphasis on the spirit side of things, for he seemed aware of all weaknesses and chinks in the adult's armour he was capable of penetrating with his cooing and with his tears.

At the ending of the final day of February the surrogate family were once again set to commence yet another journey, but this time in the opposite direction, back to the English county of Lincolnshire.

A single, additional passenger was to accompany the party this time, just a tiny one. One, to whom the railway authorities had no need to supply a rail ticket and one who's only need, was to be carried in a wicker basket or in the kindliest of arms.

***

Sir Angus Kent had failed to move of his own accord, in the firm orthopaedic bed he'd been allocated, since his arrival some six months earlier at the Royal Victoria Hospital in Boscombe as a suspected broken neck casualty.

The doctors eventually discovered that a lesion in the spinal cord had occurred at a point between the fifth and seventh vertebrae of the cervical region of his spine - which posed a severe blow to his body's central nervous system.

Indeed it was a traumatic blow to everyone, with the possible exception of one, a most terrible and severe setback that would see his body respond immediately by going into spinal shock for the whole of the first six weeks; after which, the doctors, with the help of x-rays and by testing his deep tendon reflexes, sought to be assured of the seriousness and the extent of the damage caused by this terrible accident.

For the whole of the six week period, he lay on his back, totally flat and still, with a hideous metal brace supporting his head and chin, and an orthopaedic device about his shoulders maintaining tautness between body and skull, and on the whole, making the impossibility for head movement complete.

He remained thus for a further two months after the initial period of spinal shock was over and during this extensive time he was diagnosed as being tetraplegic.

Accordingly, all parts of his body, from the neck to his toes, were affected with a catastrophic partial paralysis the immediate result of which caused the gentleman great anguish and immense difficulty in breathing; and the awful slimy secretion, partially blocking his lungs, proved frustratingly laborious to clear.

Up until the early days of March, not a soul from Sir Angus' family had visited his side; Margaret, his estranged wife had informed no one, such were her feelings of disgust and hatred for the man she had married. Even his twin brother Hamish Kent, in Lincoln, had not been notified; in consequence of this, little Jennifer Kent, his daughter, was unaware of her father's plight as well.

Joe, the stable lad, was his only visitor, his only link with the busy, outside world. And although Sir Angus was able to speak, after a fashion, his words were distorted, slow and rambling - only Joe, aside from the long-suffering nursing staff, had sat by his side holding a lifeless hand, listening to the gibberish being uttered and talking aimlessly to bring a semblance of comfort to a fading gentleman who lies by himself in a friendless room in endless loneliness.

"For loneliness is oft a mournful place in which to be ensnared. It is a place where the sick and dying go to await decision's hour, perchance to gain a respite or to go where angels lead."

***

Hamish Kent was the most amazed of men when he collected Janet and her entourage from the station at nine in the morning on the first day of March.

Janet's short, late afternoon telephone call had alerted him to expect one further unnamed visitor, and he, assuming that Janet's sister would be accompanying the party, was pleased at the prospect of meeting the sister whom he knew was special to his housekeeper.

His shock at seeing only the three who had left him months ago proved more than a little worrying but the jolt suddenly turned to joy as he watched his petite niece walking slowly towards him smiling and carrying a bundle in her arms.

Before he had had the opportunity to familiarise himself with this, his newest guest, his housekeeper took him to one side and explained to him in great detail, the events that had transpired in the life of little Jennifer Kent over the past nine or so months and how she, Janet, had wished to spare the kindly man all the scandal from the finger pointing villagers, who, she considered, had little else to occupy their dull and dreary lives but to tittle-tattle about such occasions as this and to entertain themselves with other people's business rather than their own.

She had carefully omitted her inappropriate aim in leaving the baby with her sister, Mary, of course; when for a brief moment her usual good judgment had somehow gone astray. She now realised, completely, that the right and proper place for a baby, any baby, was with its mother and so the error of her own reckonings were now skilfully ignored.

Hamish Kent laughed raucously.

'What a preposterous idea Janet, as if I would consider for one moment the importance or indeed the result of local chit-chat,' he said. 'Janet, you should have known me better than that, I'm ashamed of you.' The final part of his sentence was, quite obviously, spoken in jest, for never, not for a single second, could he possibly be ashamed of his usually most sensible and devoted housekeeper; she who had seen to his every need since the day of his own birth and will so continue in his service for always.

Being in The Old House again was like the deepest breath of the freshest spring air to the travel worn arrivals as they entered its portal and with a fondness and gaiety that was certain to last the whole day long - and way beyond.

Hamish was the first to speak in earnest by opening a cautious conversation; the subject of which was to surprise everyone. For although he had considered before this time the matter of ignoring his brothers instructions, it wasn't until now he had considered relating the matter to anyone. And so after he had apportioned champagne to all, including his niece, he commenced:

'My new family,' he said warmly, calling the buzz of chatter to order. 'I can assure you that you will most certainly not be going back to The Cottage anymore... I am most adamant about that, and, of course, that includes you Sarah. I am putting the place up for sale once again.

'There are plenty of rooms here at the Old House going spare and so I have decided that you will stay with me despite the firm instructions given me by my brother Angus; and we must use as many of the rooms as will make you all comfortable.

'I have mulled the matter over carefully and I came to this decision when you were all away... so you may deduce from that, I have not arrived at the solution lightly. Jennifer has now added to the list of reasons for your stay with me; and so I am now able to keep a close eye on all of you and especially this new arrival... my great-nephew, Jacob, oh yes, especially him.'

In spite of all that, and after he had dictated, with firmness, the revised sleeping arrangements at The Old House he added, in an excitable manner that he will be wanting to take Janet into Lincoln City, in order to purchase all the requirements for the tiny infant's needs; after she had been refreshed of course and rested herself awhile.

'Jacob will need the best of everything, you know,' said Hamish, quite unable to stop his greedy eyes from feasting the tiny infant's form. 'Cot, perambulator and all the fittings; you'll know what is needed, Janet, so when you are completely rested perhaps we...'

His words were cut short by the loud ringing of the telephone as its din echoed throughout the whole of the house. With minimal delay Janet answered the black contraption in the hall so that a degree of privacy might be upheld. Well within the space of half of one minute she re-entered the drawing room and spoke to Hamish Kent.

'It's a private call for you Mr Hamish,' said she, in a somewhat bewildered tone of voice.

After Hamish had taken the call he returned with a pallid face and a mind carrying careful thoughts but he expressed not a word of any real importance to anyone.

After a lengthy and refreshing intermission, he and Janet eventually wound their way to Lincoln City leaving Jenny and her aunt at home to look after baby Jacob.

It was some considerable time before either Hamish or his housekeeper made an utterance as they sped along the country roads that opened up the way to Lincoln later that afternoon; and Janet, polite in the expectation of her employer making headway into the opening of the conversation, which, to her way of thinking, was almost certainly to be about baby Jacob, waited respectfully still.

A gloomy silence had strangled every attempt at speech the kindly man had dared to make, and so it was quite sometime before a word could leave the overcast features of his manly mouth.

Then suddenly, without there being any logical purpose or

words of explanation, Hamish pulled the motor over into a small lay-by and quietened its engine. As he turned slowly sideways, he glanced at Janet and a look of awful seriousness dimmed his former cheery face.

'That was a lady whom I spoke to on the telephone just a few moments ago,' said he, 'a lady by the name of Jane Howe, from Dorset.'

***

It had indeed been Jane Howe on the phone that morning and in a state of nervous tension, it might be added. For weeks, no months, she had tried to make contact with Sir Angus but each telephone call she'd made to Hyde Hall had been balked by Margaret; even to the extent of refusing to convey the simplest of messages to her husband.

And so it went on, month after pointless month, so that in the end, and in nervous desperation, she visited Hyde Hall personally. This was without question and for a certainty, something she had been forbidden to do by Sir Angus - ever since she'd known the man he had made this demand of her that had to be complied with. But now, in a hopeful attempt to secure the smallest reason for her beloved's absence, she found herself carelessly ignoring each and every demand her lover had decreed.

Margaret, of course, was absent from the house, or so Jane was assured by the butler, who answered the door with irritating rudeness. Jane, ignoring the man's deliberate insolence, wandered discreetly round Hyde Hall, to the back of the place, where she hoped to gain sight of the man she loved.

She tried tentatively calling his name in a subdued voice and quickly examined the stable yard where she hoped he might be. But her calls were unanswered and her searches were in vain; and so, after retracing her steps to where she had parked her car she seated herself and pensively waited.

She thought she noticed an imprecise movement on the farthest side of the property, and so, she exited her car once more and stood awhile.

Bracing herself, and in as determined a fashion as her nerves would allow, she strode over to where she had seen the movement. All of the time she was praying that it wasn't the mistress of Hyde Hall she had seen, for a direct confrontation with that lady, just at this minute, would be more than Jane could take; but she prepared herself ready for the fray, just in case

Joe, the stable lad, was casually walking into the yard from the meadow where he had released all the horses for a free romping treat. After closing the gate he had watched them for a couple of minutes more and smiled amusedly to himself as they frolicked and rolled in the grass. And then, as they'd galloped to the far side of the mead in delightful freedom and then pranced about in a joyful mood, they galloped back to the gateway again.

He hadn't expected to see anyone that afternoon, so the presence of an attractive woman, whom he had never seen before, caused the man quite a scare.

'Is there something I can do for you ma'am?' he asked, thinking she was a friend of the family or at least a relative who had called to pay her respects.

'I have been looking for Sir Angus Kent,' she replied, with an enchanting smile settling on her face. 'I'm a friend of his and was hopeful that he might be at home, even though I haven't had any luck in finding him thus far.'

'Don't expect you've heard the news then ma'am,' said Joe, in a serious tone that instantly wiped Jane's smile away.

Jane sought the reassuring support of the crossbars of the barricaded fence beside the gateway as she was told the horrible truth about the terrible accident that had befallen her lover all those months ago and her eyes moistened quickly as she questioned his immediate whereabouts.

She had known of Sir Angus' dislike of horses even though he owned one of the handsomest of stallions, and he had, at one time, ridden across his extensive fields as freely as any other rider, but not of late. To own and ride a horse had been no more than an outer facade to impress and indulge his wife, Margaret, in the early days of their marriage, soon after they had returned from India in fact, but the pastime like the pleasure he may have gleaned from riding then had been short lived.

And so, bearing this in her mind, Jane realised there had to be some alternative reason, a heartbreaking reason that had prompted him to have ridden that fateful day.

It was in a state of complete and utter devastation that she drove her car back to Bramble Bush Cottage much later that afternoon with her mind fully occupied with thoughts of her lover.

She had called at the hospital where Sir Angus lay resting and was pointedly refused admission as the said gentleman wasn't up to receiving visitors at the moment and so she would try again the next day, and the day after that, and so on, continuously, until he agreed to see her.

It was late the following morning when Jane had summoned sufficient courage to contact Hamish, the twin brother; she knowing deep within that the dreaded Margaret had, most certainly, not bothered to relay any such news to Lincolnshire.

She had received adamant reassurances from Hamish that he would bring down a small party, which would most certainly include Jennifer, to visit his brother the following day and he had expressed his disappointment in Margaret for her non-cooperation but thanked Jane, sincerely, for taking thought to inform him.

After Jane had replaced the telephone receiver she lifted it once again and spoke to the sister immediately in authority of the staff that was attending to Sir Angus' needs that day.

She explained the situation at Hyde Hall, once again, and her relationship to the injured gentleman received another airing, and then she asked the sister, pleadingly, if she would persuade her lover to see her.

'It seems that my patient is quite adamant about not seeing anyone Miss Howe, but I can certainly appreciate and indeed sympathise with your situation and your need to see him and especially as we have had no response from our calls or our letters to his wife. The police have also called on our behalf without result. But if as you say there is a rift between the two of them then that would explain the caginess the wife is displaying at the moment. Hopefully that will change as time goes on.

'In the meantime, I intend talking to Sir Angus on your behalf with the intention of arranging a visit for you; but please, don't build up any hopes, as all our patients' wishes have to be the only orders we obey; it is they who must have the last word on a matter such as this, you see. Perhaps I might return your call in say half an hour or so to provide you with his response.'

They each replaced their respective receivers the sister in favour of a mission of mercy and Jane in favour of a much needed cup of Brazilian coffee.

True to her word the rather pleasant sister telephoned Jane three quarters of an hour later expressing a very hopeful answer to her plea.

'After much persuasion on my part, Sir Angus has given me a sign that he is prepared to receive a visit from you but with the expressed understanding that the meeting does not exceed a period of five minutes. Could you give me an undertaking to that effect and some indication as to when the visit will be convenient for you so that I may prepare my patient accordingly?'

Jane was unable to contain herself any longer, and so she suggested that one hour from now would be satisfactory. Consequently, she arrived at the hospital with ten minutes to spare.

After calling in at the sisters' office, she was, in due course, shown to her lover's side, and with tears filling her eyes at the sight of him and after kissing him, she seated herself anxiously and took his lifeless hand in hers.

'I'm so sorry my darling,' she said, as the tears spilled from her eyes and trickled down each side of her face. 'Was it me who upset you and caused you distress by not receiving you a day or two before my birthday? I told my sister Rachael afterwards that I thought you were angered by my attitude and I wished afterwards I had seen you and introduced you to her properly. But my darling, I had been up for most of the night, waiting for her to arrive from Germany and as we hadn't seen each other in years we spent much of the remainder of the night trying to catch up with each other.'

Upon hearing this, Sir Angus' own eyes filled to overflowing as he slowly rolled them in unwavering denial of her blame.

The five minute meeting drifted into an hour long visit with each holding the other's eyes in unwavering admiration and love and it wasn't until the sister gently separated the two of them that Jane left her lover in a state of extreme and agonising torment; a torment that was, from this moment on, going to agonise her for the rest of her life until it found its end.

CHAPTER EIGHT

Although Jane Howe had never met her lover's twin prior to this distressing evening she had been aware of his existence for some considerable time; for wasn't it she who had tactfully suggested that Sir Angus pave the way for his daughter's stay with Hamish in the first instance?

The disruptive girl would then live securely at his brother's home in Brenton, or close to it, where she would no longer be a nuisance to her parents and where she might at last discover a more agreeable behaviour for herself without yielding to the call of disobedience at the drop of a hat - or allowing defiance to take control of her mind without it being prompted.

Jenny's stay in Lincolnshire was deemed acceptable from the start and would be of a permanent nature. She would then remain with her uncle until she had seen the error of her ways, which, in all probability, wouldn't be until she had reached a responsible age, when a more positive and agreeable temperament will have established itself in the child's unruly mind - for everyone's sake.

Jane caught her breath for a moment after the initial sighting of Hamish had disturbed her mind; for she was overwhelmed by the similarity of the brothers and to the same extent that both Jennifer and Sarah had been dazed by the twin's remarkable alikeness when they'd first been presented to the amiable Hamish Kent.

She had heard from Angus much earlier how alike the brothers were, but the spoken word can never be compared to reality; so, coming face to face with such a phenomenon as this was a shock to her system, to say the least.

The view of Hamish as he exited his large silver car, which, incidentally, was not unlike the one Sir Angus had driven, howbeit in colour alone, was tricky for Jane to cope with.

For the briefest of moments she had to contain her emotions, hoping that the similarity between the two men, which had caused her eyes so much confusion, would be quickly made obvious, before her mind was seized by panic completely.

Even as he walked the distance of the gravelled path to her cottage door she felt her heart skip a beat and the longing for her lover's touch returned instantly to fret her.

As she abandoned her view from the sitting room window, in order to greet the man, beads of perspiration trickled down her neck and a sickening feeling lodged itself the pit of her stomach causing the whole of her frame to tremble in anticipation.

But as soon as she opened the door and heard the lower pitch of his voice when he spoke his first hello and felt the strength of his powerful hand as he clasped hers, her mind at last established the difference between the brothers and she felt comforted and more at ease because of it - for there could never be two Angus Kents, not in all the world.

Hamish had considered it somewhat unfortunate that Jane and he were not able to meet at Hyde Hall and to form a cosy threesome with Margaret there; just as an opening to their relationship, if nothing else. Such a scheme could have been arranged quite easily had Margaret been of an amicable disposition and had a more cordial connection between the three of them existed; but as it was, the idea was never put to the test and so it failed to happen.

It was Jane's suggestion that Bramble Bush Cottage should be used as the location for their first meeting even though she ought have been aware of the embarrassment that such a proposal might have caused the Lincolnshire gentleman; for it was here the lover's trysts had taken place regularly, almost from day one of the affair, and in almost perfect harmony ever since.

It was during a brief telephone conversation with Hamish Kent in the early evening of his arrival in Dorset that Jane mentioned the idea of a meeting at her home as being convenient. It ought to have been obvious to her then that a slight uneasiness would exist between the two of them; but she had dismissed her feelings straight away because she believed she was doing the right thing; besides, no alternative venue sprang to mind at the time, even though there must have been dozens of alternatives that were far more suitable - had she taken sufficient time to think or sought consultation with him.

Hamish had continued to feel ill at ease about meeting his brother's mistress in this way, even as he'd motored to the cottage that stressful evening; but because he wished to free Jane's mind of all the sadness that he realised must have gathered there lately, he decided to set aside his anxious thoughts and present a more congenial front.

But he had no need to worry unduly for never again would assignations between those two ardent lovers take place - not here at the cottage; and never again would Jane's mind be the same as it had been when immersed in carnal infatuation.

Although Jane was aware of the fact that all visits from Angus were over and had been brought to naught, she knew her love for him would not fade - not really.

She had accepted this fact as soon as she had left her lover's side for the first time - that dreadful time when she had driven from the hospital in a state of tear-filled grief. Since then, an unexpected reaction had been aroused which now dominated her mind, insisting she tolerate the futility of it all and face bravely the onslaught of bitterness - since these two demons would surely plague her being each and every moment they could.

It looked as if a very long time indeed would have to pass before Jane would be capable of coming to terms with her lover's injury, for she had considered, over the past days, he would never walk again - not now - not ever.

Neither would they be able to live together as man and wife as they both had yearned to do; and all the small, incidental things that had come to mean so much to the pair of them over the years, were now forever gone.

Surely, all of these were negative thoughts, as far as she was concerned - thoughts that should be instantly wiped from her mind. She must pull herself together now after this sad disruption to her life and although happy endings were never likely to happen for either of them there was still a little hope left to cling to - but that was all there was.

And so, in order to encourage the small amount of sanity that had been left inside her head to be restored, she resolved to remain positive. She would carry on with her life in her usual way, quite as if nothing had happened, and bring into play all the self-control she could possibly muster to deceive everyone - not least of all herself.

In reality, she knew she had to begin the dreaded process of getting used to living without her man as soon as was ever possible, now in fact; for her sanity's sake, it had to be now. It wouldn't be easy for the lovely lady - she knew that too - but the process had to begin at sometime - so why not now - before she opened the door to Hamish Kent.

Jane's dimly lit brain was at sixes and sevens as she waited for the bell to sound and being weighed down with all the disturbing thoughts that fate had so badly dealt her, her eyes were caused to glisten; and foreseeing a tear might well escape the portals of her mind, she blotted the corner of her eyes to forestall a moment's grief.

While she shook the firm hand of her lover's brother and wishing it was he, she put on the bravest face she could - just for her Angus' sake. But she lightly touched the gold locket that hung about her pretty neck for added reassurance.

It was just as Hamish released her hand that her tears began to fall more heavily - emotional tears that she was unable to prevent from flowing but which allowed her desperate thoughts to continue through the hurt.

"His being made whole again might be improbable but my faith will make it so," she gasped, whilst crying, *"I still believe in miracles. But if the time ever comes when the impossible is inevitable and I know deep down that all hope is lost and he will never be made well again... then I shall resign myself to this... with anxiety and with sorrow but with no empty thoughts touching my heart... for there will never be anyone else for me... no other man will ever take his place or come close to taking it."*

These distressing thoughts had been well rehearsed by Jane, for they had plagued her mind time and again, and all too often overwhelmed her clouded mind in moments of despair.

Hamish Kent seeing Jane's obvious distress placed a comforting arm about her shoulders and offered kindly words of regret as they stepped into the room.

Although he recognised instantly the genuineness of Jane's grief that had beleaguered the introduction to their meeting, Hamish did what he could to play the anguish down - since his only concern was for Jane's comfort at this moment in time.

He had visited this lady's most appealing cottage by himself in the late evening hour, soon after he had conversed with her over the telephone; while the remainder of his newly formed family had stayed behind at the hotel where he had booked four single rooms for a couple of nights.

Hamish had decided that an immediate meeting with her father's mistress would be too much for Jennifer to be expected to bear; not that the young mother really cared either way, for she had known of her father's affair for simply ages and had tailored her own way of thinking to that arrangement long ago. But this was her uncle's decision and so the proud young mother accepted it with good grace; after all, she was here to visit her father - not her father's mistress.

Therefore it was Hamish Kent alone who explained to Jane how his niece had become pregnant when she was still living at Hyde Hall and of course about the birth of Jacob. He placed total innocence at the feet of one so young, and, in a few words, presented the explanation that supported the likelihood of such a conception taking place.

Janet Nunn had explained the possibility of such a happening

- an event when neither participant would be aware of such an occurrence taking place. And having every respect for his housekeeper, her knowledge and her wisdom, Hamish had supported her hypothesis without question and would continue to do so until she told him otherwise.

To Hamish's delight, Jane's response was one of total acceptance; and to demonstrate this she offered to enlighten the grandfather of all that had taken place almost a year ago; and to knead his mind into the belief of these possibilities. It seems that she was mindful of a miracle such as this - as well.

As Jane was now allowed to visit with Sir Angus on a regular basis: for both the patient and the ward sister had wholeheartedly agreed to such an arrangement taking place in the future, and as she would be seeing him again in an hour or so, she would take advantage of the visit and explain everything to the incapacitated gentleman for him to mull over at his will.

Hamish Kent felt relieved by the short conversation which had taken place that evening, and after they had refreshed themselves and encouraged each other with good wishes and with Jane's promise of a phone call to be made later that same evening notifying Hamish of Angus' immediate reaction to an impromptu visit from his brother and his daughter the following morning, he departed Bramble Bush Cottage in favour of the company that had become his nearest and his dearest in a very short time indeed.

***

Sarah and Janet had remained in the back seat of the car after it had drawn up in the hospital's small car park the following morning, whilst Jennifer, carrying Jacob in her arms and Hamish by her side entered the hospital's corridors in search of Sir Angus Kent's bedside.

Jane had telephoned the hotel quite late the previous evening, after her visit with Sir Angus had, once again, ended in emotional tearfulness, and she was pleased to reassure Hamish of his brothers delight at the prospect of the visit and so it was with no reservations that brother, daughter and grandchild arrived at the door to the private ward where a nervous Sir Angus Kent was lying - all the time anxiously awaiting his visitors' arrival.

Jacob was lying contentedly in Jenny's arms as she waited awhile - nervously standing in the doorway of the sick room before she finally decided to enter.

First of all, she needed to acclimatise herself to the clinical atmosphere of this dreaded place by scrutinising the situation of her father's dire predicament before she entered it completely. Secondly she felt the need for her uncle to break the ice as it were, so that all the fear and awkwardness could be dealt with in a moment.

Then, after taking extreme courage she approached her father's side in an adult manner. After laying Jacob upon her father's arm, and without a single word being spoken, she bent that lifeless arm to enfold the infant child to his side and to hold her baby safe.

With an unrehearsed performance but a spontaneous show of fondness and with tears streaming down her pretty face she embraced her father as she had never done before.

'Daddy,' she sobbed, 'I am so sorry to have been such an unruly daughter to you, please forgive me,'

Her father failed to answer straight away: he being taken aback by his daughter's words of contrition; but with complete determination he concentrated his tearful eyes on hers in deep remorse.

After a short time he did open his mouth to speak; not as normal people speak 'tis true, but in an almost silent whisper and with a stammering that made it difficult for Jenny to hear. But his disjointed sentence was expressed in such a way that conveyed his complete sorrow and total regret.

'J Jenny,' he began, at long last; with faltering words that conveyed all that his mind was feeling. 'I lain here - months - n nothing - my mind - but - b but;' he curtailed the incoherent flow of words for a moment, as his eyes, overflowing with tears of conscience, were wiped away by Jenny with the sleeve of her dress before he could manage to continue, with great difficulty, where he had left off. '... the way - we - b behaved - since you born - badly; n never has it - never - your f fault - dear Jenny - the blame - is - ours - us - s - selfish - aimless - us - we - have - the c cause - of - problems - grief; it is - I - need - I ask - for f forgiveness - f from you.'

Her fathers faltering words, although almost unintelligible for most of the time were spoken and received with love as Jenny, placing her small finger over his lips prevented his exhaustion.

Jenny stayed in this position, with her face pressed close to her father's and her arms about his neck, for the whole of the visit.

Jacob, with never a murmur breaking his tiny mouth, eventually fell asleep on his grandfather's lifeless arm, and Hamish, after embracing his heretofore alienated brother, talked over Jenny's body to Angus, telling him about the success of his intelligent daughter's education, about the happiness she had brought him and of his intention to care for them all in Brenton for as long as his care was needed.

Eventually the relatives, with the reunion now complete and after taking their leave of an unsettled Sir Angus Kent, made their way back to the car and from there to the hotel. A resolute promise had been made to the man that lay in deep despair, stating that they would visit him again before they returned to Lincolnshire the following day.

With much sadness in their hearts, they tried to occupy the remainder of their visit in a way that might lesson the burden of their grief.

They visited the many sites that visitors tend to visit in this picturesque county but all the while their thoughts failed to leave the recollection they had of the injured man's depressing plight.

The unnecessary waste of a life would be forever there to distress them and bring them consternation; the pointless, uselessness of it all; the far-reaching and utter carelessness with a life that was barely half expended; the self-same life that could have seen contentment now in a beautiful grandchild was soon to be eradicated from the face of this world and for what? It was for a moment of unrelenting stupidity; this was the all too difficult part to accept, and so it was with solemnity and not with pleasing joy that the little party attempted to fill the lonely hours; for recollection of the emptiness that a silly accident had caused would be forever theirs.

***

It was with a feeling of pensive sadness that Jenny, alongside her uncle and holding Jacob once again in her arms, approached the sick bed of Sir Angus Kent in the morning of their return to Brenton.

They had tried to employ an air of cheerfulness and were quite successful, up to a point, but the look on the paralysed man's face didn't allow for too much flippancy and the gravity of the occasion soon took precedence.

They stayed by his side for over an hour that morning with Jenny holding on to her father with such a determination that it brought about a certain amount of confusion to Hamish's mind; indeed bewilderment, as to how a small girl of tender years could conduct herself so graciously before a man who had behaved so abominably to her for the whole of her short life.

Then, realising the obvious existence of the bond that often accompanies such a relationship, a relationship that he would never know, he abandoned his worrying thoughts in favour of appreciation for all he had.

The parting came all too quickly and with such a complete air of finality about it that it added to their misery - but as they were passing through the doorway an attending nurse called out for Hamish to return.

With shortened and uncertain steps he went back to Angus' side and inclining his head he focused on his brother's whisper.

'It was - you - f father - he - told me - it was you.'

Clearly understanding the useless words his brother had whispered to him, he turned aside; but not with anger did Hamish turn away, not with any degree of resentment for the years he'd been cheated by the two men he had so despised for the greater part of his life, but with reluctant acknowledgment and humility; he forever knowing that the importance of living was far greater to him than any title, or riches that may accompany it.

After a moment Hamish touched his brother's head as if bestowing a blessing and then he bent down again and kissed him.

'That's not important to me Angus, not any more. You can keep it... only, please... I beg of you, make sure that your daughter inherits and not your wife or your mistress, that's all I ask of you.'

Angus hinted a smile, reassuringly, as his brother left his side not for the last time but for now.

***

Hamish decided to pay a short visit to Hyde Hall after his return from his brother's bedside, hoping to establish the basis for reconciliation between Angus and Margaret before it was too late.

He drew up in front of the big house and leaving the rest of the party where they were seated he exited the car with a degree of optimism and a display of dignity in his step.

Quite unexpectedly, Margaret was in residence to receive the caller who was duly shown into the drawing room where she awaited his presence.

Her look was one of measured, spiteful meanness as she refused the hand and the kiss that were being offered. And without the hint of a smile, no matter how falsified it might have been, she indicated a chair where her only brother-in-law should be seated.

Despite this adverse treatment and before Hamish was able to pronounce his statement of determination to put an end to the unhappy divide that existed between the once happy couple and in its place to set up a friendlier atmosphere - one where a more harmonious relationship might be encouraged to flourish - the mistress of Hyde Hall briskly emphasized her response before it was even called for.

'Brother-in-law,' said she, 'if you have called on me today in the hopes of building a bridge between that useless husband of mine and myself... I apply the term husband very loosely indeed, you understand... then I am inclined to assure you that you will be wasting your precious breath, breath which I was hoping he may have used up by this time... his own at least.

'If on the other hand you have called to say that my licentious husband is already dead, then I welcome the news with open arms and of course with my sincere good wishes thrown in for good measure. But I can see from the grimace on your unfortunate face that it is not the latter and so my former assumption must be correct.'

'Margaret, I refuse to accept your heart to be as cold as you would have me believe, I had hoped that you would show a little more sympathy than this for the man you willingly married... when was it, fifteen years ago? Surely you could be generous enough to lighten his heavy burden now; now that he is so incapacitated and with his life's expectancy being sadly shortened to the blinking of an eye.'

'Hamish, your brother, for the whole of my married life, has treated me shamefully, taking to himself bloody mistress after bloody mistress and beginning when I was expecting that awful child of his.

'Pardon me if I make it very clear to you that even the mention of his name fills me with revulsion... heaped with nauseating disgust. And the sooner his life is over, so that I may reclaim my own, the better I shall like it.

'Now, have I made myself quite clear to you, Hamish? The sooner I can dance on that man's grave the sooner I shall be free of him and all of that goes for my so called daughter as well; please tell her that from me will you?

'And now if you will excuse me brother-in-law I have more important businesses to attend to this morning other than spending it in needless conversation with you.'

And with that she left the room, relying on Hamish to show himself out; which he was so relieved to do.

***

The carload of five returned to Lincolnshire later that morning with similar feelings of anguish attending each of them.

These appalling feelings had been experienced when they'd first set eyes on the all but lifeless patient of course; but the awful frustration at having to leave the man, who, in his loneliness, had shown a good deal of change in his attitude toward his fellow man, albeit because his unfavourable prospects, had not diminish.

Without a doubt, the terrible plight in which Sir Angus was so destined to be forever placed was hard to take and so their minds were laden with an unmitigated lack of hope.

The following day, after trying desperately to put yesterday's visit to Dorset behind her, the young mother rejoined her lessons with fresh determination and added enthusiasm. She had, as one might imagine, been made aware she had more to prove than she had first thought now that her uncle had made such a determined effort in repairing all of the breaches that once had isolated Jenny from her father, consequently her efforts gained energy as she battled on.

She now felt that a new approach to her learning had to be attained if only to demonstrate to her father her worth and her capabilities. She also felt more at ease with the situation of reconciliation - even though the dreaded price had been too enormous for her to contemplate.

Jacob, now situated in the cot that was stationed by his mother's side for her added and loving attention, behaved himself with equal determination and soon sought only routine consideration from his mother as he applied himself to the task of growing with tremendous speed; for that, at this moment in time, was the sole purpose of his little life.

***

A new spring had come at last to Brenton and with it the promise of a brighter year. Hamish Kent had continued with his promise to his brother and had taken Jenny and her son to visit her father for two days in every two weeks.

Eventually the paralysed patient, still with his head being firmly supported, was allowed to sit outside his bed in the comfort of an easy chair in order to welcome his daughter, his grandson and his brother when they arrived. Although he was physically unable to appreciate the experience of sitting in a chair, no matter how restful it may have seemed to others, he had found mental cheer because of the exercise - and to a huge extent at that.

His faltering speech as well had become more discernable of late; for he had learned to pronounce his words again as if he'd been a child. A specialist in speech therapy to the disabled had been employed to help with this and so the procedure sailed smoothly along.

Although the visits had passed by all too quickly, for the invalid's feeble mind to bear, at least he was now able to notice the changes in his baby grandson's progress; but the dreaded tears did all too freely flow each time of their departure.

Slowly, and with sheer strength of mind, Sir Angus began to acquire some feeling in one of his arms again. Minute feelings at first, but gradually, and with complete determination being applied, the feelings progressively increased to being useful - at least, he was now able to respond in the holding of hands and take pleasure in that superb experience once again.

Jane Howe regularly visited her incapacitated lover, tending to his every need whenever she was allowed and showering him with great affection whenever the moment presented itself.

Her sister also visited him on a couple of occasions but with each visit she brought with it a fresh amount of sorrow both to herself and to Sir Angus as well, so that the invalid, more than once, considered putting an end to her visits. Nevertheless, he stowed the thoughts once more to the back of his mind whenever they showed themselves since he did not wish for his beloved Jane to be disturbed in any way and that she should remain in her state of ignorance always - if that were ever possible.

Margaret, on the other hand, had never visited Sir Angus' bedside nor was she ever likely to do so. Not for a single moment would she consider a visit to be of any advantage to herself, you see, and without the importance of that benefit being in place why would she visit a man she so despised; and so she would continue as she'd done in the past and leave that sort of do-goodery to lesser mortals.

The mistress of Hyde Hall had learnt from Joe of the slight improvement in her husband's condition soon after one of his hospital visits had taken place. He had quite deliberately allowed a piece of information slip into their conversation: he being completely aware that Margaret's wifely duties were not being attended to in any way at all; but he wished to give the impression he was totally ignorant regarding the Kent's lack of rapport with each other.

'… good to think of Sir Angus making some sort of headway isn't it ma'am, no matter how slight,' he had said, after he'd disclosed the full bulletin - but he wasn't at all surprised at her lack of concern.

'Is it?' was all she could muster for the moment, and then she instantly changed the subject in favour of the welfare of her horses.

No further improvement in the condition of Sir Angus Kent was ever reported again. He had gained as much use in his arms as he was ever likely to gain, and that was precious little - apart from the odd feeling. And so, after he had been informed of his current situation by the specialist who had attended him throughout his trauma, he resigned himself to the fact that that was it - he must hope for nothing more.

'… and so you will never walk again…' was the abrupt report.

He received the news bulletin with bitterness by saying that he intended never to give up hope and that improvement would surely come if he tried hard enough.

He tried, but it didn't.

Eventually after months of torment Sir Angus Kent gave up the effort and settled for what he had, then turning in on himself for a while in a state of loneliness he pined for all he'd lost.

"For loneliness is oft a mournful place in which to be ensnared. It is a place to hide away from fear that harms the undefended, when cowering is the only means to pass that dread away."

CHAPTER NINE

In the fifth month of the year, reputed to be merry for one reason or another, and some four years after Sir Angus had supposedly accepted that he would never walk again, mixed-up feelings for his destiny established themselves once again in his active mind thereby frustrating his whole being and causing a particular private ward in Boscombe's Royal Victoria Hospital to be occupied with gloom.

Being of a determined and resolute nature Sir Angus secretly believed he would be able to walk again, if only in a feeble sort of way; and even though he'd outwardly accepted his fate and despite the consultant's assurance to the contrary - he still hoped for better.

Although this determined attitude continued to exist, every once in a while the incapacitated gentleman succumbed to a mixture of aggravated emotions that seemed to deny him all he hoped for. At these times, and with complete frustration attending, he would silently let off steam, thereby causing a great deal of anxiety both for himself and for his carers - but all of this was to be expected - or so they said.

Mostly there were tolerable moments when he felt he hadn't been lost or deserted in any way - these times were especially noticeable when a visit from Jane was imminent - but after the visits were over he was left with moments of despondency when he felt desperate and at the end of his tether - this is when the depression set in.

So disheartening were these moments of despair that he wished his life might end - or maybe end it himself if he knew exactly how - though he never hinted a word of this misery - not to a living soul.

Although these moods swings would continue for the rest of his days a change to his nature had resulted from his injury, for at no time had he asked for sympathy or expressed his former 'poor me' attitude in any way - not to his lover - not to anyone.

***

On the morning of the fifth day of this late spring month, the date of Jenny's seventeenth birthday, Jenny, unlike her father in far off Hampshire was full of the joys...

She had been awakened at some unearthly hour by a faint tapping on her bedroom door and so she hid her face under the nice warm coverlets in fun, for she knew exactly what the tapping was all about.

'Come in,' she whispered, at last, faking drowsiness in her voice.

The door slowly opened as if of its own accord and all was quiet for a short while. Then, without a further warning, the patter of small feet was heard, as they, with a degree of hustle, scampered across the carpeted floor. And then, silence; as the small body of Jacob leapt into the air and landed spread-eagled on top of his young mother.

Jenny quickly threw back the sheets and covers to hug her child, and to roll him about in wriggling, tickling playfulness.

'Happy birthday Mummy,' he shrieked, as he hugged his teenage mother about her silken neck. Then picking them up from the floor, where he had dropped them in his haste, he offered her his present, neatly wrapped with pink floral paper and matching pink ribbon, together with a sealed matching envelope. After reading the almost unintelligible, squiggly words on the envelope, she opened the card and carefully read its message.

"This is for my Mummy, the very best of mummies any boy could wish to have, with love from Jacob."

'Did you manage to write all of this by yourself my darling or did Aunty Sarah help you with it? It's written so very, very beautifully,' teased Jenny, smiling, 'I doubt if *you* could have written it, could you?'

'I did Mummy, honest I did. Auntie Janet wrote it out first and I copied it,' he owned, with a chuckle, 'but I did it the very best I could.'

'I can see that my darling, it is truly lovely and I am very proud of you Jacob,' she said, as a slight moistness entered her beautiful eyes.

After she had read her card at least a dozen times she replaced it in its envelope; and then with excitement charging her fingertips she hurriedly loosened the pink ribbon on her parcel and discovered a small book of beautifully illustrated childlike prayers.

Jenny unhurriedly flicked through its pages, laid it on the bed beside the card and then, gathering her son once again in her arms, she poured kisses on him almost endlessly.

'Thank you Jacob, thank you so very much; both the card and the tiny prayer book are wonderful to have and I shall treasure them both for ever.'

'Auntie Janet said you have to come down to breakfast now -

at once, she said… but she laughed when she said it,' instructed her son, with the highest amount of sweetness that could ever attend the small voice of one so young. 'I think she has a present and a birthday card for you as well.'

'OK young man, I shall use the bathroom and get dressed very quickly. I mustn't be late for my own birthday, now must I? So, I shall see you down stairs in just a few moments; is that OK?'

Ever since his birth, Jacob had filled The Old House with total joy; a little raucous at times maybe, but total joy for all that; and he had been the source and the inspiration of all the endless pleasures his young, loving mother could ever hope to have.

By heaping such happiness upon the rest of the small family as well, and in quantities beyond measure, it would have been quite impossible to have imagined a more contented, loving and cherished child; for life without him would have been unthinkable, if truth be told.

Whilst in her bathroom, Jenny pondered these thoughts and feelings, and being lost, for the briefest of moments, in the wonderment of the journey through which the years had taken her and at the good fortune that destiny had bestowed on her, she had smiled contentedly.

Within thirty of the shortest minutes, Jenny went down to the breakfast room, where her Uncle Hamish and Janet Nunn were waiting; and with cries of 'happy birthday' they overwhelmed her with presents both large and small; useful presents that would serve her well, and frivolous gifts to brighten her special day.

'Where is Auntie Sarah?' asked Jenny, when all her gifts had been opened. 'Is she not up yet?'

'I expect she is having a lie in this morning Jennifer, she was up quite late last night reading about life, and contemplating it, and then wrapping her gift for you; I shall go to her at once to make sure she is aware of the time,' answered Janet, in her usual benevolent tone, as she quietly left the room.

As soon as they were alone Hamish Kent took hold of his niece's hands and looked deeply into her beautiful eyes.

'Many congratulations on your birthday once again my dear, I hope your coming year will be filled with as much joy and happiness that you so freely give to others.

'I must say I have indeed been fortunate, Jennifer, in having both you and your wonderful son living with me in this lonely house for the past few years; you have made my life worth living again. And since your arrival, you have helped fill the aching void that my dear wife had left when she passed on all those years ago.

'I have little doubt that Janet feels much the same way and as for your aunt, well, I am certain the two of you have brought her complete joy and contentment as well, since you have been part of each other's lives.

'I only feel such sorrow for your parents though, my dear, they have missed out on so much when they might have had all the pleasure you both have truly brought to me. Still, I know I shouldn't say it, or even think it, come to that, but I'm afraid I can't help myself at times, for I reflect upon my situation often - for their loss has indeed been my gain.

'Talking of your parents, don't forget Jennifer, we are visiting your father today, so we must aim for a quick getaway,' said Hamish Kent, his features conveying a look of satisfaction as he released his niece's hands, 'I'm sure he will love to see you on your birthday and I am equally sure that the visit will revitalise him in a most positive and...'

Before he could finish his sentence a subdued request from Janet interrupted him.

'Mr Hamish,' she called, 'could you spare me a moment of your time... if you please sir?'

With haste he climbed the stairs to find Janet sitting on the uppermost step, her head was bowed and her hands were trembling.

'It's Sarah,' she sobbed, 'I'm afraid she's dead.'

***

The news of her great-aunt's death was a shattering blow and too much for the young mother to bear. In spite of the expressed concern and support from both her uncle and Janet, she broke down and wept bitterly.

After Jenny had visited her aunt to share a last farewell she went to her room for a while and lay there with her face buried and she cried till her pillow was wet with tears, all the while wanting, oh so desperately wanting, to have her wonderful aunt back with her again.

Her reflections of the loneliness, she had tolerated in the days gone by, now briefly visited her again. Awful reflections of loneliness that always seemed to hover nearby; discreetly hiding 'tis true, but hovering closely all the same; ever eager to return to clutch at her very soul; and the dreaded threat of the permanence of their return caused a panic to seize her vulnerable intellect.

But she fought back all of these malicious feelings with all the strength at her disposal, to deport them to the back of her young mind and to replace them with all of the newer memories; ones of the happier days she had shared with her much loved aunt in concert with the others.

The happy days of learning would now be demoted to a soundless memory, and the blest recall of her son's delivery, which was relieved by the compassion of an ever loving aunt - both these acts of kindness showed total commitment by a wonderful lady who was now lingering in Jenny's mind and would stay with her still, for many years to come.

Recollections of happiness with a hint of loneliness filled that fragile mind, all mixed together and muddled up with those of unabated grief. But all these recollections were to vanish in the twinkling of an eye as the gentle tapping on her bedroom door invaded her mind - and in an instant they were gone.

Her son, not entering as before with the euphoria of gift giving and the excitement of good wishes for his mother's happiness on this her special day, crossed the threshold with calm, submissive reverence, then he laid himself down in silence at his young mother's side. After placing his small arm about his darling mother's neck, he, with childlike consideration said:

'Auntie Janet told me you were here and said you were unhappy and she asked me if I would comfort you. Please don't cry any more Mummy, everything will be alright, Auntie Janet told me that Auntie Sarah has gone to see Jesus, that's all, so I expect she will be back again soon.'

Much later but in the same morning, Jenny opened the small package her aunt had left; not with ghoulish greed but with a knowing that this would have been her auntie's final accomplishment.

Hamish and Janet had both agreed that that would have been what her aunt would have wanted Jennifer to do right now, and so she completed the task just as the undertaker arrived to take her aunt away.

A small package was tipped out from its birthday wrapping onto the table; a small brown package, which contained a maroon box lined with cotton wool and upon which was placed a petite silver necklace with a heart arrangement hanging from it; and on the face of the tiny, silver heart, and inscribed in uncomplicated letters was the name, JENNY.

Reasoning the intention of the shortened version of her name immediately, and at that very same moment, she put the necklace around her neck and secured it, while she solemnly vowed never to remove it.

The formal investigation reported that Sarah Wood had died at around three in the morning of a severe heart attack; but not wishing to alarm anyone she had borne the excruciating pain alone and in total silence, with her bony fingers clutching deeply at her completely sunken chest.

The funeral being a simple affair was performed, five days later, in solemn reverence by the Anglican Vicar at the ancient village church in Brenton where both Sarah and Jenny had worshiped each Sunday morning since their arrival in the village: that is, whenever they were home.

Everyone spoke highly of the portly governess with her grey white hair sweeping back to the far reaches of her head to form the largest chignon possible at the nape of her neck. Everyone offered their sincere condolences to the young mother and to her child... condolences that were both heartfelt and sincere.

'She always found an occasion to pass the time of day when many wouldn't have bothered,' said some of the people, who had come to pay their last respects. 'A most compassionate old lady was Miss Wood; showed an interest in everyone she talked to. She will be sorely missed in these parts... that's for sure,' said others.

All of these simple, kindly words were received with the utmost gratitude by Jenny and were gently stored away for her to ponder another day when faced with quieter moments.

Sarah Wood's niece, Margaret, had been notified of her aunt's sudden passing by Hamish Kent, late in the afternoon of the day that followed her aunt's death, informing the hostile niece of the date and time of the funeral.

The communication had been deliberately made via the telephone, not only to save valuable time, but also, it was considered, so that Hamish would be assured of Margaret's clear understanding of the message without uncertainty and in so doing she would be more likely to respond in a positive manner.

She accepted the news without too much fuss by answering quite clearly that she would indeed attend the funeral.

But she failed to show.

"Not wishing to be confronted by her daughter," it was silently supposed - but not conceded.

Hamish had also telephoned the hospital where his brother lay institutionalised in a pitiful dilemma, and he had persuaded the day sister to conduct a message to Sir Angus with total delicacy so that he was aware that the now reduced company would definitely arrive seven days later than was arranged.

Sarah Wood's final resting place was in the little churchyard at Brenton village where her grave could be attended regularly by her only real relatives.

She rested in peace knowing that at last the long duration of her life had not been worthless as she once had thought and that the teaching skills she'd considered as being of no consequence, had been received with gratitude and deep affection.

As the group left the scene of Sarah's interment, Jenny lingered awhile and then walked slowly the short distance toward The Old House in complete silence. Both Hamish and Janet, appreciating that Jenny wanted to be alone awhile, walked on ahead, each holding the hand of Jacob.

'Don't forget the money you owe me,' said a familiar voice from behind. 'I know as how it's been a while since, but the truth is... I ain't forgotten.'

Jenny turned round on the spot to see the inscrutable figure of Barnabas Bell with the misaligned left eye, which was again seeking an escape route from its socket, just standing there by the same gateway he'd occupied before, with a repulsive grin occupying his restless face and showing his complete contempt for the young lady who had just passed him by.

Jenny was in no fit state to be engaged in wording battles with this disdainful intimidator and so she turned back to her family in an effort to ignore him.

'I'll take the money in kind if you like then, I'm not all that fussy,' was his response, as Jenny quickened her pace to catch up with the others.

Janet Nunn had heard Bell's subdued but demanding voice although the precise content of his words had escaped her, and she turned instantly to confront him.

But before she was able to utter a single word the inscrutable man had disappeared through the gateway and into the field of growing corn beyond. So she walked a pace or two back and placing a kindly arm about the shaking shoulders of her newly found charge they walked back to the Old House as one.

Hamish Kent, upon reaching their home, insisted on knowing, in detail, what the fuss was all about and so Jenny explained that Barnabas Bell had made certain unacceptable demands of her person for his supposed unfair dismissal from the services of The Old House and The Brenton Estate, all those years ago, and moreover, in an aggravating and lustful manner; for he considered that Jenny was, most certainly, the direct reason for all his problems.

Hamish expressed great alarm at this by saying that he would certainly place the matter in the hands of the local police to see what could be made of the unfortunate business and hopefully put an end to the repugnant harassment of his fond niece once and for all.

The investigation into the incident, which was carried out by two officers from the local constabulary the following morning, only seemed to pollute the affair with total frustration.

With continuous and adamant denial, despite Janet's witnessing support, and with the promise of a suing for wrongfully discrediting his name, the matter was instantly dropped.

In spite of this, a cautionary remark had been offered to Bell by the police sergeant, which, in all probability, would have little effect on the inscrutable fellow, if indeed any at all.

***

For three long months the three adults, living at The Old House in Brenton village, sorrowfully mourned the departure of Sarah Wood and displayed black armbands on their sombre apparel for all that time.

Each one spoke in subdued tones of respect, so markedly great was their response to Sarah's death; and the grieving each one showed for their loss was equally made manifest.

Even little Jacob, continued his inquisitiveness as to when his Auntie Sarah would return; but eventually in childlike naivety and after a good deal of persuasive undertaking, the child finally succumbed to the notion that 'never again' would be a very long time indeed.

***

One late afternoon, in the clammy month of August, so described, for the heat in this particular month in this particular year was of a particular intensity and was not made less bearable by the task in climbing an extremely steep hill. Atop this steep hill stood the magnificent cathedral within the limits of the historic city of Lincoln.

As anyone who has attempted this specific ascent in such climatic conditions as this will attest, it is indeed felt to be a notable achievement to have reached its summit.

And so it was felt to be by Jenny and Janet who had subjected themselves to this extraordinary mission in almost complete silence. Jacob on the other hand was making much less of the exercise and seemed to deal with the whole experience in significant style and in much better spirit than the adults; as he skipped around gaily and with his vocal merriment disturbing the Lincoln air.

For all the years that Jenny had lived in Brenton, not once had she visited this superb place of worship before this time. Needless to say, she had viewed it from afar when idly walking in the countryside that surrounded Brenton, and she had shopped in the lower streets of Lincoln too; but she had never come face to face with the enormity of the mount till now.

She looked up with gasps of amazement as the cathedral, suddenly coming into view, was displayed so magnificently above the many buildings which bordered its contours.

Jenny stood motionless for a while as its splendour gradually sank in; and she gazed in wonder at its spectacular beauty - at the sheer size of it all - at the sophistication of the architecture and at the heavenly splendour that all viewers experience when they first encounter this magnificent cathedral.

Whilst Jenny examined each and every spire atop each and every tower she reflected how a place of such a scale of vastness as this could be refined by the intricacy of its design. The huge, pale, brick shaped rocks that formed its walls, all cut by hand with exacting labour, seemed stacked one upon the other, as if it was their weight alone that held the building steadily erect.

Suddenly, Jenny's attention was drawn to a figure that sat alone in one of the angled crevices in the ancient wall that surrounded part of the courtyard to this holy palace.

She walked over, tentatively, to a youngish man who seemed to have grown old before his time and placed some money into the hat that lay at his badly worn shoes. The red paisley scarf, which was tied loosely about his neck, hung unevenly and was being partly covered by the long straight black hair that drooped untidily about his head.

'Tom!' she said, not daring to believe that it was him and suddenly recoiling from the thought that it might be. 'Tom!' she said again, 'is it you?'

The dishevelled man looked up instantly.

'Jenny!' he returned, without taking thought, as if he had not wanted to speak her name aloud but that it had fallen from his mouth of its own volition.

She bent down to touch his hand but before she could complete the act of tenderness he recoiled and rose to his feet and gathering his cap in his hand, he walked hurriedly away. Jenny didn't follow the man at once, but instead she went quickly to Janet.

'I'm sure that was Jacob's father,' she said, quietly, 'but I think he doesn't want to know me any longer.'

'Go after him then, Jennifer - quickly - don't you see he may be in need of your help?' said Janet, voicing her usual kindness.

Jenny, after bending down to instruct Jacob to stay with his Auntie Janet and telling him that she wouldn't be long, walked hurriedly away. The obedient child clasped his auntie's hand and stared anxiously at his mother, as she left.

Jenny thought she'd seen Tom once - in the distance; almost at the base of the sheer descent; she certainly saw someone that looked like him.

And hurrying down the steep hill that she had so laboriously climbed a few minutes earlier, she caught up with the man she'd seen; but to her regret, it wasn't Tom.

And so she walked back up the steep hill again; her eyes invading each and every doorway as she climbed to where her son stood, rooted to the same spot where she had left him, still holding onto Janet's hand in trepidation and fearing for his mother's safe return.

The whole of the scene had been closely observed by a pair of eyes that lit up at the encounter, even though the left eye did indeed wander to the far reaches of its socket from time to time; but this didn't seem to lesson his realization of all that had been said.

Whilst Jenny was bent in final attendance of her son even before she'd left the place, the owner of those eyes had instantly followed Tom and had secreted himself opposite the enclosure where the gypsy man was resting.

After Jenny had appeared and then finally returned again, he once more gathered speed to closely follow the gipsy through the streets of Lincoln and on to the outer limits of the city.

Completely unobserved, but persistent in his close pursuit of the stranger, he arrived at a small group of caravans neatly parked beyond the city's outer regions where he hoped for some intelligence, some explanation as to what was going on, and also the whereabouts of their eventual destination.

Seeing that he'd delayed his leaving the vans, and after a

single hour had elapsed, he again listened to that which was not intended for his ears to hear, as two of the male members of the group talked incessantly about their return to Dorset.

'I damn well hope the Hyde sunshine will be a little gentler to us when we get there,' said the taller of the two men, 'even though Dorset is supposed to be so much hotter than this place. Still, we shall have to take our chances and hope the summer settles to its normal way of things I suppose.'

The other smiled from time to time.

'What, you still moaning about the heat Jethro? I al'as thought you got on well with the warmer weather, leastways, you've bragged about it often enough.

'Anyways, 'tis time to wake young Tom, I reckon he's rested enough since he's bin back, and for us to make strides ag'in; no use in us a hangin' around this place any longer, as nice as it is, so, best we get underway.'

Two hours earlier Tom had left his caravan and his friends outside the city's periphery in order to view the grand cathedral closely. It was a visit he'd always wanted to make, but the long dash into the city and then the suffering climb up the steep hill in the sweltering heat had all but exhausted the man.

As he rested awhile, by seating his languid body on the cool stones of the courtyard, he leaned his depleted body against the outer wall. He had thrown his sweaty cap at his feet as soon as he had relaxed himself in order to supply his head with some freshness of air and had all but fallen asleep.

It was at this point and in this state of debilitation that Jenny had found him, and the dishevelment of his uncombed hair, which he wasn't at all proud to exhibit, dictated his embarrassment. He had certainly not wished for any inquisitive pair of eyes from some former acquaintance to scrutinize his physique; no matter how attractive the idea might have seemed to him at the time, and so, when Jenny interrupted his privacy, and without thinking, he had panicked and it was desperation alone that had decided his escape.

Now, as he lay quietly in his van he was beginning to feel that his expedition had been a big mistake. He had always possessed an inquisitive intellect and the need to see the place had been uppermost in his mind; and as the chance had presented itself so unexpectedly he had decided to take advantage of the opportunity.

At this moment, though, his needs became altered as his deeply exhausted frame took on board a quantity of necessary refreshment. He flooded his flushed face and body with a full bottle of tepid water and then drank deeply from a second. Slumping down on his bed, still fully exhausted, he fell into a short, deep sleep again without intention.

The image of Jenny's face haunted his mind as he slept and that of the youngster too, who waited a few yards away, and the pair of them, for a few brief moments looked lonely and forlorn and played reckless games upon his drowsy mind.

***

Jenny, Janet and Jacob continued the planned afternoon visit to Lincoln Cathedral both inside and out but with less enthusiasm than when they'd first decided to set out upon their jaunt.

Jenny talked of Tom with Janet, not in a warm manner, but more to promote idle conversation than anything else; at least that was how she hoped the exchange was coming across. But Janet wasn't quite so sure and so she politely probed her young charge a little more deeply as to her feelings for the gypsy when first they'd met.

'You have to remember Janet; I was but a child, a little over twelve years old at the time and under a terrible strain from the lack of enthusiasm my parent's were showing me by their behaviour.

'And so, I suppose, I was all too easily influenced and felt drawn by his kindness and his caring... almost compulsively. His protection, during those moments of my stupidity, has always meant a great deal to me and has haunted my mind on frequent occasions. My thoughts have, inadvertently, wandered back to that interlude in my life from time to time, though, and I considered him as being the strong adventurer who always needed to be part of the great outdoors, *'caring for all but worrying about nothing'* that's how I have always thought of Tom.

'But now that I have seen him again, in the cold light of day, as it were, I can clearly see how wrong I was in my estimation of him and what he has truly become; just a common beggar man quite incapable of supporting himself let alone an animal or two.

'At this moment in time I suppose I have to say he has fallen in my opinion of him, considerably, and any adventurous gypsy notion I may have had of him at one time has suddenly disappeared from my mind... altogether.'

CHAPTER TEN

The confirmation of Father Time's existence was in his hastening of the seasons all too speedily away and in the precious years being stolen as if they had been the crown jewels that were his for the taking.

During the period following her Great Aunt Sarah Wood's passing to the present time - and as that portly governess had openly predicted, Jennifer Kent developed into a most intelligent and beautiful young woman. Her long, rippling mahogany hair, which overflowed her slender shoulders to the small of her willowy back, had a lustrous sheen about it that added its own contribution to the beauty of this lovely English rose.

Jenny, still residing at The Old House in Brenton and still paying fortnightly visits to her father's sick bed in Dorset - howbeit no longer being dependant upon her fond uncle's benevolence as she possessed her own sports car these days - flew passed the age of consent and was now within her twenty-sixth year of living.

Jacob too, happy to have reached his thirteenth year, was spending much of his free time in the company of his doting uncle Hamish; learning all matters of business administration and being nursed in the preparation of philanthropic ways of thinking by looking for the more positive, straightforward and practical results in all business expertise rather than the gamble that so many of us take when beating down anyone or anything that stand in our financial path.

This energetic boy had regularly attended the local grammar school for just over two years by this time, where he was proving himself to be proficient in most subjects. But he looked forward to the day when he might continue his education at some university or other in order to further his learning, and where he would make all necessary demands upon himself in gratitude to those who had so lovingly cared for him over the years and who would eventually provide him with such a golden opportunity.

June the twenty-fifth nineteen hundred and sixty six was a date that would always stay in the mind of Jennifer Kent. It was a day of lasting sadness, for it was on this day that she received the dreaded telegram from the hospital in Dorset that would prove to be the turning point in her life and the commencement of a new chapter in her way of living.

Jenny had been busying herself in the kitchen early that

Saturday morning, occupying her time with some of Janet's more important responsibilities as the dearest of housekeepers was herself ill abed, battling with an attack of summer flu, when the awful telegram arrived by means of a young uniformed lad riding his bright red bicycle.

As soon as she had opened the door and saw the young man standing there clutching a buff envelope in his hand she realised what this call was all about. And, as her anxiety heightened and a depressing feeling dropped to overcrowd her mind, the colour drained from her lovely face in an instant.

With trembling hands Jenny took the letter from him, she broke the seal and read the depressing words she hoped never to hear:

"Sir Angus Kent stop Viral Pneumonia stop Come at once stop Life in danger stop."

She shivered inwardly as she thanked the lad - but no - there was no reply.

Hamish Kent was in his study with Jacob at the time; teacher and pupil together, both engrossed in matters of business, as they mostly were these days.

Jenny, in a distressed state of mind, hurried at once to her uncle's study and hammered vigorously on the door.

'Come in,' was the instant reply, which Jenny acted upon without taking on board a semblance of thought: her mind being blank for the time being, due to the state of extreme alarm in which she had found herself.

Feeling too distraught to speak, Jenny handed the telegram to her smiling uncle without either of them attempting to form any exchange of pleasantries.

Jacob, sensing the importance of the situation, went immediately to his mother's side and held her trembling hand tightly while Hamish read the short telegram - over and over. Then looking up, and after a two second interval had passed, he rose from his seat and went to his niece and gently pulled her to himself to provide the parental comfort he knew she needed.

'I'm so sorry my dear, but we must go to your father, the three of us... today... at once. I shall arrange, for one of the staff to stay with Janet while we're away... you go quickly and pack a few things for the two of you... I have a case always ready for such emergencies as this so I will be able to meet with the two of you in half an hour or so.'

***

Despite Hamish Kent being at the wheel the long journey was shortened by a full thirty minutes to reach the Dorset hospital at three in the afternoon.

The small group, holding firmly onto the arms and hands of one another, hurriedly made its way to the ward where Sir Angus had last been seen, and entered it with dread.

The place was empty - an anxious moment passed.

Jenny, instantly aware of a nurse stepping briskly along the outer corridor, was through the door in a flash.

Out of her mind with worry, she called loudly to know where her father had been taken.

The nurse stopped, turned round sharply and then, just as briskly, retraced her steps to where Jenny stood fearfully waiting for some reply - any reply would have done, so long as she knew where her father was to be found.

After demanding to know precisely who was asking the question and about whom, Jenny was told that her father had been taken to the intensive care unit where he was being tended for chronic viral pneumonia.

Armed with specific directions and the knowledge that her father was yet alive, they set off once again.

***

They found him - at last.

He was seen to be stretched out on the usual table arrangement associated with these places. And although reverence was well supplied by all in attendance he was still the victim of a situation almost out of control - with his having to endure the most horrific ordeal imaginable.

The clinical setting itself was bad enough but the subdued sounds, issuing from the various machines that supported the patient's life, were found to be disturbing to the anxious visitors' ears.

The three of them, walked cautiously into the room; and being fully determined - neither one looked to left or right, but steadfastly ahead.

Needless to say, this whole situation triggered a state of overpowering fear to worry them, as the subdued but nonetheless alarming sounds continued to jar their brains into a state of nervousness.

The appalling clamminess of the room's atmosphere, assisted by all of this orderly clinical commotion was felt to sap each of the visitor's strength, not completely, but enough to promote their apprehension and to destroy the small amount of hope they may have had inside.

Entangled tubes and wires, in complete disarray, seemed to exit the patient from every portal of his physically challenged body; and a suspended plastic bag, with tubes attached, dripped a colourless solution into the vein of his motionless arm by two drips in every second.

A tube, draining the patient's chest cavity of all the superfluous fluid that was gathering there, had been firmly inserted into the patient's upper body and which led to a glass bottle containing fluid of a worrying hue.

The persistent breathing sound of the automatic ventilator, which was the only means of keeping the patient alive by now, and the incessant bleep of the heart monitor - the one in discord with the other - both sought to deliberately provoke the maximum amount of panic to anyone so unaccustomed in dealing with a clinical setting such as this; both machines were competing in a never ending battle of hopelessness - but with gameness in their effort to overcome the odds.

A friendly looking nursing sister was sitting at the patients head, gently soothing his face with a moistened sponge; and with a damp swab, clamped firmly between the jaws of a pair of forceps, she wetted the patient's lips and cleared the gathering filth from around the his swollen mouth. Every so often, she would set aside these soothing tools to operate a gurgling aspirator with which to draw away the mucous from inside his oral void.

Upon seeing the three visitors she left her thankless task for a brief moment and moved unhurriedly across the room with a smile of reassurance positioned upon her sympathetic face.

After all the years of their association she had recognised the visitors in an instant and so she caused her smile to widen as she encouraged the new arrivals forward to speak to the almost lifeless man.

Hamish was first to move and bending low he kissed his brother's damp, pallid forehead; assuring him of his love and was reassured in return by the flicker of a lid.

Jacob copied the words his great-uncle had uttered as he bravely clung to a hand that couldn't stir and smiled a smile that felt all too awkward to be leaving the lips of one so young, and then he stepped aside for his mother to speak to her fading father.

'Please don't worry about me Daddy,' she tearfully exclaimed. 'We have made our peace... you and me. We love each other and have expressed that love every time we've met of late. We are both at peace with that love now and I will hold my portion of it close to my heart... everywhere I go. Please remember that, my darling Daddy.' And with that she bent her head and placed her beautiful mouth on her father's dark blue, swollen lips as he closed his eyes for the very last time.

Unbeknown to the family, Jane Howe, standing at her lover's feet and dressed in the olive garb of a carer with a green mask concealing her face, was unblinkingly staring at the lifeless form lying before her.

She had stayed with her man continuously for three exhausting days and nights, not allowing, for an instant, that slumber should take control of her mind.

When Sir Angus Kent had first been pronounced as being in a life threatening situation and was wheeled to this sterile place, she had dutifully followed and from that moment on she had been in constant prayer for her lover. And although she knew he had been taken on his final journey, while yet a semblance of life existed in his all but lifeless body - she had never left his side.

They had said their last goodbyes and exchanged words of undying love, the one with the other - with the firm assurance that they would spend eternity together; and she was happy that his only child had been the last to say her fond farewell; she knowing for a certainty that her man had held painfully on to his dying breath until his daughter came.

Jane didn't move from her station or express the sense of loss she felt inside as that monstrous machine claimed her lover's final breath - she'd not found the need to - but she would prefer to stay a little longer - but for why? No one could tell.

Just then, and with no prior warning, the doors swung open with a crash, and Margaret, his once lovely and loving wife, burst into the room with a serene smile set firmly on her mouth.

Uninvited, she strutted over to where the dead man lay and looking into the white mask that had once been her husband's face - she yelled:

'I HOPE YOU BURN IN HELL ANGUS KENT.' The voice she used to scream her abuse was so loud that even he must have heard it. Then, in a more subdued tone and with the volume turned right down - she whispered, 'May you rot in hell.'

***

After Margaret's immediate exit, the three Kents, took their leave of the hospital for the last time and drove to the hotel that had served them well over the past years.

There they drank more than one toast to the man who had been Sir Angus Kent and all the while, Hamish, the kindest of uncles, comforted his fond charges in relaxed solemnity.

Jane Howe had refused the invitation to join the small group: she being adamant in returning to her cottage in Basham Killington to where her sister waited to receive the sorry news.

***

The following day, upon contacting the funeral director and the vicar of Saint Mary's in Hyde, Hamish saw fit to let it be known that Sir Angus Kent was to be interred in the church cemetery half a mile away from Hyde Hall on the following Saturday, the second day of July.

All the local dignitaries had been arriving in dribs and drabs at the departed gentleman's former residence as soon as they learned the fate of their so called 'cherished friend'.

Each one carried feigned expressions of sadness that deliberately dulled their fickle faces and each paid their cultivated respects to the grieving widow, even though not one, of the many that visited Hyde Hall now, had considered it appropriate to visit Sir Angus throughout the years of his infirmity.

Because it clearly suited her purpose the visitors were each courteously received by Lady Margaret in person; she wanted it known, of course, she was all sweetness and light; indeed, that she was possessed of a caring character; and that any one who spoke about her differently, or in any other way, would be telling a sorry lie; and so, she too feigned a sad expression to illustrate her loss.

Whilst her husband was alive, Lady Margaret had not been considered as being a person carrying that much clout, or indeed, a person possessing sufficient character to influence anyone - not amounting to much, anyway, and certainly not within the local community. She had never sought such authority neither had she earned the acclaim her husband had found to be his; she being indolent by nature - and to the extreme.

If she wanted to change all that sort of lunacy - in other words, if she wanted to install herself within the close knit society of the landed gentry of Dorset, then she would have to tailor her character to suit the purpose - or at least give the impression of having a degree of charm about her to add to her already self-proclaimed moral worth.

All of this would be a fundamental necessity to the lady of Hyde Hall in the future - especially now that the two obstacles, which collectively had been the bane of her life, were out of her way for ever.

'I shall always need to act the part even if some may consider my existence to be a mere charade; those people can go to hell for all I care; and I shall hold fast to the title as well, even though that obnoxious husband of mine is dead.'

She spoke the words, loudly to herself as soon as the final visitor had left her presence, not caring which of the servants might hear her remarks.

Then, re-seating her posterior upon the chaise longue, she reclined her body and lifted her feet and legs to be comfortably reposed as she lit yet another long, full strength cigarette. Then placing it carefully in the even longer tortoiseshell holder, she puffed away contentedly, blowing clouds of white, billowing smoke into the capacious room, thereby causing a fuggy greyness to exist everywhere.

The half filled crystal tumbler, containing an amber fluid of sorts, which stood on the small table close to her side, was soon in her hand and was emptied in a single gulp - just as the white telephone yelled loudly to be answered.

....

Hamish had been surprised, nay, astounded at the greeting his telephone call had received when he contacted Hyde Hall extending his condolences that evening and at the same time he had enquired of Margaret if she would prefer to travel from the chapel of rest, where the body of her late husband had lain since his death, with the remainder of the family or perhaps she would be happier making her own way to the church; if, in fact, she intended to attend the funeral at all.

But the invitation alongside his sympathetic words fell like a lead balloon.

'Oh no, Hamish, you have it all wrong my dear, but thank you for your condolences and for asking. You see, I intend and, indeed, I have so arranged to follow immediately behind the hearse on my own; you may follow within the cortege if you have a mind to do so... I shall, of course, leave that to your good judgement.'

It appeared the receiver in Hamish's hand suddenly became over heated so instantaneously did he replace the confounded contraption within the confines of its cradle.

Jenny had witnessed the electrifying conversation from the comfort of their suite's settee and had smiled with some amusement at the way an unexpected seizure, resulting from mere dialogue, had befallen such a placid and tolerant man.

'I take it that the answer is no, then. I somehow thought she wouldn't wish to go,' she said, still smiling. And after walking over to her uncle, she placed a calming hand upon his shoulder.

'Oh, she's going alright, don't worry yourself about that; but she has had the shameless impertinence to make arrangements with the funeral directors so that she alone is to immediately follow your father and for the rest of the family to tag along behind - if they so desire.

'Really that woman is quite insufferable,' he said, as a tentative smile replaced his original reaction. 'Jennifer, I sometimes wonder how you managed to survive twelve years of living with your mother and still maintain your sanity, I really do. And I have little wonder at my brother seeking alternative companionship as well, if this is how she has behaved for all of their married life.'

Jacob was in bed fast asleep by this time; it had been a tiring exercise walking the streets of Bournemouth that day, seeking suitable clothing to wear for the funeral: as they hadn't even considered the need for funereal finery when they had left The Old House in Brenton.

They had completed the assignment suitably and both of them were now sat facing one another contemplating the morrow's final duty to Sir Angus, each sipping the much needed brandy that had recently been served.

'Actually uncle, if you think about it, my mother has provided the most satisfactory scenario possible for us and without realizing it... her wishing to be alone, I mean. It will lessen all the unpleasant embarrassments both for Jacob and for me... don't you think? Let her indulge herself in playing the part of the grieving widow, that's what I say... so long as it keeps her out of the way of my son. Despite any other concerns, I may have about her... that is what I'm really afraid of.

'After her worrying display at the hospital the other day who knows what she may be capable of doing or what she has in store for Jacob,' said Jenny, with quite a relieved look on her face.

'Hold on a minute, Jennifer, I'm not at all sure she even knows of Jacob's existence, I mean, how could she know? She hasn't been near the hospital for them to say anything and who else could possibly have told her... nobody!

'But yes you are quite right my dear, it will be as well to keep the dragon at arms length even though I shall be in attendance at all times if you need me to protect you both from any untoward verbal attacks or unwanted innuendo; I know far too much about that lady now... for her to worry either of you.'

***

The picturesque seventeenth century village church was, by scant tradition, set amid a group of churchyard and cemetery loving evergreen yew trees.

So popular has this variety of woody tree become to the ecclesiastical communities over the years that hardly a churchyard or cemetery, in excess of one hundred years of age, can be found without their haunting presence. The incredible width of their trunks, indicating their age, clearly stated that these particular trees had been planted on the completion of the building of the church, over three hundred years ago.

Reverently, the yews now greeted the hearse as it arrived by their standing to attention: for no gentle breeze stirred a movement to a single branch, nor yet a single twig.

It was a fine morning with the attendance of the sun making it known to everyone that it was not opposed to paying its own respects to the dead; and so it shone a radiance of great magnitude upon the pale coffin as it arrived.

The small church was filled to capacity long before the coffin arrived so that there was space for a small number only to stand at its rear. Additional seating had been made available in the aisle and at the church's periphery but these also had soon been taken; for only those suffering from acute ecclesiophobia had stayed away, such was the popularity of Sir Angus Kent - or indeed, the smallness of the church.

The long elaborate coffin, ornately draped with the Kent coat of arms, was carefully lifted from its carriage by six pall-bearers, and waltzed slowly up the aisle to the waiting bier where it would be stationed and exhibited for the duration of the service.

After following the hearse and upon her arrival at the church, Margaret had waited in the back of her black limousine until she was assured that the driver would aid her exit so that she may follow her husband closely - and reverently.

Then she, almost stumbling with frailty brought on, no doubt, by the tremendous sadness of her loss, was physically supported and steadily escorted into the church by the said driver to be independently seated by herself in the front pew - lonely and alone and with no one on either side to share in her sad loss or share in a show of sympathy for her husband's passing from this trying world.

Her black widow's weeds, it had been observed as she slowly walked the aisle to her pew, all but reached the ground and the heaviest of black veils, which covered her face and neck, achieved waist level and was held in place by a tall, feather adorned black hat, which looked not unlike a guardsman's bearskin.

She now bowed her head in the imaginary reverence of prayer and in her loneliness she fidgeted with her black gloves and appeared eager for the funeral service to be underway - or for her husband to be hurriedly placed beneath the sod - who could tell?.

With some difficulty, Jenny, Hamish and Jacob made their way through the multitude to be seated behind the principle mourner, still firmly holding on to one another as they exchanged reassuring glances.

Jenny, unlike her mother wore no black veil. Not that she objected to the wearing of such finery on such occasions as this, but she needed all in attendance to witness her presence and to appreciate the unity that had existed between her and her father, despite the many varying opinions which would have, undoubtedly existed.

Jenny was quite certain, in her own mind, that her mother would have announced her daughter's departure to Lincolnshire more than ten years earlier, together with a fabricated add-on as a fitting supplement.

Anyway, the outward appearance of a person was unimportant to Jenny, it was the feelings that existed inside the heart that counted - not some silly, frilly, bits of black.

Jane Howe had been the first to arrive at the church that sunny morning and was seated alone in body and mind. She had been adamant in refusing her sister's plea to go with her to the church - she needed to do this on her own - and so Rachael had remained behind at Bramble Bush Cottage with uneasiness as she awaited the sad return.

Jane was not sombrely dressed in black as were all the others but in a smart grey suit, the shade of which had always been considered attractively smart by her lover.

Her ensemble was made complete by a dainty grey hat, the veil of which fell to her pretty mouth; not that she had considered the wearing of such an item to be anything other than for her own concealment - and certainly not for a show of mourning. On this particular occasion she required the highest degree of anonymity to be preserved.

Like Jenny, she knew what she felt inside and no one on this planet or any other would be able to alter it or share in it in any way; it was hers and hers alone.

Situated in the rear pew, next to the aisle, Jane had calmly stood, along with the rest of the congregation, as her beloved's coffin passed so slowly by; and she reached out to touch it briefly.

No tears blinded her eyes; no black mascara stained her cheeks; she was in complete control of herself - very lonely 'tis true - but then, not really, for she had Angus with her now - all of the time - and no longer would he be going back to that insufferable wife of his - never again would Jane need to spend the lonely days and nights away from him until they met again.

After the usual spoken eulogy had been clearly expressed and after the service had drawn to a close and as the congregation unhurriedly filed from the little church, an unexpected, but truly magnanimous gesture was made by Jenny.

The occasion occurred as she reached the final pew where Jane was sitting with her head bowed not in prayer but in contemplation. Deserting the two men in her life for a while, Jenny calmly walked over to Jane Howe and reaching for her hand she quietly encouraged her father's mistress to her feet and for the two of them to stand as one in the church doorway, briefly exchanging smiles and feelings of togetherness.

And so it happened, Jenny unashamedly taking Jane's arm, caring not who should see or how they might interpret what they saw, led her out of the church and for the two of them, together, to reach the warmth of the fresh sunlit air together - the only two ladies who really mattered to Sir Angus, in the last days of his life, were now united by his love.

The family grave, where Sir William Kent and his Scottish born wife Alice had been laid to rest many years ago, had been reopened; and so, upon the reaching of its side Sir Angus, in his turn, was also carefully laid to rest on top of his father and his mother.

Handfuls of earth, gathered from the heap that was to cover the grave before the large edifice, in the form of the tombstone complete with chorused angels, could be repositioned some days later, were dropped upon the lonely coffin, as some, but not the entire congregation, filed respectfully passed.

Margaret was the first to perform the age old ritual; and as she dropped a few pieces of dried soil upon her husband's coffin she heaved a deep sigh, and with much emphasis. Then she parted her veil and with her dainty handkerchief she wiped an imaginary tear from her cheek all the while looking as though she might stumble into the trench and join her husband there.

No one was close enough to lend the helping hand she'd hoped for - no one rushed forward to drag her from the brink or to offer her the kindly support she had anticipated; and so she decided to step back of her own accord and wandered off to the big black car that awaited her direction.

Hamish Kent had witnessed his sister-in-law's orchestrated performance and had smiled inwardly at the distracted effort she had made to procure the unnecessary attention she so desperately desired.

CHAPTER ELEVEN

The celebratory gathering, which had been furtively arranged by Margaret as a self-interested tribute to her husband's life, was to have taken place at Hyde Hall as soon as the burial was over that mid afternoon.

The inappropriately 'shared by all invitation', which was verbally distributed by some of the Hyde Hall staff just as the gathering left the churchyard, may have been deliberately orchestrated by Margaret in order to exclude her daughter from the celebrations - who knows - for nobody approached the Lincolnshire Kents.

Even so, both Jenny and Hamish saw no reason why they should even consider attending such an event as this in any case, since they had no wish to play a part in any mindless wording games perpetrated by the devious Lady Margaret - no matter how well stage-managed the show may have proved to be.

'Because your mother has not thought it necessary to issue printed invitations to her guests, I see no reason to justify our absence; do you Jennifer?' said Hamish, as they walked towards the car. Jenny shook her head. 'And so, I propose we return to our hotel straight away and travel back to Brenton first thing in the morning. All unnecessary confrontations with your dear mother can be shelved for a later date when I don't doubt, for a single moment, she will do her utmost to upset us both. In the meantime I suggest we employ caution in our avoidance of the lady.'

It was just as Hamish Kent was about to enter his big silver car, that he was approached by a graceless but not altogether unpleasant looking gentleman.

The inelegance of the gentleman's lack of height was more than compensated by his extremely fleshy waistline, which was tightly covered by a pair of black trousers and a rather tight fitting, black waistcoat. The unfortunate waistcoat, however, was seen to be gaping below its matching jacket - gaping that is - because one of the six buttons that was supposed to be holding the garment together, a central one, was found to be neglectfully missing - or left undone; it made no difference which - the result was still the same.

The remainder of his black suit was also lacking tidiness and the afore mentioned black jacket, which was decidedly crumpled, had been left undone for obvious reasons - in fact his entire ensemble was in urgent need of a steam iron's pressing engagement.

Puffing heartily away at a largish briar, bent in its stem and flat in its wide bowl, the shortish corpulent gentleman introduced himself as Colin Tooke, the Hyde Hall Estate solicitor, personal friend, advisor and confidant to Sir Angus Kent.

The tall man and the shorter man's firm shaking of hands and the exchanging of polite pleasantries had preceded the solicitor's forcefully delivered information; viz. that it was he, Colin Tooke, and he alone who had been appointed by Sir Angus Kent as unconditional organizer to oversee all of the legalities relating to the Hyde Hall Estate. At the same time, and because the estate matters were so involved and complex by nature, or so it was firmly stated, it was his intention to appoint members of his own firm of solicitors to carry out the greater portion of the legal legwork on his behalf. It would, however, be Colin Tooke, and he alone, who would oversee all subject matters which held the greatest merit in the distribution of the deceased's properties and certain other modifications that the law demanded.

The short, corpulent solicitor had, apparently, been summoned to Sir Angus' bedside seven months earlier; long before the invalid had been stricken by the deadly virus that was to finally take his life.

It was on this occasion and with great difficulty, it must be noted, that he had received detailed instructions from Sir Angus Kent regarding certain adjustments and alterations that were to be made to his existing will.

He had then, two full weeks later, returned to his client's side with the revised testament in his hand, and slowly and with much emphasis he had read and reread, several times over, the completed complex will aloud as Sir Angus Kent listened intently to all that was being explained.

Being assured that Sir Angus had fully understood everything legitimate, Colin Tooke had duly urged the paralytic to sign the lengthy document, page by page by way of a mark, in the presence of the nursing sister who had willingly been seconded to act as the official authenticator of this illegible quasi-signature.

All of this had been meticulously explained to Hamish Kent since the new will, still in probate, had inscribed within its pages, certain bequeathed advantages to a particular underage person and it was hoped that he, Hamish Kent, would present himself as trustee for this particular underage beneficiary and be diligent in exercising certain powers in relation to the funds, which he should hold in trust until the underage person had attained the legal age according to the law.

It didn't take a mathematician to work out exactly who that certain minor beneficiary was to be, and so he, Hamish Kent, had willingly agreed to the undertaking.

As soon as the firm of solicitors was in a position to have completed its work and was also, after acting upon the wills complex instructions, in a position to set aside a date and time for the all important and inevitable meeting for the reading of the will to take place, Hamish would be notified via telecommunication by the said Colin Tooke himself in order to allow Hamish Kent the opportunity to manoeuvre his own business matters accordingly. This would, in turn, accommodate the stout solicitor's busy schedule; bearing in mind, as well, the other important beneficiaries who would have to be conveniently notified in order to rearrange their own particular affairs.

And so, the short, corpulent solicitor, after shaking hands with Hamish Kent once again and with a complacent grin that stretched the full width of his wide physiognomy, waddled off to attend the social gathering at Hyde Hall and to imbibe the long awaited, refreshing tipple that would heighten his busy day.

***

One hour and thirty minutes after the late Sir Angus Kent had been placed to rest within the confines of his parent's grave, the so called commemorative celebration, which was more akin to a banquet for the living than an appreciation for the life of the dear departed, began in earnest.

Everyone in attendance seemed relieved that the party was not the sombre affair they had anticipated: for the merrymaking was undeniably going swimmingly from the start.

Lady Margaret had abandoned her guise as the mournful widow by this time and was chatting freely with all her guests in turn and with her late husbands closest friends the Melchamps in particular - that is, Lord and Lady Melchamp who had travelled from East Sussex early that morning to be present at the funeral.

Now being settled in one of the most capacious rooms available at Hyde Hall and being totally discarded by her husband, Lady Melchamp, (nee Warren, Bunny to her closest friends, of whom there were precious few these days), presented herself as being rather elfin in size and shape and of a delicate disposition.

Being a rather insecure sort of lady, particularly on an

auspicious occasion such as this, she was nervously clinging to the seat of her chair by holding onto it firmly with both hands. Her left hand clutched the left side of her chair's seat, her right hand the right; and although she may not have felt it, she did appear most strange and flushed of face; almost as if she was straining upon the seat of a velvet covered toilet seat than a luxurious chair; and as it was observed, said ne'er a word to a living soul.

The nervous little creature was mainly concerned about the floor between her legs, than anything else, for she gazed continuously at her sable clad feet that showed beneath her long flowing, black dress, and at the ornate sable clutch purse cum handbag, which lay hidden and abandoned beside them.

Aside from all that, the unassuming little lady was contemplating nothing of particular importance, and only occasionally did she raise her drab hatted head in the direction of her husband, as his booming voice grew so high in volume that, on the odd occasion, it was distinctly heard above all else; including the mind-numbing music being played the whole time.

Lady Melchamp, in fact before she had become so conferred, seemingly centuries ago, had never considered herself worthy of moving within the same company of people as Alfred Melchamp. She, being plain to the extreme and without having the slightest impression of an interesting personality about her, had always assumed she would eventually be left by herself and on the shelf of no hope.

It was after she had been bequeathed a considerable legacy, nay, a large fortune by her doting father, upon his untimely demise, that her dire situation changed and life for her began to take on a new meaning; as a somewhat altered and improved social phase in her existence emerged - and to a remarkable degree at that.

Consequently, the then unattractive young lady, it seemed, had something going for her after all - now, what a surprise!

It was immediately Melchamp heard of her father's death that he decided to seek Bunny's friendship. Of course, the plain young lady became so bowled over by his charm and by his flamboyance that she became totally besotted with him; and seeing the positive affect that was resulting from his persistence, Melchamp wasted no time in the reinforcement of his influence over her.

In the first few days, after their initial connection, he began indulging her with all the extensive and continuous attentions imaginable and from which, needless to say, she felt unduly flattered. The faked compliments, the likes of which simply dripped from

Alfred Melchamp's mouth, caused the visibly unattractive young woman to become a falsely enhanced individual who languished in pretence.

They had courted for just two months before she was forced into an unlikely marriage with Melchamp; but a baby was due, so nothing else could be done but to go through the rigours of matrimony despite there not being a ha'p'orth of the crucial commodity of devotional and committed love existing between them - it seemed that Bunny's mania for the monster had dwindled by this time.

Unfortunately for her, the longed-for pregnancy miscarried four weeks after the wedding ceremony had taken place and so she had been left childless and would remain so for the rest of her days.

She had felt dejected by this event and somewhat saddened by the utter futility of it all. Being barren and weighed down within the confines of a loveless, lifeless marriage was enough to disturb the most secure of people let alone someone as unstable as Bunny. But in time, the plucky little lady was able to continue with her life regardless of her misfortune, and in her usual and unalterable way at that.

The egotistical characteristics of Alfred Melchamp were poles apart from those of his wife. He was tall and colourful while she was short and drab. He possessed an athletic figure, while she was fast becoming lean and looking seedy.

Not unlike his friend, Angus Kent, he too had found himself attracted to the opposite gender and was certainly not surprised to be held in high regard by the most unlikely of ladies, while Bunny was the dowdy girl she'd always been and to whom no one gave a second glance nor yet a tinker's cuss.

Melchamp had met with Angus Kent when they'd both served in India as young officers in the British armed forces, and quite a while before Alfred Melchamp had succeeded to his title. They had both returned to that country's shores later to help reorganise military matters before that country's independence was established.

Their two young wives, the one most beautiful, the other not, had accompanied their husbands in the service of their country, and at the time, had found the life on offer there to be very much to their liking.

It was during this final bout of service and six and a bit years before India's final independence was achieved that Jennifer Kent was conceived and born. The Kents had returned to England's shores almost immediately after the birth of their daughter; such was the influence Sir Angus Kent held with the British Army at the time, whilst the Melchamps had stayed on for the full term; quite irritated at being left behind.

Even so, both men had remained fairly close in their friendship with each other over the years with only the flimsiest of differences in opinion existed between them.

Although this intimate bond had survived between the two men, Lord Melchamp had not once visited his paralysed friend during his hospitalisation; not wishing, to be involved with sickness of any description, it might be supposed. Even more probable was his total fear of hospitals in general - maybe the aroma, which existed within their environments, offended his sensitivity - who knows.

But he and Bunny had both decided to pay their last respects to his old comrade at this unalterable moment in time; at least he had made the decision and she had followed - such was their marital relationship.

And so here they both were, she a wall flower sitting by herself and he an old lecher not wasting any time in flirting with all and sundry and Lady Margaret in particular.

'I must say you are looking extremely fetching today Margaret, but then, black has always suited you; at least I have always thought so; and, if I may make so bold, it enhances your most beautiful face and figure with a high degree of sensuality, which I find most irresistible; but how one can improve perfection, is quite beyond me,' said Lord Melchamp, with a rakish grin about his mannish features; he then bayed inwardly like a demented dog as he continued in eagerness. 'I'm pleased to see you are over the bout of uneasiness that I noticed in you at the old boy's graveside a while ago. Don't do y'know, all this down in the dumps nonsense; shows bad form m'dear, that's what I always say! It is best to move on as quickly as possible, straight away, if you ask me; take up with some hobby, Margaret, that's my advice... or better still take a lover!'

'Are you offering Alfie?' responded Margaret, coyly, as a rather seductive look, issuing from her eyes, rested on his mouth. 'Oh don't you worry yourself about me Alfie; I'm free at last to do exactly as I please and I intend to do just that. I have been shackled to a marriage that has not suited me for far too long and I have remained faithful to a man, who I have despised, since I don't remember when.

'Now I intend to take full advantage of that newly found freedom and exploit it for all its worth... hmm... now you just watch me, Alfie. I intend to be completely unbridled, liberated from hell at last to be just me, which is all I have ever wanted out of life in the first place. Answerable to no one, that's what I intend to be, and certainly not to a ridiculous man in some ridiculous marriage.'

'Ditto old girl, well said, I know exactly what you mean, couldn't agree with you more, I feel exactly the same way m'self,' replied Lord Melchamp, as a feeling of licentiousness entered his mind and everywhere else at the same time. 'But unlike you, Margaret, I'm unable to do anything about my desires; you must see that. If I left old Bunny over there where the hell would I be? A pauper, I shouldn't wonder. I rely on the old girl's fortune just to get by these days... which she would undoubtedly take with her if I ever left her or played around so that she left me. You see, unlike Angus, hardly any financial security accompanied the jolly old title I inherited.

'Not only that, but it's not possible to be discreet about these things, not these days, Margaret; too many busybodies on the lookout for a bit of tasty scandal y'know; too many looking for the filthy lucre to enhance their miserable lives... and who can blame them? Not I for one; not unless it was me at the centre of attention of course.

'But if life became really unbearable, heaven forbid, and poverty weighed me down... I expect I would be more than willing to sell a story or two to the press for a few pounds; if I was up against it, that is.

'But that's precisely why you've kept yourself so squeaky clean all these years, if I'm not mistaken; am I not right my dear... so there are no tales to be told and only wealth and status to be inherited?'

'Yes Alfie, you are perfectly correct,' replied Margaret, dropping her seductive smile awhile and temporarily replacing it with one more attuned to a feeling of belated ire. 'Angus had played around for most of his married life, you know, taking to him mistress after mistress and while we were still in India at that, *and* while I was with child. Can you imagine it Alfie? I was encumbered with his child in my belly while he was playing the field and laying anything and everything he could lay his filthy hands on.

'I was determined, there and then, not to let on about everything that that man had been up to, and to keep it securely wrapped up in here,' she said, tapping her head twice. 'I didn't wish to rock the boat for myself you see, and I suppose, looking back, I was right... and I'm glad I didn't; saving it carefully until the time was right, seemed more appropriate to me somehow.

'But the time is never right is it Alfie, not really. At least I had the pleasure of telling the man a few home truths more than a couple of years ago... but no one else knows about all this, except you.' She paused awhile as she pondered what she had just said and to a man who was supposed to have been her husband's closest friend. *"I must put this right... straight away,"* she quickly thought to herself.

She then produced a most alarming extension to her already alarming statement; a statement which had given all the lurid details of her failed marriage and to a man who should not be privy to such secrecy; especially hers.

'So, you think me to be looking rather fetching in black do you Alfie?' she said, at last, her seductive smile suddenly returning to her fast changing face. 'Why don't you follow me upstairs Alfie, and I will prove to you just how fetching black can be?' She added the intimate suggestion with a chuckle; and with that she walked calmly away not turning her head once to see if he was following or no - but feeling inwardly confident that he was.

"I shall do it with his best friend and on the day I buried the obnoxious whoremonger," she thought, as she laughed inwardly to herself - almost uncontrollably.

Lady Melchamp had noticed her husband talking closely, almost intimately, with the widow of his close comrade. Her attention was instantly drawn to them the moment his voice had been lowered to normality. She had surveyed them both, from the corner of her eye, as their conversation grew in its intensity, and had looked discretely away as the couple glanced in her direction.

She had watched as Margaret Kent walked toward the door and she noticed the seductive smile on her face and the transparent look in her eyes as she did so. Then, by stretching her neck and straining her eyes, Lady Melchamp watched, as her husband, with his face flushed with deceit and looking about him - followed his fate.

"Poor idiot," she thought.

She pursued her husband up the stairs and along the corridor at a discrete distance, staying well back and out of sight as she avoided the backward glance he gave; she watched furtively, and carefully noted the room her husband had entered.

Bunny then returned to her seat in the capacious room and seated herself more contentedly.

Ten minutes later, she grabbed the arm of a passing servant and marching him, reluctantly, to that very room, she opened the door briskly; and entered without a word; and together she and the man-servant watched as her husband, making every effort in his attempt to conceal his nakedness and not giving a jot about the woman with whom he had occupied the bed, quickly departed the bedroom with oaths of extreme anger trailing him - and dressing himself hastily as he went.

The worm had turned and turned most decidedly.

***

That very evening, at the stroke of midnight, when all was still and deathly silence had caused an awful eeriness to fill the air, a lone motorcar made its way to rest itself outside the drystone wall of the old Hyde churchyard. And although the place was lit by the fullest moon that night, the lone figure, that exited the maroon car would not easily have been recognised by any secreted observer whether sheltering from the night or hiding in terror close by.

The solitary figure fearlessly made its way to the recently filled in grave without hesitation, and walked unceremoniously and irreverently over the loose earth that covered that place of rest. Its hardened heart was filled with abhorrent hatred and its evil mouth, distorted by the lurid laughter issuing from its portal, would have seemed repugnant to even the devil's ear - and the gladdened feelings in its heart were unconcerned by the lack of respect it so repulsively displayed.

***

Just two short months after she had returned from Dorset with her uncle and her young son, and in the very early hours of no particular Saturday morning, Jenny awoke with a sudden start from the deepest sleep she had had in years.

A terrible, muddled dream of great intensity had awakened her. A dream so real it illustrated her father's dire dilemma and her aunt's final piercing pain so vividly that she arose from her bed instantly and sought her image in the full length mirror to establish reality once more.

Jenny still regretted her great-aunt's passing, of course, it went without saying and she would continue to miss the portly governess with her grey white hair for years to come; but gradually, in the fullness of time as they say, the yearning would one day lose its intensity and eventually be replaced by a memory or two of the happiness they both had shared in the short while she had known her as her dearest aunt.

The missing of her father, on the other hand, was somewhat different; for in the earlier part of her life she had known him to be the uncaring man he truly was. She had, for awhile, remained somewhat pleased he had had his tragic accident that was to eventually take his life.

But she wished no one in the world the excruciating agony or the torment of mind and body that had suddenly descended upon her father; and so continuous had the agony been felt by him throughout the long years of his suffering, that it was to become unbearable at times.

And yet, because the accident had brought about a change in his character, a change that allowed them both to enter into a lasting closeness for the first time in her existence, she had indeed been thankful. And so, from that aspect, together with the result of the many visits she had paid him over the years of his incapacity, she missed him also - and sorely regretted his passing.

Jenny's bedroom in The Old House was comfortable and large and was situated at the eastern aspect of the property. All comforts imaginable had been fitted for her pleasure and convenience when she'd moved there permanently with her son; and she was delighted to have been able to apply her own creativity to the room to make it truly hers.

She now walked, in earnest, back and forth in that room; plagued with uneasiness as she considered the dream that had so suddenly disturbed her and had finally been the cause of her waking. The worst of bad dreams, which had so shaken the young woman into a state of fear, troubled her to such an extent that she was now trembling with nervousness.

The nightmare had been set in an opulent bedroom; a room she had known but rarely entered - a room that she instantly recognised as that belonging to her mother, back at Hyde Hall in Dorset.

Her father, at least she considered the tall male figure to have been that of her father although the detail of the form that had been presented to her was faceless, had entered her mother's bedroom carefully and with a degree of uncertainty in regards to its entitlement in being there at all.

She had watched the mannish figure as it neared the bed on which her mother, clad only in a black negligee, was reclining. The figure was taking off his clothes as he crossed the room and was dropping them carelessly on the floor behind him as he eagerly moved toward the bed. He then clambered impatiently to be next to her mother, and all the while they were both engaged in laughter that was both hideous and devoid of humour.

No coverlets covered the couple as they teasingly played. No pillows were in place as pillows usually are, though they were still there on the bed or on the floor in complete disarrangement - as if they had been thrown in playfulness. No discernable words were being spoken as shameful activities were entered into; activities that were both loathsome and nauseous to Jenny's innocent mind.

Suddenly, the bedroom door was thrown open and Jenny's great-aunt Sarah moved swiftly and angrily into the room and commenced to rebuke her niece, Margaret, forcefully; and indeed, berated her far beyond the wildest concepts of any dictionary explanation of the word could ever hope to state.

The stringing together of words, being jumbled and running into one another, made no sense at all but they completely illustrated the ferocity that her great-aunt felt inside. And the flailing of her arms, as though attempting to take flight from this filthy scene, was most alarming to Jenny's innocent state of mind.

The faceless form of Jenny's father gathered its clothes and rushed passed her Great Aunt Sarah to the door - endeavouring to dress itself as it departed in total panic.

Margaret gathered a couple of pillows and placed them haphazardly behind her dishevelled head and laid her naked body back with no attempt at concealing her embarrassment or her shame as she continued to laugh untiringly at her tomb garbed, white haired aunt.

Jenny continued to ponder the vile dream until the darkness finally gave way to the bright August sun as it showed itself through the tall elms that surrounded the inside of the walled perimeter of the garden. It wasn't until she had finished the witnessing of the rising of the sun that she left the window where she stood. She bathed and dressed herself, then went down the stairs to breakfast with her dear son and her admiring uncle, but with unsavoury questions harassing her usually placed mind.

CHAPTER TWELVE

Ever since Sarah Wood had departed this world, Janet Nunn had been encouraged to dine with Hamish Kent and his family at all times and to join in all family social activities no matter what the occasion. The thought behind this move was that Hamish, being so full of concern both for Jenny and Jacob, considered that the family would be complete once again if Janet's presence was evident.

As a result of this, and for the past eight years or so, Janet had been pleased to oblige her employer and the strategy for all that time had worked successfully; for both Jenny and Jacob had become fervently attached to the sprightly Scottish housekeeper without deserting the memory of their fond Aunt Sarah in the slightest.

The place was completely deserted when Jenny first walked into the breakfast room that bright Saturday morning; as all of the household working staff was rarely expected to be employed over the weekend, accept on the odd occasion when entertainment was anticipated. As a result of this it was left to Janet or Jenny to prepare and serve each of the weekend meals which they were both pleased to do.

Mealtime habits, especially Saturday breakfasting, was routinely viewed by the Kent family as being the most important meal to get the weekend underway. This practice was steadfastly required and encouraged by Hamish, who always and without exception, enjoyed his full cooked breakfast to include everything available and for it to be consumed in the most cordial of atmospheres possible.

It was now six thirty in the morning; a little early for Janet to be up and about just yet and so Jenny queried in her mind if it would not be more sensible to return to her bed in the blessed hope of recapturing a few more valued minutes rest. Nevertheless, the same unfortunate thoughts continued to plague her mind at this moment and so all prospects of sweet repose were wiped away in a flash.

As a direct need for the nightmarish thoughts to be eradicated as soon as was ever possible, Jenny resolved to walk the attractively designed and well established garden until it was time to set in motion the cooking of breakfast; at least that would give her time to come to terms with her night of fear... or so she had hoped.

As she slowly walked the garden paths, and with her eyelids being caused to flicker by the early sunlight's glare and with her mind being caught up in a state of confusion, she totally ignored all the garden flowers that usually filled her heart with joy.

Muddled, aimless thoughts had taken control of her mind and would so continue for some time yet, when they should have been sorted in order to conjure up some kind of meaning to the outlandish dream; however, the ability to unravel the confusion the nightmare had left behind escaped her altogether.

She then considered that by using sound reasoning, instead of guesswork, and by trying to understand the dream in a more intellectual manner, might easily be the way forward and help her find the meaning to this ghoulish illusion more quickly... assuming, of course, that brain power in the guise of sound reasoning might be all that is needed to gather level-headed logic from a few confusing notions. But that too proved futile, for she found no sound reasoning on hand for her to use.

For one whole hour she walked the beautiful garden, during which time she had repeated the circuit more than once and had stopped on each occasion by the large koi pond and watched the huge colourful fish as they swam around for her distraction.

Still nothing sprung into her futile mind during all that time and so she continued strolling as before; though now weighed down with disappointment.

It was after the fourth and final noiseless stroll, and while she was seated on the small wall that surrounded the pool's edge and with her chin firmly resting on the palms of her hands, that Janet Nunn, upon noticing Jenny from the seclusion of the kitchen window, settled on engaging her charge in early morning conversation.

Moving slowly and silently toward her seated ward Janet startled Jenny; and as she offered her the warmest of highland smiles she failed to notice the alarm her presence had caused.

The lovely young woman raised her head sharply in complete surprise.

'Good morning Janet,' said Jenny, 'you gave me quite a start.'

'Hello Jennifer my dear. Oh did I? I'm so sorry; it wasn't my intention I can assure you of that,' returned the Scottish housekeeper. 'But I do hope everything is alright with you all the same; only you looked so forlorn just sitting there all by yourself in that odd fashion, quite as if you had the whole of the world's troubles resting on those fragile shoulders of yours; and so I felt I had to find out if you were completely all right.'

'Not so fragile as you might think Janet,' returned Jenny,

equalling the smile that was being offered to her. 'My shoulders are quite deceptive and are much tougher than anyone might really suppose... but yes I'm OK thank you.'

'A mere figure of speech my dear, I didn't mean to imply that I found you to be wasting away at all,' rejoined Janet, with a chuckle. 'But really now, is everything good with you? Only you did seem to be lost in thought. Perhaps you didn't enjoy a full night's sleep; is that it? I know only too well how troublesome it can be to have one's night frustrated by sleeplessness; when in the early morning's hours all our problems seem to be intensified beyond reason.'

'Janet, I was awakened by a fearful nightmare in the early hours, that's all; a nightmare, I might add, that I do hope will not be of a recurring nature.

'I don't expect you possess any talents for the interpretation of nightmares or dreams do you? Only I have searched my mind for a solution ever since I've been awake and have drawn a blank at each and every attempt. I am a resolute believer in such nonsense, you see, Janet, and in the past I have found dreams to be quite... how shall say, yes, quite relevant; well, to a certain extent at any rate.'

'Well now, why don't you tell me all about your nightmare Jennifer? I may not have the ability to remove curses or the like; for believe it or believe it not, I am not a Scottish witch, but it may help you to have a second opinion; you never know what two women's minds like ours might produce if we put our heads together and our thinking caps on straight.'

Upon saying this, Janet sat herself on the low brick wall beside Jenny as the two ladies conversed and meditated about dreams, nightmares, imagery and many other forms of the supposed paranormal; not that dreams or nightmares in themselves could ever be considered as being paranormal, but the interpretation of them might.

Eventually Jenny did come to the crux of the matter that had so concerned her from the early hours and which was still causing tension to besiege her usually tranquil mind.

Jenny related to Janet, in grisly detail, everything unseemly and sickening to her mind that had occurred in her nightmare even to the extent of detailing the sexual activities that she found to be so disgusting and she felt comforted as she revealing each chilling aspect.

'That is indeed quite some nightmare Jennifer and one that would cause nauseous feelings to the most hardened of stomachs...

I'm quite sure of that.

'I suppose you are hoping your dream is telling you that you would have preferred your father and mother to have been reunited in wedded bliss, all those years ago, is that it?' asked Janet, with dubious assumptions in her reasoning. And not entirely convinced that Jenny's mind was fully attuned to her reply, she continued. 'You see my dear, if, as you have just said, the gentleman in your dream was faceless how can you possibly be sure the impression you received was that of your father? I mean it could have been almost any one; why even…'

'Because,' interrupted Jenny, 'his shape, his upright posture, and the way he was so formally dressed was exactly that of my father after dinner.'

'But Jennifer, the man was faceless; you admitted that much yourself, so I don't see how you can be totally sure that it was your father; unless, of course, you wanted it to have been him… as I have just this minute said.'

'Yes I suppose you are right Janet, I hadn't thought of it in that light,' said Jenny, and after taking some rapid rational thoughts she added, 'perhaps that's it; perhaps I did want it to have been him. I wanted nothing more but for my parents to have behaved in a way that normal, fun loving people behave. But it wasn't like that, Janet. They weren't like that. They weren't at all normal or loving.

'Do you know, in all my days since I was old enough to remember, I have never seen my parents exchange a kiss or even touch each other in any way that could have been construed as being intimate… or normal. Why, even when they were going away from Hyde Hall and leaving each other for days, weeks or months on end, there was never a demonstration of affection from either of them.

'And I suppose because of that, there was never a demonstration of affection for me either. Oh, how I longed for either of my parents to have shown me just a little affection, just a touch of my hand or a stroke of my hair would have done, but no, there was nothing for me. Still, that has very little to do with my horrifying dream, so I shall pass on that one.'

'May I ask you, my dear, have you, at any time, ever suspected either of your parents to be involved in extramarital relations… other than the one we already know about, that is?'

'Father was always self opinionated to the extreme,' said Jenny, colouring slightly, at the thought; and the question provoked a slight embarrassment to pain her mind a little. 'I am sure he harboured the notion that all women, whom he ever came into contact with, were more than willing to jump into bed with him and without the need of gentle persuasion or coercion. Not that I thought of it quite in those terms at the time, of course,' she smiled discreetly, 'but looking back from where I now stand, yes, that's precisely what I thought of him and so it came as no surprise to me to learn about Jane Howe.

'But Jane appears to be somewhat different from my concept of 'the other woman'. I don't know if you share my opinion from what I have told you about her, Janet, but to me she seems to be a really caring person and that it is quite clear, even to my clouded mind, that she loved my father totally, and without any of the little doubts or hindrances that may get in the way of her loving a married man. And she still does love him I suppose, in her own way, even though he's gone... I'm quite sure of that.'

'Yes I must say I was favourably impressed with what you have told me of the lady's qualities but we must eliminate her from your dream, Jennifer, as nothing in it applies directly to her. It is the members of your dream and those alone on whom we should concentrate our thoughts at this moment, namely: your mother, your father and your Aunt Sarah; everyone else, it seems to me, are quite irrelevant.

'First of all, I am quite certain that the man in your dream is not your father at all.' At this juncture, Janet paused for a moment to take thought while at the same time she took Jenny's hand into her own and smoothed it gently with thoughtfulness before she continued: 'You see, my dear, since your father's unfortunate accident and before his untimely death, you had been on good terms with him, and you have told me before that you have forgiven him for his neglect to you over the years and with no misgivings in your mind at all.

'With Jacob entering your father's life at the fitting moment he did, and being by your side at all times while you were all together, I fail to see how the vision of a faceless figure in your mothers bedroom could possibly be that of your father. I mean to say, why would you wish to make your own father so unreal when you were at peace with one another? Why on earth would you feel the need to exclude a man who has come to mean so much to you over the years and with whom you had made great strides in reconciliation? It just doesn't make sense to me, Jennifer, surely you must see that. No, I think we must look elsewhere for the faceless figure's identity and in any direction save that of your father's.

'Now, can you recollect anybody... anyone at all, mind you,

who could possibly fit the description of the male figure that was being so attentive to your mother; excluding Mr Hamish of course?' She smiled at her utterance of the final part of the sentence.

Jenny thought for quite a while, and she went over, in her mind, each and every male visitor she had ever seen at Hyde Hall, one whom she might have considered to have possessed a physique like that of her father.

Search as she may there was no one; no one at all who possessed, or shared equal characteristics with her father or was of a comparable size or stature to him... no one that came to her mind immediately, anyway. Of course there were a few oddballs who frequented the place, such as the estate solicitor but he was nowhere near the correct height or shape of profile and neither were all the others. Then she considered those further afield, those who visited her parents only rarely.

'There was Lord Melchamp of course, his physique and my father's were almost identical,' said Jenny, 'but he was my father's friend of long standing; my father's closest friend in actual fact and he would be the most unlikely of candidates to have been so intimately caught up with my mother.'

'Close friends or not; that sort can be very deceiving, Jennifer,' offered Janet.

'No really! Lord Melchamp served with my father in India and was attendant to my father at his wedding. He was also my godfather, or so I believe. But he, to my sure and certain knowledge, has never accomplished anything that approached a meaningful responsibility to me, or for me, come to that; I never saw much of him anyway. But I would, without a shadow of doubt, have trusted his loyalty to my father... implicitly you might say. And in any case, I would never have considered my mother to have been the sort of woman to have taken a lover in the first place, she is much too selfish and demanding for that sort of thing," said Jenny, protectively.

'Be that as it may Jennifer; one frequently find the closest of our friends to be guilty of wrongdoing at times; whether the offence be adultery, theft or even murder. Those closest to us should be watched more closely than those furthest from us.

'Tell me, is Lord Melchamp married and if so is his marriage stable and secure, to your knowledge, Jennifer? What I mean is... has there been any scandal linked to his marriage in any way that you are aware of?'

'Janet, you seem to have it in for dear old Lord Melchamp, and I can't think why,' responded Jenny, with a degree of flippancy in her voice as she laughed outwardly in disbelief.

'I know these matters may seem implausible at times Jennifer but we are attempting to understand the meaning of your dream... if you remember? That is, if indeed there is one,' returned Janet, raising her left eyebrow as she cast a disapproving look in Jenny's direction because of her flippancy.'

'I'm sorry, Janet, please continue; I didn't mean to be superficial and I really do wish to get this worry off my mind.'

'A thought has just this second crossed my mind, Jennifer,' said Janet, replacing her eyebrow to its original position as her eyes lit up with a surprising suggestion. 'I wonder if Mr Hamish has crossed paths with your Lord Melchamp in the past. If he has, then I am sure he would be pleased to enlighten us. What do you say we include your uncle in our little debate over breakfast? Or would you prefer to keep the matter just between the two of us?'

'Oh no, not at all,' rejoined Jenny, with a relieved look of approval passing her pretty face, 'let him join the debate by all means: if you think he would be at all interested; so yes, let's do that. First of all, though, we must prepare breakfast, as I'm sure he will think much more clearly as his tummy is being filled.'

During the preparation of the meal the two ladies continued their dialogue at an even more heightened level as Janet enquired of the relationship that had existed between Sarah and her niece, Margaret, even though she was aware of Sarah's disappointment in the way her niece had behaved towards Jenny - her husband too for that matter - in the early days anyhow.

'I think they interacted well enough with each other, although mother has little time for anyone other than herself as you already know. But I have never witnessed Aunt Sarah reprimand my mother or behave toward her in any way that might be construed as being corrective. She wouldn't dare; you must remember that Hyde Hall was the only home she had at the time, and so she would never have jeopardised that... not for the entire world she wouldn't.'

Just then Hamish Kent made his cheery entrance and after greeting both ladies he seated himself in his usual place at the head of the table.

'Quite a promising morning for the commencement of the weekend, don't you think, Jennifer? Is that son of yours not up and about yet?' he asked, in anticipation of yet another interesting weekend in the company of his enthusiastic great-nephew.

'No, not yet Uncle,' she said, as she seated herself beside her uncle.' I expect he's having a lie in this morning; besides, he was more than likely studying till all hours last night; you know how enthusiastic he is about his learning.'

'Yes indeed, quite a remarkable lad is that son of yours; never known another like him. He is so intense about his work it's quite difficult to believe sometimes.

'Well, what do we have for breakfast this fine morning? Something smells jolly good!' said Hamish, in his usual friendly and cheerful manner.

The question was answered by Janet as she walked in from the kitchen, with a tray fully laden with all things expected.

'Well Jennifer, have you asked your uncle about Lord Melchamp yet?' she asked, casting an eye in Jenny's direction, 'Best get it over and done with before Jacob makes an appearance; not the sort of debate to be entered into in front of the wee laddie.'

'Yes you are right Janet,' said Jenny, turning her head in the direction of her uncle; but before introducing the dreaded subject yet again, she asked, 'Have you any knowledge of a Lord Melchamp, uncle? I believe he lives or lived on the south coast somewhere and was once a close friend of my father's.'

'Yes that's right Jennifer,' returned Hamish. 'He lives in West Sussex I think. Your father and he were in the army at the same time and I believe them to have served in India together; a couple of times, if my memory serves me correctly. A great one for his stocks and shares was Lord Melchamp, again if my memory is accurate; never made a fortune out of it though; always going for the long shots, or so I believe, and never for the certainties.

'He married a most peculiar looking woman though; one who inherited a fortune from her father. She, being the only progeny, received her father's total wealth. That, to my way of thinking, was the big attraction in the first place for Lord Melchamp as his own father left him with precious little other than a title and massive gambling debts; leastways that was the tittle-tattle at the time. Haven't heard his name mentioned in years though. Why, what's the old reprobate been up to now?'

'You said that last bit as though you know him to be an undesirable character uncle. Is he? Or has he been?' queried Jenny, with a soberness about her face that betrayed a feeling of loyalty to someone she didn't really know, and had rarely seen since she was a child; except at the funeral of course and then no conversation had existed between them. But that was Jenny, always ready to praise and rarely did she put anyone down without just cause.

'Good heavens no, not a bit of it, he is squeaky clean as far as

I know. To be perfectly honest with you, I never knew the fellow that well. He was best man at your father's wedding, I know that much. Come to think of it, it was at that particular function I gathered all the titbits about him.

'I noticed that he and his lady wife were at your father's funeral although I failed to provide myself the opportunity of entering into conversation with them; we, like you, merely passed the time of day, that's all. But as far as his integrity and his honesty are concerned they're not sullied in the slightest Jennifer, no, not at all. Perhaps you would be good enough to explain what these questions are all about.'

And so Jenny began, once again, to speak about the nightmare that had caused her so much anxiety. When she had finished her kindly uncle rose from his seat and walking over to his niece, took both her hands in his and gazed tenderly into her eyes.

'I'm so sorry you have been so disturbed my dear,' he said, calmly, 'but really, you oughtn't to place too much emphasis on dreams or nightmares of this nature. Don't you think they are the result of the dregs from your imagination or the effect of some book you may have read at sometime in the distant past? Please don't allow such a matter as this influence your thinking, Jennifer; not by placing an importance upon it above all reason.

'I couldn't possibly extrapolate anything whatsoever from the loathsome, faceless gentleman in your dream or draw any conclusions at all from what you have just told me.

'Clearly, this thing has upset you terribly and I can only feel for you and offer you my sincere support.' Then in an attempt to lighten the mood of breakfast he added: 'perhaps we should spend today in taking a trip into the country or better still, maybe a trip to the sea might be just the thing to brighten up the weekend for you; what do you say? I'm sure young Jacob would enjoy a day off from my company alone, especially on such a sunny day as this; shall we ask him? '

And so the pseudo family of four fully occupied themselves in an exhausting but frivolous day by the sea, walking the cliff tops and doing all things normal in a customary excursion of this nature, and, on the whole, they spent the entire day taking pleasure in the trip - not immensely, 'tis true, but they profited from the fresh sea air if nothing else.

Even so the male members of the party were never far from each other, and together they debated as many commercial and industrial problems as they would have done had they been home.

Jenny, on the other hand, remained thoughtful for most of the time: she not being fully able to escape the neurotic nightmarish experience of the morning's early hours. And although spending time with Janet was a joy, her usually carefree mind seemed bogged down and was continuous in its anxiety; and so she remained all but silent throughout the day.

Gradually though, and after a good deal of thought, Jenny succumbed to the notion of Lord Melchamp being the main architect of her uneasiness. The noble lord, being the main character in her night's disturbance was to her mind extremely worrying - not to say inconsiderate; but she now believed it to be more than a little likely for it to have been he who had invaded her sleep.

Nevertheless, not wishing to pursue her newly established reckoning straight away with ill-mannered accusations, Jenny withheld her reasoning for quite sometime, for the whole of the day in fact and it wasn't until the family group were returning from their trip that she considered broaching the subject yet again, but only to Janet this time.

Jacob was seated in the front of the vehicle chatting away to his Uncle Hamish in constant boredom about all matters of commerce with accentuated ease, at least both of the ladies considered the male conversation in those tedious terms. And as Jenny and Janet occupied the rear seat, it was quite easy for Jenny to return to the same topic but in a discreet yet tactful way.

'You know Janet, I am now beginning share your opinion and am fast coming to the conclusion that it was Lord Melchamp who took the predominant role in my nightmare last night. I say this because of how Uncle Hamish described Lady Melchamp. This of course was supported by my remembrance of her at the funeral. She is most certainly a very plain looking lady indeed... and that's putting it mildly; while he is the most colourful character one could possibly imagine and not without a good deal of appeal either. And as their marriage was brought about by financial gain on his part, again according to Uncle Hamish, I can well imagine why he would feel the need to make some sort of conquest in order to make his life less dreary.

'But as I have said before, I have never considered my mother to possess a flirtatious temperament; but now that my father has gone... well who can tell? I have heard her clearly say, and on more than one occasion, that life was tediously passing her by and that it was being filled with very little excitement these days... so yes, perhaps she is now about to make up for lost time... who knows.

'But I wonder if there will ever be a way of finding out for sure if any credibility exists as to the reason for this wretched nightmare of mine, which is fast becoming a wretched bore.'

Janet thought for awhile.

'Who knows Jennifer, perhaps when you go down to Dorset again you will be able to find out more answers to your dream and if it had any genuine meaning to it… or maybe it was your uncle who was more correct in his assumptions.'

CHAPTER THIRTEEN

Not long after the family excursion to the nearest coast had taken place and at about four thirty on a particular rain filled afternoon, Hamish Kent received the awaited communiqué from the Hyde Estate's corpulent solicitor, summoning Hamish and Jennifer Kent to attend his office in Dorset for the reading of Sir Angus Kent's last will and testament.

It is somewhat unusual these days to hold an official meeting of this nature, but as already mentioned, the affairs of this particular estate were unusually complex and involved and so it was considered reasonable and practical for everyone concerned to be so assembled in order to take delivery of the information simultaneously; not only that but it seemed to be essential in order to satisfy the solicitor's unlikely starved ego....

The gathering was to be held at the offices of the Tooke Empire, as already mentioned; at three thirty p.m., on Friday the thirteenth August nineteen hundred and sixty five, to be precise.

Hamish Kent, after reading the date of the scheduled meeting, smiled amusedly to himself, for he had, just a few days earlier spelt out to his lovely niece the futility of her probing into superstitious nonsense. Hamish, being a rational person by nature, had always failed to give any credence to worthless beliefs of any description - but now, here he was hoping that the unfortunate date would not influence the journey ahead in a detrimental way or indeed the meeting itself.

Bearing this in mind he now looked skyward for some sort of inspirational response. None came. And so he laughed aloud in a jovial manner.

Hamish had not been notified of the meeting by telephone as was originally guaranteed by Colin Tooke during their drawn out introduction after the funeral, neither had he been convinced he would take delivery of such a communiqué by that means. For this reason, and because he was of a kindly disposition, he had thought little of the matter over the passing weeks: he supposing it to have been an impromptu statement on the solicitor's behalf, which was not to be totally relied upon.

Hamish Kent, also being a man of discernment in the ways of business correctness, read through the letter he now held in his hand extremely carefully, and he, understanding the value of such a communication totally, was pleased to have been given at least a few days notice in which to rearrange his own business schedule. He would now apply his mind in this direction in order to complete the necessary adjustments needed with all speed; but, in any case, his worthy estate manager, who was a boon to Hamish at times like these, could be relied upon to step into the breach and act on his own initiative with little inconvenience to himself.

It wasn't until the evening that Hamish was able to share the pertinent communiqué with Jenny and then not until the family was assembled at the table once more in readiness for their usual evening meal.

'I certainly hope my father's testament doesn't alter my life style too much, Uncle,' exclaimed Jenny.

And as she read the short letter for a second time a sense of foreboding filled her mind, quite as if it was conveying some sort of omen to her, a dread even, for her to be apprehensive about; and a look of apprehension clouded her nervous face, which she attempted to cover with improvised words.

'I can quite see how annoying it would be to have journeyed all the way to Dorset, with you once again, only to find that my father's last wishes were for me to present myself at Hyde Hall at some future date and to once again be permanently living there. All the awkward problems that will undoubtedly be brought about by simply being in the same house as my mother, will not be welcomed by me... or by her either, come to that.

'Not that I have any objections to running the estate, no, not at all; in fact a stimulating challenge of that sort would be something to look forward to; but living with my mother once again, yes well, that is quite a different matter.'

Then upon reflection, she arrived at a more logical conclusion to the problem which lightened her anxious feelings at once and her face brightened appreciably because of it.

'Still, that is hardly likely to happen seeing that my mother still enjoys good health.' She smiled cheerily. 'I mean, she would be more than capable of looking after all matters of importance as far as the estate is concerned, don't you think? And without her experiencing too many difficulties either: assuming of course she is able to move herself in the right direction and summon up sufficient energy to do the job properly... both at the same time.

'Anyway, if she found herself to be out of her depth and not up to the task in spite of everything, well, she could easily employ an estate manager, as you do uncle, just to bear the brunt of things so that she is still able to continue a life style that suits her best; I'm sure my father will have considered all that anyway.'

'Please be aware, Jennifer, it is much safer for us not to anticipate matters of this nature without having at least some indication as to what your father had been taking into account over the past years. All sorts of possibilities may have entered his mind regarding the estate as he lay upon his sick bed and with little else left for him to do but contemplate matters of this sort.

'Remember, your father had been an intelligent and shrewd business man for all his life, if nothing else, and had always been an excellent judge of people's characters as well.

'His mind wasn't affected by the accident you know, only his body, and so it's with a degree of certainty that I advise you to rely upon your father to have exercised great mental insight in the drawing up of his testament.

'In any case, he is not likely to have offered an incompetent person the helm or someone that would be capable of exploiting the estate for their own benefit, now would he? Not that I consider your mother to be incompetent... not by any stretch of the imagination, and I should hate for you to think that I implied anything of the sort; but really, would he have left everything to someone who is capable of destroying an estate that the Kent dynasty has built up since time immemorial, whether deliberately or through lack of judgment? No, I think not! He will have had in mind a competent farm executive, someone capable of managing and further developing this estate, which is to be left... in perpetuity if you like; whatever that may mean these days.

'But it won't be just you or your mother who your father will have been thinking about, Jennifer, but Jacob also and Jacob's children and theirs after that. So you see one has to look a long way ahead and study the broader picture in these particular instances.

'In the meantime, if your father considered your mother to be the person for the job, then so be it; I know he will not have arrived at that decision without due consideration, and, quite possibly, with taking advice.

'In any case, please remember Jennifer, the same applies today as it did all those years ago when I first promised you I would look after and care for you. I still consider that to be my duty and indeed my pleasure, in spite of all that has happened recently. And so, whatever the outcome of today's meeting, I shall be with you every step of the way, guiding you in all matters... whether they are farming matters or not... if in fact you need me, that is. No matter what problems may overtake us in the future, Jennifer, I shall be there for you; please bear all of that in mind, my dear.'

***

Friday the thirteenth arrived after taking precisely ten middle sized days in the doing. As prearranged, both Hamish and Jennifer arose early to allow the maximum amount of time for their journey to Dorset.

Leaving The Old House at Brenton at eight sharp, amid drizzling rain, was not an easy task for either of them; for a toothsome breakfast should never be rushed; but the time for departure came all too soon.

They assumed they had allowed enough time to arrive at their destination long before the proceedings were expected to have been under way and so no further worries were anticipated.

The inclement weather had other ideas, though, for it slowed their motor down considerably, thereby causing the finely tuned calculation of their journey to be somewhat imprecise. Even by going directly to the solicitor's office instead of checking into their hotel first, as they had planned to do, they were still thirty minutes late in their arrival.

As they climbed the stairway that led to the corridor that in turn led to Colin Tooke's personal office, and knowing that her mother's insufferable presence would be there just waiting to beleaguer her mind as usual, Jenny caught hold of her uncle's arm as an unexpected bout of nervousness rapidly distressed the whole of her body.

In fact Jenny had no need to worry for it was a most affable Lady Margaret, or so it first looked, who was seated at the corpulent solicitor's side when they opened the door.

She was seen to be calm and in a state of complete control, though not a word of greeting passed her lips as the couple entered. Colin Tooke, on the other hand, looked more than a little nervous at being so tightly trapped by the mistress of Hyde Hall - she being his only visitor.

Both Jenny and Hamish Kent stood noiselessly together. They felt no need to break their silence for they were caught in complete surprise at seeing both Margaret and the solicitor sitting alone in this way and being locked in serious debate with one another - or so it first appeared.

But the moment the identity of the new arrivals had taken hold of Mr Tooke's mind he became so relieved and reassured that he gave the distinct impression of a condemned man, who had just that moment cheated the hangman's noose. His chubby face lit up and the lips of that chubby face became stretched with a smile - though it twitched incessantly.

As he wobbled hurriedly to the office doorway, still holding on to this high degree of relief, he was observed to greet the visitors from Lincolnshire with the vigorous shaking of their hands, that were more attuned to the motion of well-oiled water pump handles than anything else, and which were accompanied by over-exaggerated words of cordial welcome.

The Lincolnshire Kents finally seated themselves with discreet nods of greeting in Margaret's direction, as the smartly attired, unresponsive lady conjured her handkerchief from the sleeve of her dress to conceal her awkward face.

The lavish office would have been more impressive had the solicitor's flat bowled, curved stemmed pipe, with its obnoxious smouldering, not been in operation. But, as it was, smoke seemed to fill every corner of the large office and, because no window had been opened, the intolerable smoke was causing considerable discomfort to one of its inmates by the watering and reddening of her eyes and in the congestion of her lungs.

So much was the pollution being felt by Margaret that she began employing the services of the recently acquired handkerchief and she coughed, continuously, to free herself of the misery she was enduring.

All at once, as if wishing to impress the newcomers or rather to remind them of her forceful temperament, her relaxed attitude changed to one of excessive discontent as the Margaret of old shone all the way through the fug.

'For goodness sake Colin, put that obnoxious pipe of yours to one side before I take the wretched thing away from you and throw it out the window,' said she, as she gutturally cleared her throat and blew her nose at the same time. 'And open that blessed window as well, will you, before I pass out and have to be taken to hospital to be resuscitated by a full tank of oxygen,' she added, as the intensity of a bout of raspy, chesty coughing reached its climax.

'Yes of course,' said the corpulent solicitor, as he eased his way to an adjacent window; and upon opening it to the complete width of its wideness, a most welcome freshness of dampened air rushed swiftly in to permeate the whole office immediately.

He lingered by the window for the shortest moment, selfishly filling his own lungs with the revitalizing air by exercising his diaphragm to inflate his chest to its full extent, before he resumed his position at the table.

Once seated, he became rather anxious; all the while contemplating his gold wristwatch in silence, as though waiting for a fifth member to complete the gathering.

Just as Colin Tooke was about to apologise for the unfortunate delay to the commencement of the official proceedings, a gentle tapping on the door was heard to be barely discernable. Nevertheless, it was loud enough to prevent the short corpulent solicitor from having to explain the hold-up to the now visibly impatient Lady Margaret.

After a hastily delivered invitation for the person to enter, the internees all turned simultaneously to face the doorway and to observe the shapely Jane Howe standing there. She looked about herself in an undecided fashion as she walked slowly into the room.

'God, I'm not going to be subjected to pernicious prostitutes at this meeting as well as repugnant relatives, am I?' asked the malicious Margaret, in such a derogatory tone that she drew everyone's attention to herself - rather critically in fact - and not without just cause, for each member had recoiled with revulsion at the shameful remark.

Jane faltered somewhat as the contemptuous words were spoken, and moved into the room rather cautiously; and in the hopes of avoiding any further discourteous comments from the mistress of Hyde Hall, she inclined her head instantly.

Upon seeing the demoralizing sensations expressed in Jane's eyes, Hamish stood at once and walked toward his late brothers lovely mistress, and, relieving her of an extremely wet raincoat he kindly escorted her to the chair where he had been seated - next to Jenny; who not unlike Jane had also taken great exception to Margaret's caustic remark.

Uncharacteristically, Jenny felt the impulse to make reply - some verbal response in order to take her mother to task for the unseemly words she had spoken; but catching her uncle's disapproving eye, she glared somewhat critically instead. Her mother, on the other hand, failed to take notice of the censuring stare or she had deliberately ignored it - who could tell?

Hamish draped Jane's dampened coat over an empty seat adjacent to the door and seated himself next to the newcomer so that she was adequately protected on both sides; with him now neighbouring his insufferable sister-in-law.

'I'm so sorry to have arrived late,' offered Jane, after she was seated and addressing her apology mainly in the direction of the corpulent solicitor. 'I do hope I haven't caused an inconvenience to anyone, but unfortunately I picked up a wretched puncture from a protruding flint in my lane just twenty seconds into my journey and I have been waiting all this time for some assistance to arrive.'

Jane seemed meek and a little apprehensive as she looked about herself seeking a degree of friendly reassurance from somewhere - anywhere would have done! And so, Jenny, feeling under the table for Jane's soft, moist hand, tenderly stroked it and then held it in comforting support. The two ladies then exchanged polite and understanding smiles with one another as the solicitor's calming words were spoken:

'That's quite alright Miss Howe,' said Colin Tooke, with a benevolent smile. 'Mr Hamish and Miss Jennifer Kent arrived just a few moments before you and so you haven't missed a thing; in point of fact I was just about to open the proceedings when you entered.'

So saying, he began to relate all matters relevant to the death of Sir Angus Kent and the Hyde Hall estate in a most official and forthright manner with steadiness and a complete sense of purpose in his voice - hoping for total approval from his captive audience, it might be assumed.

'Firstly may I assure you all of my fullest, my most sincere and heartfelt sympathy for your sad loss. Sir Angus and I have shared each others company over many years and so you will appreciate the loss of such a valued friend to me as well.

'The nature of his testament, which I might add, has been acted on without showing precedence to anyone in attendance, has required me applying myself to the obtaining of certain directives from law to ensure the correctness in the procedure of this will and so it has been this endeavour that has caused much of the delay in the completion and the drawing up of this complicated testament.

'Nevertheless, everything now being accomplished, I am at last able to deliver Sir Angus Kent's written and agreed last will and testament to you all this afternoon.'

After further explanations of delay in the promotion and endorsement of all matters legal regarding Sir Angus' business affairs and the clarification of certain relative aspects to the business itself, a certain fidgeting occurred from Lady Margaret's direction as if a particular level of impatience had filled the lady's mind, thereby annoying her intensely.

'Cut all the legal claptrap and silly piffle, Colin, if you please, and proceed to the more pertinent matters in question,' said she, exercising her usual rudeness coupled with unseemly irritation. 'I have other, more important concerns that are in need of my attention this afternoon, therefore I'd appreciate rather more directness from you. So perhaps a more speedy continuance of this ridiculous procedure should be installed; if it isn't too much to ask.' The final seven words of the sentence were spoken with contemptuous spite and bile.

'Yes of course,' offered the corpulent gentleman as a slight flushness tinted his wide face, 'I fully understand your eagerness, but we have to remember the importance in making clear, to all concerned, precisely what Sir Angus proposed when he related his intentions to me in the preparation of his will and as the law demands. And so, if you will please bear with me a moment or two longer I should prefer to communicate this reading in the right and proper manner.'

Margaret was furious at being put in her place in such a succinct and polite manner. She was only used to dictating her desires to others and to having her own way in all things relevant to herself. And so she didn't take kindly to being pulled up by anyone, no matter how soothingly; the net result of which caused the lady's powdered countenance to turn slightly crimson as she employed her handkerchief to cover her embarrassment.

It now looked as if the corpulent solicitor was deliberate in taking his time over the communication, which seemed to fire further irritation into the heart and mind of Margaret - and with great intensity to boot.

When he eventually arrived at the most important part of the will that told of how Sir Angus and his father had ruthlessly prevented Hamish Kent from succeeding to the inheritance that was rightfully his, her annoyance reached an almighty climax.

She stood immediately to utter her hysterical protest to that which had been so forcefully stated.

'What!' screamed Margaret, defiantly, 'what are you telling me? Is it... is it that for all this time and ever since his father's death my late husband has been enjoying a situation that was not rightfully his?' The solicitor nodded and lowered his eyes to search the papers in front of him as a discreet smile appeared at one corner of his mouth. 'Well where the hell does that leave me?' The afore reddening of the widow's countenance had by this time deserted her; and all blood, now being drained from her face, was replaced with a shade of ghoulish whiteness as her whole body trembled in angered uncertainty.

'Margaret' interrupted Hamish, quietly, 'please sit down and exercise a degree of restraint within yourself. I am sure Mr Tooke will then be able to enlighten you regarding your personal entitlement, as far as Angus' will is concerned, all the more quickly if you do'.

She turned on Hamish with a blazing look of hatred issuing from her eyes, and if looks could kill, Hamish would have joined his brother in the blazing heat of hell's inferno at once.

'Calm myself?' she screamed. 'How in god's name do you expect me to calm myself after a bombshell of that magnitude has been dropped on my head?'

'Because, Margaret, if you don't, then we shall be quite unable to proceed, and that will be in no ones interest... least of all your own,' said Hamish, attempting a reassuring smile and placing an angled hand a little above the table close to where she sat and in a calming gesture that was unmistakable.

Margaret seated herself reluctantly and commenced fidgeting with the hem of her handkerchief; all the while staring at Colin Tooke with great intensity as the flow of blood gradually returned to her face once more.

'As I was saying,' rejoined the solicitor, once again, with a degree of frustration in his voice, much from the fevered interruption than from any disappointment his declaration may have caused.

'From now on,' he continued, with a cheery smile now settled on his face, 'Sir Hamish Kent will be able to assume the family title, and jointly with Jennifer Kent to receive all hereditary entitlement to the Hyde Hall estate, if he so desires. If, on the other hand, and if Sir Hamish so wishes, he may be sole owner of that which is rightfully his and therefore, in his turn, bequeath the estate to whomsoever he consider to be most worthy and capable in its administration after his demise. But Angus Kent had hoped that his beloved daughter, Jennifer Kent, would eventually inherit and in the interim period be in partnership with his brother and that she should receive suitable training in the administration of the said estate by him. If in partnership, then they both should receive incomes as Sir Hamish Kent deems appropriate.

'From my personal fortune I bequeath the sum of three million pounds to Jacob Kent, to be invested and controlled by Sir Hamish Kent as trustee, until he becomes of age. It is hoped that my blessings will rest upon him always, together with my undiminished love and good wishes.

'Bramble Bush Cottage I leave to my beloved Jane Howe

together with an income of ten thousand pounds per annum to be linked to that of the country's price index until such times as she should marry. She, I have loved in a particular way above all else and will continue so to do until we meet again.

'To Margaret Kent I leave an income of one thousand pounds per annum to be also linked to that of the country's price index. Her continued residence within the walls of Hyde Hall will most assuredly be at the discretion of my brother Sir Hamish Kent; but it is hoped that he will exercise sufficient goodwill to allow her residence there to be for the remainder of her days.

'Should she remarry, however, or take on a wifely role then she would most certainly forfeit all allowances made under this testament and be required to relinquish her home.

'The remainder of Angus Kent's personal wealth is bequeathed to Jennifer Kent, his daughter, for her to purposefully use and to increase in perpetuity for her lineage.'

A new unavoidable battle descended onto Margaret. The battle, which was now powerfully raging in her mind, caused her to engage a drooping posture with the weight of it all; the hunching of her narrow shoulders, which were usually so straight and well defined, affected her in such a way as to make her look, somewhat misshapen.

Suddenly she sat bolt upright once more as a look of complete amazement instantly covered her face; quite as if a bout of the dreaded, feverish ague had seized the whole of her body, thereby causing a shivering fit to take hold of her. All of this was unmistakably brought on by intense intimidation and humiliation - Angus' bequeathal to Jacob Kent, it would appear, had taken its time to sink in - and a bitter pill to swallow.

'And who, may I ask, is this Jacob Kent that is to receive such preferential treatment?' she asked, in feigned calmness as she rose from her seat once again; this time with the placing of her fingers outstretched and separated upon the table, and the transference of her weight to them was intended for added emphasis.

Jennifer was jarred into action by her mother's stance and so she also stood in defence of her child and in defiance of her mother, as a look of calm and tranquil assurance possessed her.

'Jacob is my son,' she exclaimed shamelessly, 'and therefore your grandchild: if you care to acknowledge him as such.'

'Oh I see it all now, an illegitimate heir to the Hyde Hall throne in the making is it? And that is putting it politely. And who may I ask is the father of this so called grandson of mine? Not you I hope Hamish!" she smiled a sinister smile before she carried on. 'No, no need to answer me now, I am sure everything will all come to light in the fullness of time and it will be all the sweeter to savour then; and, it will be at that time when I shall gain my satisfaction in the knowing of it all… and not at this moment.

'It is perfectly clear to me, from the look on your immoral face, that you haven't the remotest idea who the father could possibly be anyway, so I shall not labour the point now, only suffice it to say, you have obviously taken a leaf from your father's book… is that not so, Jennifer? Nothing ever changes, does it, my dear?'

Jenny looked away from her mother and re-seated herself. The moment she did she felt Jane's comforting hand seeking and finding hers; drawing it closely to herself as a reassuring response for Jenny's own caring.

'Well, Colin Tooke, this isn't the last you will hear of this little matter. I shall certainly contest the will as you will no doubt have been aware; in fact I shall be in touch with my own solicitor this afternoon. Oh, I quite forgot… you are my solicitor aren't you Mr Tooke? Well I shall now be dispensing with your services in favour of one who might show me more allegiance in the future; in the interim, I wish you all a most unpleasant afternoon.'

And with the mildly offensive statement leaving her mouth to be left dangling in mid air, a most disagreeable lady stormed out of the room.

After Margaret had abandoned the meeting, the small gathering was stunned into silence and for some considerable time at that; with a disagreeable feeling of clammy moistness attending each person; even though the window was still wide open.

Jenny did attempt to engage Jane Howe in some sort of womanly repartee but the inclination for wittiness on both their parts was somewhat constrained and so the quietness and sweatiness that had been in attendance throughout the meeting continued in its unpleasantness.

Feeling most encumbered inside, he being weighed down with the complexities of Angus Kent's instructions, Colin Tooke did what he could to smooth the fevered brows, as it were, by way of offering an apology to his visitors for the unseemly outcome of the meeting. His had been an arduous and loathsome task but as uttered later by Sir Hamish Kent to his niece:

'… I should say he carried out the responsibility of settling the estates interests with thoroughness and great fortitude; all the same, it will be interesting to see if he will be able to exercise the same determination when responding to your mother's official appeal.'

CHAPTER FOURTEEN

The rain-drenched street, alongside the Tooke Empire's offices, glistened continuously whilst oil stained patches reflected the rainbow's tints upon its darkened face.

The pouring rain had ceased in its attempt to flood the place completely, for all cloudiness had vanished and in its stead a turquoise blueness coloured the open sky; and the sun's brightest rays were being reflected from across the way by the glass covered openings of the assorted retail shops.

Jennifer Kent was first to leave the office block after the official meeting had drawn to a close; and so she waited in the foyer a good fifteen minutes before her uncle eventually caught up with her.

Casually slipping her arm through his, when he eventually arrived, she smiled kindly at the man she had complete confidence in and loving regard for.

They lingered and chatted awhile longer and then turned as one towards Jane Howe, who, in bringing up the rear, smiled in gratitude at their waiting.

'Jane, would you care to accompany us to our hotel, so that we might share dinner together?' asked Jenny, with compassionate concern encompassing the words of her invitation.

'That's very kind of you to offer, Jennifer,' replied Jane cheerfully, 'I should love to have dinner with the two of you.' Then, for the briefest of moments she further considered the words she had just spoken. "But maybe not at your hotel; that would, I fear, be pushing the bounds of hospitality a little too far, especially after the outcome of this afternoon's meeting.

'Why don't you both visit me at my cottage and allow me to prepare a tolerable dinner for you? I should love to cook for you both, particularly now that I am on my own. You see my sister, Rachael, returned to her home in Germany a couple of days ago and so your company would be much appreciated at the moment, and provide... a welcome break for me, especially as....'

Jane failed miserably in the completion of her sentence and the inflection in her voice compelled the others to direct their eyes towards her with expressions of understanding and compassion.

Jenny quickly glanced at her uncle for a positive response to the shared invitation and was delighted to have received it immediately - by the nod of his head.

'Thank you Jane,' replied Jenny, refreshing her smile, 'that would be lovely… we would both like that very much.'

And so it was settled.

Jenny and Sir Hamish Kent then walked off to the car park to collect their car and from there to the Derek Hotel to check in and freshen up, whilst Jane hurried away to her car, with the deflated tyre still on its wheel and the wheel still in the tiny car's tiny boot, and thence to Bramble Bush Cottage to prepare the tolerable meal she'd promised.

After Jenny and her uncle had taken care of all the personal attention the long day had caused and had dressed in a more appropriate style, they wandered down to the hotel's largish lounge where they treated themselves to an aperitif or two.

Still standing at the highly polished bar, with its tempting array of colourful bottles and the mirrored tiles behind them, Jenny turned to face her uncle with a cheerful smile warming her face.

'Although you may consider my congratulations to be unnecessary, Uncle, I shall offer them to you all the same, both on this afternoon's disclosure and in the manner by which you attempted to calm my mother?' The warm smile then deserted her as she extended her remarks. 'Actually I was surprised to learn of the appalling deceit grandfather used when he bequeathed the Hyde Hall Estate to my father, and, of course, the title that went with it.

'It can't have been easy for you, wondering what it was that compelled grandfather to make such an unfair decision as that: one that pushed you to one side in order to give preferential treatment to my father. Maybe something was said or done to annoy the old chap… I can have no idea. But it must have made you a mite suspicious by being excluded in that way all the same, and maybe filled you with a degree of disapproval at being ignored. But now, well, I am very pleased that you have finally received what is rightfully yours.'

Jenny's warm smile returned as she embraced her Uncle with the biggest hug his neck had received in a long time; despite the fact there were others in the room that looked on her behaviour with a certain amount of disdain: this hotel being that sort of place. But she treated the stares with the greatest contempt possible as she propelled her uncle to a small table in a more secluded corner of the room before she continued.

'Tell me Uncle, how long have you known about the deception; was it many years ago or was Mr Tooke's disclosure as big a surprise to you as it was to the rest of us?'

'On the second of our visits with your father, he called me

back to his bedside... just as we were leaving, if you remember, Jennifer.' Hamish began his answer with a certain amount of caution in his voice: in all probability due to the countless years of avoiding the subject. 'He at last, and without hesitation, confirmed everything that my mother had suspected all along. But because being ignored in that way had proved to be of little importance to me I instilled in your father's mind that it should be you who gained the legacy and not me.

'But your father seems to have gathered a great deal of wisdom over the years, which I never believed him to own; and so, in the end, he decided that both you and I should be involved in the running of this large estate. So yes, I was, indeed, quite shocked at that aspect of the declaration.

'But why he felt the need to include all of that in a testament of this nature in the first place, and in such a condescending way too, is quite beyond me.

'It would appear that my father had already told him I was older than he by at least ten minutes, so how could I possibly inherit something that already belonged to me? The answer to that one, my dear, will have to remain a mystery, I'm afraid.

'You know, Jennifer, the more I think about it the more I am convinced that my own father was to blame for your father's unpleasant attitude and the scheming way he went about his life.

'I realise one shouldn't speak ill of the dead, but you should know that my father was more than a little unjust in his approach to life and his attitude must have rubbed off onto my brother.

'Father was a dictatorial man as well, Jennifer, no, not just so far as his two sons were concerned, but the whole household as well... staff included. He much preferred to verbally bludgeon into submission everyone he came into contact with, including my mother. His overbearing ways in going about everything seemed to be of prime importance to him. He cared for no one, you see, and anyone who stood in his path would be pushed to one side with contempt.

'And the arrogant attitude he exercised at home where the family was so naively concerned, was quite unbelievable. He even made family decisions that were no concern of his; decisions that were my mother's and hers alone to make. In doing this he sought to belittle my mother at every occasion; thinking he'd cause her self-esteem to falter, no doubt. Of course, he wasn't at all successful in this, for she remained resolute to the end.

'As you most probably will have realised by now, Jennifer, my mother was a prosperous lady in her own right, which was how I was able to purchase the Brenton Estate after her demise. You see, as father left the Hyde Hall Estate, yes, everything to your father, so did my mother leave all her wealth to me; and looking back it was more than likely to have been in keeping with sweet revenge than anything else.

'My mother and her two siblings had shared the inheritance of vast Scottish lands from their father; lands of great value I might add; however, she sold her portion of the legacy soon after she married father. Don't ask me why she did such a thing... I can have no idea; it is unlikely she divulged her motives to anyone, least of all to me; but I suspect it was to prevent my father's interference in matters that would have been private to her.

'But she invested her capital wisely and at the end of her days she proved to be a very wealthy lady indeed.

'Mother's wealth, always needled my father, and whenever there were difficulties between them; and there were many such occasions, believe you me, this contentious subject would almost always be brought to the surface.

'You see theirs wasn't the happiest of unions... no doubt Janet would choose to tell you differently; but my mother, with her subservient attitude to life, always surrendered to my father's opinions in order to keep the peace and she made it appear that we all lived in perfect harmony and bliss with one another.

'Anyway, that aside, your father has done a great job with the estate since it has been in his keeping and we should be eternally grateful to him for that. What with the release of more acreage to the tenant farmers and the increase of the dairy herd, which, to my way of thinking is always less of a gamble than arable farming and not forgetting, of course, the newly established modern dairy; that alone must have increased the company's profitability enormously. So yes, all in all, he has done remarkably well.

'Needless to say, had I been kept up to date with the estate's progress at all times I would have known all of this; but, as relations between your father and me had become so strained over the years I had no way of knowing how well the old place was doing.

'Colin Tooke, after he had performed his duty so eloquently this afternoon, kindly took me to one side and informed me of all the improvements that your father had so successfully accomplished at Hyde Farm. That was why I was a little late in following you down.

'But I can assure you, Jennifer, my involvement in the routine running of things at the Hyde Estate will be kept to a minimum; don't forget I have the Brenton farm to contend with as well.

'And so, for this reason alone I propose we employ an experienced estate manager to serve in a temporary capacity to help and advise you when I am not on hand. That way nothing should go amiss in the farm's day to day management and with everything being kept in line with the plans we make together. How does that sound to you my dear? Do you think you might consent to that idea?' Jenny nodded thoughtfully, as Hamish carried on in the same confident tone.

'Oh, I know that you mentioned your abhorrence at the thought of living at Hyde Hall again, especially with your mother still being there to exasperate you at every turn, as she most assuredly will do; but I am sure you are more than a match for her now, Jennifer. And as Jacob grows he will also be there to give you any moral support you may need.

'As far as Margaret contesting the will is concerned, you can forget it; the estate was never really your fathers to give away in the first place so the only claim she'd be able to make would be upon your father's personal account. The small annuity he has allowed her will come from these funds you see; the residue of which he has left to you... which I found to be most gratifying.

'I think it would be advisable for you to keep this separate from your own private account as the need to make monthly payments for both your mother and Jane Howe will have to come from these monies and not from your own account or from the Hyde Hall business coffers either; anyway I'm sure Mr Tooke will arrange all that for you.'

For all of this time Jenny had nodded attentively and smiled agreeably, *"there could never be anything in this man's exchange of words or action of deeds that could bear him blame or reproach,"* she thought.

'I know I was rather reluctant to even consider a move back to Dorset when we were in Brenton; but as the instructions from my father appear to be so decisive, with everything being determined for me... well, more or less... I intend going along with it.'

'But nothing is set in stone you know, Jennifer. If you decide you want out completely or to play only a minimal role yourself, then so be it my dear, the choice will always be yours.'

'No, I should hate to let both you and father down. I'm sure everything will go smoothly once I'm settled in the old place once again; and who knows, it could be fun bandying words with my mother from time to time, and it will help me to become more self-sufficient... if nothing else.

'Talking of mother, I was rather ashamed of the way she handled herself this afternoon. I'm sure her zany display failed to do her cause much good... not to my way of thinking, anyway. I mean to say, all her hostility turned out to be rather embarrassing in the end... and made her look contemptible and quite small.

'I don't know why I'm so surprised at her manner, but I am; how fortunate for her that you were on hand to help control her tongue; she would be raving still if you hadn't calmed her.

'Having said that, I do see her point of view... to a certain extent anyway... and, I feel sorry for her as well. After all, she has now lost everything she had been used to over the years.'

'Ah yes, that was a little unfortunate, wasn't it?' returned her uncle, with a sympathetic smile lighting his face. After a slight pause he added: 'but if you think about it, she hasn't lost a thing, not really. She will still be living where she has lived since the day she was married; she'll still have her meals provided for her and still be able to enjoy all the incidental benefits she took pleasure in before your father's death; like the horses, the stables and access to the lands, together with all of the other social activities she indulged in.

'And her income isn't really that dire, not by today's standards and it will keep pace with the cost of living so don't look upon the matter with too much despondency, Jennifer... she'll be just fine.

'I don't know about you but I have no idea as to your mother's upbringing,' he continued, more pensively. 'Sarah Wood's brother, that's Margaret's father and your maternal grandfather, was head of a boy's grammar school in or near Oxford, in his latter days... or so I believe; and so I should have thought him to have been a firm disciplinarian all those years ago.

'If so, perhaps his attitude regarding other people rubbed off onto your mother; like yourself, she had no siblings to take any of the fiery wraths flying about the place at the time... so she probably took the full brunt of it herself.'

'Yes you're probably right uncle; but really I have no idea either, at least no idea at all about her family history.

'You see, mother never confided to me anything regarding her childhood, even to the extent of never mentioning her father or her mother by name. Perhaps they both died before I was born, I really have no idea.

'It wasn't until Great-Aunt Sarah turned up so unexpectedly all those years ago that I was aware my mother's father even possessed a younger sister. What a shock that was!

'Still I'm glad to have known my Great-Aunt Sarah, although she too was a bit of a tyrant to start with and it wasn't until we both went to live in Brenton that she became more relaxed and allowed the trueness of her beautiful character to shine through.

'She has played a major role in the development of my life, you know that don't you Uncle, and in a most purposeful and affectionate way; and she was the kindest of tutors any child could wished to have. I do miss her so very much,' said Jenny, as her eyes sparkled with a dewiness that was closely observed by her uncle.

'Yes, Jennifer, I miss her too, as I am sure does Janet and Jacob but I am equally certain that your aunt would not like for us to sit here right now getting all sentimental over her,' said Sir Hamish, glancing at his watch.

'I phoned for a taxi to collect us just before we came down, thinking I wouldn't subject my motor to the unutterable torture from that appalling lane any more. It most certainly should have been here by now. Only hope that the puncturing of tyres isn't contagious in Dorset otherwise we could miss out on tonight's special treat.

'Jennifer, I do hope you won't mind me asking, but are you sure you are up to this evening's arrangement; without your feeling too embarrassed, I mean; only it's being provided by your father's ex-mistress you know, and at the place where their most personal meetings always took place?'

Jenny's face reddened and she took a little time to consider the question. At the end of the pause she made her reply.

'Uncle, I consider Jane to be a very lovely lady and I can quite easily see the magnetism my father found in her.

'When I eventually return to Hyde Hall I shall be glad of all the friends I can find and I sincerely hope that Jane will be one of them - if only to exchange notes on my father's life I suppose; and of course some sort of guidance with Dorset's local supermarkets, which seem to be springing up all over the place these days.'

Her uncle smiled kindly and together they walked through the foyer's revolving doorway and into the fresh evening air and to claim the now awaiting Taxi that would take them to dinner

***

Sadly, Jane had indulged her passion for the amber liquor prior to her guest's arrival; that much was obvious to them both as soon as they entered the cottage, but it failed to have any effect on the dinner turning out to be the strange affair it did. Not meaning by that statement that the food was in any way unpleasant or muddled, with custard being served in the soup bowls or gravy being poured over the apple tart, no, the meal was perfectly acceptable, despite the hostess being ever so slightly tipsy.

But the after dinner conversation; now that was a little weird. It lacked all the sophistication necessary for polite discussion and was considered to be one-sided in the extreme.

Jane insisted on talking incessantly, and in needless detail about the affection she held for her lover. Jenny found this to be unnecessary, and quite as embarrassing as her uncle had earlier predicted; for both Jenny and Hamish had observed the affection the couple shared in the past - if not in fact, but certainly by the implications provided by both lovers during earlier conversations.

Jenny considered the usual after dinner chat to be insulting to her own principles as well; particularly at this present time when the death of Angus Kent was still fresh in the minds of everyone concerned.

An avid love affair, being described in such an intimate way and to two almost complete strangers, was tantamount to admitting and glorifying adultery; which, after thinking about it, that was indeed what Jane was doing. But it had never been referred to as such, not in so many words, and certainly not by Jenny or her uncle. Okay, Margaret had openly made such accusations and with some force, she not being at all backward in the pronouncement of such condemnations.

But, being dubbed a harlot, a promiscuous trollop or being labelled any other such name by Margaret, was one thing, but accusing oneself of breaking one of the Lord's sacred commandments, especially the seventh, well, that was quite different. And not only that, Jane was also bragging about the support and encouragement she had given her lover regarding his infidelity to his wife - which infuriated Jenny to the extreme.

The admission of guilt that Jane was taking great pleasure in claiming for herself was a solo performance, so far as Jenny could make out. And going to the great lengths she did in failing to lay any blame on Angus in a culpable way, seemed absurd; especially when one assume it to have been he who started the affair in the first place.

Jenny also felt uneasy that she was unable to see a hint of remorse anywhere - not without there being a high degree of self-acclaim being present, anyhow.

This, it seemed to Jennifer, was Jane's very own recital, one in which she alone was to take centre stage. The entire ovation - every single handclap - she would claim for herself - and wasn't she enjoying it.

It looked as if Jane was assuming, rightly or wrongly, that all her sins would evaporate if she owned up to them or went on about them long enough.

It was most strange, but it now appeared that Jane actually believed that the more blame she could be seen to carry the greater the benefit she would derive; that, by claiming all heights of impropriety for herself, so that no one else could share the blame, was the best way forward for her. She considered that by doing this, everyone would then focus their sympathy solely on her; that way she would no longer be considered the immoral woman she believed herself to be. If her innocence was to be brought about, then all liability for the sins she had committed must be truly hers - and hers alone - it was a must.

Nevertheless, Jenny weighed up the matter quietly to herself, while her hostess droned on continuously.

As a result of this weighing up, Jenny decided that it might be somewhat unkind, mean spirited even, to attempt to curtail Jane's wanderings simply to prevent Jane's reputation from condemning her. In other words, Jenny considered Jane should be allowed to carry on to her hearts content and immerse herself in the emotion of it all in order to free her mind from the dreadful grief she was facing.

After clearing all undesirable opinions completely from her own mind, Jenny sited in their place positive thoughts to encourage her host to clear her brain of all those awful feelings; anything and everything Jane had horded over the months and years which had been the cause of so much anguish must now be eradicated from her mind - and be held at bay for as long as possible.

But how that might be accomplished Jenny had no way of knowing; maybe when she got to know Jane a little better she might suggest she obtain some sort of psychiatric advise.

That aside, Jenny observed that Jane had not, thus far, placed any blame at Margaret's feet for driving Angus away from the marital home and into the open arms of another woman in the first place. No, this feature of her mother's role in all of this had been purged by Jane and so Margaret had escaped the whole affair squeaky clean; an aspect which Jenny found to be astonishing but heart-warming all the same.

"To be fair, the greater number of people in Jane's position would have willingly searched for such excuses for their immoral

*behaviour and directed them most vigorously at any unsuspecting
candidate. So why hadn't Jane done this? Probably due to too much
alcohol being imbibed before we arrived I expect... either that or
there is more moral fibre in this woman's character than she is
willing to lay claim to... some sort of religious belief maybe, which
will probably come to light at some future time, possibly after I get to
know her better,"* thought Jenny.

***

After she had settled herself and had shelved her guilt hang-up in a
more favourable way, Jane went on to describe in detail the moments
of her first meeting with Angus.

It would appear that the couple first met at a June function
which had been organised on behalf of some obscure charitable trust.
The social get-together was held in some small village on the south
Wiltshire border by a mutual friend, a score or so years ago.

Apparently the house and grounds, where the event was
being held, were very prestigious, with sweeping lawns leading
down to a listless river which marked the southern boundary of the
gardens. And floating upon this almost stagnant water, two skiffs
were seen to be available to anyone daring such an adventure. But as
there were no takers for the quest, the skiffs remained at their
mooring in total stillness.

The social gathering was rumoured to have been an all
married couples affair, so obviously it should have been only those
entwined in wedded bliss that were to have been invited and
therefore attending.

It was thought that someone, probably a friend of the host
who had known both parties, possessed a roguish sense of humour
and had deliberately suggested inviting Jane and Sir Angus Kent
along just to see what the outcome might be; for they were the only
singles there.

They were eventually introduced to one another simply as
Angus and Jane - no other names were called or asked for. This
introduction was briefly performed by a certain mutual friend,
probably the host, who proposed they connect with each other as
temporary partners for the evening - as a result of this 'joining
together' the numbers would then be made even, so to speak.

Sir Angus hadn't minded the minor mischievous
wrongdoing in the slightest, he considering it to have been great fun
to have been taken advantage of in this fashion, especially as Jane

was so attractive.

Jane, on the other hand, had felt differently. She had considered it to have been a foolish ploy on the host's part. For to deliberately bring two people together in this way, especially when they had no knowledge of one another, was a strange undertaking and might easily be construed as being decidedly harmful.

But that wasn't the only feature Jane thought most strange; for almost all of the guests appeared to be acquaintances of her so called partner, right down to the waiters and waitresses that flitted about the place; all of whom seemed to hold this man in the highest regard, while she knew no one except the host.

As a result of this, Jane gave way to the notion that she had aligned herself to an extremely popular and stylish gentleman, indeed; and one with whom she ought to have felt privileged at being so acquainted.

So here they both were - two strangers thrust together in a situation, not of their making, but a situation all the same which would most probably culminate in some seedy love affair - which they would both live to regret, given the fullness of time.

But then, that was the whole idea in the first place wasn't it - to sow the seeds of lustful discontent then sit back and watch the situation develop. And as cupid's arrows flew about the place they hoped, of course, that a few would eventually hit their target and by so doing partially destroy the lives of two unsuspecting people... such bliss!

From the beginning, they revelled in each others company immensely as they dreamily listened to the tiny orchestra playing some minor classical pieces in the warmth of this particular summer evening. And as they conversed with one another, with barely a moment's pause interrupting their flow of words, each set of eyes hardly strayed from the others....

Of course they sipped a drink or two just to ease the casual conversation along, but the drink or two they sipped only served to grease the tongue rather than prove a detriment to the brain.

The annoying home grown midge's interest were quite continuous and in plentiful supply as they hovered above the lawns of this particular country house at this particular time of evening. But they failed to be overly bothersome - not to this exclusive couple who all but failed to recognise their existence for the whole of that romantic evening.

After the twosome had savoured a few crumbs of the offered refreshments and after they had indulged in idle chit chat with one another, they had taken great pleasure in dancing together; and for some considerable time at that - continuously in fact - right up to the evening's revelry was announced to be drawing to a close; which was brought about much too soon as far as the two of them was concerned.

During the whole of the evening's festivities, Jane, had apparently, received no admission from Angus that he was a man of some distinction, a married man at that, with a wife and a small child at home; or that the wife in question had a fondness for her own society to the exclusion of all others, including that of her husband and daughter. No, that had not been mentioned - none of it - not then - that was to come later - three weeks later to be precise.

They had reluctantly disentangled themselves - the one from the other and went their separate ways after the party had ended, with nothing else untoward going on and nothing else untoward being exchanged between them - nothing worth a mention that is - except maybe the electrifying glances that lingered - particularly when the time for parting came; and so they left one another quietly - but thoughtfully.

Nevertheless, there is one other feature worth a mention at this particular juncture; it was revealed later that something had been sadly overlooked. Even though each had desired to see the other again, the couple had neglected to swap personal information including surnames, private telephone numbers and the like and so a dilemma now existed that was not easily overcome.

In the interim period, that is the immediate period that existed after their first rendezvous and before they accidentally met in town a week or so later, the two of them had each ceased to think of the other for the whole of that time and both had endured the never ending sleepless nights and the all too frequent moments of regret at not exchanging their essentials, for neither of them knew how a reconnection between them might be brought about - not in a confidential way, anyhow.

Of course Jane might easily have applied to the evening's host for the express identification of her temporary partner the following day, but not wishing to appear desperate in her need for male companionship, she hesitated. And Sir Angus too, he also hesitated, but for other reasons, far too obvious to state here.

Unbeknown to them, however, the dilemma was soon to be resolved. For three weeks after the Wiltshire soirée had taken place, and with deep purple rings decorating the cheeks beneath her beautiful eyes, Jane had journeyed into town on the pretext of buying a frivolous something or other for her self-indulgence or more importantly, to perk up her lonely day in order to promote her own happiness. But in reality it was to occupy, what would otherwise have been, a most boring Saturday afternoon when the only thing she wanted was to be with him....

She was approached by Angus as she came out of, what proved to be, a most expensive store. Angus had offered to carry the impressive shopping bag that Jane was holding and at the same time he asked her to re-enter the prestigious store once again so they might share tea together.

'We had such a wonderful time, him and I, just doing things that normal people do; with dear Angus, having left his wallet at home... requesting me to pay the bill,' said Jane, smiling as her mind floated back to that Saturday afternoon in pleasured reminiscence.

'At long last we exchanged surnames and very stupidly I gave him my telephone number... upon his insistence, of course... just in case he should find the need to call me anytime, which he assured me he would; and then he spoiled the whole of the afternoon by telling me more about himself.

'It's strange isn't it, when someone is about to tell you something how you, in some way, already know what it is they are about to say? That's how it was with me. He told me of his position, his unhappy union with Margaret and how he couldn't escape any of it.

'... Being devoid of excuses for a divorce on the grounds of embarrassment to his standing....'

'That was how he put it. A little pompous I remember thinking at the time. But I somehow knew all about him... that he was married already... everything; even before he'd opened his mouth to tell me... I did. After all, how could a man as lovely as he not be married?

'I told him immediately that I would not be seeing him again and that my religion strictly forbade me to associate with a married man: me being a dedicated Catholic at the time; but the magnetism... it was far too strong for me, and so after his countless telephone calls I eventually gave way to his persistence and we saw one another again... and again....

'What a fool I was to have given him my number that afternoon, what a complete and utter fool. He would still have been alive today if I'd had sufficient insight and saw what would happen if we got together. I should have known that no good could possibly have come out of a relationship like that.

'Of course, I had spoken to my priest for guidance and was plainly told of the Bible's protestation at such a relationship. But I paid no heed to the warning; I knew immediately I asked the question I would disregard the answer. He was the man I loved, you see, and would forever love. So now I must pay the price for my sins by living the rest of my life in utter loneliness.'

"For loneliness is oft a mournful place in which to be ensnared. It is a place where a torn in sunder heart seeks tender healing refuge, 'till long lost love is eventually restored forever; but for the while, in that warming solitude, be soothed from heartfelt sorrow."

CHAPTER FIFTEEN

Upon their return to Lincolnshire, Jenny made all haste in the necessary arrangements concerning her move back to Dorset. In so doing, she had busied herself with the sorting of her collection of clutter that most ladies of her age and temperament horde over a period of twelve of the most fleeting years imaginable, and was satisfied with the outcome.

On the Saturday morning following her return, Jenny was up bright and early and making her way to the local village store fully focused on an errand for Janet. Although a stretch of dark clouds hovered above the far horizon, she was not at all put off by the prospects of a casual shower or two, even though she wasn't dressed for such an occurrence.

Jenny had always felt it her duty, her pleasure even, to oblige the aging housekeeper with an errand such as this - whenever the need arose. Occasionally it was to pick up some unforeseen supplies the cook had run short of, if the need was urgent; although more often than not a phone call would have seen the delivery made within the hour. Nevertheless, as the store's trade bike was temporarily out of action on this particular day, a visit would have to be made instead.

And so, Jenny was using a sprightly step in her stride to make the mile seem shorter and all the more pleasing. A truly cheerful mood also attended her heart as she walked the distance and she listened to the warble of a blackbird calling from its perch on the tall wall that encompassed the far side of the Old House gardens as she passed and which added to the cheer she already felt inside.

All at once Jenny decided to put an extra spring in her step, coupled with a lengthier, loopier sort of stride which she considered would be of benefit to her fitness. She also had it in mind to skip along the road as she had as a child skipped the mile, so extreme was this light hearted feeling that existed within her; but deciding she was a little past such energies at her age, she continued with her lengthened stride instead.

It was during this particular visit to this particular provider of provisions that the heavens opened and a sudden deluge was heard reverberating throughout the store's shelf-lined, shelf-packed walls. It rattled with some intensity upon its corrugated roof as well and in such a way as to fill everyone inside with a good deal of apprehension.

One or two curious customers ceased cramming their baskets at once in order to glance out of the glass fronted doorway to establish the intensity of the deluge and then they returned to their basket filling exercise as soon as their fascination had been satisfied.

The jamming in the mechanism of the only till open in the store that day, caused a further delay; for it was more than a few minutes before the manager was summoned to attend to the fault: although the checkout lady had been tinkering with the wretched thing for all that time.

When at last he arrived he seemed a little baffled over the adjustment he was supposed to be making; he being unsure which knob to press or pull in order to correct the fault. All of this tampering about only added further delay which caused a great deal irritation to many of the customers who were carping needlessly to one another about the unnecessary waiting.

Not so Jenny it seems. For in view of the fact she had walked to the shop this morning, quite unprepared for rain, she was content to outwit the storm by taking advantage of the place as a providential shelter. She knew full well she had time on her hands anyway, so there was no need for her to hasten her departure in the slightest.

A further ten minutes saw all business transactions completed with Jenny feeling delighted with the extra purchases she had made.

Then, as she emerged from this particular store the rain exerted itself yet again, not completely 'tis true but enough to cause discomfort in the dribbling of the wet stuff down the backs of necks of anyone so ill-advised to take the risk.

Jenny was not suitably attired to deal with rain of any intensity, as afore mentioned, and so she took shelter beneath the shop's canopy until this added shower had passed.

While she willingly waited, Jenny exchanged a few optimistic words with a couple of passers-by, who, like her, had found themselves in a state of unpreparedness for the rain's unexpected deluge. Not unlike her, they too had decided to gain a little shelter for themselves until the skies had cleared.

Cheery chatter occupied a good few minutes of their time and as they were so humorously engaged the rain eventually slowed down until only a few intermittent droplets were felt before it stopped completely.

Taking her leave of the two ladies in a jolly sort of way, Jenny started off on her short stroll back to The Old House again with an absence of determination in her step this time but with the added hindrance of one bag of shopping in her hand - filled to capacity.

As she walked along she allowed her mind, almost inattentively it seems, to drift awhile over years that had brought her so much happiness in this friendly village.

She continued the mile with a degree of breeziness still overflowing her mind, and allowed a melodic air to repeat itself within her head - over and over it went, somewhat drearily at first for there was no release from it, and then she allowed the simple tune to escape her mouth; the melody and the words together. All at once the simple song became almost tolerable though very soon she missed a note or two and it was then that the tune became somewhat discordant in a strange sort of way; for whatever else she may have been, Jenny was plainly no Maria Callas.

Jenny had walked two hundred yards - no more, when suddenly she felt a clammy hand fingering the top of her bare arm.

The offensive touch, which brought her to an immediate halt, filled her with an instant degree of alarm and a feeling of repulsion swept over her, causing her an involuntary shudder. She turned in an instant to see who was helping themselves to a modicum of intimacy at her expense.

Jenny's heart sank as she saw the form of the insufferable Barnabas Bell standing before her with a sickly grin on his face that distorted its features beyond reason.

The licentiousness about this man was as intense now as it had ever been - more so even, though he tried to hide his lustfulness behind the stated sickly grin. And as the piercing gaze from Bell's right eye pored over Jenny's figure from the top of her head to her knees, so too his peculiar left eye wandered to the outer perimeter of its own socket and rested there awhile before it was stilled completely.

Unlike Jenny, Barnabas Bell had not grown at all in height since they'd last met over eight years ago, as the top of his head was seen to barely reach the crest of Jenny's shoulder. The width of his frame had scarcely altered with the passing of the years either, although his hollow chest had become more pronounced.

'Why Mr Bell, how nice to see you again,' lied Jenny, as an awkward smile that might easily have been mistaken for a look of utter disgust crossed her silken face. 'We haven't met for some considerable time, have we? Where have you been hiding yourself for all that while?'

The instant Jenny's words, no matter how insincere they

may have been intended, reached the ears of the heinous creature standing before her, the unruly left eye, belonging that of Barnabas Bell, shot into action by performing its usual routine - just the once though, and then it ceased its performance almost as suddenly as it had started.

'Hello to you as well Miss Kent. I do hope I do see you are well,' his words were slightly jumbled. 'Oh, I've been living down in the southern counties for all that time,' said he, regaining his nerve. And with a devious smirk that matched perfectly the rest of the man's hideous appearance - he gloated. 'Got myself a job as a waiter in sunny Bournemouth... I have... a nice little number it is too; and the hotel I work for is posh and all; although the money ain't up to much and not at all what I deserve. But still, that is more than made up for by the tips I get: me being such a kind and obliging sort of fellow, as you may well recall from when we first set eyes on each other, all them years ago.'

Jenny was taken aback by this astonishing piece of intelligence, for never in a million years would she have expected such a revelation. But she managed to conceal her surprise with elegant ease and betrayed not a single indication of fear for the hideous creature to latch onto.

'That is indeed good news, Mr Bell,' said she, followed by a slight pause. 'How long have you been living in Hampshire?' She asked the question without appearing to focus too much interest on the subject but all the time her mind was infuriated by this bizarre coincidence; and she wondered how much of it might be attributed to an unexpected piece of information that had been passed to him regarding her own connections with the county, which, bordered that of her own.

Of course, Jenny had no way of knowing that a family of wandering gipsies had stimulated his curiosity with some innocent word or other, thereby allowing him to be privy to their plans. This, in some strange way, may have encouraged a feeling of revenge to occupy his twisted mind, who knows? But sooner or later Jenny would end up at her former location, he had been sure of that and it was there that the gypsies had been headed. His calculating mind had plotted well ahead and all because he had already witnessed the close relations that existed 'twixt her and the gypsies?

All at once Jenny recalled the last words that Bell had offered on the day she had buried her dear aunt, the day when he had frighteningly threatened to undertake recompense in kind for all the harm she was adjudged to have caused him.

She had hoped Bell had put all those silly notions behind him by this time, but he being the kind of evil person she had always considered him to be - she knew, deep down, he hadn't.

And so she was sure that plans for reprisal would still be uppermost in his tardy mind and she wondered how far those plans had progressed.

Jenny had certainly conceded that Bell's schemes would be a good deal further evolved than anyone might imagine. Meaning, that even if he was capable of carrying out any devious plans - he would certainly not admit them to anyone - maybe not even to himself - for they would all be unconsciously formed in his wicked mind. She was also sure Bell would not have the ability to purposefully create evil anyway: it would be second nature to him - surely.

How wrong she was!

But she resisted the urge to press the loathsome creature for any further details of his expedition to Hampshire, she knowing that his own insecure tongue would eventually provide the answers she sought - which of course it did.

'Oh, I drifted down that way a few months after we last met; when you were coming away from the old churchyard that day, if you cast your mind back a bit; you know, after you had been burying that overgenerous old aunt of yours... you may well remember the time,' he answered; and his grin increased in width at his own contempt. 'Of course, I've been back and forth a couple of times since then; just to visit my dear old mother who had grown so poorly over the years; but as she passed away just last week, I won't be coming back here quite so often - not now - not unless... I've got something special to come back for... if you get my meaning.' The convulsive left eye commenced its movements again as the words left his drooling mouth and the fingers at the end of his sweaty palms became extended then moved apart and quivered with excitement as he concluded the insinuation in his sentence.

Jenny was not at all impressed with the innuendo and was immediately jarred into moving things speedily along.

'Well I'm sorry to hear about your mother Mr Bell and I do wish you well and hope you have a safe journey back to your home in Bournemouth,' said she, again with faked sincerity in her voice, as she hurried herself away from the situation to continue her walk back to the Old House by a dozen steps or so.

All at once she stopped and listened to his chilling voice as it followed her up the road.

'Oh I don't live in Bournemouth Miss Kent,' he called out to her, with his obnoxious head raised high in the air to gain more directional and far reaching power to his voice and more effect to be felt from his mocking words as well. 'Oh dear me no, Miss Kent,' then with minor undertones to his voice he added, 'I take it that you *are* still Miss Kent, as I don't see no ring on your finger that might tell me different.'

A longish pause followed, which allowed his remarks to sink in, before he considered how next he might intimidate his prey. 'No, I only said I worked in Bournemouth... not that I lived there.'

Then more loudly still so that his victim might gain the full impact of his words, 'you see, I live in a pretty little village in Dorset that sits close to Bournemouth; a quaint little place it is as well... called Hyde, Miss Kent...' Another short pause punctuated his sentence which allowed for further emphasis.

'I bike to work every day from there you see. It's a fair old distance, Miss Kent, I can tell you that, but I manages it alright, and it keeps me fit and my legs strong, what with the exercise of it all; see here,' said he, as he extended his right leg; and by placing his two open hands around his thigh he illustrated the compactness of his minuscule muscles; at the same time his hateful grin hung around his face a while longer, hoping his words would eventually achieve their intended effect.

All of a sudden, Jenny experienced a condition of extreme lividity, causing her to feel somewhat dizzy, and a bout of faintness began to overtake her at the sound of the information being called out so pointedly.

And so she turned round again in a state of shock and took ten or so weak paces back to her intimidator. And as she furtively battled to maintain her own bodily balance a bout of paranoia began to dominate her mind.

"This is more than a coincidence," she told herself. *"Coincidences like this just do not happen... not ever. He must know all about me, where I am about to live, about my father and his death, about my mother, about Hyde Hall... about everything. It is so obvious. He has deliberately situated himself where I am going to live in order to torment me... or something much worse.*

"He is fully intent on turning up when I expect him least... ever present as he has always been... and with me looking over my shoulder all of the time... and for the rest of my life too. Whatever shall I to do? Don't deny it... face up to him... call his bluff and brave it out!" she thought, as she pulled herself together. *"For goodness sake... don't allow him to see your fear."*

'What a coincidence Mr Bell, you seem to have pre-empted my relocation precisely; but then, you knew that all along didn't you? You know exactly where my home is to be, don't you? What a cleaver little Ding Dong you really are Mr Bell,' she said, her voice displaying all the shameless nerve and boldness her usually unassuming temperament would not normally allow.

'Well, let's hope you behave yourself a whole lot better than you did when you were employed by my uncle, otherwise you won't find me to be the frail, timid little girl you readily abused over ten years ago.'

Barnabas Bell's smug grin was wider and scarier now than it had been before; and so, setting aside any disparaging response he may have considered using he totally disregarded the deliberate accusation Jenny had made.

Instead he ferreted about in his trouser pockets as if his hands were in need of some distraction of their own and so they sought some alternative amusement to occupy their time.

'Now ain't that a coincidence Miss Kent? It surely is the greatest coincidence ever,' he returned, as his hideous smile further perverted itself with the contemptuous remarks.

'Don't tell me you are going to live close by me after all... now ain't that nice. Who would have thought it; that take some beating, it surely do,' he further added, as he removed his hands from his pockets and exercised them by lightly rubbing them together in front of his hollow chest.

'So, you and me are going to be near neighbours once again are we... in spite of everything, eh?' he said, as immeasurable amusement accompanying the dubious question issued from his face and with all the awaited eagerness of a winner of the football pools who had just learned of his good fortune.

Jenny, after completely ignoring the contemptible ignoramus, walked hastily away.

***

Sir Hamish Kent was bent over a table in the drawing room, sorting papers and moving them from one pile to another as if searching for some special document of great importance, when Jenny walked in seemingly filled with despair. He straightened up immediately and turned round at almost the same time and appeared surprised by his niece's attendance; and the pale complexion that tainted Jenny's face, at the moment, disturbed him immensely - causing him to become horrified.

'Jennifer!' he exclaimed. 'Whatever is the matter? You look as if you've seen some ghostly apparition, or something equally disturbing.'

He walked over to her and took her two hands in his with utmost parental concern; as he always did when his soothing comfort was needed by his lovely niece; and with the gentlest of smiles, he offered her his full attention.

'I have just this minute received a most devastating shock uncle,' said Jenny, her brown eyes wide with exasperation. 'You will, no doubt, remember that obnoxious man, Barnabas Bell, who caused me so much trouble soon after Aunt Sarah's funeral and who used to be in your service until he was dismissed by Janet, well he has made his presence felt once again and in the most threatening way imaginable.

'He stopped me as I was returning from the village store a few minutes ago and informed me that he had moved to Hyde eight years ago and he has found himself employment at a hotel in Bournemouth. It is quite obvious to me that his move to the south has been quite deliberate and that he fully intends to continue with his persistent pestering and harassment. What on earth am I to do about the man Uncle? Wait until he recommences his obscenities or have the law on him straight away?'

Clearly, Jenny was in a state of deep distress by what she considered to be a very worrying dialogue, and she looked helplessly weak as she claimed a nearby chair and buried her face in her hands for a brief moment of relief.

She was totally confused with what she imagined were the prospects that lay ahead of her and appeared unable to deal with the situation in a rational manner.

'If I understand you correctly Jennifer, this man has been living down in Dorset for the past eight years; then surely his moving there can only be regarded as an unfortunate coincidence. After all, the man is at liberty to live wherever he decides to live - or at the very least find a liking to live... within the whole of the UK if he so desire; presumably where he can find employment, I should have thought.

'It can't be easy these days, not for a fellow with such a limited potential as his, for he doesn't seem to be the brightest of people does he?' said Sir Hamish, his countenance alight with reasonableness as he spoke. 'So one shouldn't place too much emphases on the matter my dear,' he continued evenly. 'Please, try to stay calm and not overreact by the few words he undoubtedly wished to provoke you with; I'm sure the whole event is quite harmless, Jennifer, and the man Bell, well, quite innocent of all charges you seem to have set against him.

'I'm not saying that he hasn't made a few discreet inquiries since he has been there; that would indeed be quite natural coming from a man with even the smallest degree of inquisitiveness; which undoubtedly, must have got the better of him. And as our name, not being an everyday sort of name, well, it must have cropped up in conversation from time to time, especially since the recent death of your father: that by itself will have been a prime subject for discussion. And so, it would not be unreasonable for him to couple the Lincolnshire Kents with this newly found species in Dorset. And as I have just said, in all probability he will have made some discreet inquiries merely to satisfy his own curiosity. But that is where the matter must surely end, my dear, don't you think?'

Jenny wasn't at all sure that her uncle had fully grasped the implications or the severity of the situation or indeed the awful repercussions that might arise in the future should her suspicions become an established fact.

When someone of Bell's devious capabilities live so close to the home of someone he despises and when the bitterness he undoubtedly feels for her is activated in his mind, well, anything could happen.

Although Barnabas Bell had failed to mention the matter of his dismissal from The Old House, Jenny felt sure that for all this time the hateful man still harboured a grudge in his minuscule mind and would be truly delighted to launch some sort of reprisal against her, her family, or both, no matter how long it took him and no matter what lengths he might have to go to achieve it; for hadn't he mentioned retribution in kind on their previous encounter - whatever that may mean.

Jenny now emphasised all her fears to her uncle, embellishing them openly with all the exaggerated details her imagination could summon up.

'Oh, dear me!' exclaimed her uncle, with a smile of perplexity now replacing the one of wisdom. 'You do seem to have it in for poor Mr Bell, Jennifer. And you also appear to be harbouring distaste for this man in the extreme, which is so unlike you. Is he really as bad as the picture you are painting, Jennifer? Or is this an obsessive disorder you have suddenly built up in your mind?' He laughed a little at his own questioning. 'Oh, I don't doubt your sincerity in your claims, my dear, and I didn't mean to dismiss any thorny ideas you may have regarding his history and what you may imagine or consider him capable of performing in the future. But really, we have to take all that lies ahead as it befalls us and not go anticipating problems before they arise.'

Jenny was very disappointed at the level of support she was getting from her uncle and was clearly relieved when her son entered the room apparently looking for his Great Uncle Hamish to solve a particular problem he had uncovered in a particular project the two had been working on over the past month or so.

'Don't worry Jennifer;' said Sir Hamish, as he fondly touched her arm before following in the wake of Jacob, 'you really have nothing to worry about my dear, I'm quite certain of that.'

Jenny returned his smile reluctantly and waited a discreet moment before walking outside seeking Janet Nunn who she felt sure would offer her all the support she now felt she needed.

She found the aging housekeeper returning from the vegetable garden and sallied up to her at once.

The kindly woman was slightly surprised by the burst of energy from her ward and smiled as she thanked her for the provisions she had bought.

'Jennifer my dear, what on earth can be the matter, you look as if you've seen a ghost?' Janet aped the words of Sir Hamish's greeting, almost to the letter.

'Janet, over the past years you must have come to know me pretty well,' said Jenny, as she attempted a faked smile of limited proportions. Janet nodded a little insecurely; 'and so you have to admit that I am not one given to silly exaggeration or indeed to any unnecessary and foolish anxiety.' Again Janet nodded but more thoughtfully this time, as Jenny continued. 'As I was returning from the village shops earlier, I was once again accosted by that awful man Barnabas Bell.

'Now, I am a grown woman Janet, and I should be able to cope with an incidence of this nature without the need for parental support of any kind. But I am at this moment in time, very much in need of such support and advice, which, I am sorry to say, doesn't appear to have been forthcoming from my Uncle Hamish.'

The existing smile on Jenny's face diminished as she continued. 'You see, this monster Bell has informed me that he now resides in Dorset, in the very village where I, seemingly, will be spending the rest of my life.

'He clearly told me of his present position in a very

contemptuous manner and it was obvious from his remarks that he wishes to terrorise me in the most alarming way possible - it's as though he wants to achieve, and indeed, maximise all the enjoyment his tiny warped mind will be able to find, by terrorising me and by maltreating me in any way he possibly can.'

Janet Nunn considered carefully the accusation that was now being laid at the feet of the hateful man. She remembered clearly the conversation that had preceded the appalling row she experienced with the insufferable character when she fired him from his employment at The Old House all those years ago; after she had witnessed, of course, all the obscene remarks his filthy mouth had uttered.

'That is news of the worst kind, Jennifer,' said the kindly housekeeper, with a look of the deepest concern firmly rooted in her age worn face. 'So you consider him to be up to his old tricks once again, do you my dear? I can surely understand that you would do, given the circumstances of his past history and his knowledge of your origins.

'How long has it been since he was last on the scene here in Brenton, Jennifer? Let me think now, it must be well over eight years ago, am I not right?' she said, answering her own question with the utmost gravity. Jenny nodded her head in the affirmative vigorously. 'Well now, time doesn't seem to have mellowed the man, for if indeed he has moved to Dorset in all innocence then there could be no reason at all why he wouldn't have told you the fact in a more congenial manner. No, I think you have every right to be concerned Jennifer, and I say that with all sincerity. You say you have approached your uncle with your dilemma, is that right?' Again Jenny nodded her head. 'Well, what did he have to say about the matter?'

Jenny told her of her uncle's disappointing reaction.

'That is not the response I would have expected from the man, Jennifer, most unlike him, that's for sure,' she said, as she inclined her head deep in thought. 'My guess is that he doesn't wish to worry you excessively or to cause you to have more distress than is absolutely necessary, but that he means to have words with our Mr Bell and put him straight over a few things or at least ask the local constabulary to offer a few words of advice on your uncle's behalf. You may take it from me, Jennifer, that is surely your uncle's immediate plan of action and by not saying anything more to yourself or further involving you at all would be his way of discreetly handling the unfortunate situation.'

Jenny placed a thankful hand upon the attentive and considerate housekeeper's arm.

'Thank you Janet, you have put my mind at rest completely and so I shall put the matter to the back of that seemingly over anxious mind of mine, attempt to be at ease with the world once more, and concentrate on organising my move back to Dorset.'

The two ladies exchanged harmonious smiles then linked arms affectionately; and keeping pace with one another they walked slowly back to the house, perfectly at ease in each others society as always and with the worrying subject placed firmly out of Jenny's reach.

Janet, on the other hand, did continue with her thoughtfulness as feelings of anxiety traversed her own mind and she decided to approach Sir Hamish herself in order to ascertain the full extent of his views upon the subject.

Janet did this at the earliest opportunity; which was in point of fact two days later and was most surprised to learn from her employer that the constabulary's visit had been completed and that Mr Bell was no longer living at the address they had written in their records. They also confirmed the death of Mrs Bell to be accurate.

PART THREE

CHAPTER ONE

One misty morning in late September when essential freshness had failed to cool the already warming air, a brown and white removal lorry, paying little heed to the local inhabitant's need for sleep, disturbed the serenity of Brenton village by turning up at The Old House at some unearthly hour; revving its engine most alarmingly and, on the whole, creating an awful din.

All scheduled excursions had been satisfactorily logged on the removal company's docket at least a week ago, and by the driver himself, so he knew he had the day right - it was the timing that was wrong, two-hours-too-early wrong, in fact.

Because of the blunder, twenty man sized fingers (thumbs included) could now be seen drumming on the cab's dashboard, keeping time with some obscure tune that was loudly emanating from an ancient portable radio - for the whole of the locality to hear.

And so, as the two man crew hung around for an indication that someone soon would be moving about the house in order to put an end to this tiresome bout of waiting, their annoyance grew by the minute.

Presumably because he had little else to occupy his mind at the moment, the lorry driver, without warning, decided that the lorry ought to have been more suitably parked for the loading of furniture than where it had been casually left on arrival.

And so, he carried out a few noisy manoeuvres so that the jumbo furniture carrier was now facing in the opposite direction and pointing toward the wrought iron gates through which it had just entered. He then backed the vehicle to a position at the bottom of the steps that led to the portico of The Old House.

The cantankerous driver's intention to make an unpleasant situation worse, by exercising as much din as was possible, was quite obvious by this time.

Be that as it may, a further fifteen minutes saw the lorry driver and his mate empty themselves from the cab with all hope seemingly lost.

They were about to place their feet on the first step of the portico in order to rouse the inhabitants when the front door was thrown open and a beautiful young lady was seen to be walking from the doorway, all smiles and wondering what the rumpus was about.

Of course, this vision of loveliness coming towards them, with a pleasant smile lighting her face, caught the lorry's crew completely by surprise - but pleasingly so, and with no further protests issuing from either one of them but with eagerness now decorating each of their faces, they selected a gear that would move them both forward simultaneously and at a steady pace in order to get the lorry loaded quickly.

Every piece of furniture that Hamish had bought for Jenny and Jacob over the years was to be loaded onto the lorry - together with all their personal possessions; despite Jenny's earlier expressed disapproval at leaving both rooms bare.

Allowing two rooms to stand empty was, to Jenny's tidy mind, quite unthinkable and unnecessary; after all, she considered there would be more than enough furniture at Hyde Hall for the two of them to share.

But the very best of uncles had told Jenny he wished for everything to go with them so they would feel more at home when they eventually arrived at Hyde than they otherwise might have felt, and that both rooms at The Old House would then be identically refurnished ready for niece and great nephew when they returned for their expected visits; it seems there was to be no arguments.

Jenny's Lotus Elan 26R sports car, with its famous steel backbone chassis and its vivid yellow, glass fibre body supporting a black removable soft top, was quite a different matter, she would never have left that 'thrill' behind, no matter what circumstances prevailed.

This superb apparition of vehicular delight being the envy of virtually all of Brenton's local inhabitants was frequently seen to be speeding along Lincolnshire's rural roads in recent days. The splendour of driver and car in motion, heading in the direction of who knows where, was an amazing sight to see from any distance, far or near and the passionate sensation of daredevil driving defied description particularly when applied to a young lady of Jenny's ilk.

Jenny had sold her ancient sports car and bought her treasured toy directly after she had buried her father: she knowing full well the importance he had placed on vehicular splendour and how greatly he would have wished for her to own and enjoy such a prized beauty as this.

In actual fact, the purchase was more by way of a cheering up exercise than the need for a new vehicle and on the whole this outstanding sports car achieved that objective rather well.

Jenny brought her four-wheeled pride and joy to the front of the house and parked it ahead of the lorry while she went back inside to say her fond farewells to her Uncle Hamish and Janet Nunn and to claim the hand of her beloved son.

She skipped noiselessly up the steps once more and smiled at the uniformed removal men as they moved, with great difficulty, through the wide entrance hall.

The two men, desperately struggling with each extremity of a massive wardrobe that had housed almost the entire collection of Jenny's clothes since the day she first moved into The Old House, were far too busy with the job in hand to return any pleasantries that might be owed to the trim young lady; or else they were still in a strop over their own opinions of the day's hour in order to make the effort - who knows?

Now, quietly standing in the hallway awhile, alone and unattended and glancing out off the doorway, Jenny felt surges of uneasiness engulf her whole being as her steady gaze settled on the final piece of furniture being stowed in the lorry's cargo space.

This surge of uneasiness, she knew very well, was the result of the intense panic she was momentarily feeling inside. An inescapable panic - a panic of fear as a new chapter in her life was about to open out before her much sooner than she had anticipated, in fact, and at her old home in far-off Hyde where the social order of things would be uncertain and unreliable.

This brand new chapter, she felt, would certainly contain an excess of responsibilities, far greater than she could ever hope to manage on her own. And these, no doubt, would be thrust upon her from day one, causing her inadequacies to show. The thought of such a task as this now filled her mind with horror and feelings of doubt and uneasiness made headway in her brain.

Because of all this horror she now believed that happiness might never be forthcoming from Hyde Hall - not yet - not as this brand new chapter immediately unfolded, anyway - and not as she had hoped might have been the case if intervening years had passed her by.

In addition to these misgivings, a strange suspicion that something bad would happen the moment they reached their journey's end plagued the young woman's mind as she stood there engulfed in pitiless doubt; and she was overwhelmed by a strong feeling of fear of having to meet the hostilities from the mother who, in the past, had been the cause of much of her solitude.

The awful dread of having to live again with this iniquitous woman who had initiated all the grief her young mind had had to tolerate for its first twelve tortured years, now descended upon her with a sudden burst of awareness - desperate in its need to persuade

Jenny to remain in the here and now rather than to go forward to deal with the unexpected.

But these weird sensations, not unlike all the other disadvantages she had listed in her mind, would have to be ignored, for her own sanity's sake they had to be - she knew the truth of that.

Suddenly a voice entered her intellect as she stood in the quietness of the hallway. A kindly, familiar and inspirational voice - a voice she'd remembered through the annals of her youth, but which had been absent from her memory for the past eight years or so. A silent, loving voice, one that brought her encouragement, hope and cheer, one that warmed the inner parts of her heart with the affection she had so deeply missed - but a voice that in reality had never been so very far away.

"You have a son now Jennifer, a truly wonderful son who must be encouraged to aspire to the station in life that has befallen him and which, one day, for his descendents' sake and for yours as well, my dear, he will make his very own by putting his mark upon it so there can be no doubt at all what he, with God's help, might accomplish. So, don't hold back anymore dearest, Jenny, go forward with confidence, for you will not be on your own anymore; and may God, with his good grace, go with you."

Her dear Aunt Sarah's voice came restlessly to her from far away, beyond the forbidden horizon that placed them far apart. With comforting words she came, words that caused Jenny to smile with joy, both inward and without, and they gently soothed the doubt away that had gathered in her mind.

Collecting her thoughts once more, she felt happy that the first twelve years of her son's young life had been spent in the company of the wisest, kindest man that she had ever known - one who would always be ready to assist both her and her beloved boy in any way he could; so long as his earthly body gasped sufficient breath to live.

The farewell wasn't as emotionally tearful as Jenny had expected and Jacob was most eager to claim his seat in his mother's brilliant car.

After the warmest of embraces from her Uncle Hamish, Janet came forward and holding Jenny closely to her aging breast she fondly kissed her cheek.

'No uncertainties now Jennifer, if you please,' said she, firmly, although a moistness was clearly to be seen in both her own weary eyes. 'We are only a phone call away, you know, and will always be ready and willing to talk with you; and don't forget your uncle will be visiting you very soon to see how well the two of you are settling in.' Janet used her words sparingly but with fondness for all that, as if she was speaking to her own child.

Having the young mother and son living with her for so long had been a wonderful interlude in the life of the Scottish lady who was now experiencing the evening of her days, and she wished with all her heart that Jennifer and Jacob could have remained at The Old House to make the end of her own life seem a little easier.

But that wasn't to be, she knew that, and so she reconciled herself to a future without them and to face the unknown's emptiness as bravely as she could.

They drove away from The Old House without too much ado and so it was with cheer, coupled with just a tinge of sadness that Jennifer Kent, together with her son Jacob, made her way to her old Dorsetshire home in the village of Hyde where who knows what unpleasant happenings may lay before her there.

....

At four thirty in the afternoon of Friday the twenty fourth of September nineteen hundred and sixty five a bright yellow sports car closely followed by a largish removal lorry drew up at the wide double steps outside Hyde Hall.

Vehicles and visitors alike were observed with discreet awareness by prying eyes that had waited over an hour for the small procession to show. They now investigated every inch of the two vehicles and their occupants through a small divide in the closed curtains of a certain upstairs window on the second floor of Hyde's most stately house.

The trip down from Lincolnshire had been rather pleasing and warm sunshine had attended the small procession for much of the route as it wound its way through England's central counties to Dorset's southern shores.

As the two vehicles reached their journeys ending, an air of cheerlessness filled the Lotus car whilst its occupants remained seated in the hopes that someone from the big house might come out to greet the new arrivals.

But no one came.

"No love awaits you here, Jenny... so why did you imagine there might have been a welcoming reception for you, or receptions of any sort at all, come to that," she thought disappointedly to herself.

Reassessing this unpleasant situation and being furious at being ignored, Jenny exited the car and marched unfalteringly to the big oaken door; and pulling the handle of the ancient bell, she waited.

Eventually her dogged perseverance was rewarded by the presence of Spiller the butler.

'Good afternoon Spiller; Miss Jennifer Kent and Master Jacob Kent have arrived.'

Spiller was dumbfounded.

An uncomfortable pause followed.

'I take it that you are expecting us?' said Jenny, brusquely but positively.

James Spiller, a tall, upright, balding man in his early sixties, was taken aback by the terseness of the introduction, as he sadly failed to recognise the child of yesteryear, now fully grown to maturity, both in stature and in beauty.

'No Miss Kent, I have received no such directive regarding your arrival.' His eventual answer was abrupt, almost nervously so - to begin with anyway, and the corner of his eyelid twitched with anxiety. Soon, however, he gained a little more confidence to his manner. 'Perhaps I should check with Lady Margaret to establish precisely what is to be done, Miss Kent.'

'No such person, Spiller, I am the mistress of Hyde Hall now, so I suggest that you realign your allegiance very carefully and very promptly; if you wish to keep your position secure within this household, that is.'

Jenny's demeanour was acutely hostile at this point in time, and deliberately so; not that her hostility should have been directed towards Spiller of course; the poor man had obviously received no prior warning regarding her arrival and his loyalty and obligation to the family had never been in question in the past.

But it was Spiller who was now taking the full brunt of Jenny's unwarranted but freely expressed aggression; aggression, which, in point of fact, ought to have been saved for her mother, for it was she who had been notified as to the expected time of arrival of the new owner of Hyde Hall and by Sir Hamish Kent himself; while Jenny had stood at his side witnessing the telephone conversation so there could be no dispute.

Spiller stood warily still. Quite unable to take in all that had been so blatantly said to him; not knowing which way to turn or who to acknowledge as his current employer.

After a moment more of uncomfortable uncertainty Jenny came to his rescue and explained the events that had transpired since

Angus Kent's death.

At last a light shone in his eyes, a light of approval; well, maybe just acceptance, but he still remained motionless, quite unable to decide his next course of action.

'Spiller, I take it that my mother has not explained the situation to you in easy words for you to understand as I have just done?' said Jenny, trying to recover a few of the social graces that had been neglectfully absent from her attitude since she'd arrived.

The butler slowly shook his head, almost daring not to utter a word. And so, with some irritableness still accompanying the line of her questions Jenny continued while she still held the man's attention.

'So I take it that you have not had rooms prepared in readiness for us to use?' said Jenny, she knowing full well that the answer to even a suggestion of such a question would be in the negative.

'No miss. As I have already stated, I have received no instructions regarding your arrival,' he replied curtly.

Jenny, now detecting a certain amount of obstinacy in the butler's tone stood her ground with renewed vitality to her voice.

'Then Spiller,' she said, calmly, 'may I suggest you attend to it; straight away if you please.'

'Yes Miss Kent. Am I to understand that you will require your old bedroom to be prepared?'

'No Spiller, you may understand nothing of the sort. My father's bedroom is to be prepared for me and the smaller adjacent room is to be prepared for my son. I take it that both rooms are empty and free of clutter, and if so, please direct the removal men accordingly. We will both be in the drawing room awaiting your presence when everything is complete.

'If you would be so kind as to inform Agnes of our precise location, Mr Spiller, then perhaps she will serve refreshment to us there; if she is still employed here, that is.'

'Yes Miss Kent, I will do that at once.

'In actual fact, Miss Kent both those rooms were cleared of all furniture, cleaned and have been redecorated soon after the death of your father,' he said, with the hint of a smile breaking his narrow lips, feeling, that at last, he was one step ahead of his new over-assertive mistress.

"Yes, I bet they were. I'll bet the old witch couldn't wait to rid herself of everything that belonged to my father," thought Jenny, to herself.

The butler was still feeling somewhat flustered, and a certain amount of perplexity still harassed his mind to some extent, and the apparent absence of any communication that should have been forthcoming from his former mistress regarding the changes should have angered him too - but it didn't.

Despite his inner feelings, or because of them, he strode off with lengthened strides to see to the bidding of the new mistress of Hyde Hall and in no time at all he had everything organised and well under his control; although he did find time to consider carefully the matter of 'allegiance' that Jenny had referred to, and precisely how he was going to deal with working for two domineering women in the same house at the same time and who would most certainly be at variance with one another for most of that time.

After Jenny had left her butler to his duties she wandered back to the car and sat awhile holding her son's hand.

'Well my darling what do you think of your new home?' she asked, with a radiant smile lighting her face.

'Seeing it only from the outside Mummy, I consider it to be very big, yes, very big indeed and much bigger than I remembered it to be. I was just wondering how I might avoid getting lost in such a big place as this. Does it look as huge inside as it does from the outside? Or are all the rooms tiny and out of proportion with the outside of the place?' asked her son, with a level of hesitation on his face.

'Why don't we both go inside and find out Jacob? Who knows, you might be pleasantly surprised.'

They both exited the car and closed their respective doors simultaneously. Then, with his caring arm tightly holding onto his mother's and her pulling his arm even closer to herself, they walked towards the house.

They had barely reached the entrance to the six pillared portico with its wide double steps and its ornate ceilinged roof, when Margaret appeared within the confines of the arched doorway, as if by magic. She bore an unexpected look of civility upon her aging face, which, for her, was to be regarded highly: civility being a rare commodity these days so far as the ex-mistress of Hyde Hall was concerned.

Gone were the days when beauty alone shone out of those august, hazel eyes, now narrowed with dire hate; when every stud from miles around sought her company and her laughter and longed to romp the long dry grassy mead with her and to wander in excitement beside the tranquil waters of the fragmented coast at the cove of Lulworth, close to where she lived.

But those were golden days of long ago - halcyon days for her; an earlier period in her life when she, still in her youth, had never known the name of Kent, and now, in her leaden, later years, she pleaded for her ignorance of the name she'd come to loathe.

'I see you've arrived then Jennifer.' The words poured from her lips in the time honoured fashion of disdain; for never could she despise another woman with the same intensity of hate that she heaped upon her own daughter. 'And I see that you've brought along your...' she caught herself before she'd let the vulgar word slip that she longed to use and clung onto it for all she was worth - 'your son.' She spoke the word replacement quickly as though she wanted it fast out of the way.

Jenny, being determined not to do battle with her mother on their first day, quickly removed Jacob's arm from her own and taking him gently by the hand led him to where his grandmother was standing.

'Jacob,' she said, looking down at the face that meant the entire world to her, 'this is your grandmother.'

Margaret tried her utmost to move forward to greet her grandchild but found herself firmly rooted to the marbled floor; and so, Jacob, seeing that nothing could be gained by waiting, moved forward himself with a confidently outstretched hand.

'I'm very pleased to meet you, Grandmother,' he said, with unfaltering words.

Margaret was quite taken by surprise at the correct politeness the young boy had exhibited. And so she bent down from the waist and inclined her head so that the lad might kiss her cheek - which he did, and with slow deliberation.

'I'm most pleased to make your acquaintance too Jacob and I do hope that we will prove to be the closest of friends.' The words seemed to stick in Margaret's gullet a little although a flicker of a faint, false smile did briefly pass her mouth and not unlike any other time when she had found herself distributing niceties she could ill afford, she was reluctant to place too much emphases on them.

Jenny, feeling that for Jacobs's sake and his alone she ought to attempt to display a hint of affection toward her mother, moved optimistically forward but with a good deal of expected repercussions already forming in her mind.

Exchanging a worthy air of fondness in a somewhat artificial and staged situation, is never easy, therefore, in order to add as much impact to the sincerity of her attitude as was humanly possible, Jenny reached out both her hands for her mother to take.

Although she shouldn't have been, Jenny was somewhat saddened and disappointed by her mother's expression of total disinterest and by the flagrant disregard she expressed in not allowing such a personal demonstration to take place at all; for upon seeing and indeed in the anticipation of Jenny's well meaning intentions, Margaret moved backwards a couple of paces thereby avoiding all possible contact with her daughter.

Margaret, of course, considered she was being used in an alien manner - a way she did not care to fall in line with; and quiet rightly so, one might possibly suppose, for having any interaction forced on her, or any show of affection at all, for that matter, would be totally unacceptable to her; and so she would consent to none of it; not if it was beyond her better judgment - no matter how sincere Jenny's feelings of warmth may have been.

Why should she indeed? All Margaret wanted was to be shrouded in mystery and by so being she felt she would be able to demonstrate to the whole of Dorset that she was still the lady of Hyde Hall, who wasn't to be trifled with; at least that was what everyone thought.

Jenny, upon seeing this obvious snub, immediately gave way so that a pact of acceptance rather than desire might exist. She, realising that only a compromise, a peaceful coexistence even, between the two obstinate and conflicting parties of mother and daughter was the sole arrangement to be expected, and that never could there be an amicable understanding of peaceful harmony to be regarded as being possible - not now - not ever.

While Margaret, without furthering another word, retraced her steps to her room Jenny and Jacob walked unhurriedly across the marbled hall and along the brightly lit corridor that led to the drawing room and reached it at the same time as Agnes, the senior parlour maid, who doubled as cook at times, was arriving.

'Hello Agnes,' said Jenny, as brightly as she was able: bearing in mind she was still smarting from the pangs of resentment her mother had just delivered. 'How lovely to see you again, I was hoping you were still in service here, as it's always pleasant to see a familiar face.'

The senior parlour maid looked slightly bewildered at seeing the two newcomers at first, although a smile did eventually break through the mask of uncertainty.

'Miss Jennifer?' asked Agnes, in stunned surprise, 'is it really you?' Her face lit up in final recognition. 'Mr Spiller informed me that we had visitors and would I serve refreshments in the drawing room straight away, but I had no idea at all who it was that I was expected to serve the refreshments to, no idea at all; but I'm so pleased it's you.

'How wonderful to see you again, and you, all grown up and looking as pretty as a picture that I'm sure I hardly recognised you at all. And who is this young gentleman who looks so handsome that I'm sure he will break all the young ladies hearts in a few years time... if he hasn't already done so?'

'Agnes, this is my son Jacob,' said Jenny, as she glanced and smiled with pride at her son. 'We shall both be living here now that my father has gone; as I expect you will soon find out: if you don't already know.

'You see, I am the new owner of Hyde Hall, Agnes, and as such, will be running this house and the estate in the future. And my mother... well, she will now be retiring from all involvement in business activities and from the day to day running of this place as well; although she will still be living with us of course. And so, if there are any problems in the future, or even if no problems exist at all, then I am always available to speak with you and indeed with any of the staff who may need my attention... as and when the need arises. So please don't hesitate to approach me directly at any time at all, Agnes.

'Anyway, Mr Spiller will certainly be staying with us and continue to be engaged in his usual capacity, as indeed, I sincerely hope, will the rest of the staff; for their jobs are perfectly safe here, and so there will be no need for any of you to be concerned about the security of your future employment at Hyde Hall.'

It seemed to Jenny, at the time, that she had taken advantage of an opportunity to explain the up-to-the-minute situation regarding that of Hyde Hall to a senior member of her staff and for that member to broadcast the situation to the rest of the household as she saw fit.

How wrong she was. For almost immediately Jenny and Jacob had acquainted themselves with their new rooms and Jacob had then taken off to explore the remainder of his new home while his mother was now familiarising herself with her father's old study, that an impatient knocking was heard upon the door to that particular room. And Jenny, looking up from one of the drawers in the polished mahogany desk she was examining, encouraged the entrance of an irate Mr Spiller who forcefully berated the new owner for undermining the said butler's position within the household.

Mr Spiller firmly asserted that Jenny, whom it should be

noted was immediately taken aback with a huge level of disbelief by the accusation, was said to have exposed him, the senior man of the household, to a circumstance of calamitous proportions by maliciously discrediting his position.

'Miss Kent,' said Spiller, as his features struggled with a reddishness of embarrassment. 'I fear you have denigrated my position in this household by usurping my authority, thus leaving me no alternative to the offering of my immediate notice of resignation.'

Not only was the reddening of his features worsening by the minute but his whole body appeared to be shaking with extreme emotional confusion.

'What on earth can be the matter James, sorry Mr Spiller? Please tell me at once, what is it that you are finding so unacceptable? What have I said or done that is causing you all this... obvious anxiety?' asked Jenny, in the meekest of voices, for she had no idea what could have provoked such an attack of the jitters and in such a way as to cause the poor man to react in this unlikely manner.

Spiller then raucously re-enacted the whole episode of his conversation with Agnes when she disclosed, most innocently, to him what Jenny had said regarding the new administrative arrangements at Hyde Hall. He told Jenny that it was his express responsibility to make the staff aware of any changes of circumstances surrounding the house and especially with anything regarding their own personal employment. He now felt that he should have been consulted first before Jenny disregarded his position.

'But Spiller, I did in fact tell you of the revised seating arrangements of the house; as soon as I had arrived here actually, if you remember. It is hardly my fault that you have been caught up in events which prevented you passing on the information to the rest of the staff, and I did say to Agnes that she may already have been aware of this particular bulletin of household news. I considered that it wasn't unreasonable to assume you would have imparted that information when you instructed her to serve tea earlier. No, you didn't do that did you Mr Spiller? You didn't even have the decency to inform Agnes of the identity of the so called 'visitors' to whom she was about to serve refreshments, and besides, your responsibility is to the male members of the staff and not to the female members. So yes, I shall be pleased to receive your resignation as soon as I have it in writing. Until then, I wish you a good afternoon Mr Spiller.'

Mr Spiller lost no time at all in searching out his former

mistress so that he might relay to her exactly what had taken place and what was being said behind her back.

"Well done Jennifer," said Margaret, to herself, with the full width of a self satisfied smile decorating her features. *"Didn't take you long to upset the whole household, now did it my dear?"*

CHAPTER TWO

Almost all of the broadleaved trees that were to be seen in the Hyde Hall estate's extensive forest were beginning to show golden tinges to their leaves far earlier than usual this year. And the adjoining grassy parkland that swept on down, past the big house all the way to the river's dried up edges and which formed an essential part of the estate's vast acreage, was scorched by the intense heat of the summer's sun as well.

All of the shrivelled grass merely served to stress the desperate need for the wet stuff to get onboard a cloudy nim-bus pretty quickly and zoom along to disembark instantly - if not sooner - having said that, sodden earth is oft a muddy hindrance whereas total dryness is undeniably a farmer's dread.

The grassy, unfurrowed fields, used for grazing, appeared to be in reasonable condition - seriously on the dry side 'tis true, but at least the cattle munching them found little to complain about.

But the wild meadows, where once lush grass had grown, had been left unattended and were providing quite a different problem. These fields had felt the need for the reaper's sheers months ago but with no one heeding their pleas they began to lose their freshness and wither away. Now each wilting blade was crying out for a long sustaining drink to revitalize its dying life or at least be cut to urge some sweeter shoots to show.

During the long years of Angus Kent's incapacity, the farm's foreman, Andy Hedges, had made decisions as far as the agricultural side of matters were concerned but needless to say only after his instructions had been approved by the then Lady Margaret Kent. Most of the time he courteously liaised with her Ladyship to make sure all of her ideas were inline with his own. But his discontent at discovering the lady's unsuitability for running a farm soon escalated for all to see; and the longer she was under his feet the shorter his temper became.

His rising frustration, brought on by this impossible state of affairs, worsened after an official meeting with the mistress of Hyde Hall had taken place one steamy afternoon.

'Please don't get me wrong ma'am,' Andy Hedges had ended up saying, 'I love my job and have al'as done so since startin' here some twenty odd year ago; but unless you give me more freedom in decision makin' without your interference ma'am or at least pay me well for putting up with your blasted meddlin', then I shall have to think hard about me stayin' here.'

Upon hearing these brusque words the lady was taken aback and felt rather bewildered and humiliated at being accused of incompetence in such an impolite way; and by a mere farmhand at that.

"Clever ruse Mr Hedges," She thought. *"However, I can clearly see through your trickery. You will, most certainly, not be getting a weeks money in lieu of notice out of me, as I have no intentions in firing you. I am well aware of all my faults and failings, thank you very much, Mr Hedges and so I have no need for a mere peasant dictating the dos and don'ts regarding farming practice to me. And what is more, I do not plan to be the victim of blackmail either."*

Margaret withheld all these thoughts and opinions and kept them to herself. Normally she would have dismissed the man on the spot for gross insubordination but fearing being left to her own devices she decided in favour of silence, *"after all no farmhand is going to wheedle unearned money out of me by making such threats,"* she cunningly surmised, and so she ignored the man and allowed the matter drop.

In the end Hedges became totally disenchanted with the situation; and finding the lady's lead to be less than useless and her stubbornness far too burdensome to bear, he abandoned his position in favour of a job at the local plastics factory which offered him four times the rate of pay Hyde Hall was willing to afford.

In past years Angus Kent himself had taken the helm of all workforce coordination, but since his injury and subsequent death there was no one to take control of the agricultural side of things - apart from Andy Hedges that is.

It is true the dairy side of the business was safe; meaning that the cows were milked regularly; the two dedicated cowmen had seen to that. But the arable side of farming was quite a different matter and was now in desperate need of transformation.

Not a single farmhand possessed sufficient drive or interest in the farm to step into the breach and attempt to reorganise the place themselves. No, they had seen what had happened to Andy Hedges and realising that all his efforts had been thrown back in his face, they thought twice before interfering. Jeopardising their own jobs in that way would have been a huge issue for them to deal with, and in any case it was doubtful if they would have been up to the task anyway.

Because of the absence of Andy Hedges, appalling neglect

now blighted the once highly rated Hyde Home Farm. And until solutions could be found and brought to bear upon this grim situation, and the farm hands organised into the workforce they once were and the new owner's attention drawn to fresh proposals that must be long overdue by now and for those proposals to be stung into action straight away, then nothing could be expected to be accomplished in this dire situation and so everything would stay as it had been since the foreman left - sluggish at best - lifeless at worst.

Jenny realised that all this mess would not be put right until she and her Uncle Hamish had put their heads together and worked out the necessary strategy that would revive the farm. Then again, not until they had explored the more long term solutions that would be needed for the future smooth running of the place; but time was moving fast - far too fast it seems.

The last week in September had been a trying time for the new mistress of Hyde Hall, for not only had her mother criticized her at every given opportunity but she was still finding great difficulty in obtaining a suitable replacement for Spiller. The butler had deserted his post immediately he'd presented his letter of resignation, which, needless to say, was without the usual terms of notice to quit being observed.

In that uneasy period, Jenny had found it necessary to promote Agnes to the position of temporary house keeper. She stated clearly that the arrangement would be provisional and that Agnes must not regard the post as being permanent in any way.

Jenny had summoned her senior parlour maid to her study early one morning and placed the proposition before her; she then asked if she clearly understood the offer.

'Yes Miss Jenny, I understand, course I do. I should love the chance to show you that I can handle the job to your liking. After all I have been senior parlour maid here for a long time now Miss Jenny... came to Hyde Hall soon after the war, which you won't be able to bring to mind, I know; but I have watched Mr Spiller as he went about things; so I'm sure I can copy him.'

'Alright Agnes, I will allow you this opportunity to prove yourself but you must remember this is an acting post I am creating and you must not consider it to be anything other than that. You see it is important for me to find an experienced butler, Agnes, so that I am able to concentrate on running the estate and leave the administration of the house to him... so long as you understand all this, Agnes...'

'Yes Miss Jenny that will be fine by me... as I said I understand all you say. Just give me the chance to prove myself, that's all I ask.'

And so that was how the matter was left. Agnes was now temporary house keeper although the matter didn't rest at all well in Jenny's mind.

October's allotted time drew quickly to a close but still there was no replacement for Spiller; and although Agnes displayed all the necessary enthusiasm for her new position she was totally unable to use her initiative. In order to shore up this failing, she continually sought Jenny's approval of her own answer to even the smallest order.

But Jenny said nothing more to Agnes and allowed the situation to remain and for it to extend itself of its own accord.

In spite of this, Jenny had found herself to be under a continuous strain. Her own freedom from household restrictions should have been in position by now so that her mind could focus on the all important estate issues.

But that wasn't to be. Jenny now felt that the butler problem had been all too hastily resolved, recklessly so in fact; for she couldn't free herself despite knowing Agnes was in charge - or, more than likely because of it. It had been a decision that Jenny would later confess as being brought about by a state of hesitancy - a panicked decision in fact.

Jenny's excuse at the time was that she was being held in turmoil by reams of problems speeding through her mind ten to the dozen, and in such a continuous and perplexing stream that would have tried even the most experienced of organisers. All of this was indeed true. It was also true Jenny had foreseen this would be the case and not that long ago either.

Consequently, it was now vital for Jenny to find that special someone. Someone enterprising and forceful enough to get to grips with the situation. A man or woman, she held no preferences, but certainly someone who'd had experience in sorting out staff grievances with fairness and confidence; someone who could exercise initiative and someone with sufficient aptitude for organising without Jenny having to take the leading role in the day to day running of the house.

***

In the final week of October, Sir Hamish Kent paid the long awaited visit to Hyde Hall to satisfy his natural curiosity regarding his much loved niece's wellbeing. He also needed to assure himself that Jenny had overcome all difficulties and obstacles, which he knew would have littered her path and that she was now in charge of the demanding situation in which she had been so abruptly deposited.

Jenny had thoughtfully notified her mother of the precise date and the expected time of her uncle's arrival, hoping she would maintain some effort in 'the art of sociability' during the period of his visit.

But that wasn't to be. The explanation on offer was that throughout those particular two weeks Margaret had intended to take a 'much needed holiday', one which she claimed to have planned some months in advance.

Precisely where this holiday was to be spent was not disclosed, not at the time and it wasn't until much later that Jenny discovered her mother had spent those prearranged weeks in the company of a recent divorcee, one Lord Melchamp no less, and at his newly acquired downsized home - still situated in the county of Sussex.

Jenny, in the fullness of time, came to realise that a certain connection had existed between the two parties for some considerable period, which failed to surprise; not to any extent anyway. She was already aware of the nightmarish relationship that existed between the two parties anyway. All the same, the juvenile secrecy that now existed and which concealed her mother's holiday location at this moment was a mystery to Jenny.

Jenny and her uncle spent much of the two weeks in promising debate about the estate and also in the calculation of profits to be expected at the end of the company's financial year: which would be reduced but not calamitously so as Jenny had first imagined.

They had organised the late cutting of grassland which then had been dried and stacked ready for winters use and they had also, after a short debate, decided to employ an estate manager, although the suggestion had already been mooted and decided awhile ago, soon after Angus' death in point of fact.

After long and careful consideration they finally decided to offer any proposed candidate a ten year contract to take effect after a nominal trial period had taken place. It would be at the end of this ten year phase that Jacob will have become of age and be in a position to take the reins of the estate - if he so desired.

And so, they would now be seeking a mature and experienced man, one who would be looking forward to retirement at or around the end of that particular period of time.

Casually walking around the stable block on the final afternoon of Sir Hamish's visit, they engaged Joe, the stable lad, in a rather laid-back conversation just as he was about to groom his grey mare after they had taken a long and arduous gallop together.

Jenny had introduced Joe as the one who had found her father lying in a state of unconsciousness, after he had fallen from his horse, all those years ago.

Joe had visited her father's sickbed at every given opportunity, which had pleased and reassured Jenny; at least someone from Hyde Hall had cared; and for that reason alone the stable lad had ranked highly in her estimation.

Later that same afternoon, and after Sir Hamish had declared his opinion of the stable lad - finding him to be intelligent and of a pleasant disposition - he once again sought Joe's presence; this time to ask if he was aware of any suitable candidate that might be considered for the responsible position about to be created.

'No, I don't know of anyone off hand but I shall certainly keep my ears open for you and if I hear of anyone at all likely I shall definitely report to Miss Kent straight away,' he had said, with complete self-assurance in his voice.

Sir Hamish had thanked Joe for his cooperation and walked back to the house. It was later that same evening when the telephone rang and Joe's confident voice was heard as he focused on an amazing coincidence that had just occurred.

'I have just this minute heard that my uncle is soon to be leaving his employment. The owner of the place, where he now works, is disillusioned with farming and wants to sell up; and feeling more than a little insecure after learning the news, even though a commendation to any prospective new owner has been promised, my uncle has decided to seek alternative employment so he is now looking round for a new and more permanent job.

'He's about the age you are looking for and he has a wealth of farming managerial experience behind him. If you like, he could come over tomorrow and have a word with the two of you to see if he might be up to scratch and what you may have in mind for the job; if it would be convenient to the two of you of course.'

And so it happened, Joe's Uncle, Alf Abrams, paid his first visit to Hyde Hall early the following morning, before Sir Hamish had left for Lincolnshire - was found to be most suitable and was duly offered the position of farm manager, and not as estate manager as first envisaged, and that he would commence his duties at the beginning of November.

***

Time, like a runaway motor on an endless ribbon of road, was speeding along without restraint. And with the newly appointed Alf Abrams now firmly at the helm, the oiled wheels of Hyde Hall estate's home farm moved more easily thereby freeing Jenny, at last, to concentrate on important estate matters.

Christmas passed in the usual celebratory fashion with Jenny and Jacob spending both feast days at The Old House in Brenton. But although the short Christmas vacation was, in every sense of the word, most glorious, the various impending problems stacking up for her back in Dorset compelled Jenny to cut short their visit.

And so it was that both mother and son prematurely returned to Hyde Hall on the day following Boxing Day.

Margaret was, quite predictably, found to be absent when Jenny and Jacob arrived back at the big house in the early part of the evening and a strange sense of desertion surrounded the place when they arrived.

With no lights to be seen serving its rooms, Hyde Hall presented a miserable and sinister sort of place and a feeling of unfriendliness entered Jenny's soul where a feeling of homeliness should have existed.

Fully realising that all of the household staff would be absent from the big house over the holiday period: each of them celebrating Yuletide in the warmth of their respective homes, Jenny had relied on Agnes to hold the fort. And Agnes, wishing to establish her relatively new position, had readily agreed to remain at Hyde Hall for the short period of Jenny's absence.

Nevertheless, upon her return from Lincolnshire, Jenny was rather disappointed to find this arrangement to have been strangely disregarded.

Immediately Jenny walked through the large oaken door, and as she fumbled for a particular master switch which she knew would illuminate the whole of the lower area of the huge hall plus all of the downstairs passages in one specific movement, the telephone's ringing was heard to piercingly reverberate throughout the whole house, thereby accentuating the Hall's eerie emptiness.

'Hyde Hall,' exclaimed Jenny, after picking up the telephone's black receiver and wondering all the time who could possibly be calling at this particular time of the evening and so close to the Christmas recess at that.

'Oh, Miss Jenny,' the tremulous voice of Agnes came across in a most anxious fashion. 'Thank goodness you're in; I've been trying to get hold of you for hours. I telephoned that number in Lincoln you gave me and was told you had already left, and so I have been trying this number ever since.'

Jenny, not finding Agnes' distraught voice to be helpful or indeed reassuring, attempted to soothe her housekeeper:

'Agnes, please take hold of yourself and tell me what it is that's causing you all this silly panic,' she said, remaining perfectly calm herself.

'Well,' she said, still in a state of extreme anxiety, 'very early this morning I had a visitor to the Hall asking after you, by name, he did. He looked to me as if he was an extremely suspicious sort of bloke; in point of fact more like a gypsy he was than anything else.

'He scared the living daylights out of me, I can tell you, what with his dirty face and all. For even when I asked him, and in the most polite manner possible, he wouldn't go away. So I told him I was going to fetch the police if he didn't move himself from off the premises but still he wouldn't budge. So I shut the door in his face Miss Jenny, and I telephoned the police.

'Well, they weren't much help, no help at all in fact. They asked me where you were and when I expected you back. Well, I told them everything and they said that so long as the man hadn't harmed me or threatened me in any way I should forget about it, for it ain't any crime at all to ask if someone is in and could they speak to them.

'But that gypsy bloke, he fare upset me, I can tell you, and so I locked the place up and went home: not wanting to put myself in any sort of danger, you see.'

Jenny digested all that Agnes had said and found she was most disappointed in the woman whom she had placed in a position of authority. After she had battled with the situation in her own mind Jenny considered Agnes to have panicked at the least provocation.

'Look, I'm at home now Agnes, so why don't you take the rest of this evening and tomorrow off and I shall see you in a couple of day's time. I am more than capable of coping with the preparation of a few meals for my son and myself so you are not to worry about anything, OK?' said Jenny, replacing the receiver thoughtfully just as the doorbell echoed its need for attention.

Jacob, who had been by his mother's side during her conversation with Agnes, moved quickly along the corridor, across the wide hall towards the front arched door and opened it to reveal the recently appointed farm manager standing there with his hat in his hand and a broad smile on his face.

Alf Abrams was a tall, broad shouldered, fine-looking man with a weather beaten complexion and matching red hair. Being dressed mostly in tweeds he always exemplified an efficient farm manager. The attitude and the general demeanour of the man inspired confidence in everyone he happened to be speaking to.

'Hello, Master Jacob,' he said, his wide, straight smile expanded even further when he saw it was Jacob who'd replied to his summoning. 'Is your mother in and able to exchange a few words with me?' He looked over Jacob's head to where Jenny was standing at the far end of the wide hall as he spoke; he then shuffled his feet as if wishing to be invited in out of the cold.

'Good evening Mr Abrams,' called out Jenny, from the distance that separated them; and with a hint of confusion clearly expressed on her features - she deliberated:

"Dear me, not another problem so soon, and from another member of my staff not being able to cope with their job.... or could this be an extension of the first one I wonder?"

'Please come in and share a pot of tea with us, Mr Abrams; we have just this minute arrived home and I was about to put the kettle on as we both feel the need of a warm pick-me-up.

'Come this way, into the kitchen Mr Abrams,' she added, as he crossed the large entrance hall beneath the wide staircase and into the long parade of corridors that seemed to endlessly serve the whole of the lower regions of Hyde Hall. At the bottom of this particular passageway they reached the largest kitchen he had ever seen.

After pulling up three wooden seats to the outsized kitchen table, whilst Jenny brewed a pot of flavoured tea, he made himself comfortable.

'I've just had Agnes on the telephone telling me all about some phantom caller who appears to have been seeking me by name early this morning. Have you heard about the problem or is yours of a different nature,' she asked, hoping nothing too difficult was to be presented but also realising that this was still a holiday period and that anything incidental would surely have been shelved for at least a further day or so.

'No ma'am, it's the same problem I'm afraid. Apparently the police called round here earlier this afternoon and when they found there was no one at home they called in at my house: they not knowing where Miss Agnes lives; though how they come to know that I now worked here, lord only knows, it seems to me that news has a habit of travelling at a rate of knots in the countryside at times ma'am.

'Anyways, they needed to satisfy their own minds that everything was OK up here at the Hall and so after they found this place empty, they came to see me as I said. I've just popped out to take a look round the place for myself, just to make sure everything was alright, and when I saw your car outside and the lights on I thought I should pop in and let you know what's been going on. I take it that everything is alright here ma'am; only you can't be too careful these days.'

'Yes everything is fine Mr Abrams, thank you for your concern. I haven't seen any unlikely characters mooching about the place… not yet. But still it does seem rather odd that someone should be asking after me, and using my name as well.'

'Did Miss Agnes say what the caller looked like ma'am? Only, like you say, it does sound a mite improbable that any stranger would know about yourself… you only been living here for such a short time and all.'

'She told me that she thought the man's features resembled those of a gypsy, Mr Abrams, although I'm not at all sure what that is supposed mean.'

'Did she now? Well that puts a different slant on things altogether. You see, I was out walking with my old dog on the far side of the forest on the Sunday before Christmas, when I happened to notice some smoke rising through the trees. Well I was fearful that a forest fire might have been started by some young boys; well you know what kids are like; not that anyone could get much of a blaze going this time of year though. But when I reached the spot where the smoke was coming from I saw four or five caravans parked in a semicircle and half a dozen or so travellers all seated around a blazing camp fire.

'Well I asked if they had had permission to be camped there and the spokesman, he told me they hadn't but that they had parked their vans here in past years and that nobody had minded or complained at all.

'What with Christmas coming on and me not wanting to bother you with the matter, I took it upon myself to approve of their stay; 'but for no longer than a week after Christmas is over, mind you,' I told them. I hope I did the right thing ma'am but I felt I should start acting on my own initiative; I always have in the past and haven't been found to be wrong all that often.'

Jenny's eyes widened with a degree of excitement as her

manager revealed his recent encounter with the gypsy travellers and fidgeted with increased uneasiness as the cup she was placing to her lips shook a little so that she moved it from one hand to the other as if it was extremely hot. When at last she replaced the cup to its saucer she still seemed a little flustered and it was a few moments before she hesitantly enquired for further information.

'Mr Abrams, this spokesperson, what did he look like and how did he speak?'

'A very personable young man he seemed to be, very polite in his manner. About thirty years, I should have placed him at, yes about thirty, maybe a year or so older, afraid I'm not that good with ages. He's a tall handsome looking chap with broad shoulders and longish black hair. His skin is well tanned, but that comes with living in the out doors I expect rather than from any ethnic origins. But he spoke with a sort of educated voice with no hint of a foreign accent at all; only some, they speak with a sort of Irish drawl.

'But I'm sure we will have no bother with these particular people ma'am, no bother at all; they all seemed very harmless to me, just wanting to get on with their own lives and in their own way of doing it; if you gets my meaning. Still, if you plan on having a shoot this year I expect we shall be a few partridges and a pheasant or two short,' said the farm manager, with an infectious laugh, as he finished his sentence.

'That's a point, when do you intend starting the first shoot of the season,' asked Jenny, now feeling less edgy and more relaxed.

'Well now, first of October sees the commencement of the shooting season in this country but Boxing Day is the traditional day for a good shoot in these parts, but I guess we're a little late for that. Actually it's not a bad thing to miss a season though, gives the local birds a chance to catch up with their stock, and as we haven't a gamekeeper on the estate at the moment to move things along we wouldn't be able to organise a shoot anyway.'

Jacob was intently listening to the conversation and squirmed about on his seat as he awaited an opportunity to speak.

'What's a shoot Mother?' he asked.

The farm manager, noticing some hesitancy in Jenny's reply answered Jacob's question for her.

'A shoot, Master Jacob is an occasion when people, usually other local farmers, are invited to pay a fee for the privilege of shooting in an organised party. Game and rabbits are flushed out by a team of beaters who create the devil of a din by hollering and banging about on trees in the woods so that the game fly up in the direction of the guns to be shot then cooked and placed on the table for you to eat. I expect you like the taste of a bit of pheasant and partridge don't you Master Jacob? I know as how I do.'

'Yes I do, Mr Abrams, but I'm not so sure about the shooting bit,' replied Jacob, glancing at his mother. 'Is there no other way of catching the birds besides shooting them? Only a good few might only be wounded and then have to die a most agonizing death.'

'That's not likely to happen, Master Jacob. You see the shooters, they all use twelve bore shot guns and the pellets spray out by the time they reach the bird so they don't usually miss so the birds don't get wounded. They might be missed altogether though, if the gun goes off at half cock, so to speak; so then the bird flies away to safety. No I reckon that shooting is about the kindest way of picking them out and much better than running them over with the wheels of a motorcar.'

Jacob looked a little uncertain, but he didn't continue the discussion further.

'Thank you Mr Abrams, perhaps we will overlook the shoot this year then; but perhaps another year? We'll have to wait and see.'

Alf Abrams, finishing his cup of tea, rose from the table as if to leave, collected his hat from the stone floor where he had deposited it and touched his right eyebrow in a gesture of respect to the small family. He then commenced his walk slowly towards the door and the passageway beyond, immediately followed by Jenny, while Jacob remained at the table.

'Mr Abrams, thank you very much for all the trouble you have taken this evening and the patience you have shown,' said Jenny, with a grateful smile lighting her lovely face. 'I would like you to know how much it is appreciated.'

'Ma'am, it was no trouble, no trouble at all... really; all in a days work as they say.'

'Mr Abrams, one other thing. Would it be too much to ask you to pop over to those travellers, say tomorrow or the day after... or whenever you are due back after your holiday break and ask their spokesman to call in to see me? Perhaps you would accompany him... if it would be convenient. Perhaps we might be able to sort out some agreeable arrangements between the three of us, some sort of permanent time schedule for their stay, if they are as amicable as you say they are.'

CHAPTER THREE

As soon as Alf Abrams had left Hyde Hall the amazing news, concerning the likelihood of Tom's presence being on the estate once again, immersed itself in Jenny's brain leaving her with naïve and unrealistic thoughts of romance that were unworthy of a lady in her position: for she wasn't a child anymore and thoughts like these should have been over and done with long ago. Yet, here she was, all starry-eyed and giddy; and the more she thought about her gypsy man the more excited she became.

It wasn't long, however, before all this excitement started to lose its intensity and feelings of niggling doubt began to take its place; for even though she had received her manager's assurance that he had seen and spoken to Tom and that he would be seeing the gypsy once again within the next few days, there were still doubts; and so she should have employed an attitude of indifference in her behaviour - that indeed would have been the sensible way forward.

But it appeared that Jenny was being burdened by an assortment of emotions at the moment, emotions that were spinning round alarmingly in her muddled mind within a spectrum of two extremes: delight on the one hand and disbelief on the other but with delight finally getting the upper hand.

Throughout six of the longest days Jenny had ever known, she'd occupied herself within the precincts of Hyde Hall, not daring to leave her home and endeavouring to ply her brain with matters of the estate. But for all that time she had found it virtually impossible to concentrate, since this state of uncertainty was far too great to handle.

But those six long days had now vanished; leaving behind no evidence as to their having existed in the first place: for nothing had been achieved during that lengthy period, that's for sure.

In view of the fact that a single word had yet to be received from her farm manager, regarding at least some sort of contact he should by now have made with Tom, Jenny was sadly disappointed.

"Surely Alf Abrams must have paid a visit to the gypsies encampment by now, it's not too much to ask of one's farm manager to be a little more obliging than this, and a little more attentive to his own promises as well," she had thought. *"Surely he should have been more communicative with me as well... keeping me in the picture, so to speak; I'm quite sure I would have done had our rolls been reversed."*

Jenny quickly reassessed her opinion of Alf Abrams character. She finally decided him to be of a sluggish disposition without possessing any sense of urgency at all; and certainly not a sense of urgency that ought to have stung him into action before this time.

"Had a really vital matter existed that required his instant attention he would have been left standing at the starting gate; still mulling matters over in that dreary head of his," she thought, unsympathetically. *"Then again, maybe he hadn't seen through my facade of indifference that I tried to use at the time and so he failed to realise how hugely important this particular visit is to me. If that was the case then I'm not surprised he has been so sluggish in displaying the attention to his duty that I so badly need."*

Because the previous days had taken their toll on Jenny's wits and the duration in their passing had been found to be irritating in many ways, anxiety in the form of extreme nervousness shaded Jenny's mind, so that in the end she found it necessary to reroute her brain in the direction of positive thinking.

And so she nursed her head in cupped hands, as she seated herself on the chesterfield again, and considered all that had led to this day - this hour; for the likelihood of a fresh meeting with her gypsy friend seemed further away now than it ever did before.

Despite the fact that the original piece of news should have proved to be more than a little probable to her, Jenny suspected she shouldn't have placed so much emphasis on it; she certainly should never have felt completely certain that it really was Tom's vardo that was parked on the far side of the forest at all, or that the man her farm manager had spoken to was actually Tom. He surely could have been anyone, anyone at all; someone who had taken on Tom's roll as leader maybe: if ever Tom held such a pretentious roll as that in the first place; but after Jenny had searched her heart she knew she was desperate for it to be him.

As the wait was giving the impression of going on for ever, and in order to help the time along, Jenny tried to engross her mind in other, more important matters once again. Matters of the estate, as already mentioned, and those of Jacob's education were top of her list of priorities but even those bore little significant success in providing her mind with the diversion it required.

Because her once energetic brain seemed now to have its own ideas about the way it chose to function, she, in the end, consigned all efforts, regarding its behaviour, to the assemblage of lost causes, and allowed her unfettered intellect to mull over thoughts of its own choosing and in its own time.

It was way past ten in the morning on the sixth day after Jenny had asked Alf Abrams to arrange for the gypsy's leader to visit her. And with her anxious mind still in turmoil after that heady conversation, and finding the possibility of a reunion with Tom to be bewildering, the telephone had rung urgently - at around eleven.

'I regret not getting back to you sooner ma'am but I have been caught up with so many other things I just haven't had the chance of a visit till this morning.

'Anyway I've had a word with the spokesman at the gypsy camp, he will be most pleased to meet up with you this afternoon, if that would suit you at all ma'am.' The voice of Alf Abrams had come over as if he had been somewhat short of breath. 'I thought it quicker to go home to phone you than go all the way up to the Hall and risk you being out, so I hurried myself and ran some of the way, that's why I'm huffing and puffing - sorry about that ma'am.'

'Mr Abrams, will you please stop calling me ma'am. I really don't mean to sound impolite, but I do find the title somewhat pretentious. Miss Kent or Miss Jenny or even Jenny will suffice equally as well in future if you please.' Jenny had answered Alf Abrams in this abrupt way as a faint frown of doubt had engaged her forehead at the thought of this staid man's ways ever changing.

She had also answered her farm manager in this unusual offhand manner hoping to throw him off the scent, as it were, hoping he would consider the meeting to be of no real importance.

'Well now, I don't know about that ma'am... I'm not used to such familiarity with my employers, but I shall do my best if it would make you feel more comfortable.'

'What time will you be here Mr Abrams, as I have to be available for a visit from one of my tenants later in the afternoon?' She had been somewhat sparing with the truth by this statement, just for once in her life, as no such visit was earmarked for today's agenda. 'And what is the gentleman's name who you will be bringing to see me?' she had quickly added.

'The man's name is Hawke ma'am; he didn't offer a Christian name, that will have to come later, if you need to know it, that is; and we will be with you at one thirty sharp.'

In complete restlessness, but still not feeling able to leave her home for fear of a further report coming through, Jenny had occasionally moved from room to room within the boundaries of the substantial downstairs region of the house, eager to occupy herself with at least some form of dignified time wasting.

259

At this moment, however, and not unlike all the other moments in the six days of her waiting, Jenny sat once again on the dark green chesterfield in her spacious drawing room in fidgety nervousness as the previous encounter with Tom drifted back, troubling her usually well engaged but now extremely weary mind.

She remembered most vividly, the last time she had seen her gypsy man, the father of her son, just as she had recalled the account a hundred times before - when solitude had kindled such memories to take control.

"It was August, nineteen fifty seven, a few months after my seventeenth birthday and the death of dear Aunt Sarah Wood," she told herself. *"That day had been the hottest day ever, the day that I had walked up that awful hill to visit Lincoln Cathedral with Jacob and Janet.*

"Sticky perspiration flooded my face and the rear of my neck and ran down the small of my back in torrents; I remember that well enough. And it was there directly opposite the cathedral doors that I saw him; sitting with his back against an old brick wall begging like some misfit... like some down and out drifter."

Jenny now remembered the extent of his haggard and fatigued appearance and how ill he seemed to look. The terrible shock she had felt at seeing her one time friend in such an agonisingly run down state was the reason for her pity.

"Obviously, he had become a common beggar by this time, anyone could see that" she added the phrase, slowly, to the list her recollection of the man had brought to mind,

"But my panicked feelings, at the time, had been the cause of my hindrance. I now wish I had stayed calm and been able to find him in those narrow streets or at the very least had taken more time in my search for him. But I had completed all I could, within the limited time when I ran all the way down that frustrating hill in the hopes of finding Tom. Having the opportunity to attend his needs and to care for him, as Janet had plainly urged me to do, was important to me."

Although the finding of Tom wasn't to be, it hadn't been Jenny's fault that her attempt had been in vain or that the exercise had been aborted with despair.

But all of that was a long, long time ago indeed.

It was now fifteen minutes past one, and Jenny had once again parked herself on the green chesterfield after mooching around for a while and once again her mind was being dominated by feelings of dread or hope.

She had poured herself a schooner of oloroso and swallowed it a single gulp in the hopes it would settle her nerves; but as the drink had little affect - she poured another.

Jenny repeated the name 'Hawke' over and over to herself as she waited for the big hand on the grandfather clock to move off the three - but it seemed to have stuck there somehow and so she examined her own watch to reassure herself of the big clock's accuracy.

'I make them to be the same.' She spoke the all too disappointing words loudly to herself, 'still fifteen minutes left to go, then.'

Jenny had never known Tom's surname and had doubted his ever needing one; now she considered how improbable it sounded.

'Tom Hawke? No, not in a million years; sounds too much like the character in that Devonshire song, what was it? Something about someone lending someone else a grey mare,' she said, more loudly as she glanced at the clock once again - still no movement.

"Whatever shall I say to Tom, if indeed it is him,' she wondered, *'I shall certainly not introduce Jacob to him... not as his son, anyway?*

"Although it occurred all those years ago I have often examined the likelihood of us having Jacob together; it always seemed so improbable to me somehow... especially when I have no recollection of him even touching me that night... not in that way... save for the secureness of his arms when he held me tight during that appalling storm. But Janet had recognised the possibility and she, with so much experience behind her after having been a midwife for all those years, should have known... unless... she was merely trying to protect me from something. Still, I imagine he was more than close enough to me when he unconsciously exploded in his sleep... that must have been it.

"But however did he manage to allow such a decline in his standards to follow, I wonder? He was so full of himself and displayed plenty of exuberance when I first met him as a child. He seemed well aware of the difference between good and evil then; and right and wrong seemed uppermost in his mind and was the principle for his life; at least that's the way it looked to me at the time.

"He positively brimmed with self-sufficiency and was even forcefully confident when he stood up for me against father that time." She allowed her thoughts to stay awhile, as a warm smile

radiated her lovely face at the remembrance of that occasion. *"How his attitude shook daddy's foundations - poor daddy.*

"*But going on from being a young man of supreme confidence to a lowly beggar... well, I just don't get it; I don't understand how it could have happened... he was also without any real worldly worries either, or so it seemed to me; and being concerned where his next meal was coming from was about all there was to fret him.*

"*He looked so healthy when first we met, filled to the brim with a casual attitude and peace of mind, just as if nothing in the whole world could ever shake or bother him; a free spirit, just bobbing about the countryside doing exactly what he wanted to do and when he wanted to do it, that's how I remember him... always will I suppose.*

"*I wonder if his appearance has changed at all. Still as handsome as ever I expect - Alf Abrams seems to think him to be very handsome and not the dishevelled beggar I saw in Lincoln. Anyway, that was indeed a prized compliment... coming from another man and....*"

The loud clanging noise of the doorbell interrupted Jenny's musings and she glanced at the clock and then at her own timepiece, they were indeed synchronised, both were now showing the anticipated half hour.

She rose nervously from her chair, straightened her clothes and walked slowly down the long corridor, across the wide hall to the heavy oaken door; cutting short Agnes' emergence with the wave of her hand as she went - and opened the door to its limit.

'Miss Kent,' said her farm manager, remembering the new designation he was asked to use and which his employer openly preferred. His wide smile now changed into a mischievous grin as he introduced the guest.

"*Maybe Mr Abrams has guessed what this is all about after all,*" she thought - noticing his impishness - she had no idea.

'This is Mr Hawke, ma'am, the gentleman from the other side of the forest who you wished to meet.'

Tom Hawke stepped forward with a look of unrehearsed surprise at seeing Jenny and an air of controlled self-assurance lit his handsome face and a gleam in his eye too that bore the recognition of twelve and a half long years.

He offered an outstretched hand towards the beautiful lady whom he was being presented to. And Jenny, taking the hand she had thought never to hold again, smiled a heart warming, welcoming smile.

'How nice to meet you Mr Hawke,' she said, quietly, meaning to say more and with greater fortitude, but with her manager standing close by she felt stuck and was unable to do so.

'Likewise, ma'am,' returned Tom.

Alf Abrams, acutely perceptive of moments when he knew his own presence was superfluous to other people's needs interrupted the commencement of the meeting.

'Miss Kent, I wonder... would you mind if I took my leave of you. I'm sure you are able to handle matters from now on... only I have some urgent business that needs my attention.'

'Yes of course, Mr Abrams, if you consider it to be important. Yes... I'm sure I shall be alright. Although...' she hesitated awhile before continuing, 'perhaps you will be good enough to call in later to see me; before you finish for the day, if that would suit you... I may have something of interest to discuss with you.'

'Yes of course ma'am; good afternoon to you both.' And with that he left, with an incredibly cheery smile flooding his florid face.

The sun had found a break in the clouds by this time and was dimly shining its rays through to the hazy January afternoon as Jenny and Tom Hawke entered the house and made their way to the warm drawing room, with Jenny feeling just a little awkward at the situation she had created for herself but which in the final stages had burst upon her with such rapidity.

Despite her feelings and after she had guided Tom to a comfortable seat, she pulled herself together and offered her friend a drink which he accepted with some eagerness. She poured two glasses of the agreed beverage and after handing one to Tom she seated herself rigidly opposite him.

'It's good to see you again Tom;' said Jenny, as a pale cherry blush enhanced her face, 'it's been a long time since Lincoln hasn't it? I did chase after you, you know, when you left in such a hurry that day. I wanted so much to help a friend who had fallen upon hard times but you seemed not to want to know me.'

Tom was quite taken aback by the frankness of Jenny's statement and felt more than a little piqued that she should have even considered him to have fallen on hard times - let alone to mention those ancient feelings to him now.

'Fallen on hard times? Is that what you thought?' he said, not allowing his wide smile to diminish. 'Then all I can say, Miss Jenny, is that you misread the situation completely.

'It was a blistering hot day, if you remember, and, as I was in a hurry to see the cathedral, I ran all of the way from my vardo which I had left parked outside the city's boundary and in the care of my family. Don't know if you realise it at all, but that's some fair distance away; and not wanting to keep my friends waiting I sped along at quite a pace.

'I was fair done in by the time I reached the top of that hill I can tell you, so I sat down to recharge my batteries, so to speak, and threw my sweaty cap on the ground at my feet. That's when you came along. Not wanting you to see me in such a state of fatigue all oozing with sweat that soaked both my body and my clothes, I made a quick exit; far too embarrassed, I suppose... and I didn't get to see inside the cathedral after all.

'That was all there was to it, Miss Jenny, not really a beggar at all as you may have supposed at the time but merely a man who was exhausted with the heat of the day,' said he, amused at Jenny's misconception.

Jenny's face immediately turned from her existing cheery hue to an inelegant shade of crimson as she rose from her seat and walked over to Tom; and feeling completely mortified at the mistake she had harboured for all those years, she knelt at his feet, and taking both his hands in hers she lifted them to her mouth and kissed them, gently.

'I'm so sorry Tom, I should have known better; but for all this time I have felt that I had neglected you in your hour of need, when you had been so kind to me in mine all those years ago.'

'Miss Jenny, you should never feel indebted to me. I did for you what was needed to be done at the time and would do again... if the need arose.

'But your father, he didn't take too kindly to me did he, what with you staying overnight in the wagon and all,' said Tom, as a fleeting smile flickered across his face. 'But tell me, what else could I have done, given the circumstances at the time? When I think back, it was a pretty dumb thing for you to have done: you following me the way you did that day. I said so at the time if you remember, and we knew too how badly your parents were going to take it. Still no harm was done in the end and I expect your father eventually got over the shock.

'How is your father, anyhow; only I haven't seen him around lately? I often used to catch sight of him about the woods and hide from him when I thought he might be getting a bit too close?'

'He died in June of last year, Tom. He fell from his horse and fractured his spine some time before, but he lived on in agony for years after and eventually died of pneumonia.'

Tom's hands tightened on Jenny's as he looked into her moistened eyes.

'I'm really sorry to hear about that Miss Jenny,' he said. And as his fingers gripped hers so tightly, he felt the need to place his arms about her and to comfort her, but he remembered his place in time and remained seated. 'I'm sorry for you, not for him. He's in a better place now, you must know that, free from all the pain and sorrow of this world. My only hope is that the two of you were able to make up your differences before he went; only I remember you saying how badly he had treated you when you were a kid.

'I always think there can be nothing worse than leaving this world with a whole string of regrets lying about the place, and old animosities and resentments as well. If they are all left unattended to you might have to leave behind a heap of sadness for those that are still on earth.'

'Yes, Tom, we were at peace with one another; but I still miss him so very much.'

Jenny took advantage of the period of hushed stillness that followed, and allowed her eyes to trace the contours of Tom's weathered face. She felt it looked much the same as when she'd first seen him, when the two of them had buried Bluey together. A little older maybe, but not that much, for he still held the same strong handsome features he held then.

She broke the stillness at last:

'How long are you staying, Tom, before you and your family move on again, I mean?' The question was spoken gently and with concern and not at all in the wanting of them to be gone from off her land - it was taken in the way Jenny had meant it.

'We had hoped to stay till spring Miss Jenny, but I think your man might have other ideas and have us gone in a few days time; I thought that was what this meeting was to be all about and not intended for the two of us to sit here just talking reminiscences and drinking all your fine booze.'

Jenny smiled.

'Yes, you're right of course Tom, but it is rather pleasant to catch up with each other and to exchange thoughts of the past... at least I think it is.'

Jenny had hoped for much more than this meeting was offering. Perhaps she wanted Tom to declare his undying love for her, to sweep her off her feet and take her away with him to who knows where; as a child she had wanted nothing more, but she soon came to herself and put all romantic notions firmly behind her.

'Tom, as far as I'm concerned you and your friends can stay here for as long as you wish. I have it on the very good authority of my farm manager that he has every confidence in you all as being trusted residents and that I should have nothing to fear from you staying where you are. So yes, please stay as long you like; you will soon feel the brunt of my wrath if anyone abuses my lands or anything on my lands come to that, or indeed if I should be given any cause at all to change my mind.'

Tom laughed and Jenny smiled at the insinuation of her statement, both knowing full well that he could be trusted in every area Jenny had mentioned - well, with the possible exception of a rabbit or two going missing and perhaps the odd pheasant straying onto his dinner table - as Alf Abrams had hinted.

'That's very generous of you, Miss Jenny, very generous indeed. But you may rest assured we have no intentions in burning down the big woods yet awhile and we will be keeping the site both clean and tidy and make good any damage caused by our presence... I shall make sure of that; so you will have no need to worry or complain on that score.'

They talked and smiled together in this vain for some considerable time, each enjoying, enormously, the company of the other with four hands clutched firmly in the middle for all of this lengthy period. And it wasn't until after Jenny had decided she would bring forward a notion that had inadvertently been sown in her mind by her farm manager, and which she had pondered both day and night ever since, that their hands became unclasped once more with Jenny resuming her seat. They did not separate by desire but more by way of the event of the conversation being extended; the idea that had dominated Jenny's mind, needing an airing anyway.

'Tom, I do hope you wont consider me to be completely naïve or impertinent in my asking, but have you ever been engaged in permanent employment? I ask this because I find I have the possible need for a permanent gamekeeper on the estate and I thought that you may consider the position for yourself: you being well versed in countryside manners and natures good. There is also a cottage that will go with the position, if it would suit you. No pressure at all for you though, just something you might like to consider as time goes by... if you ever decide to settle.'

Immediately she had made the proposal she knew how

inappropriate and preposterous such a suggestion would be to a man like Tom.

"This man is a free spirit," she told herself, *"what on earth would he want with being tied down to a job?"* but she ignored her doubts and let the matter ride.

'I thank you very much, Miss Jenny, for thinking of me in that way, but I'm a contented man doing what I do. I love God's nature and would do all I could to preserve it. But to my way of thinking gamekeepers are people who are hell-bent on rearing birds for other peoples sport. Now please don't get me wrong, I have nothing against killing a bit of game, I do it myself when my belly is empty but there is something wrong in killing just for the sake of killing. Oh, I know they would say that every bird killed finds its way to someone's table, providing tender meat that is eaten with much appreciation, but its how the thing is carried out that bothers me.

'Did you know that eggs are collected on the shoot area and bought from breeders too; they're hatched, reared then released into the wild to supplement nature's population? Not much wrong with that you might think. But the birds are reared by cramming them in heated buildings by the thousand. Then, after they are but a few weeks old, they are put into release pens to acclimatise them to the wild.

'Adult breeding birds are fitted with devises to stop their natural aggression, when, in the wild the weak can easily escape the expectation of some sort of pecking order. Their wings are clipped when they are about seven weeks old to prevent them escaping over the top of the fencing and if this doesn't work, the outer, fine, juvenile feathers are pulled. Their beaks are partially amputated as well in order to cut down damage through aggressive pecking and the killing each other. All of these practises are commonly used today and they are, to my way of thinking, barbaric in the extreme. And so, all in all, it is a very cruel business indeed, Miss Jenny, and I will have no part in it, no part at all.'

Jenny looked aghast at what her friend had told her; little did she realise the implications attached to the preparations of the much acclaimed shoot.

'How on earth do you have all of this knowledge Tom?'

'Me being so mobile about the countryside, Miss Jenny; that's how. I picks up bits of information from time to time, and there is more, much more, to it than I have briefly told you, things that your tender heart would find to be quite sickening, so we'll say no more about the ghastly subject.

'Now if you've a mind to, and when you have a free hour or so to spare, why don't you pop over for a visit to the camp? It would only be fair for you to meet and get to know all my people and who it is you are showing so much kindness to. I shall be pleased to introduce you to my new wagon as well; it's so different to that old Bow-Top caravan you stayed in that stormy night.'

Jenny deliberately showed an avid interest in Tom's proposal and promised to pay him a call fairly soon; however, she failed to set a date for the visit and the matter was finally left in abeyance.

Nevertheless, a slight feeling of disappointment in the way her gamekeeper proposal had been placed to one side did enter her head and it continued to jar her on the odd occasion.

"Still, he didn't say a definite 'no' and surely he wouldn't find the need to use such barbaric methods as the ones he'd talked about," she thought.

CHAPTER FOUR

As in the case of countless other enthusiastic children of twelve significant years who face disruption to their schooling, Jacob Kent, also found the unwanted break in his learning to be an inconvenience - a nuisance even - in spite of everything; the cause of which was not of his making in the first place.

He had realised that moving to a new school might be a trifle worrying at times, even before he and his mother had left Brenton, although he failed to convey his concern to anyone at the time: he assuming, quite rightly, that he was worrying unnecessarily.

Throughout the preceding years, Jacob had grown to admire his old Lincolnshire Grammar School by taking to heart its traditions and its principles. Added to this he had become friendly with most of the boys in his year and with some that were older than he as well. But because his regular place of learning was being replaced by a school in Dorset, he had found the change to be just a little disconcerting; besides, he was older now and possessed a higher level of respect for education and so he had not wanted any changes to occur at all.

So, ill at ease he most certainly was; that is, before his mind had had the chance to become fully attuned to the idea of change. And even then, not until he had been fully initiated in a school that would hopefully provide him with his individual comfort zone and one that may prove to be the concluding stage in his middle years of learning.

He tried to set-aside all worrying thoughts by not allowing his mind to dwell on the matter that often. Of course, he had expected a few problems in the early days - that would have been quite normal to his way of thinking; and that the move might prove be life changing in many ways. A little thought provoking at times, for good or bad, but one that would be special in the creation of new friendships and new endeavours as well, which, with the passage of time, would promote fond memories for his mind to recall - in the future year's quieter moments.

Despite all this uneasiness flooding his young mind he was still pleased to be resuming his education once again - and at a Grammar School to boot.

The location of this new school, being so close to Bournemouth and no more than half a dozen miles from where he lived, was an added bonus; for it provided his mother with the convenience of being able to deliver Jacob and pick him up without too much rushing about the Dorset countryside.

Being an amenable sort of boy, Jacob had tried to put across all the right expressions for this new episode in his life - on the outside, at any rate, so that his mother might feel reassured; though it was with only limited eagerness mixed with feelings of anxiety that existed deep within.

He had sought encouragement by the fact that he would be faced with many exhilarating, fresh-found challenges as soon as his studies got underway; by that time his usual degree of confidence will have returned.

Nevertheless, because he was no longer within easy reach of his Uncle Hamish's learned guidance, he feared he would be hindered for support; for he adjudged, no matter how mistakenly, that his mother's feminine advice could not to be favourably compared with that of his uncle's manly counsel, no matter how well-meaning her intentions were thought to be.

For this reason alone, Jacob had felt somewhat frustrated by only being able to converse with his uncle Hamish remotely, by telephone in fact, when more physical clarification of his schooling problems would be necessary and more immediate, as it had already been proved.

But he had no need to worry himself unduly as his uncle would always make himself available to him, day or night. He would always be willing to expend as much time on his beloved nephew as was indeed necessary, to aid, guide and encourage this much approved young man to excel in all matters of education; or, indeed, to offer his advice on any other difficulties that life may have in mind to hurl at him from time to time; whether it be by phone, mail or indeed in person, if that were ever necessary.

In keeping with all the first days in the history of pupils attending new, awe-inspiring places of learning, Jacob's first day was also found to be slightly scary. Not in the manner regarding his education but in a different aspect altogether; for he had considered that he might discover some difficulty in establishing new and lasting friendships; friendships that would have had to come from the huge number of pupils already happily settled there. But it was because they were already settled there that he considered the task to be more difficult than in fact it was.

After Jacob had revealed his fears to his mother during their first journey to school, and as she delivered him outside the school gates early that dank opening morning, she reassured her son as only devoted mothers can:

'Darling,' she had said, smiling at his uncertainties, 'I have every confidence in you. I am sure you will soon find your feet within this school and bond with many new friends very quickly - if you want to, that is. After all, you had no difficulty in making new friends when you started your last school - now did you?'

And so it proved to be, for as soon as Jacob entered the largish cloak cum locker room, which had been previously shown to him on his final preparatory visit just two weeks earlier, a firm but welcoming voice was heard from across the way.

'New boy here are you Kent?'

The summarized question was asked from the wide opening to the locker room adjacent to the classroom where his inquisitor now stood. And when Jacob turned to register the questioner's identity, a tall, well built youth, about twelve months older than Jacob and with a full mop of fine, unruly, straight blonde hair, stepped forward and smiled openly at him; showing himself as being a well mannered youth by any standards.

'You seem to have me at a disadvantage,' replied Jacob, confidently. And walking over to the blonde lad he politely offered his hand which was willingly taken. 'How did you know my name? - Eh?'

'Fredrick Worth, that's Worthie to any of my many well meaning friends, but you, may call me Fredrick, I don't much care for Fred, or Worthie either come to that.

'Anyway, I usually make it my business to get to know all the new boys at the start of each term, just in case they're *worth* knowing. Get it? *Worth* knowing - Fredrick *Worth* - ah well - forget it.' He paused awhile as soon as he realised his pertinent joke had rebounded. 'So what's your Christian name young Kent, what handle do you prefer?'

'Jacob; my name is Jacob and I don't much care for that to be shortened either; not that there are many ways you could shorten it,' returned Jacob, with a faint smile and looking for all of the world a most confident young man who might easily have been mistaken for a fully fledged pupil of long standing at this aging grammar school, when deep down he felt it not to be the case.

The proposal of a private tutor educating Jacob at home such as Jenny received had been put forward by Hamish - was briefly discussed - then promptly rejected by the mother - quite adamantly in fact - the suggestion being totally out of the question.

'My son is precious to me, Uncle,' she had said, 'and he is not, repeat not, to be subjected to the torturous loneliness that I had to endure as a child, I am wholly uncompromising on that point.' Jenny had been steadfast, despite her uncle's questionings.

And so the red bricked, traditional, late Victorian building now being used as a grammar school, with its jaded and antiquated look of inhospitality and with the date 1900 being uniquely inscribed above its doorway, was finally selected as the only option in the search of a school for Jacob.

Although it was not the most cleverly maintained place of education in the nation, and sadly, not at all to be favourably compared with Jacob's previous grammar school in Lincolnshire, it did present itself as being the only school of its kind within an area of seventy or so square miles.

Of course, as always, there had been other mildly suitable alternatives; some of these ought to have been investigated more fully, one might suppose, but because of parental fussiness they had been largely ignored. The excuse being that they had failed to come up to the expectations expressly sought by Jenny.

One such school was a fee paying public school. This time it was Jacob who censured the notion, he being most adamant; and with no opportunity for logical debate he stated his rejection most profoundly:

'A public school is out of the question as far as I'm concerned, Mother; I cannot possibly consider such an idea... not for a single moment.

'I mean to say, do you seriously expect me to attend a public school where I can be abused at every given opportunity, by burly six form boys? You see, I knew a young lad who had been very unhappy at the public school he went to in Lincolnshire; too snobbish and unfriendly by far, with younger boys being physically abused by older pupils - continuously in fact. In the end his parents removed him and allowed him to come to our school.

'From what I have since found out, most of these so called public schools are pretty much the same these days... the country over. So, even if I were to be taken on as a day boy, the answer would still be a firm no.'

That was that, the reason given for the refusal was taken on board by Jenny, and no more was said about the matter.

Earlier that drizzling morning, Jacob had found himself walking through the open gateway feeling reasonably confident but with a questioning look upon his face that seemed to contradict those feelings.

Jacob had stared in dismay at the measure of scaly flakes of dirty, off-white paint he saw hanging from the wide doorway he was about to enter. And as he looked up to the tall curvature of its supporting timbers, most of the paintwork was seen to be peeling there as well.

The lower half of the walls, forming the immediate corridor, that the young lad had walked along, were badly scuffed by the boots of bawdy boys; and although dark green in colour, which should have posed few restoration problems for any worthwhile decorator, the walls had been completely neglected.

When Jenny had taken her son for an introductory visit she had formally remarked to the school's principal about the extremely poor presentation of this grammar school and she had been assured, at the time, that the décor problems were being considered but held in abeyance until certain financial problems could be resolved - probably at the close of the half term or at the very latest during the summer recess, which, at the time, seemed much more likely to Jenny.

The walls of the cloakroom cum locker room, where Jacob now stood, were not unlike the walls of the corridor that past its wide opening and along which he had walked a minute or two ago. These walls also looked as if they were in need of a coat of obliterating paint. At the moment, they were all flimsily covered with the same dark, glossy green colour, which matched the passageway - well, as near as made no difference. But it did look as if paint had been splashed about at least a century ago and with a balding paintbrush being used.

A narrow, grooved dado rail separated the green section below from the grubby cream colour above, each colour contrasting the other with formal unsightliness.

The lower dark, gloss green section of the décor in the locker room had been mostly scraped, scratched or gouged quite deliberately with some sharp instrument or other; and a sizeable quantity of etched graffiti markings and a variety of inappropriate designs were also plainly visible.

Other improper words were also written and other names inscribed as being, presumably, the initials and pseudo names of the ham-fisted artists involved.

Some scrawled graffiti, especially those of the obscene variety, had been unsuccessfully painted over with a miss-matched dark green colour so that the writings were still visible as lighter shades beneath the obviously botched attempt.

A double rail in the centre of the cloakroom area and one of the walls were strung with rows of hat pegs, some of which hung lifelessly down with but a single screw holding them to their original positions; all looking extremely disorderly and likely to cause harm to some unfortunate youth - sooner or later.

The back wall to the cloakroom supported a series of lockers, two tiers deep. The doors of these were fastened by a variety of insecure padlocks; string or wire or both were also used. A similar arrangement of lockers was repeated on the immediate part of the wall in the corridor outside.

More than a couple of locker doors here were broken, dented, or merely left hanging despondently with no apparent owners wishing to claim them.

This spectacle did not pass Jacob's notice at all favourably and he adjudged the spectacle to present an offensive recommendation for what was considered to be, the school's educational excellence. He also thought the sight did not provide a pleasant reception to a young man who was presenting himself for middle education - and for the first time of asking at that.

After discovering a spare undamaged locker, Jacob had begun to stow away his belongings when first he'd been approached by Fredrick Worth and now the two youngsters faced one another with a degree of affability filling the room.

Even though twelve months separated the two boy's in age, as already established, a mere half an inch in stature was seen to be the differing measurement between them - for Jacob was also tall of stature.

'You're a local lad I expect!' quizzed Fredrick Worth, with a degree of idle curiosity - as a few other boys began to mill about the place.

'Yes, I live in one of the local villages called Hyde; Hyde Hall to be exact.'

'Hells bells, then what the blazers are your parents doing in sending you to a squalid dump like this for? They must be loaded, if you don't mind me saying so; and if you live where you say you live then I should have thought they might easily have afforded some other school, one that would be much more suited to a posh kid like you, and without there being too many money problems for them to deal with, either.'

'Don't know about that, it was my choice to come here in the first place. You see, last year I was being educated at a super grammar school up in Lincolnshire, so it seemed more sensible, to my way of thinking, to continue my education in the same, or at least, a similar syllabus. I didn't want to add to the difficulty of moving from one school to another by unnecessary changes, now did I?

'I suppose I could have been enrolled at a public school; actually that was put forward as a suitable alternative, but I didn't really fancy that idea very much.'

Just then the loud ringing of a bell resounded throughout the whole building, summoning pupils to their classrooms.

'Catch up with you at break time young Jacob, or maybe lunch time and we'll have a further chat together then,' called Fredrick, as both boys went their separate ways.

Obviously, Fredrick had considered Jacob to be an important sort of lad - important enough for him to develop a friendship of sorts; although for some unknown reason he had failed to make him aware as to how he knew his surname.

The day's lessons went much as Jacob had expected and his eagerness to learn was especially evident.

Very few changes to the curriculum set at his previous school were evident and so Jacob Kent sailed through the day with ease.

Fredrick Worth, being as good as his word, met up with Jacob at all three break periods. And at the close of the school's working day he was waiting by the gate for the two of them to be engrossed in even more chitchat.

Jenny was delighted both with Jacobs's enthusiasm for his new school and with his finding a new friend so quickly; one with whom he could build a close and long-lasting relationship, she hoped.

'Chamber's Farm, Mother, that's where Fredrick Worth lives,' said Jacob, while they were still halfway through their journey home. 'His father's name is Fredrick as well. Isn't he one of your tenant farmers Mother? Only I seem to remember you speaking of someone by that name fairly recently.'

'Yes you're quite right darling, the Worth family has held a legal entitlement to its tenanted land, from the Hyde Hall estate, since time immemorial, or so I have read. I have also found out that Mr Worth and his father before him have worked Chamber's Farm for at least forty years and further back than that, I should have thought.

'In fact, Fred Worth's farm, is one of the most profitable

farms in this region, next to the Hyde Hall home farm that is,' she asserted, without any noticeable smugness. 'I'm sure that is how Fredrick must have been familiar with your name darling, as I was speaking to his father, only a few days ago.

'I mentioned to him at the time that you would be starting at the local grammar school in the new term. Funny why he didn't mention at the time that his own son was already at that school; didn't wish to sound presumptuous, I expect.

'But he is a very amiable sort of gentleman, and shows himself as being very hard working indeed. He is very industrious and innovative as well in his farming methods... according to Mr Abrams, anyway.

'Maybe it might be a nice idea to invite your new friend over sometime, you will most probably gain quite a lot of help from him if you do, as he will undoubtedly be slightly more advanced than you and has probably already covered the same or similar subjects that you will soon be taking.'

'Thanks mother, that sounds like a good idea; I shall drop it into the conversation when an opportunity presents itself.'

And so it came to pass, Fredrick Worth became Jacob's first firm Dorset friend and the two youngsters were soon to be seen in each others spirited company at every given opportunity; seriously learning from each other, exploring each others farmland and fishing in the local river Avon. And when not in one another's society they would keep in touch by telephone so that when Jacob came across a problem with his homework he was able to consult his friend - without the need to bother his Uncle Hamish after all.

***

It had been a full four weeks since Jenny's meeting with Tom Hawke at Hyde Hall, and spring weather, it was hoped, would soon be on its way - helping to supply a positive start to a brand new farming year.

Jenny had put Tom's suggestion, regarding her possible visit to his gypsy encampment, to the back of her mind and although he'd eagerly proposed the visit she hadn't allowed her thoughts to become bogged down or excited by the idea in any way at all.

In her quieter moments though, and on more than one occasion during the past weeks, Jenny had occupied her mind by going over the meeting she'd had with her gypsy friend, particularly taking into account the part when she had put forward the gamekeeper proposal to him. And although she'd grasped the reasons for his abrupt rejection of her suggestion completely, she was still disappointed - extremely so - and wondered if it would ever be possible to somehow change his mind for him - for it was perfectly clear he would be unwilling do so by himself.

'But he hadn't turned me down flat, not in so many words. He had just failed to assert himself in the direction I had hoped for, that was all.' At least that was what she told herself time and time again.

Not that Jenny's long delay in visiting the camp site could be regarded as a payback for Tom's rejection in any way, no, no; the lovely lady would never stoop to such pettiness as that. It was just that a visit no longer seemed quite so appropriate - that was all - not in her opinion anyway.

Nevertheless, what with winter's bleakness being so persistent and she being weighed down with estate business Jenny had tried to ignore all subjects relating to Tom, as soon as they entered her head, in fact, and to treat them as she would a passing thought. Though, she was persistent in finding Tom's rejection of the keeper proposal to be vaguely irritating.

"Surely he wouldn't feel compelled to adopt the horrible techniques in pheasant mutilation, he described so forcefully, if he were to accept the position... he could use more conventional gamekeeper practices just as easily... more so, I should have thought," she considered regretfully, to herself. It was obvious, even to her, she was not letting this issue go; she would surely resurrect it later at least one more time.

As Jenny was seated in the solitude of her bright bedroom a few evenings later she rekindled her feelings on an assortment of matters and the need to develop a meaningful relationship with someone, popped into her head.

She had failed to stimulate a worthwhile friendship with anyone of consequence since she'd been in Dorset and the notion of involving herself with any of the local institutions had been ignored by her. She finally decided it was Tom's society she sought most of all, and not that of any other well meaning individual.

So, with no further appropriate thoughts attending, she, in the end, promised herself a visit with Tom to be now relevant in spite of everything, and so she decided to undertake such a call the following day; and it being Saturday, would be a most convenient time for her.

As Margaret had still not returned from her lengthy Christmas break, she had telephoned her hoped for friend, Jane

Howe, inviting her for dinner on the same Saturday evening, feeling that she should retain at least some sort of rapport with her father's former mistress - if for his sake alone.

"*... but my dropping in on Tom's site shouldn't get in the way of Jane's visit or confuse or hinder it in any way at all,*" she thought.

....

The Saturday noonday was bright and sunny. A few, white, fluffy bits and pieces drifted over the horizon 'tis true but nothing that posed too much of a threat to Jenny's visit.

The weather had, in actual fact, been friendly the past day or so, and seemed set to continue in that mood for a while longer. And it was with this fact of assured commendation from an almost cloudless sky that Jenny decided to walk through the broad leafed forest, taking the same path she had taken as a child, when she had followed the gypsy to his van - instead of using her car along some lengthy road she was unsure of.

Even so, the going was difficult and decidedly wet under foot, but she was reasonably confident she could remember the way. "*It's the other side of the forest, directly opposite... I'm sure of it... if indeed the camp site is in the same place it had been when I made the trek before,*" she thought to herself; and so she commenced her ramble at a cautious pace.

Jenny's questioning mind bothered her a little as she strolled across the meadow that passed alongside the forest's margin, and she wondered if the homemade, cross-shaped marker, she had so carefully crafted for Bluey's grave, could still be where she had placed it all those years ago. But, upon reaching the spot where she knew her old friend had been buried, she found no cross, not even a rotting trace of one. Even the small mound, which had indicated Bluey's interment then, had been flattened by the passing years and grass now grew with lengthy blades so as to disguise all forms of its existence.

She stopped awhile - then heaved a sigh.

Moving on, she scrambled over the netted fence which had enclosed the broad leafed forest for many a year and caught her jeans on a rusting spike in her haste. It was not without some difficulty that she managed to free herself and as she completed the awkward task she glanced down to see a small three corner tare where she was sure it didn't show.

Her jaunt through the large wood was pleasant enough with barely a breeze stirring the supple branches of all but a couple of evergreen trees.

Many vocal chords, mainly issuing from birds of the black variety, were distinctly heard close by and in the distance too, and their warbling tunes delighted the beautiful lady immensely as she passed along the way.

Isolated patches of pale yellow primroses were shown to be freshly born in unopened loveliness with more flowers yet to come, countless more: if the densely packed carpets of green were anything to go by.

And the tall, deciduous beech trees, with their dark grey coverings of the smoothest bark, were now to be clearly seen with newly formed buds on each branch of the lofty entangled ceiling.

Jenny knew that each bough and twig were already adorned with perfectly formed buds, almost as soon as the old leaves had fallen in fact and would now be waiting for the miracle of spring to enable the tiny leaves to unfold and for the yellowish-green flowers to ultimately show themselves.

It reminded her of a poem she had written when still a child; and she tried desperately to bring it to mind.

'How did the blessed thing go,' she said, quietly to herself. Her response was positive. 'Ah yes, I remember it quite clearly now:'

This oh so sombre glade
Will, in a while, display
A clearer, brighter shade
Of green for springtime's day.

Spring has e'en now endowed
Each bough with buds yet hid
Then openly avowed
That blooms will burst as bid.

The warmth from infant spring
Will hearten flowers to grow.
And with ne'er a din, will herald in
The awaited summer's glow.

'Ha, now how did that last bit go? Something, da de, da, de, da and de da de da... something about Mother Nature's eternal ring - I have it:'

*And Mother Nature's blest
Eternal ring will shun
The old leaves from the best.
Then comes the fall, when all in all,
The cycle will have run."*

'I don't know - it was something like that - I'm sure of it...
that is, of course, if my memory hasn't deserted me altogether.'

Jenny knew her poetry was dull, juvenile even, more so now
than when her uncomplicated words had been scribbled. For
although Jenny had loved poetry as a child she'd had little help from
the then austere Miss Wood. But she had battled on with her aimless
doodling all the same.

All of this, and much more too, enchanted Jenny's dancing
senses as natures beauty unfurled itself before her lovely eyes and
encouraged her jaunt of occupied attention to stay with her to the
forest's end.

The welcoming aroma of burning wood was the first
indication of the camp's company being present - as the blue sky
once again showed itself through the forest's final branches.

And then the curling white smoke at the forest's edge, as it
moved through the trees in Jenny's direction, caused her to cough a
little; and so she skirted round the cloud to avoid being totally
choked.

More carefully this time, Jenny clambered over yet another
netted fence that skirted that side of the forest.

And then, all at once, she saw the five vans; not one hundred
yards away; each meticulously placed to form a circular pattern and
all neighbouring the sizeable, billowing campfire that had caused her
throat's discomfort.

A black, bowl shaped cauldron was hanging above the
flames with the protruding handle of a ladle moored to its outer rim;
and an oversized lid was precariously balanced over its mouth. And
as liquid in the cauldron bubbled away, so too the balanced lid was
being caused to rise and fall - again and again.

A delicate smile broke Jenny's beautiful lips as she eyed the
gypsies' Heath Robinson goings-on in the art of nomadic cuisine; but
the distinctive aroma issuing from the cauldron caused her nostrils to
flare, somewhat, with heady delight.

Tom was sitting on a large log with a forked stick in his hand
poking aimlessly at the fire and chatting to a couple of his friends

who were similarly engaged.

His broad back was towards Jenny as she silently approached and a faintly disguised expression of 'Hey up, visitors,' made Tom turn to look in Jenny's direction.

Upon his recognition of the lovely lady, his face instantly broadened to a wide grin as he stood to welcome his guest with two extended arms.

'Miss Jenny! Welcome, welcome to our humble homes. I never thought you'd summon enough courage to make it through the woods on your own; but I'm mighty glad you have.'

The gypsy took Jenny's two hands in his and stood there for a few brief moments as he filled his senses with the wonderment of the vision that stood before him. And then, dropping one of her hands and lifting the other, he drew it gently to his lips and kissed it tenderly, in a fond hello - or so everyone thought. But to Jenny's senses it meant so much more than a mere gesture of welcome.

She was pleased to find herself in the company of this man; however, she did colour up - just a little - in mild embarrassment as certain thoughts invaded her lively mind.

'Hello Tom,' she said, as she awkwardly returned the greeting. 'As it is such a fine day, though the wetness persists underfoot simply everywhere, I thought I might risk a walk through the forest and accept your kind invitation to a visit with you all... at long last.' She turned her head as she spoke the final few words of her short sentence so that there could be no mistake by the statement she had uttered and that it was meant for the whole camp and not for Tom alone; for she had no intentions in disclosing her feelings, whatever they may be, to any casual bystander let alone to Tom's closest friends.

Because the whole of his family had expressed their appreciation after he had revealed the glad tidings, Tom called out to each and every one to step forward and to meet the new lady owner of the estate who had been so generous in allowing the company of travellers to stay on the site for as long as they desired.

And so, with happiness shining from their faces, both young and old, men, women and children alike, stepped forward and gathered to surround and greet their benefactress. With a small degree of obliged servitude being automatically, but willingly expressed, they each in turn shook the delicate hand of the mistress of Hyde Hall.

'Where's Mr Bee?' Someone in the crowd chanced to think; and then he shouted the name more loudly. 'Mr Bee, step forward!

Come out from my van and be politely recognised, and express your heartfelt gratitude to this here beautiful young lady, same as the rest of us... will you man?'

The summons was adhered to, not immediately but within a few seconds of the call being made; and Barnabas Bell, the scourge of Jenny's childhood, stepped forward to be presented by standing on the uppermost step of the furthest vardo from the group of people, with a sickening grin that stretched from ear to ear. The misshapen figure of the man, with his wayward left eye, who had caused so much grief to Jenny, was unmistakeable.

Upon recognition of the man she so despised, Jenny ran hurriedly from the scene, and in the direction of the forest - the way she had come - without a single word of farewell or excuse for leaving breaking her lips for anyone to hear.

CHAPTER FIVE

Jenny was beside herself with rage.

Indeed, the anger that welled inside her at this moment was beyond belief, for never, in the whole of her life, had she been tried by so much loathing for another person. How could she have been, when it was alien to her nature to feel revulsion for any living creature?

Why, even her mother's appalling behaviour had failed to affect Jenny's mind in this manner, or in any manner close to it; heaven only knows she had behaved badly enough and often enough, over the years, to merit such feelings.

But there it was; a brand new emotion had now entered Jenny's nature thereby forcing her opinion of this creature, Bell, to be filled with unmitigated hate. Of course, she had felt a loathing for him on numerous occasions in the past but nothing that had reached such intensity as this.

Not only was she enraged by Bell's hideous visage but she was also confused by the idyllic scene that had been set before her a minute or two ago.

"A tranquil scene it had been then but one which I now consider as being a ridiculous charade. The whole act was staged in a heartless fashion in order to cover up the shocking goings on within the camp itself and within its families as well," she thought; her unreasoned emotion getting the better of her.

Jenny's anger towards these gypsies was brought about by her sighting of the vile Barnabas Bell standing on the wagon's step in open defiance of her; and the sickly grin that hung around his mouth only added to his insolence. In performing such an audacious act as that, he had made it quite clear, he knew it was Jenny who had turned up to be welcomed as guest of honour and not some unlikely stranger.

But the man, merely being in residence with Tom's friends was more than Jenny could stomach; and she had to breathe deeply - again and again - to prevent her from being physically sick.

Despite all this, she questioned in her own mind how it was that Bell could be so well established in the camp. She knew the cretin resided in Hyde: he had made that piece of information abundantly clear when last their paths had crossed; but, since she was fairly certain he would not have been able to afford a van from his own resources, she was perplexed as to how he managed to exist?

"Someone must be housing him... I'm sure of it; living in someone else's van can be the only logical explanation; perhaps he's living with Tom himself... who knows?"

Jenny considered this alternative fairly rationally, without any additional nerves being exposed; for the event of the summoning voice that had motioned Bell from his place of hiding, had not fully infiltrated her brain for the while.

As expected, new reservations were now beginning to form - reservations that brought into question Tom's principles - and they were building up inside her mind at a rate of knots, thereby causing her rising rage to culminate in a state of out of control fury. This out of control fury left her deprived of all virtuous opinions of Tom, and in a way she never thought possible.

The heated anger that accumulated inside her mind because of Tom was bad enough - surely - but now it was being increased by the realisation that it was her land that was being used to provide Bell with his free sanctuary and consequently his comfort as well.

Adding both these insults together only served to swell the frantic lady's rage in a way that was beyond her comprehension and caused feelings of hopelessness and extreme frustration to exist in her spirit and her soul.

She was now terrified of what to expect from Bell, where to turn, or what to do next.

Tom's action was completely out of character as far as the beautiful woman was concerned - she had always considered him to be more thoughtful than this; and she failed to produce any justification for the gypsy man's behaviour. Any pretence at understanding this situation had been slung to the back of her mind - as soon as she had left the place, in fact - since all of these insufferable gypsies had behaved so badly - yes - the whole lot of them.

All of this distress only served to heighten Jenny's fear of Bell and caused her to be ever mindful of the cruelty he was willing to inflict on her. Mental torment or physical violence, it made no difference - since both afflictions were as bad as each other; but the thought of either, alarmed her already panic stricken brain.

"This obnoxious man is a complete moron and is capable of anything to harm me... anything at all. And Tom as well, isn't he as bad? Hasn't this gypsy let me down so badly? How could he give sanctuary to the madman who has caused me so much grief? And by deliberately harbouring him he has placed me in the impossible situation I now find myself." She screamed the illogical words

inwardly to herself in fear and panic as blood drained from her silken face and tears of fury filled her eyes.

After a few moments, she calmed herself a little - temporarily - and slowly she retraced the morning's jaunt, in her mind that should have meant so much to her.

"The walk here had been so lovely, even beautiful at times as I anticipated seeing Tom once more and I had looked forward to being acquainted with the closest of his friends, who he had told me so much about. How could he have been so... thoughtless as to sully our friendship in this way...?"

She now found herself shaking inside as her temper took control again thereby encouraging her mind to freeze itself in a mixture of frustration and stress - for she had now reached a point that was tugging at her emotional tether - a point, beyond which, she was not prepared to go; even if she could.

"No, not for anyone will I allow my benevolence to be taken for granted or used in this way. And I will not cease from heaping my vengeful retribution on all gypsies, even on you Tom Hawke; so you can all go to the bottom of the bottomless pit for all I care... and rot there... the lot of you.

"This obnoxious man, Barnabas Bell, has the foul morals of the devil himself and is a demon from hell. Not only has he abused me both sexually and mentally as a child but later on, prior to my return to Dorset, did he not torment me with the vile innuendos of a fiend and with me not knowing which way he would continue his repugnant behaviour. Even so, I had chivvied myself to ignoring all the dirt that was spilling from his filthy mouth and evaded all the disgusting insinuations he threw in my direction.

"This man has been an evil curse on my life from the day I first set eyes on him; an irritation that will not go away and cannot be relieved with the soothing lotion of persuasion; for hasn't the dearest of uncles not applied such a balm and failed in his attempt?

"If this man, being the dregs of humanity that he is and a loathsome blemish upon the face of the earth as well, thinks he is benefiting from my generosity... well, he had better think again... because I can tell that cretin here and now... it will be over my dead body...."

Jenny weighed up all of these declarations and fears in her head only slightly calmer than she had said them to herself. But seeing that all the anger still raged within the dimness of her mind the conclusive statement of her thoughts was intended as a seething threat.

She waited awhile for Tom to catch up with her, as she knew he surely would, and so she placed one foot in front of the other very slowly.

She had scaled the netted fence once again and was heading in the direction whence she came when she heard the echoing sound of Tom's trailing voice calling out her name, anxiously and clear.

She stopped and turned as she waited for the gypsy's arrival - her bitterness still showing.

'Miss Jenny,' he said, breathlessly when he came at last to where she stood. And with his outstretched arm resting its hand caringly upon her shoulder he added: 'Whatever is the matter? Why did you leave us in such a hurry? Was it something I said, or did, to make you respond in such a way?'

Jenny brushed his hand away almost as soon as it had touched her.

'No Tom, it's nothing you have said at all, but I feel I must now cancel my approval for your stay on my estate and I shall now need you gone from here by the end of next week... sooner if you are able.'

Jenny's words descended like a proverbial bolt... and as Tom held high the hand that had rested briefly on her shoulder in an act of submission, he stood aghast at the instruction she had uttered.

He sighed heavily.

'Yes of course, Miss Jenny, we will be gone from here tomorrow, if you desire it. But won't you first give me some reason for your change of heart. An indication at least as to why you are looking so distressed and why such a reversal of fortune has been shown to me so that I can at least pass on to the others why there has been an abrupt change of plan.'

Jenny, her mind more stable now, was suddenly filled with remorse at hearing Tom's plea for a required explanation of the adjustment to the favours her lips had delivered a week or two ago, and she knew at once that his appeal was being coupled to innocence.

And along with the remorse, or because of it, there came a final sinking feeling in the pit of her stomach as the sudden realization at last penetrated her mind.

Yes indeed, sad to say, the penny had dropped at last, exposing Tom's integrity; and all the accusations she had imposed on him were deemed flawed and all these unsavoury feelings were now stuck - firmly - in her gullet.

"Why on earth didn't I consider the possibility of Tom's innocence before; instead of assuming the worst in him?" she

thought, with a trembling feeling inside.

Instantly, Jenny opened her eyes wide and covered her mouth with the palms of her hands in horror as shocked panic at the offensive way she had treated Tom - and with such determination and lack of self-control at that - struck home.

Now a fresh dilemma existed to be bravely coped with: how could she possibly justify her hasty order for Tom to leave without first explaining the worthless cretin that had slyly concealed itself within the confines of Tom's hospitality?

Any explanation given at this stage would look bad for her in Tom's eyes - or so she thought. And it would, as well, without doubt, inspire the man Bell to amass all vengeances imaginable against her, if she named him now for what he truly is, and he would dump all of it on her head and with all the fervour at his disposal. He was more than capable of performing each and every variety of venomous revenge against her, with little thought for her, or anyone else for that matter; and with no regret at all being evident either.

She reasoned with herself quickly:

'Tom, I cannot in all honesty give you a logical explanation for my decision without releasing certain foul information about a member of your tribe, which, I am sure, you would not wish to hear. So we had better leave matters as they are and go our separate ways: you to your way of life on the road and me to the running of this place.'

The words seemed to stick in Jenny's throat as she realised the earth-shattering decision she was making; for it was regrettable to have to close an episode in her life before it had scarcely begun. *"But it has to be done all the same,"* she thought.

She looked deeply into the mystified eyes of the anxious man that stood before her; with sadness and regret in her own heart for allowing such a maniac to come between the two of them.

'No Miss Jenny, I can't leave things like that be. If you have something against any one of my friends then 'tis better you say it now so that I can at least try to make matters right between us. If someone has harmed you in any way, any way at all mind you; well then, I shall certainly need to know all about it. It's no good locking these things away you know!

'As I said before, when you told me of your father's death, we must never leave matters to be unresolved so that they fester in our hearts. It would be nigh on impossible for me to leave the matter hanging about like this, and I should hate for us to part with any animosity existing between us; because, well, we may never get the chance to put things right again. So I'm not moving from this spot until you explain yourself to me; I shall follow you all the way to your home if needs be and I shall still pester you till I leave this place for good - never to return.'

Jenny's demeanour changed dramatically at the hearing of Tom's words and she moved closer to him and taking his hands into her own she looked up and gazed into his hazel eyes.

'You are truly a lovely man, Tom Hawke, and I bless you for wanting to preserve our friendship.'

The gypsy gathered her into his strong arms and held her comfortingly, not overly close but close enough to disturb the minds of the two of them.

It was but a brief moment before the realisation dawned on him that he may have overstepped the mark, and the perception that his station in life should be kept safe and preserved at all cost, was uppermost in his mind; and so he released her, and in so doing he looked to the ground as if ashamed of the liberty he had taken.

'Please don't look so sad Tom; we have done nothing wrong, only goodness can possibly exist in an embrace - you must know that. But please, don't compel me to say something you will not wish to hear; and when this person's colours are fully exposed, as they most surely will be, then please come straight back here to me again, where I will be waiting, so that we may continue with our unsullied friendship.'

'OK Miss Jenny, have it your way,' said Tom, as they both turned round to go their separate ways, 'perhaps you're right after all.'

And as he and she disappeared from each others view, his voice echoed through the tops of the tall trees, as it had before.

'See you again then I expect, Miss Jenny.' and then his voice was stilled.

***

For all the time that had passed since her return home, Jenny had been in a tortuous state of disbelief at how badly her visit with Tom had gone that afternoon. And she questioned if he had truly accepted their parting as an amicable solution to the dreaded impasse they had reached, or whether he held her reluctance to disclose all she knew against her.

"He'll be gone by next Saturday, I know he will; he's a man of his word - I know that much about him. But he'll be back again,

I'm sure of that as well; but even if we were to be doomed never to meet again I shall still have my memories of him." She thought in silence as a lonely tear escaped its place of making. *"And I shall vigorously hold on to all the memories I have of him... till the end of my days. No one, but no one can ever take the place of my son's father, so they best not try."*

***

The doorbell sounded loudly, arousing Jenny from her deep thoughts as she pottered about the large kitchen preparing the meal that was to be shared with Jane Howe that evening.

Agnes had been given the evening off, thereby allowing Jenny the privilege to indulge her culinary skills.

Jacob was in his room attending to his homework and spending an hour or so in quiet conversation on the telephone with Fredrick; for it wasn't only the newness of their friendship that stimulated the two boys chatter these days, but a mutual interest in all things wholesome that compelled such fascinating repartee.

Jenny had dried her hands and was removing her apron as she sallied forth leaving behind the transitory concerns that had engaged her mind since her return from seeing Tom. And the recollection of his final promise quickly caused her mind to change from despair to one of delight; and as she crossed the hallway the feeling lingered in her mind and she allowed a lovely smile of inner warmth to take the place of all unwanted gloom - which Jane Howe mistakenly thought was meant for her.

As the door was opened fully for the mistress of Angus Kent to enter, she coloured slightly in response to Jenny's mood.

'Hello Jane, how nice to see you again,' said Jenny, as the brightness still lingered upon her face. 'It seems absolutely ages since we last met... I do hope you are keeping well.'

The greeting was kept as casual as Jenny was able: bearing in mind she experienced a feeling of friendliness whenever she was in Jane's company. And so she wished to be openly congenial to her guest even though she felt that the same liberal gestures were not always fully reciprocated - not in exactly the same way.

'Thank you Jenny, I'm well,' said Jane, as she stepped inside the huge hall and exchanged a double peck on the cheek with her hostess. And then, after taking off her weighty fur coat she revealed her dress to be so daringly cut that it revealed the most risqué cleavage that Jenny could ever imagine.

'I wasn't at all sure if you were entertaining other guests this evening or whether we would be alone, so I dared to dress suitably formal just in case.'

Jenny wasn't at all certain if Jane had meant by her remark that she had dressed formally for the benefit of other guests or whether the statement was meant for the second clause. Anyhow she decided not to allow Jane to elaborate.

'No Jane, we shall be quite alone; that is unless Jacob decides to join us for dinner a little later; he said that he might do so, as he is always willing to accept the odd glass or two of wine.

'I felt we had some catching up to do, that was all, and as I didn't wish to neglect our friendship any longer, I considered I should do something about it; after all you are part of the family, in a manner of speaking, and I am sure my father would have preferred us to remain good friends even at the risk of my mother's disapproval; she, I hasten to add, isn't here; she's still absent even after the four week period she had taken for her Christmas holiday; although where she exactly went to… I have no idea.'

'Don't you really Jenny? I thought you would have known all about your mother's comings and goings. Well I can assuredly put you straight there. Its common knowledge that your mother has taken up with a Lord Melchamp and visits him at every given opportunity… well, since his divorce from his wife, anyway.'

Jenny failed to respond immediately to the free intelligence being offered, howbeit with some difficulty; instead she escorted her guest to the prepared dinning room where she had set up a smaller than usual table with a three place setting - and instantly offered her guest an aperitif.

Somewhere or other in this narrative it has almost certainly been mentioned Jane Howe as being a most curvaceous lady. Although she was now enjoying her forty-second year of living, she still looked rather pretty, not ostentatiously so, but she did carry a certain air about her that held an alluring fascination for the opposite sex to dwell upon; this facet had most certainly been borne out by Angus Kent, when he was still alive.

She usually spoke with a quiet, faltering sort of voice, quite unsure of herself at times, but on this occasion the volume was turned up a tad; well, high enough to indicate to Jenny that her guest had already partaken of the amber fluid, to which she knew she was particularly partial - most probably to calm her nerves. And although Jenny considered Jane to have lost a little weight since she last saw her and her features were looking rather more wan than usual, helped no doubt by the sparsity of her makeup, she kept these observations discreet, thinking that the affect of her lover's death was still proving to be a little burdensome.

A most convivial atmosphere abounded throughout the whole of the meal with both ladies taking in turns to serve one another and both were absent from the table and in the kitchen when Jacob popped his head round the door.

'Hello Mother, hello Jane,' he said, with a flushed look upon his face that betrayed a sharp discomfort. 'I'm so sorry, but I fear I will be unable to join you for dinner this evening. You see I have this awful headache which doesn't want to leave me; been on the phone too long exchanging banter with Fredrick I expect.

'Anyway if you will both excuse me, I think I should retire for the evening in the hopes of feeling better in the morning. You see, Fredrick is popping round to see me tomorrow and hopefully we shall be spending the whole day together; if that's OK with you Mother.'

'Yes, of course it is. Darling are you sure you are alright though?' asked his mother, quietly and in the concerned way that every doting mother does when an only child is ill. And walking over to her son she placed an open hand upon his forehead. 'You seem to have a slight temperature, Jacob; have you taken an aspirin tablet or anything else to help the wretched pain away?' she asked, to which Jacob nodded positively. 'Then maybe you are right dear, perhaps bed is the best place for you. But no reading, mind; your head won't get better if you bombard it with too much concentration.'

After a further exchange, Jacob excused himself again and left the ladies to the conclusion of their meal.

'So how long has my mother's relationship with Lord Melchamp been a reality to you Jane; what I mean is, how long have you known... if you are absolutely sure the thing to be true, that is? Only I know that even the most innocuous interactions between people can quite often be misinterpreted by those who are all too eager to discredit the unsuspecting and blameless innocents.' said Jenny, her inquisitiveness at last getting the better of her.

They had finished the meal and both ladies were sipping from glasses of brandy, interspersed with coffee from petite coffee cups.

'Yes, you are right there Jenny, I know that to be true, only too well; as I shall tell you in a moment,' returned Jane, with the forefinger of her left hand curled casually around her bottom lip and the remainder of her fingers installed on and below her chin; she not really knowing if it would be correct in continuing the subject or no. She finally decided to go ahead despite knowing that it was Jenny's mother who was being so blatantly accused.

'Firstly, I can assure you that the allegations regarding your mother's affair with Lord Melchamp are perfectly true. I have heard from a reliable source that he has moved from Sussex and is now living in Bournemouth and I saw them myself going into the Bloomsbury Hotel both giggling like a couple of teenagers,' continued Jane, allowing her hand to drop to her lap at last. 'Their hands were most lovingly clasped and the couple almost danced as they entered the foyer... and with a grin on the face of Lord Melchamp that betrayed everything his mind was contemplating.

'It was all too obvious they were together, Jenny; not that I blame them, of course; after all, they are both free agents now and are at liberty to enter the most loving of relationships available, and without anyone pointing a finger of disapproval in their direction, either.

'Apparently there was no mention of your mother being cited as co-respondent at the divorce courts, as a mention in the local newspaper, published a few days, later insisted that the marriage had irretrievably broken down of its own accord.'

'Well good for her. Perhaps this will free the rest of the world of her aggravating pomposity and allow me, at last, to be liberated from her continual criticism. Heaven knows it's about time.'

'Yes I do agree with you Jenny,' returned Jane, now carrying a meaningful look upon her faintly tinted face. 'But as I was about to tell you a minute or so ago, the interpretations of situations can all too often get twisted. Many times I have suffered, unjustifiably so, I might add, by being pointed out as a fallen woman, and by people who don't really know me that well.' Jane paused awhile, as she carefully considered her following words; she then smiled widely. 'Yes, it is most certainly a good thing that the darkness had fallen by the time I arrived here this evening, Jenny, for had I been seen by anyone... and without any other guests being evident... then you most certainly would be tainted with the same reputation as myself.'

Jenny's forehead became unusually furrowed as a deep frown indicated her inability to understand what her guest had implied regarding her own indiscretions. And so she hesitated a little with a couple of attempts at words that were struggling to escape her mouth.

'Whatever do you mean Jane?' Jenny's look was as

perplexed as she sounded.

'Well since your father died, my sister Rachael, for reasons best known to her decided to visit me on several occasions, mostly at weekends actually; she, probably thinking that my loss was far too great for me to handle on my own.

'I am fully aware that Rachael and I do not look remotely like sisters and that people wouldn't be able to tie up the fact that we are related just by looking at us, and as nobody knew about your father and me, not local to me, anyway, loose tongues apparently started to wag.

'Seeing me with my sister so often and her staying with me almost every weekend; well, people have kindly put two and two together and have somehow come up with some obscure number. Apparently they now believe us to be having a wild female affair which I consider to be quite hilarious... but not so Rachael. You see, she now refuses to visit me at all, saying I should go over to Germany if ever I feel the need to see her.'

'Lord is that all? Sorry Jane, I didn't mean to make light of your problem, but I was beginning to think that someone was saying awful things about *me*. But this must be terribly unpleasant for you Jane; you must be devastated with this ridiculous situation. How on earth do you know that people have this ridiculous opinion of you and are talking so obscenely? Usually the talked about are the last to hear the gossip being spread about themselves: at least I have always considered that to be the case,' said Jenny, as she reached across the small table to extend a comforting hand and to rest it gently on Jane's slender fingers.

'Oh, I have received at least four anonymous letters with the same hilarious accusations, plus a couple of obscene phone calls. I have been to the police of course but they seem helpless in cases like this.

'Anyway, thank you for your concern Jenny, but really, it is wasted on me. If people talk about me then at least they are leaving someone else alone, besides, the gossip may be true for all they know. I mean how could I possibly be able to prove to them otherwise?

'If I need the gossip to end, then the only way to bring it about would be to move and I love my dear cottage far too much to take such drastic steps. No, gossipers will soon find something else with which to occupy their wagging tongues, and until they do, well, I'm not about to worry myself sick about it or lose any sleep over it either.'

Jenny, feeling they would be more comfortable in the drawing room, suggested they took their glasses and retire to a more relaxed atmosphere; and after reviving their drinks the two women walked casually from the table taking their glasses with them.

The room was warm from the glow of a roaring fire that Agnes had lit earlier in the day and so they found the moderate environment to be most pleasing as they seated themselves on the long, deep comfortable sofa.

With the effect of the table wine and then the brandy's stimulation, the couple soon found themselves to be in a mood of intense, cosy conviviality and were beginning to giggle rather more than was acceptable - although both ladies were able to hold their liquor completely - well almost completely.

Jenny explained to Jane about her meeting with Tom but managed to exercise sufficient control to omit the ill-fated encounter with the obnoxious Barnabas Bell: she not wishing to be seen as being incapable of controlling the despicable situation that had existed between them and so she limited the description of the meeting as being no more than pure happenstance.

'Apparently they will be leaving here before the end of the week so we will be seeing nothing more of each other until their eventual return; if indeed they do decide to return, that is.'

Jane felt temporarily dejected by this piece of impromptu information, she feeling a little envious of anyone having feelings of intimacy for others, be they fabricated or an established reality, when she had no one who she could consider with extra special yearnings or who could occupy her mind with thoughts of passion.

'So, I take it that you haven't told him of your suspicion that he might be Jacobs's father then,' she said, 'only I should have thought that to have been paramount in your mind. Maybe some...'

Jenny immediately interrupted her guest by raising her forefinger to her mouth, and by pursing her lips she created an extended 'shush' to fill the room.

'Sorry Jenny, I didn't mean to cause you any sort of embarrassment, perhaps we had better close the subject, as one can never know whose ears may be listening,' she whispered.

But it was too late. Jacob was about to enter the room when he overheard the poignant conversation, but being a level-headed young man he failed to go through the half-open doorway and crept silently away, back to his bed, instead.

"Some things are private,' he thought to himself.' *I have complete faith in my mother; she will speak to me about it when she*

considers the moment to be right... I'm sure of that."

But throughout the night his curiosity ran riot and caused him a degree agitation that amounted to near sleeplessness.

Jenny had thought she had heard a movement behind her but upon going to the partially open doorway to investigate she saw nothing untoward, and so she closed the door firmly to lessen any intrusion.

CHAPTER SIX

It was fairly late the following morning when Fred Worth and his son Frederick arrived at the imposing entrance to Hyde's most prestigious house.

They stepped lightly from their vehicle more or less simultaneously, but with a degree of watchfulness being employed by Fredrick as his movements were hindered, to some extent, by the jeep being parked overly close to the bottom step that preceded the front of the elaborate portico, thereby leaving little room for the young lad to manoeuvre his feet in safety.

Driving the large, mud encrusted four-wheel drive Jeep, that he always used for local trips, caused feelings of importance to occupy the big farmer's mind; not that the muddy state of his prized farm vehicle was anything to boast about, but at least it did indicate the strapping farmer's level of agricultural busyness, in a strange sort of way: he allegedly not finding enough time in a twelve hour day to keep the monster clean.

The years had moved all too speedily, as far the farmer was concerned, and an unlikely ten years had come and gone since Fred had found the necessity to visit Hyde Hall. (Father and son, it might be pointed out, had never attended the place together, for in the short time that Fredrick had been acquainted with his newly found friend, the distance had been achieved on foot).

If there had been concerns over Fred's tenancy in the past, they had always been dealt with at his own place, Chambers Farm, between himself and the then, Sir Angus Kent, and so this specific visit came as a renewed pleasure for the tenant farmer.

After father and son had climbed down the steps of their sludge coated vehicle, and after a couple of brief remarks had been made by Fred: implying that a certain amount of embarrassment ought to have been felt because of the Jeep's appearance - but wasn't, a smile broadened his cheery face as he gazed in amazement at the width of the steps that led to the awe inspiring house.

Fred Worth had quite forgotten the enormity of the place, it seems, and so he turned his head to his son and with the winking of his eye he nodded his apt approval.

Inside Hyde Hall and occupying the second from bottom step of the marble staircase that descended to the centre of the floor of the great hall, Jacob was already waiting for his friend to arrive. As he sat impatiently, and in order to engage his mind in helping the minutes pass more speedily, he untied then retied his shoelaces three times in a row - in a double knot configuration, although, this focused attention didn't work that well, for it failed to hasten the time along at all. And so an air of expectancy existed causing a degree of anxiety to occupy his mind.

Not wishing to disturb the whole household, Jacob had tiptoed down the stairs some fifteen minutes earlier; and long before either his mother or Jane had left their respective rooms.

Actually, Jacob had been somewhat surprised when he'd looked from his bedroom window to see Jane's car still being parked outside. *"Nothing had been said last night regarding her staying over, so I wonder why the necessity arose; it had to be some obscure reason, that's for sure; I doubt she'd had car problems so maybe it was the result of too much booze,"* he thought.

His mind now conjured an impression of his mother's guest; her personality and her appearance - as he was still desperate in his need to fill the time.

He considered her to be a fairly pretty and amiable sort of lady, for her age; but one who wouldn't be in the habit of being overly talkative to middle sized boys; not that the two of them had idled away that much time together - none at all in fact, but he thought she was pleasant enough for all that.

"It's no concern of mine if Jane Howe was incapable of driving home last night; if she'd knocked back too much alcohol so she couldn't drive her car safely, well, that's her business and her own silly fault. Anyway, they'll both be nursing pretty big headaches this morning, if I'm not mistaken, and far bigger than the one I had last night, too." He smiled cheekily to himself as the thought crossed his mind.

"It serves them both jolly well right... that's what I say... maybe it will teach them a lesson in moderation that they'll both remember in future. Still, as Agnes is back at work this morning maybe she will be kind to them both and maybe take some tea up to them. But then again, perhaps it would be even kinder if she allowed them a lie in this morning so they are not disturbed at all.

"Anyway, I suppose they'll both be consoling one another for the rest of the morning and dosing themselves up with aspirin; then once they're fully sober I expect they'll be chatting away to each other like billy-o about things only women chat about; so, I guess they won't miss me if I make a quick exit without me saying my goodbyes."

Jacob was pleased to know his mother had allotted sufficient time to entertain a house guest, as she'd had no visitors since her return from Lincoln; save that of their dear uncle of course.

He now considered his mother's needs in socialising to be of paramount importance, if her life was to have any real meaning, and she should encourage such occasions to be more frequent and not the rarity they had been in the past. He also hoped Jane's visit would prove to be a prelude to further visits and a way of brightening the monotonous life for his young mother, and one he hoped would develop into a lasting friendship; not unlike the one she had hoped for him.

As already implied, Jacob found Jane to be vaguely acceptable as a friend for his mother although he had hoped she would find other friends as well; possibly closer to her own age and of the opposite gender - if that were at all possible. But he steered clear of all thoughts of gypsies after he'd eavesdropped their conversation the previous evening.

"I think it's high time I had a father of my own; though he would have to be a pretty special man if we are to be at all suited. But she's the only one who can make it happen... with some encouragement from everyone else of course; especially me... I suppose. But I can't see it happening, not yet awhile anyway, particularly if she isn't prepared to go out of her way to do something about it herself.

"Hope she isn't waiting for someone to turn up on the doorstep and sweep her off her feet; I'm sure that's what loads of females dream about these days; according to the magazine I was reading the other day, it is. Well, she can take it from me, it just doesn't happen that way.

"Still, maybe she doesn't want to be married; I mean she's never been out with a chap; at least not to my knowledge. But I really hope something exciting happens for her pretty soon.

"I know the very thing. Why don't Fredrick and I encourage his father to be interested in mother? He's a bit older than she is, well, quite a bit older, in actual fact; not that that matters; and I don't think he has a wife; at least I've never seen one about the place whenever I've visited their farm. But he's a nice enough sort of chap and they both share the same interests in farming, so perhaps they would make the perfect couple. But before all else, I suppose I ought to find out if he's married or not."

Jacob had continued in this frame of mind until his musings

were interrupted by the expected arrival of the Worth Jeep. As soon as he heard the continuous purr of its engine his mood changed and he smiled with delight at the thought of his friend's company for the rest of the day.

He raced to the door before the bell could be noisily produced: for he was now particular in not wishing the ladies to be disturbed, especially on a Sunday morning.

He reached and opened the door just as Fred Worth was raising his brawny hand to activate the bell.

'Good morning Mr Worth, good morning Fredrick, are you both OK?'

'Yes we're both fine thank you Jacob; hope you are the same.' This was Fred Worth senior returning Jacob's welcoming greeting. 'What time would you like me to collect Fredrick later? Only I need to be busy for most of the day by finishing the ploughing of one of the twenty-five acre fields that I started earlier; so I can have it ready to sow my maize; can't sit around all day doing nothing when there's work to be done... even if it is a Sunday.'

'Please don't worry about that Mr Worth, I'm sure my mother will be pleased to drop Fredrick back home after we've eaten together this evening... if that would be alright?'

'That's fine by me; thank you Jacob. Now I will wish you both a good day together and be on my way.... Only hope you won't be getting up to too much mischief the pair of you; still, I guess you wouldn't be boys if you didn't have a little fun and it seems to me you can't have fun without a little bit of mischief being thrown in.' A smile creased his weathered face as he turned to go. Then, just as the farmer was about to take a stride across the portico floor, his move was interrupted and so he turned.

'Hello Fred, nice to see you again.' The feminine tones of Jenny were heard from the centre of the hall. She hastily reached the small group and stood smilingly inside the open doorway, cutting short Fred Worth's movements.

'Brought Fredrick over I expect. Oh hello Fredrick... didn't see you there. How are you both? What a glorious day for the time of year; we really are most fortunate with how the New Year has started; weather-wise, I mean. Or perhaps you prefer the seasons to stay as traditional as possible?'

'Good morning, Miss Kent. Makes no difference to me either way, although I suppose fine weather does allow us to get on with things a little more easily; at least my lads won't be sheltering from the rain in my old barn just frittering away their time by mending sacks all day long and the ground will be warmed nicely for my maize. So, as I was just saying to Jacob here, we have to take advantage of the good weather when we can.

'Still, I suppose you are well ahead of yourselves here at the Home Farm, now that you are being organised by Alf Abrams. Good man is Alf; that one knows a thing or two about good farming... I can tell you; and he always seems to enjoy what he's doing, too; always deeply concerned, if you know what I mean?'

'Yes he really is a godsend, Fred, and I consider myself to be very fortunate in having him here. He also seems to have settled in rather well; so things appear to be satisfactory all round.'

'That's good to hear, only I know he rates you pretty highly as well Miss Kent. Says as how you're easy to get on with and keen to learn; that means a lot to a farm manager that does.

'Well, I had better head off home, got a million and one things lined up to do after I finish the ploughing I started earlier. Not enough hours in the day, Miss Kent, that's the trouble. Jacob tells me as how you might be willing to bring Fredrick home for us this evening or when you're good and ready; if you're quite sure it will be alright, that is?'

'Yes of course Fred, quite alright. I have no idea what these two have got lined up for today, not too many surprises I hope, but I'm sure they will enjoy themselves all the same; they usually do.'

Fred Worth forced a smile as he turned to walk back to his muddy vehicle. After he had turned his Jeep round, he smiled again and produced a most unexpected wave that didn't seem to register as being that important to Jenny. Then he slowly headed up the lengthy drive.

'So, I'll leave you two in peace then, shall I? Don't forget I will be here all day if you should need me. Oh, I believe Agnes has some breakfast ready this morning for anyone who wants it... if you wish to take advantage of her kindness. But there, I expect you have more important things in mind, am I not right?' said Jenny. And as no immediate answer was forthcoming, she walked away in the direction of the staircase.

Jacob and Fredrick chatted away to one another so urgently that their words overlapped from time to time as they moved steadily away from the big house and in the direction of the forest.

Jacob had not planned to discuss his earlier thoughts with Fredrick - though his mother was still on his mind. But, the timing, it had to be right for a personal matter such as that.

'I know I shouldn't have, because it was a very private

conversation, but I couldn't help overhearing the discussion my mother was having with her friend last night. It appears that some gypsies have parked themselves on the far side of our forest. They won't be staying around for very long it seems, so how do you feel about the two of us paying them a visit... at their camp? After all, they *are* on my mother's estate, so I reckon I have every right to call on them today or at any other time, come to that. What do you think? Do you think it would be too rude of us... or are you up for it?'

'Sounds like a good idea to me, Jacob, I have never seen a gypsy camp before; not close to, anyway; so it's surely worth a morning's visit... so yes, it might be great fun... and if they get a bit bolshy we could always tell them to move themselves on, straight away.'

The two friends laughed at the fascinating idea as they steadily walked down the long meadow together; and after picking up sticks they slashed at the tall nettled foliage on the way.

They crossed the wire fencing at much the same spot Jenny had crossed it the previous day but without the same thoughts in mind or a similar mishap occurring.

It was a long trek through the wide, dense forest, a dampish one as well and one that Jacob had never undertaken before; even though he had often considered such an exploit. But undertaking a hike of these dimensions alone had always seemed rather pointless to him, without there being a significant reason - that is. Still, he had a reason now and he had a friend to share it with - and that made all the difference.

Coppiced hazel thickets were clustered together and looked rather sinister neath the wide canopy of lichen covered oaks - together they formed the forest's darkened scrubland. And the huge gesticulating beech trees, with their tightly twisted branches, paid their contribution to this timbered, shadowy place as well, and made the setting seem even more forbidding - causing a little uneasiness to remain in the minds of the two young lads awhile.

Eventually, the tall trees and shrubbery separated and sunshine was to be clearly seen through the leafless branches. This brighter feature, visible in the distance by both the boys, caused their excitement to rise; for they realised they were about to reach the forest's edge.

The damp, dark-green fields, adjoining the forest's margin, and from where tree-packed hedgerows were observed bordering a lane beyond, were preceded by yet another barrier over which the boys had to climb; and not unlike the one on the other side of the forest, it too brought little in the way of a challenge to their agility.

But the smoky aroma of burning wood that greeted them was a different matter, for it irritated their sensitive nostrils and caused their eyes to water.

After they had fully scaled the fence they turned to their left, and there, standing about fifty yards in front of them they caught their first glimpse of the five large caravans; each positioned in a traditional semicircle for convenience or for comfort (they were unsure which) and with a small number of people milling about the place attending to their chores.

'Hey-up visitors,' called out the same voice using precisely the same words he had identified Jenny with yesterday and in the same surprised tone of voice he had used as well.

This time, Tom was descending the steps of his van and a questioning smile traversed his face as he watched the two boys crossing the clearing. With hurried steps he walked over to the newcomers before anyone else could greet or question them.

'And who might you two lads be, who so brazenly stride into our camp?' He said, instantly. And although his searching words were felt to be a little hostile at first, this was cancelled at once by the huge grin on his face, which put the two young lads at their ease.

'Good morning sir,' said Jacob. 'My name is Jacob Kent and I'm the son of the owner of this estate and this is my very good friend Fredrick Worth. The two of us were curious enough to want to come and pay you our respects by calling on you this morning, which we hope will be well received and not taken as some impolite intrusion.'

Tom's wide smile seemed to grow even wider as Jacob completed his greeting and which the tall gypsy admired so openly.

'Is that right? Well that's an extremely fine speech young Jacob and I am very pleased to make your acquaintance,' said Tom. And as he reached out and took Jacob's hand in his, a mysterious feeling overcame him; an inexplicable feeling that somehow a bond had already been set between them, a bond that he wished to express, but somehow couldn't find sufficient words to exemplify a meaning. 'Tom Hawk's the name and you're both very welcome here, very welcome indeed,' he added. He took Fredrick's hand in a similar welcoming gesture, but all the time his eyes remained firmly fixed on Jacob's face.

Tom motioned the boys to the big log seat beside the campfire where he had hoped to sit awhile with Jenny. And the three of them sat together as old friends who had recently renewed a past acquaintance sit together; with the drinking of flavoured tea which Tom had offered.

'So how is your mother Jacob? Was it she who sent you over to see me this morning?'

'No sir, she doesn't even know we're here. But I did overhear her telling a friend last night that you would soon be moving on and so we thought it might be a good opportunity to meet up with you before you went away. I do hope that that's alright sir.'

'Of course it's alright Jacob. Why wouldn't it be?'

'I don't know sir; I think maybe you might consider our being here... an intrusion when it's not meant to be. We are only being curious, that's all, and mean no harm whatever.'

'Please don't fret yourself Jacob, all is well between us... I can assure you of that.'

The two boys and the tall gypsy chatted easily with each other for a while longer until Tom said at last:

'As you must know, it's Sunday today and me and my family of friends, well, we usually sit round the fire on Sundays, about this time of the morning, in actual fact. We read a little scripture from the Bible and sing a couple of hymns together and then we say a prayer or two. I should like very much for both you lads to join us; if you've a mind to, that is; but there is no need to feel compelled to stay... not if you don't want to... or if you feel unhappy about taking part in such an event. We only take about a half an hour from the start to the finish of our little service, in any case, so we won't be keeping you long; then we share something to eat together which you may wish to share as well... if you've a mind to.'

Both Jacob and Fredrick were astonished by the invitation being so freely offered and after looking at each other they smiled their approval and appreciation openly.

A small number of Tom's family of friends moved slowly to gather about the now flaring, smokeless fire, each carrying a black book in their hands and each with a face adorned with smiles of perfect serenity.

In less than a minute, the rest of the tribe arrived in the same peaceful mood, now bringing the number up to fourteen - including the two boys.

No grand piano or harmonious organ assisted in the singing that morning; no heavenly choir was heard leading that little group, and although the melodies may have sounded slightly tuneless at times the splendour of their singing was up to and way beyond any bishop's apt approval.

A hushed, meaningful reverence attended the small gathering, as they bowed their heads in prayer, sang their ancient hymns and listened to the Holy Scriptures being read. So movingly together had this little group gathered that a spiritual atmosphere of vast proportions seemed to have been created and which covered them all in a divinely inspired mantle of enchantment.

Suddenly and without warning, a female voice was heard to cry out above the rest with strange utterances; the effect of which had little bearing on reality and was perceived by both of the boys as being incomprehensible gibberish. Even so, quietness still filled the mood of that little flock as their heads hung in reverence, whilst the woman's emphatic statement continued in unabated love and sincerity - bestowing heart-felt blessings upon them all.

Jacob and his friend, both being totally unprepared for hearing the surprising spiritual gift of speaking in tongues, were mystified and they held their breath in the wonderment of it all.

And then, as soon as the communiqué had been completed another female voice was heard from the back. This time with clearness of diction and forming an understandable statement that set out the interpretation of her friend's verbal message.

After the ritual had been completed, and they had sung their final hymn, the members of the group went to each other, and with the exchanging of a Christian kiss and the firm shaking of hands they offered words of deep respect to one another.

'May the peace of God rest upon you my friend?'

And a blessing on the two lads was also given; the same blessing as was so generously bestowed upon each other - and by each and every member of the group .

China bowls and metal spoons were then produced as if from nowhere and Tom, taking each bowl in turn ladled out a measure of the broth from the cauldron that had been suspended over the campfire for the whole of the morning and he served it to each member and to the two strangers. The flavour was found by Jacob to be so delicious he mopped his bowl with some offered bread and he recognised, with deep appreciation, the simple, homely meal that had been so freely offered.

All but a few of the group dispersed after half an hour or so of convivial conversation, leaving Tom and his acquaintances sitting alone in congenial chatter.

'Was our little service to your liking my friends or did you find its message to be overpowering?' asked Tom, with a smile of satisfaction settling on his lips after the remnant of the little group had finally dispersed.

'Both of us, I'm sure, found the service to be quite wonderful Mr Hawke,' said Fredrick, 'but we didn't wholly understand the funny foreign language the lady was using.'

'Yes, I understand that speaking in tongues can seem a little weird to the uninitiated but to the believer it is the inspired and important proof that God exists and that we are forever the children of our Father. It vividly shows, to the believer, the most basic principle of the Christian way of life, which is to trust in the word of our heavenly Father with all our hearts.

'The use of tongues isn't the employment of any words known to man but rather sounds from the heart, giving Him our praise and our blest thanksgiving. Even the honey bee makes sounds with its dainty wings which man can never understand but they are really thanking God for the nectar they sip and the freedom they share with their fellow bees, as do the whole of the Lords creation in their various ways.

'Beyond that, speaking in tongues is a special gift from God, as is the interpretation of tongues and it is a wonderful way to get around the limitations of our native language and it enables us to tell our heavenly Father that we love him and are thankful for all his wonderful gifts to us.

'I hope that explains matters a little better for you, but when, and if, each of you feel the calling from Gods Holy Spirit then I am sure all things will be made clearer to you then.

'Now you two, how would you like to see inside my vardo? That's my home over there,' said Tom, pointing to a most intricately decorated wagon, spotlessly clean, highly polished, and painted with the most vivid colours imaginable. Each colour contrasted markedly with the other two, creating the utmost brilliance possible. The maroon, golden yellow and white colours appeared so bright it was as though they were still wet from being freshly painted.

The trio walked over to the wagon and climbed the five steps that led to its front porch; with its ornately carved sides affording a welcome. The top to the stable-type door was open and the boy's faces lit up as their eyes feasted upon the elaborately decorated walls inside; homely, yet so sparkling clean that they feared marking anything that was in easy reach of their grubby fingers.

'This is my Reading Wagon; some call it a Kite Wagon because of its tapering walls. I haven't had it long. It was left to me by a dear friend of mine who passed away last year; that's why I have the black ribbon still attached to my arm. But I was so privileged in being left it, as the old custom is for the owner's wagon to be burned soon after his death, alongside almost all his belongings as well. But as that don't make good economic sense these days, the tradition is fast slipping away.'

The trio stepped further inside and as they did Tom proudly pointed to a highly polished, blackened, cooking stove that was empty of lighted coals.

'So what do you think of my old cooking stove? A little beauty isn't she? Made of cast iron that is, but I only use it if and when the weather's so bad that I can't do my cooking on the campfire outside.'

Above the stove, and precariously perched on an intricately carved mantelpiece were two most appealing porcelain figurines from Greek mythology; one of Aphrodite the other of her lover Adonis, both looking as though they might topple off if the vardo unexpectedly lurched as it trundled along some uneven country road, if they hadn't been fixed by some canny means.

Next their flitting attention was drawn to the narrow ceiling with its painted biblical scenes. These were uniquely illustrated and similar to no other; though, at first glance, they might easily be compared to the ceiling of the Sistine Chapel, for their individual and separately bordered patchwork of artistry was so meticulously painted it could have been a masterpiece. The most striking of colours were used - colours so vivid that they begged belief. Bright shades of blue and warmer colours too, all blending together to form a work of harmonious beauty that was absorbed by the eye of any beholder - completely.

Polished mahogany cupboard arrangements were seen to be filled to capacity and even the smallest of alcoves occupied such cabinets - each covered with glass doors, all encasing beautiful china and gleaming glassware.

'I have never seen anything like this before, Mr Hawk; it is so truly amazing I can't wait to tell my mother all about it. How do you manage to cram so much into such a small space and keep it all looking so clean and tidy? It really is most incredible,' said Jacob, as his big brown eyes widened to their fullest extent.

'Well, that's the secret you see. A place for everything and everything in its place, as the old maxim goes. If I apply this all the time and clean the place regularly each day, then there can be no real problem. But I love my vardo so much that it's easy to keep it as it is; it is only me who use this place, and nobody else, you see I have no family at all to mess things up for me - unfortunately.'

As they carefully climbed down the slightly curved steps once again, Barnabas Bell was seen to be walking hurriedly across the open space that was formed by the circle of wagons and turning his head to look at the trio he increased his stride as his face became agitated.

'We didn't see that man at the service earlier, Mr Hawke,' observed Jacob, casually. 'I would have noticed him had he been there.'

'That's Barney,' returned Tom, with a smile. 'No, he doesn't join in with the rest of us that much. Maybe he's an unbeliever, I'm not really sure. He hasn't always been with us... joined us in Lincoln about five or six years ago. He's a nice enough sort of chap; though he does tend to keep himself to himself more than he ought. He seems to get on alright with old Noah though; that's the old boy who Barney lodges with.'

Jacob's face became more serious.

'That's a coincidence, Mr Hawk, mother and I used to live in Lincoln; well close to it; a small village called Brenton, only about five or six minute ride away from Lincoln's centre, in the car.'

'Did you now? Well that is indeed a coincidence, because I believe our Mr Bell came from that very village. I wonder if he knows of your mother at all. I shall have to ask him; not now, but when you've both gone... maybe later on this afternoon, or maybe tomorrow when I can be alone with him... in private... so to speak.'

CHAPTER SEVEN

Following the chatty departure of Jacob and Fredrick, Jenny returned to her room to discover the insufferable throbbing pain that penetrated her forehead earlier, had totally disappeared, thus causing a mood of comfortable relief to occupy her mind for the first time that morning.

The instant Jenny entered the tranquillity of her spacious bedroom, she wandered over to her outsized dressing table with its array of mirrors perfectly angled to maximise the reflection of the bright white luxury that existed there. The brightness seemed to encourage Jenny to confront the day ahead with happiness - rather than allow any complications to trouble her.

After withdrawing the deep cushioned stool from under her dressing table and retrieving the silver handled hairbrush that she had abandoned earlier, Jenny seated herself to recommence the task of brushing her long ebony hair, yet again, with lengthened strokes.

Then, leaning her body toward the mirror and tilting her head forward, twisting it this way and that, she allowed her shiny tresses to cascade down until they covered her face completely. She then continued the grooming once more but this time with increased vigour and in all directions imaginable.

A gentle tapping on her bedroom door compelled Jenny to straighten herself immediately and she returned her head to its original position without delay.

Jenny immediately assumed the tapping was being caused by Agnes seeking trivial instructions for the day, as was her practice - or even more plausible was Agnes discovering a simple challenge which she was unable to unravel by herself: she being in need of her mistress' guile to explain the puzzle for her.

Anyway, despite all her logical guesswork, based on Agnes' earlier performances, Jenny invited the caller to enter and was most surprised at seeing Jane Howe's image being clearly reflected in her mirror. Her guest, standing rather elegantly in the doorway, was wearing the pink dressing gown Jenny had loaned her the previous evening.

Catching sight of Jenny sitting at her dressing table like this and being absorbed by such a personal task, caused Jane to hesitate a little as her look of elegance changed to one of uncertainty; quite as if she had suddenly felt uncomfortable at finding Jenny in this way - and she seemed at a loss in knowing how to deal with the situation.

No serious offence had been committed, obviously; though something was on Jane's mind otherwise she wouldn't have presented herself at Jenny's door in the first place - uninvited in this way.

Jenny, turning her head slowly in the direction of her guest and away from her mirror, smiled warmly.

'Hello Jane what an unexpected pleasure. Do come in, sit down and talk to me while I finish brushing this mop I call hair.'

'May I sit here?' asked Jane, in her usual timorous voice indicating the edge of Jenny's bed and paying no attention to a comfortable armchair that stood close by.

'Yes of course, sit where you please, Jane, no need for you to stand on ceremony with me.'

Although Jenny was most surprised at seeing Jane this early she was more than a little peeved at witnessing her state of unpreparedness for the day and she watched with some curiosity, once more by way of her mirror, as Jane perched her bottom on the corner of the bed.

Then, after laying her body back a ways, Jane slowly and deliberately curled her limbs in an unseemly manner to display her figure for Jenny's entertainment - and obvious approval.

After supporting her head with her hand and using her elbow and arm to take its weight Jane straightened one of her legs whilst the other remained curled beneath it and in such an improper fashion that it caused the pink dressing gown to carelessly gape a little where it oughtn't to have gaped and gape a little where it was most inappropriate for it to have gaped.

Upon seeing Jane's performance, Jenny readjusted her line of vision and immediately engrossed herself in her hair grooming exercises once more; but this time with a feeling of slight uneasiness disturbing her mind.

'Did you sleep well?' enquired Jenny, gathering her wits together: she being eager not to appear alarmed at Jane's posing antics, which she was anxious to dispel from her mind quickly, for fear of embarrassment.

'No, not at all well, actually,' answered Jane. Her voice sounded bright enough although her unsmiling expression betrayed a degree of anxiety as though she had picked up the headache Jenny had abandoned earlier and kept it for herself. 'I found it most strange sleeping in the house that once belonged to your dear father, that was all and I felt quite unable to settle for thinking about him... I still miss him so very much.'

'Yes, I expect you do, Jane. I miss him too you know. I'm sure it's going to take us both quite some time before we get used to the idea of him not being around anymore... if we ever do. But we must battle on... he wouldn't want us to grieve for him indefinitely you know, I'm quite certain of that.'

Jenny wasn't at all sure why Jane was showing such undue emotion this morning as there was no hint of this state existing during the previous evening. *"She seemed happy enough then... in fine form, actually; so, why the change I wonder,"* thought Jenny, now considering her father's mistress ought to have been in control of any feelings of melancholia by this time; certainly more than she was displaying at the moment, anyway.

"I wonder why Jane has really decided to visit to my room right now." Jenny asked herself, with a hint of suspicion existing in her mind. *"Surely it isn't just to tell me of the pitiful night she has spent alone... just thinking of my father. No, it's much more likely to be some sort of excuse to scrutinize my bedroom or maybe she is seeking a remedy for the headache she has decided to have. Now that's much more like it."*

'So what brings you to me this morning Jane? You'll be in urgent need of a couple of Aspirins I expect, after last night's unwavering session of drinking you are probably feeling a little under the weather; am I not right? You know, never in the whole of my life have I consumed so much alcohol; you must have a terrible influence on me Jane Howe!' Jenny laughed sheepishly at the docile accusation she had uttered, though Jane's face remained unchanged.

'No, I'm feeling alright thank you, Jenny. I took a couple of pain killers as soon as I awoke this morning; I always carry a few for an emergency and they seem to have worked perfectly well. No, it's not that; I came to ask you what you had in mind for this morning and if you fancied a walk to blow away the cobwebs before I leave for Basham Killington; or if you wanted me gone straight away so that you can get on with some work.

'Actually I thought a stroll might be just the thing to ease my mind of the unfortunate lonely sensations left over from last night; I also thought I should ask you for any suggestions you may have for the ridding of them altogether. I never realised, before now, how devastating loneliness can be.

'The loneliness I felt last night was so intense, Jenny, it was more in keeping with the feelings you have described experiencing as a child and I wanted to go to you and have you comfort me. Laughable, in the cold light of day, isn't it? I ask you... me... a middle aged woman seeking the comfort of a child,' she said, as a distorted giggle escaped her lips. 'But that was how I saw you last night, in the confusion of darkness... as a young child.

'It just shows you how illogical the brain can be in the small hours... when everything is mixed and muddled up and all problems are magnified beyond reason. Jenny, I have never experienced such loneliness before. I'm sorry to harp on about it as I know I must sound a little tiresome; but this loneliness was really too big a problem for me to handle by myself, it was so extreme I couldn't wait for the sun to rise. I wanted someone to rid me of those feelings so much I could only think of knocking on your door for you to give me comfort; well, that will show you the depleted condition I was in. And I would have done it too; had not the good sense prevailing prevented the idea.'

'You mean you wanted to crawl into my bed... beside me? Jane, what an absurd idea? I've never heard of such a thing. Well maybe you should have... I don't know; I have never slept with anyone before, well, except Tom, that stormy night and of course on the odd occasion when Jacob may have been disturbed; but only then when he was very young. So yes, maybe you should have come to me, if you are not prone to bouts of the fidgets, that is; what a novel experience that would have been. Well, if we are ever together again and you are left completely on our own as you were last night, and you feel the same need to dispel your loneliness, please, you must do just that... come to me.'

Jenny chuckled quietly, in her innocence, at what she regarded as being a bizarre idea; but a look of relief crossed Jane's face as a feeling of liberation filled her mind at the realisation of what she now considered to be Jenny's complete approval of such womanly closeness.

Feeling more relaxed at this point, Jane adopted a look of fascination for her friend's beautiful hair as Jenny resumed her routine. And a soft smile flitted across Jane's face as she stared, with excitement, at witnessing the uninterrupted grooming performance. Every now and then, a little vigour crept into the strokes, but in a stress-free manner, as Jenny moved her head from side to side, back and forth.

'You are brushing your hair far too intensely Jenny, may I come over and see to it for you?' she asked. And with no expressed approval being forthcoming, she left the bed and walked over to Jenny and stood attentively behind her.

Without answering but smiling like some obedient child,

Jenny handed the silver handled brush to Jane, and, sitting bolt upright, in a vivacious posture of anticipation, she awaited the unexpected but thoughtful act of care she was about to receive; for never before had she remembered such an experience of intimacy that someone brushing her hair might provide. Why, even as a small child she had always attended her hair herself, if her memory was intact, and she wasn't prone to visits at the hairdressers that often either.

As Jane took on the role of Jenny's personal coiffeuse and as she commenced her gentle attention to those gorgeous ebony tresses by applying slow, constant caressing strokes, all at once an immediate feeling of unexpected pleasure filled Jenny's body; from the tips of her curling toes to the tingling sensation that traversed her spine. All of this, and much more, caused Jenny to arch her back in a careless manner so that her head rested on Jane's stomach for a fleeting moment.

Immediately, Jane's smile widened as she carefully repositioned Jenny's head. And easing it forward with her long, cool fingers, she resumed the pleasurable and agreeable exercise once again.

'You have such beautiful hair Jenny; its wonderful sheen is so inviting that it ought to have all the loving attention we can give it. But your scalp seems tense and in need of a gentle massage to free it from its rigidity… here, let me see to it for you.' And so saying, Jane handed the brush back to Jenny who coloured-up for the briefest of moments as she carelessly mishandled the implement, thereby allowing their hands to touch.

Jane's slender, tapering fingers diligently infiltrated and explored the depths of Jenny's hair; reaching deeply but caringly into her tightened scalp. And as she moved those fingers with slow, gentle stimulation, the whole of Jenny's head relaxed with the pleasure of it all and to become wholly eased of its rigidness. And as she ceased her five minute labour of love, Jane bent down slowly and kissed the top of Jenny's head; she then resumed her position upon the unmade bed.

Jenny had certainly felt the kiss but she considered it to have been a maternal gesture, rather than anything for her to worry about: Jane being so much older than she, and childless. And so she failed to comment in any way at all and allowed the matter to close as if unnoticed.

'Well, that was marvellous Jane, thank you. I must say you certainly do possess a most gentle touch; it was so soothing that I wouldn't have minded you continuing for the rest of the morning and you have left my scalp in a delightful tingle as well... all over.

'But it's such a wonderful day, Jane, that ten minutes in the fresh air will do us both the world of good and as you say, it will blow away all those dreary cobwebs; and then I must get on with some paperwork.

'So, if you care to get yourself ready, I will meet you back here in a few minutes time,' she said.

After taking thought, a problem entered her mind. 'Wait a minute, Jane, you haven't brought a change of clothing with you; you certainly can't walk about the countryside in that lovely evening dress of yours. Perhaps you won't mind wearing a pair of my trousers and a suitable jumper; a jacket also might be useful as the weather is still so very bracing outside, even though it is such a pleasant day.'

So saying, she hurried over to her outsized white wardrobe, and searching the extent of its rails she produced a pair of light brown, needlecord trousers, a sweater and a jacket. 'Better try them on Jane, I know you are an inch or so taller than me but perhaps they won't look so bad; anyway, who's to see you?'

Jane's manner became a little indecisive and she looked at Jenny as if to say:

"Are you really sure about this?"

Instantly she allowed the pink dressing gown fall to the floor thereby revealing the scantiest underwear Jenny had ever seen and which left nothing at all to the imagination.

Jenny caught her breath in embarrassment as she viewed Jane's voluptuous body and tried to incline her head and her eyes away from the display on offer but without too much success; at least, her head moved but her eyes were firmly rooted to the parts of Jane's anatomy that were supposed to be private; and Jane noticing Jenny's dilemma, beamed within, as she reached out for her support in the struggle she was having with the trousers.

Jenny and Jane walked slowly toward the meadow arm in arm and were filled with delightful harmony inside, but discreetly so; each enjoying the warm company of the other with immense pleasure and both chatting away as though they had been friends of long-standing.

Then, passing the spot where Bluey was resting, they stopped awhile as Jenny shared the memory of her dear fluffy friend and of her meeting with the gypsy who had played such a large part in her younger days. Because of these shared memories, an emotional choking sensation issued from Jenny's throat and she felt Jane's kindly, reassuring arm being placed around her slim waist awhile.

They then continued on toward the stream that led to the wider river beyond.

Jane, now feeling well-established in the seclusion of Jenny's friendship, seemed to sense an emotional tie to her young companion, which was totally unexpected, but it was an attachment that satisfied her immensely.

Halfway between Bluey's grave and the narrow stream the two linked fingers - caused by nothing more than a sudden feeling of togetherness - but instinctively so - quite as though neither of them had been aware of the act ever happening and certainly with no resistance being voiced or a sense of shame being felt by either of them.

And so they continued, hand in hand as consenting women often do at times like these; both of them offering light exchanges, the one with the other, and without a care in the world or the smallest amount of awkwardness existing between them.

They crossed the narrow rickety bridge and stood awhile, their senses attuned to the sights and sounds before them.

A darting flash of greenish-blue and bright orange dived head-first into the water, catching a tiny, wriggling minnow in its long pointed beak. The small jewel-like bird then lifted itself to the safety of a pliant branch of a coppiced willow tree; the first such tree of many that lined the river's edge. The bird perched awhile, and after experiencing difficulty in swallowing the fish with a single movement of its head - as it would normally have done - in a moment of hesitation it dropped its catch into the silvery water.

'Kingfishers are beautiful little creatures don't you agree Jane?' said Jenny, turning her head toward her friend, 'but I didn't think they were quite as clumsy as this one appears to be.'

The couple stood on the spot, still loosely holding each others fingers and still watching the little bird as it flashed away once more. Then slowly they turned round to head back the way they had come. Although the stroll had taken less than fifteen minutes of their time both agreed that enough fresh air was enough and as a result they sought the warmer climes of Hyde Hall once more.

Remaining in the clothes that Jenny had loaned her, Jane quickly went to her room to collect her evening dress and wrap, while Jenny returned to her bedroom to wait for her friend in order to facilitate her departure.

Jane popped her head round the doorway as Jenny, walking toward her, offered to escort her to the front door.

Then, standing in the open doorway, the two ladies faced each other.

'Thank you Jenny, the meal last night was simply lovely and almost as wonderful as the company I was able to take pleasure in. You must allow me to return the compliment... and soon; I simply can't wait to entertain you in the same generous manner you have entertained me,' said Jane, dropping her dress to the floor. And then, after the shortest of short pauses, she moved closer to her friend as she continued: 'Jenny, I am unexpectedly feeling a fondness for you, a fondness which I find very difficult to describe, let alone to understand.'

Then, enfolding the beautiful young woman in her arms so that one of her hands was placed to the small of Jenny's back the other just below her neck and Jenny, with her own hands being awkwardly placed on Jane's shoulders, they both gazed steadily into each others eyes without the hint of a smile existing between them.

In an instant, Jane gently manoeuvred her friend a little closer and to a position more fitting for her; but she became disappointed when Jenny turned her head sideways in preparation for a peck on the cheek. Jane quickly changed the position of her hand and placed it to the back of Jenny's head and rotated it gently to give her the access she required.

Feeling unable to escape for the moment, Jenny felt her own face being drawn towards Jane's.

And then, seeking the most desirable mouth she had ever hoped to find, Jane gently pressed her own lips into it; touching it with sensitive emotion.

Confused feelings flooded Jenny's brain. And as her face reddened with extreme embarrassment, she felt her heartbeat quicken - frighteningly so. And then, standing back a little, she turned her head away from Jane; for her eyes, it seems, sought a safer haven - a new situation - anything at all that would distract her from the current embarrassment she was finding so hard to cope with.

"Perhaps that was nothing, nothing at all; perhaps that is the way ladies say goodbye to each other these days... I don't know!"

These confused feelings aroused Jenny's emotions in such a way that they caused her to quiver inside and for her to doubt the validity of her own naivety.

After a while Jenny was able to encourage her own face to

brighten a little and so she returned it to Jane with a pseudo smile as though she had been filled with fear of accepting the event that had just taken place and which she had considered to be so strange.

With awkwardness still hanging around, she urged her wits to steer clear of modernity and all its wiles.

The effort wasn't easy, for modernity had already installed itself in Jenny's innocent mind and she felt her pulse quicken to a most alarming rate and beat more strongly than she had ever known it beat before - as unseemly feelings of inadequacy invaded her mind.

Jenny accredited these unseemly feelings to her own failure in providing the necessary encouragement for Jane, and they were absorbed by her emotions in such measure that they swamped all the fears and doubts that had previously settled there.

After a while, Jenny took control of her mind once more; however, she still hoped a more familiar routine would quickly be established.

Eventually, they joined hands again and together they walked along the corridor that led to the marbled stairs.

Both allowed no awkwardness to take control of the situation as they walked the length of the passage; for awkwardness was deliberately concealed by both ladies.

It wasn't until they were halfway across the wide hall that Jenny made reply to Jane's earlier declaration and she did so with simulated smiles emanating 'neath a countenance of concealed concern.

'Yes, it was an enjoyable evening Jane,' said Jenny, at last; still with stifled feelings from the embrace but as brightly as she was able. 'I have taken pleasure in your company too, and yes, I will look forward to seeing you once again as well... but perhaps with not quite so much brandy being on offer next time, eh?'

They laughed together as they reached the closed doorway and they briefly touched, before Jane left Jenny for the loneliness of Bramble Bush Cottage in Basham Killington.

But unanswered questions lingered in Jenny's mind; awkward, unanswerable questions that she knew would encumber her still further.

***

After she had waved her friend off, Jenny made her way back to her bedroom with all haste and throwing herself headlong on the bed she stared up at the ceiling in total disbelief.

After pulling the long bell rope to attract Agnes', attention, Jenny waited; her head still spinning in the uncertainty of what had just occurred.

"What is it about this woman that has claimed my mind so completely?' she asked herself, as she, in her entangled thinking bit fretfully into her lower lip. *"Surely I'm not attracted to the female form. Many times I have seen girls on the beach, clad only in their bikinis; many are the times that I have seen the erotica of girly magazines decorating the shelves of seedy newsagents, exposing themselves in a manner of extreme titillation; all of this, and much more too, but still I have never felt the allure of the female figure. Never have I felt the urge to embrace another woman either; a man, yes, of course I have, but never a woman.*

"Then Jane comes along and suddenly I'm bowled over with the beauty of her voluptuous body. She has most certainly created a need in me that seems to have surpassed all other of my physical needs. She has managed to build a fascination for me and in me that has created this desire for more intimacy with her, but I was too frightened to move things along in providing the obvious encouragement we both needed.

"Why, even yesterday when Tom took me in his arms and gave me a beautiful hug... the effect of it stayed with me for hours after; but it never stirred the same emotions in me that Jane has stirred.

"So, which is it to be, is it Tom or is it Jane? Man or woman? Or perhaps it's neither; perhaps it's merely a strange fascination for the unexpected or a mother figure that has been sadly missing from my sheltered life. I have been in Jane's company on many occasions before this and have never even considered her to possess such magnetism or to possess such an appealing body."

Another tapping on her bedroom door, the second one this morning, disturbed Jenny's mental meanderings as she rose from her bed to answer the summons.

'Oh Agnes, please come in. Look, I am popping out for a while later and as I am expecting both Jacob and his friend back about dinnertime, I wondered if you would be good enough to organise a bite to eat for them. Nothing to grand mind, maybe a few fish fingers or something of the kind will do.'

'Yes, Miss Jenny, I most certainly will be pleased to do that for the young gentlemen, you just leave it to me. I will serve them something good and hot; if they've been out all day in the cold... well, they'll certainly need something warm inside them. And what about you Miss Jenny, will you be dining in this evening?'

'No Agnes, please don't worry about me, I had so much to eat last night I feel I have enough food inside me to last a whole week, and maybe even longer than that.'

'So will that be all Miss Jenny?'

'Yes that will be all Agnes, thank you.'

Then as Agnes reached for the handle of the door, she dithered awhile; she then wheeled round quite unexpectedly with an awkward expression on her face.

'I do hope last nights dinner with Miss Howe went well for you both Miss Jenny.'

'Yes, very well indeed thank you Agnes; as I have already said, I really did eat too much and I am still feeling the effects of gluttony, I'm afraid.'

Agnes retraced her steps into the room by two paces, looking quite perturbed.

'Miss Jenny, I really don't wish to overstep the mark and I really don't know how to say this without sounding... well, too familiar, but I thought you ought to be aware of the rumours that I have heard about Miss Howe...' Agnes hesitated somewhat as if seeking the correct way to proceed and she was immediately helped along by her mistress.

'What is it Agnes?' she asked. 'What rumours have you heard concerning my friend?' Her voice was stern but her face was sterner. 'Come along Agnes out with it... what have you to say?'

'Well Miss Jenny, I've heard tell as how she has taken up with female company in an unsavoury sort of way and she has now become one of these liberated kinds of women, everyone talks about these days. They are now saying that, since your father passed away, she has been beside herself with grief, so much so that she seeks female company of an intimate nature. And that a lady associate of hers visits her at each weekend and they get up to all sorts...'

Agnes' words were abruptly interrupted by Jenny as a look of extreme irritation coated her features.

'Agnes I don't know which quarter this absurd and dangerous tittle-tattle is coming from but I can assure you that they are completely unfounded. I can tell you now that the lady in question, who visits Miss Howe so regularly, is her sister and she visits in order to relieve Miss Howe's grief. So, now that you know this, I would be obliged if you would quell all such nonsense in the future, as soon as you hear it in fact, and not indulge yourself in such ridiculous rubbish in any way. I hope I am making myself clear to you Agnes, as the last thing I need right now is for you to gossip about my friends or myself for that matter, not ever, do you hear me? Really, Agnes I thought you to be beyond twaddle of this sort, it really doesn't become you, you know.'

'I'm so sorry Miss Jenny, but I was only concerned about you and your good name, I can positively assure you that I only listen, never, but never, do I pass on anything that is none of my business, you may rest assured on that Miss Jenny, really you can. And I now appreciate and quite understand the information you have just given me.'

Agnes turned once again to engage the handle of the bedroom door but she was once again halted in her stride.

'Agnes, on a lighter note, who was it who attended my hair when I was a child? Only Jacob's hair has grown to be so long now, it is in need of a trim.'

'Why, I used to look after your hair myself Miss Jenny, always did, ever since you were a baby. And as for Jacob, well I could see to that for him as well; I did all my children's hair for them when they were young; still got all the hand clippers and scissors as well. I'll have a word with Master Jacob if you like, that way you won't have to bother yourself about it.'

When Agnes had finally left the room, fresh doubts and fears crept back into Jenny's mind; doubts and fears that her maid servant had brought unexpectedly to the surface, and although she was already well aware of the rumours, they were now concerning her greatly.

"So, Jane's reputation as being a ladies lover is still doing the rounds, and perhaps there is no smoke without fire on this occasion, who knows; perhaps she really has hoped for female company as an alternative diversion but never found it. And because I am the one closest to Daddy she has chosen me. But that doesn't take into account my own feelings.

"I must erase all of this fantasy nonsense from my mind at once, for that surely is all it is, useless fantasy; and concentrate on the more down-to-earth side of life."

Jenny had changed her mind about her departure that afternoon, or it was never in her mind at all, but merely an excuse to summon Agnes to her room in order to put an end to her own feelings of embarrassment... who knows?

Nevertheless, Jenny was still at home when Jacob and Fredrick returned to Hyde Hall and because of their successful visit to the gypsy encampment they were rather eager to seek Jenny's attention and share with her all that had occupied their day so favourably.

They found her behind the house talking to Joe as she stroked Snowball's tender mouth. Upon seeing the two boys she excused herself from Joe and his horse abruptly as she relayed a greeting to the two young lads from across the yard.

'Have you both had an exciting day? Tell me, what awful pranks have you been up to that have kept you away for so long?'

'Mother, we took a walk over to the gypsy camp,' answered Jacob, excitedly.

Jenny put a hand to her anxious mouth and gasped.

'Mr Hawk gave us both a magnificent reception and allowed us to visit his fabulous wagon, to attend a religious service they were holding and to eat and drink with them all as well.'

'Jacob, I... those gypsies will not be staying for very much longer. You see I have issued a directive for them to quit my estate and I have been assured they will be leaving by the end of the week.'

'But Mother, you can't do that; they are really such lovely Christian people and wouldn't hurt a fly. Please say they can stay; they won't do any damage to anything, I can promise you that, and they keep the place so neat and tidy too; so please say you'll change your mind'

'No Jacob, certainly not, orders have been given and if they are still there this time next week then the police will be notified to move them on. I expect Tom Hawk has sent you to appeal to my better nature, has he?'

'No Mother he hasn't,' answered Jacob, brusquely and he turned to go just as his grandmother's car was heard in the driveway. It was brought to a sudden halt directly in front of the Hyde Hall entrance - out of view of mother and son.

CHAPTER EIGHT

It was a cold, bleak, wintry day that persisted throughout the following Wednesday and days beyond: the severe, unexpected depth of snow that in the space of a few hours had fallen on Dorset had caused it to be so. And because of it, silence in the form of total emptiness now existed on every local byway.

Moreover, because of the suddenness and indeed the lateness in the changes to the weather's pattern, no snow clearing or road gritting operations had been arranged, let alone for them to have yet been considered, despite all the recommendations that had been so freely given by the forecasters. The council officers' failure to stubbornly heed the meteorologist's warnings was to blame for this dismal situation - and everyone knew it.

"But these are England's most southerly regions" was their pathetic response - *"snow can't possibly fall here... not at the end of such a moderate winter and not at the commencement of the first day of spring's most tranquil months, either;"* they had argued... *"can it?"* Yes it can, and it did.

As a direct consequence of the council's obstinate disregard, the entire population of Hyde had to remain in their homes longer than was convenient; all outside jobs were left undone - employment was lost and all outings of importance were missed - for the foreseeable future anyway.

The whole of the area, surrounding Hyde Hall, was particularly affected, seeing that it possessed an exposed northerly aspect; and so a ten inch blanket of the white snow caused all the roadside borders to be buried, all the road markings to be hidden, and every road-sign to be masked, thereby making travel in each and every direction to be extremely hazardous - if not downright impossible.

The feeble excuses for the council's negligence in dealing immediately with a situation of this magnitude irritated the village parents greatly; however, it had the opposite effect on their elated broods, as all the children, with the possible exception of Jacob Kent, embraced the widely circulated school closure bulletin with shameless excitement, no matter how short lived the vacation was thought to be: they being only too keen to amuse themselves in ways that young children throughout the ages have amused themselves in snowy conditions such as these.

But, as already mention, not so Jacob Kent. This young man

would always consider a situation of this kind to be a total inconvenience, even a setback to his education.

Although he was particularly fond of his new home and the white flakes with equal bliss he was such an avid pupil that he grew frustrated when having to be kept away from his place of learning, whatever the reason - snowflakes included.

Margaret, on the other hand, hated the snow, but that wasn't why she had remained detached, cut off and freed from all social engagements since she'd found her way back to Hyde Hall. No, there were other reasons; private reasons existed that were for privileged ears alone to hear.

The two part-time employees at Hyde Hall merely assumed they knew why Margaret had remained isolated in this way; the permanent members of staff were surer: bearing in mind that the disapproving talk, surrounding her questionable relationship with Lord Melchamp, had been in existence for some considerable time. And after a good deal of covert tittle-tattle had been exchanged, this reason for her seclusion was assumed undeniable.

But stifling a report of this magnitude, be it true or false, would prove to be a most difficult task indeed: seeing that a senior member of the Kent family was directly involved, and especially as this particular story cum rumour was of a personal nature - as was this piece of hot gossip.

And so, by isolating herself in this way she thought she had discovered a canny way of preventing all the wagging tongues from broadcasting her business; anyone wishing to nosily inquire directly would, quite rightly, be put in their places at once; for everyone's private affairs ought to be private, especially where Margaret Kent is concerned; so that was the end of the matter.

Of course, garbage of this sort ought to have been nipped in the bud, before it started to bloom and would have been had Spiller still been at the helm; but he wasn't - and so the rumours flew about the place like wildfire; gathering speed and embellishment as they went their wilful way.

With the disciplinary measures of sacking being removed from their executive powers, most ex-employers are all too often seen as being easy targets for domestic gossip. After all, any piece of intrigue, in the early days, will appear to be thrilling for most people's mouths to spread and so it will continue 'till the source of the gossip has been smothered or tedium sets in.

And so it proved to be with the ex-mistress of Hyde Hall; and in order to protect her own privacy, she would keep all information of a personal nature locked away from all interfering noses - and especially where her own daughter's prying nose was concerned.

Consequently she remained in the seclusion of her own room at all times of the day and night - well more or less; and by incarcerating herself in this way, even at mealtimes so that one of the maids was obliged to accommodate her every whim, seemed the only way for Margaret to continue her life without her being made aware of the above twaddle taking place.

Only on two occasions was she seen to be furtively prowling about the place and on both of these occasions she inadvertently stumbled across her daughter with unnecessary embarrassment attending.

Although Margaret had felt compelled, in both instances, to exchange the time of day with Jenny, each meeting resulted in much rudeness being displayed; together with words of aggravation; both of which were heard to be issuing from Margaret's disruptive mouth.

During the second occasion, however, Jenny, with a determined effort to contain this impossible deadlock, ignored all the histrionics as she tried to soothe her mother's emotional behaviour - at least, that was her intention. She had deftly backed Margaret into a corner and pointedly asked if she had enjoyed her temporary break from the family home, which, for one reason or another had become extended beyond the Christmas period. This was performed with the most tactful verbal skills on offer.

'Yes I did,' was the curt reply, with no expression of appreciation regarding the enquiry or any reciprocal comments being available, but, as always, she was skilful enough to sully the reply with expressions of complete unpleasantness.

This was followed by a period of quiet during which time Margaret eyed her daughter with utter disgust and loathing.

'I hear you have been entertaining that trollop, Jane Howe, since I've been away, and here, at my home too,' said Margaret.

Jenny was horrified.

Despite this, her mother continued as before: 'And I have to say, Jennifer, by using your usual lack of respect for me by taking advantage of my absence.' Her words came with a bitterness that engulfed the whole of her mocking face. 'Now, why wasn't I surprised to hear that; birds of a feather flock together, as they say; and all lesbians find a partner sooner or later; at least that's what I've been led to believe. But then, perhaps this particular lesbian has already found a partner... in you; am I not correct in my assumption, Jennifer? You are Jane Howe's lady lover aren't you? Or am I jumping the gun a little? Well if you are not, then I'm damn sure you soon will be; if that whore gets her claws in you.

'Still, I shall find no need to put up with your shameful shortcomings and lack of virtue for very much longer, Jennifer; I'm moving out you see, so you will soon be able to entertain all the whores you desire, from the near side of Bournemouth to the outer limits of Timbuktu, for all I care… and to your hearts content at that, and long may they remain to scandalise and malign your name.'

'Mother, your sarcastic comments and your utterly ridiculous and ill humoured remarks do you justice, for they cause you to sound totally despicable and fully deserving of my contempt. I hope you realize what you have become… you are a despicable old woman who provokes hatred wherever she goes; my only hope is that Lord Melchamp will be able to make something of you or at least tolerate your ludicrous behavioural patterns and foul mood swings half as well as I do.'

Margaret was stunned by the unexpected disclosure of this piece of privileged intelligence her daughter was evidently privy to.

'What? Damn you… who in hell's name told you where I was going?'

'Don't worry Mother I know all about the two of you and how you managed to seduce him on the same day you buried my father. No, don't bother to deny it.'

'Go to hell … you liar! Who have you been talking to that is so willing to malign my good name with such evil lies as that?'

Jenny ignored her mother's enraged question and walked away from her with complete contempt covering her face; although critical reflections did thrash about in her mind as she left.

She questioned if it had been Agnes who had expressed her treachery with an unfathomable display of disloyalty to harm her reputation by revealing Jane's visit; or maybe it was Jane, herself, who had been overly zealous with her tongue.

But either way, Jenny had had no need to concern herself, not with this particular issue and not at this particular moment because not ten minutes later she received a mysterious telephone call from a quiet, almost jaded but well spoken, feminine voice.

Jenny was in her study when the call came through but it was a voice she couldn't bring to mind no matter how she tried. For some unknown reason, the caller had felt the urge to keep her identity a mystery and so the name had been rudely withheld from Jenny's ears - and although Jenny had had the opportunity to ask for her identity - even before the conversation started - the moment passed her by.

'May I speak to Miss Kent please?'

'Yes, speaking.'

'I don't wish to alarm you, Miss Kent, but I have it on very good authority that your mother is having your comings and goings monitored.'

The dull purring sound that followed indicated that the short, one sided telephone conversation had been brought to an abrupt end.

Jenny was furious.

As already stated, Jenny had no idea whose voice it could have been at the other end of the phone; certainly not someone within her household - she was pretty sure of that; but she didn't care - not for the moment anyway - that would come later; she now had a more important assignment to attend to.

She stormed up to her mother's room and without a hint of civility in her move she flung open the door.

The room was empty.

She rushed down the stairs again almost stumbling as she went to pursue the drawing room but this time she contained herself a little, before she entered, even though her feelings of anger still dictated her mood.

She found her mother in her customary position, casually lying on the chaise longue with a lighted cigarette in one hand and a glass of whisky in the other, casually thumbing through some glossy magazine.

Margaret failed to look up as Jenny entered.

'Mother, you completely disgrace the Kent name and of being my parent, and so I intend to use the term 'Mother' inaccurately, yes, very inaccurately indeed,' said Jenny, summoning up all the uncontrolled resentment she could find that had built up in her mind for a very long time indeed. 'Tell me; are you intent on having my every move monitored when you are away and living with the dubious Lord Melchamp? Or will you consider that shameful and despicable practice to be beyond your financial resources? These, of course, will be lost altogether should you marry the gentleman; ah, but then again, he may summon sufficient courage to walk away from you before long and leave you to your own evil devises; what do you think?'

There was no answer to the impertinent statement.

Only the deep drawing on the long, tortoiseshell holder encapsulating one of her full-strength cigarettes, the lengthy exhaling of the light grey, wispy smoke before it drifted toward the slightly opened window, her diligence in the faked perusal of her glossy magazine, and of course, the flavour of the single malt whisky which she savoured with relish at each and every sip. These actions alone constituted the wordless reply. These and these alone were her sole responses; these and these alone provided Margaret with her interest and her innermost desire - for the time being. All else, especially words of contrition and those of affability, failed to issue from the ex-lady of Hyde Hall's mouth, for only the most sickly of sick grins imaginable was seen to be settled there.

'Lady Melchamp, or whatever it is you prefer to be called or be known as these days, you are the most despicable person on the planet and no longer do I wish for you to remain here... under my roof. I want you gone from Hyde Hall today... this very minute; do I make myself clear?'

A verbal reply came forth at last.

'Hardly my dear; have you looked outside lately in order to review the weather?'

***

The following day brought with it a little more zeal, and a little more kindness too, for not only had the snow settled down to a faint flurry but the snowploughs had ventured forth in significant numbers so as to reinstate the comings and goings of the local populous. And it was at two thirty in the afternoon, on that very day, when the sky produced a bluer, brighter hue and Margaret Kent had departed Hyde Hall, that a ringing reverberated through the halls of the big house, making it clear that the heavy, oaken door was in need of being answered.

It took Agnes a full three minutes to reply to the summoning call and to find a handsome looking man awaiting her attention.

'If Miss Kent is in I should very much like to have a quick word with her... if that is at all possible, please ma'am.'

'And who should I say wants to speak to her?'

'Hawke, my name is Tom Hawk ma'am.'

'If you would care to step inside, Mr Hawk, so that I may close the door in order to keep the cold out, I will see if Miss Kent will receive you.'

As Agnes vanished Tom waited within the confines of the big hall admiring a couple of pictures that hung on either side of the immediate two angled walls adjacent to the doorway. And being thus preoccupied, he failed to notice a pair of young eyes peering down at him from a covert position at the rear of the upstairs gallery; and a smile widened the striking young face of Jacob Kent as he waited for his mother to show or Agnes to reappear.

It was Agnes' return that ushered the gypsy across the hall and down the lengthy corridor to the now familiar drawing room.

'Mr Hawk is here to see you, Miss Kent.'

'Thank you, Agnes... that will be all for now.'

As Agnes left, closing the door quietly behind her, Jenny stood up from her seated position and slowly walked to her gypsy friend with her face radiating a glow of intense happiness. And the reciprocated smile issuing from Tom's face settled her mind, dispelling all doubts, and told her all she needed to know.

'Tom,' she spoke his name quietly and effortlessly and not at all how she had spoken it on the final occasion of their meeting; and with her hands reaching out, she clasped his, welcomingly. 'How lovely it is to see you again. I more or less guessed you would pay me a visit today... or at least very soon.

'No doubt you will be seeking an extension to your stay with us, seeing that the weather is so awful at the moment; which I approve most willingly; but only for another week mind, after that the weather will have changed permanently... with any luck.'

'Yes, Miss Jenny, in a way that is why I have called to see you today... but that is not the only reason... there is more to it than that... in reality. First of all... a much more important matter has to be sorted out between us.' Tom's look was one of uncertainty as he oddly stumbled through his sentence. 'You see, I was never very happy with the way we left each other the other day; or with the way that matters were left hanging in the air between us; worrying it was, I can tell you... for me at any rate. And although I did try to work things out in my own mind, well, as best I could... I gathered little success with my reckoning... no success at all, I have to say... not at the time I didn't.

'And then, quite without warning, I had a breakthrough. I don't know if you are aware of it or not, Miss Jenny, but your son, Jacob, he paid us a visit last Sunday with one of his friends. Truly, Jacob is a lovely boy Miss Jenny; he's a real credit to you and does you, his father and your family proud. Still I've not come here to tell you what you must already know,' said Tom, as his face widened to make comfortable the smile that still existed there only to find that his flow was being interrupted by Jenny's impatience.

'Yes, my son did mention he had visited you Tom; totally uninvited and on the spur of the moment, or so I have been led to believe. The venture, I have to say, was not at all approved or suggested by me,' she hastily added. 'I do hope you realise that Tom. But it seems he was much taken with you also, and told me all about his visit in great detail.

'But that's not why you're here, now is it? I'm sorry, please carry on Tom, I've interrupted you and I can see by your face there is much more than a trivial discussion with me about my son to be unloaded from your mind.'

'Well, Miss Jenny, it was while young Jacob was with me that he pointed out someone who I knew came from a little village near Lincoln... where you and your family once lived, for a while, or so Jacob told me; someone by the name of Barnabas Bell. Now, I have no idea if you were ever acquainted with this particular fellow or not. That is really why I'm here, you see; to find out if you ever knew him.

'Nevertheless, I did face Barney with that very question on Monday, that was the day after Jacob's visit, but he tended to evade the question for some reason or other, even though I had only put it to him out of casual curiosity; I mean to say, I wasn't accusing him of anything, no mater how he may have viewed it.

'Anyway, the very next day, early in the morning, before all else had stirred, he left the camp and hasn't been seen or heard of since.

'Now this bothered poor old Noah; he's the chap that Mr Bell has been lodging with, and he came to me and asked me if I had seen his friend at all. Of course, I was as puzzled as he was; but as all of Barney's things were missing from the vardo, we realised that his leaving was deliberate and that nothing at all unpleasant had happened to him.

'I should now like to know, Miss Jenny, what the connection between the two of you actually is... if there is one of course; and is it his presence alone that is determining whether we are able to stay on your land or not?'

'I told you once before Tom, I'm not prepared to tell you anything you may not wish to hear and especially something that may have an effect on relations within your camp.

'The last thing I want is for you to discover any sort of bitterness or hostility existing within your family because of me; or for my disapproval of anyone to come between the closest of your friends for whatever reason. Some of them must surely have been friendly towards him, Tom... your friend Noah for instance; he surely must be closely acquainted with Barnabas Bell.'

'Ah... So I am right, from the way you speak you certainly

did know the man.'

Jenny felt somewhat misled into revealing her awareness of the man she loathed, and she felt she had been clumsy in not being more selective in her choice of words. But she smiled at her unfortunate blunder and finally admitted the regrettable knowledge of the man that had plagued her life for so long.

'Alright Tom, yes you are right, I did know Barnabas Bell. He was employed by my uncle some time before I even moved to Brenton. But I have no idea why he couldn't have admitted that fact to you, when you spoke to him... unless, of course, a great deal of guilt hindered his tongue. Tell me Tom; are there any young children at your camp?'

'Yes there are, five or six actually. But two young sisters in particular, one is five and the other about ten, seem pretty close to him as I've often seen them playing with Barney. They both seem to have a fondness for him and I've always thought him to have the same mentality as them, as they play about together in all innocence... when he's home from his job, that is. And I'm not the only one to notice their innocence in playing together... why; even the children's parents have remarked to me how happy they are to have Barney about the place.

'You see, he doesn't have much to say to anyone else at the camp except to old Noah as I've just said, but what have these kids got to do with the issue here Miss Jenny? Why do you ask?'

'Well it doesn't really matter, not now that he's left you.'

'Miss Jenny, I understand totally your reluctance to discredit anyone in my camp, or anyone at all, come to that. But we are homely, honest people, and not at all how most folk may imagine us to be; we're content with our simple way of life and live in rare harmony with one another that suits us well... least ways, most of the time.

'Now, I think I have the right to ask if you know of any reason why that harmony might be put to the test or broken in any way. I don't know what Barnabas Bell's intentions are regarding his living with us any more; he's said nothing to me... he may return tomorrow, for all I know, he may even be returning now... as we speak. So if you have any knowledge that may be detrimental to my people's wellbeing or their safety, then, for our friendship sake, speak now, for if something happens that could have been avoided then I'm sure you will never be able to live with yourself... not for the rest of your days.'

'Yes you are right Tom; I have vacillated far too much

already and have been silly in holding out on you for so long too. But you see I have valued our friendship too highly for it to have been jeopardised with any careless talk. Even my dear uncle considers me to have overreacted in my estimation of Barnabas Bell. But really, Tom, I consider him to be a most dangerous man; capable of anything in order to get his own way, and so I fear for my own and my families safety too... while he's around.

'Why, even at Christmas time he visited Hyde Hall while I was away, asking after me by name; and he upset my maid so much she had to call the police; so you can see how carefully I have to tread. Nevertheless, I shall dither no longer and tell to you all I know about the man....'

Jenny then described in great detail the sexual abuse and harassment she had experienced. All of the threats Bell had made to her, all the fears she suffered for her own and for her families safety, all of these and many more feelings of unease that had worryingly been instilled in her mind in Lincolnshire; and all because of this imbecile.

Tom listened, attentively. But no utterance left his mouth, only a humourless expression covered his face for the whole of the time Jenny was speaking.

After she had finished, a silence existed; and since Tom's head was now buried in his hands he appeared deep in thought as if his mind was carefully weighing up any problem that could be added to this dire situation.

Finally he looked up at Jenny and smiled; but the smile seemed to offer no solutions and any answers to the difficult situation seemed far away - so uncertain was his gaze.

'I can now see the dilemma you felt in your telling me about this man, Miss Jenny. Bell, however, has done nothing that warrant's his arrest or our retribution; everything he has said or done to you is open to conjecture and would be considered by many as being his word against yours.

'OK, your uncle's housekeeper heard him make improper suggestions to you that she had not been keen on him making and which she eventually fired him for, but these would hardly land him in jail, Miss Jenny. And as far as I know, he has committed no offence since living with us; he has not harmed the children in any way; not that I've been told about. He has proved to be a comfort to an old man in the final stages of his life... that is all; and besides, he keeps himself to himself for most of the time he's with us; well I can hardly banish a man for doing that, now can I?

'I now find myself to be in a fix, Miss Jenny, equal to your own it seems. If he returns to the camp and I forbid his stay I risk him heaping his vengeance on you, as he already knows where you live, and I also risk upsetting poor old Noah, though I might easily overcome that by quietly explaining to him what Bell is really like. And if I allow him to stay with us, well then, we have to move on as soon as we can to accommodate your demands and by so doing we put the children's wellbeing at risk: if what you say about the man is the slightest bit exact... which I don't doubt for a minute.

'Well, that's it then, in a nutshell, as they say; if he returns we will indeed go immediately. So, will you trust me not to deceive you Miss Jenny so that we may stay a little longer? I mean I could easily tell you he's not with us and at the same time keep his presence a secret from you... just so we can stay a few extra days.'

'Tom, you may stay where you are as long as it suits you... so long as that man is not benefiting from my estate. But I will not be seen harbouring a man who I consider to be a perilous threat to me and mine. I can't emphasise that enough... I'm sorry, but my refusal in accommodating such a man on my land is not open for discussion.

'So, in answer to your question, yes, I trust you implicitly. So all we can do for now is hope that Bell doesn't return, at least not before the better weather has arrived; I take it that you will be keen to move on soon after that anyway.'

'Yes Miss Jenny, we have been here for some time on this occasion, though we tend to keep to Dorset... most of the time. It is a pleasurable enough spot and we're glad for it to have provided us with shelter over the winter months and I cannot thank you enough for your hospitality. But when the late spring and early summer months arrive... well, we will all want to be moving on then, to feel the freedom of the road under our feet and the open sky over our heads, once more.'

Jenny walked her friend to the door and lightly touched his hand when the time for parting came.

'If ever your son feels like a visit with us please don't discourage him, Miss Jenny, for as I have already said, he is a very likeable young man and one with whom I should like to become better acquainted.'

After exchanging words of fond farewell, Tom left.

An odd, haunting feeling compelled the gypsy to look back as he walked away from Hyde Hall that day, not to the doorway where Jenny was left standing did his glances stray, but to one of the upstairs casement windows where Jacob stood behind its shining panes.

Tom eventually stopped, and after turning round he and Jacob exchanged meaningful glances; and the discreet wave of hands of a special, personal nature were given and received simultaneously.

***

So that is how the situation was left; Tom and his friends stayed on at the site where they were now happily settled until their need for the open road once again surged through their veins.

Tom did have a confidential word with Noah explaining Barney Bell's absence; but making the reason as light as he possibly could in order to save the old man unnecessary distress.

On the whole, the old gypsy took the news pretty well, considering he was the type of gentleman who preferred not to think badly of anyone until a rhyme or reason could be established; one that demonstrated matters to the contrary. If that were the case he would then lean heavily on the offender with considerable force.

But as no further statement or communication of any description had been received from the direction of the encampment, Jenny assumed that Barnabas Bell had failed to return to Noah's van and that the matter of his disappearance was therefore closed.

Jacob did visit the encampment on two subsequent occasions: once in the company of Fredrick and the second time he braved the forest by himself. But with each resulting visit boredom began to set in: there being a limit that a young lad like Jacob need know about the gypsy way of living or indeed their history; and so, no further visits were made until well after the school's spring holiday.

Because Jenny now felt fully at ease about the situation at the Hyde Hall Home Farm - mainly due to Alf Abrams' managerial ability - and with the estate's business being in good order as well, and after brushing all thoughts about gypsy encampments to one side, she decided that as the school spring holiday was growing steadily closer, it would be a good opportunity for her and Jacob to plan a short break.

There were underlying but significant problems being harboured within Jenny's mind that continually plagued her subconscious and which were simply crying out to be aired; and she knew but one place where this could be best achieved.

CHAPTER NINE

Following Jane Howe's unfortunate visit and after her sleep had been disturbed night after dreary night, Jenny wrestled with her own conscience as she questioned if it had been she, who had stimulated the intimacy that had occurred between them and which had taken hold of her mind so fervently ever since.

Something had to be done, if she was to regain at least some semblance of normality in her life, that much was obvious; and so, because Easter was in the offing she decided that a visit with her Uncle Hamish would be appropriate; she would then be able to seek the advice she needed from his sympathetic housekeeper, as she had before sought it.

After revealing her intentions to her son, though omitting the reasons for such a visit, and in order to yield to Jacob's unrelenting pestering, urging his mother to invite his friend Fredrick along for the ride and after acquiring the all important parental permission from his father, the invitation was timely placed.

As anticipated, it was with a high degree of eagerness that the invite was received and then answered amid loudening shouts of joy issuing from the two boys. And so the proposal was firmly established with no further questions daring to be asked.

The bright yellow Lotus Elan, crammed with three animated occupants and three bulky sets of luggage, and looking as though a month's visit was on order rather than a mere three day's jaunt, took its leave of Hyde village very early on a bright Saturday morning. And with no time for easy cruising it sped across the countryside, with varied scenes passing on either side, exhibiting a show of fleeting beauty - though blurred in the extreme.

Since this special car was maintaining a healthy speed throughout the journey the ability to hear let alone understand each other's jovial chatter had been reduced to impossibility. The engine's noise would have been mainly to blame, of course, but the rushing of the wind that was caused by the motor's black roof covering being wound back and made fast, also played a part.

Anyhow, with no exciting experiences existing to assist the lengthy time along and with only two short convenience breaks being taken on the way, the keyed up group were relieved to have arrived at The Old House in eight hours flat - almost to the minute, intact, and with twinges of hunger making demands on each of their stomachs.

Jenny felt a surge of chirpiness envelop her as the Lotus entered the driveway on that sunny afternoon, and a sudden wave of childlike enthusiasm overtook her; and as she glanced from left to right her grinning face was placed on view for everyone to see.

Now, this action may easily have been purposely feigned for her host's benefit, who knows; but the chirpiness and the grinning certainly wasn't - it came as a surprise - even to her, for during the journey she had felt somewhat apprehensive about her return to Lincolnshire on this occasion; even though a short space in time separated her previous sojourn.

Being back in Brenton village again, however brief, would have a positive affect on Jenny, but it would cause her to feel a little hesitant, a little uncertain and cautious at times - more so than when she'd arrived here for the Christmas break.

Maybe, all that had taken place in the interim, back in Dorset, would be the cause of her discomfort this time - after all that was the real reason for her mission.

But the many periods of time that had been filled with happiness whilst living here soon dominated her emotions; these were the spans of time that had seen Jenny through her unusual childhood.

Still, all those years had scurried by so fast a mere blinking of an eye had seen them pass away but the memories of those halcyon days would be forever hers, stored away in her guarded mind, to be revived at a moment's notice at a different place - a different time.

As an enormous, glowing smile prepared itself to overrun her beautiful features a tiny tear escaped its channel to run down the side of her lovely face; and ease, in the form of serenity, overtook her once more; so happy was she to be home again.

She sounded the horn twice to indicate the Elan's arrival just as the aging housekeeper showed herself to be first out of the oaken doorway; a little slow of movement by this time, but with an abundance of zest still abounding. With but a few seconds passing, the tall handsome figure of Sir Hamish Kent followed her, offering the visitors a discrete wave of his hand and a beaming smile to equal that of Jenny's...

'How lovely it is to see you both again.' This was Janet, mopping up floods of tears from the cheeks of her sunken face, quite as if it were emotions of farewell being discharged rather than the warmest, welcoming words she could ever hope to give.

The two ladies, young and old, held each other affectionately and continued with the lengthy embrace until it became - well, almost a sight of inelegance.

After Jacob had been almost wrestled to the ground by Janet, Hamish Kent arrived to take his fond niece and nephew in his arms; the two of them together. And heaping gestures of love on them both, he walked, unhurriedly in the midst of them to the inside of the house whilst the white haired housekeeper politely introduced herself to a slightly confused and neglected Frederick, and Sir Hamish Kent also was introduced to him, from a distance.

As soon as the new arrivals entered the house they were settled with sandwiches in abundance, tea, cake and conversation.

After a long drawn out period of the previously mentioned had taken place; Jenny couldn't help but notice a suppressed yawn of boredom emerging from Fredrick's mouth. At almost the same time her eyes were distracted by someone outside the window. It seemed, to her eyes, a newcomer was on the scene - a thickset figure, struggling with suitcases. He was bent double and had a pained look on his florid face that indicated a fair bit of exertion was being spent. He then allowed the suitcase in his right arm to slip a little even though his effort persisted.

This youngish lad, of roughly fourteen years, appeared to be in a good deal of bother; for it was obvious to Jenny that the cases were far too big for him to handle by himself, though, from a distance he looked determined with his obligation. Twice Jenny saw him stumble, and twice she saw him regain his stance - the solution to Fredrick's boredom and the suitcase carrier's dilemma, were instantly made obvious to the considerate lady.

'Jacob, do be a dear and pop outside to help that young man with the luggage. I'm sure he would appreciate some help as he looks as though he might do himself a mischief any moment. His attempt at carrying our suitcases, and at the same time, looks to me to be an impossible task for him. Perhaps you might take Fredrick with you so that you can carry a case each.'

Eager to attend Jenny's bidding, thereby freeing themselves of the afore mentioned tedium and leaving the three adults with the cosiness of conversation, the two set off without delay as Sir Hamish distracted the ladies with more chat.

'I must say it was an unexpected pleasure to receive your telephone call the other evening, Jennifer,' he said, after the three were quite alone, 'but I must say I was rather concerned, when I realised the call was from you, just in case some underlying difficulty had arisen at Home Farm that had prompted your call. My mind was rather relieved, I must say, to discover your only need was to pay us a visit.

'When I hear nothing to the contrary I automatically assume that everything is in good shape down in Dorset and that Mr Abrams is fulfilling his potential as we both hoped he would; at least I always expect that to be the case.'

'Uncle, we were so fortunate in finding that man and I will be eternally grateful to Joe for recommending him to us in the first place,' said Jenny, as a wide smile of reassurance gleefully decked her face.

Jenny then went on to extol her farm manager in every way imaginable: his dedication, his pleasant way with which he carries out his duty in fact every aspect of Alf Abrams shone through, reassuring both Sir Hamish and herself.

'The only fault I can find with him is that he spends so much time at his post that I fear for the social aspect of his life. Why, only the other day... on his day off mind you... he noticed a gypsy encampment on the far side of the large wood, which, I have to say, is a regular visitor to our estate; though he was unaware of it at the time. He looked into the matter straight away then reported back to me, immediately, instead of leaving the incident until his return to work the following day as most men in his position would have done. I mean, he didn't have to do it, not there and then; it wasn't a life threatening emergency... so it could easily have waited.

'But Mr Abrams likes to keep on top of things you see. 'Keeping everything tidy' I expect would be his way of putting it; and so he clears up at once... as he goes along. So yes Uncle, Alf Abrams is an excellent farm manager and worth his weight in gold; you know, I think I should strive to be more like him.'

'That's good, Jennifer, I am relieved to here it; it's just as well to keep abreast of things, I know that to my cost at times.

'Now I wonder how those two lads are getting on. Perhaps I should take a stroll to see if everything is in order eh? And maybe leave you two ladies to catch up with all the gossip. I'm sure you have a great deal to talk about; if not, I'm sure you will soon find something.'

Jenny and Janet both grinned at the insinuation as they watched the kindest of men disappear from the room each knowing, deep down, how much he delighted in his great-nephew's company.

The ladies brought each other up to date with the goings-on in both counties - well, more or less, and sat in idle chatter together; both finding the other's society to their liking, just as they had in the past enjoyed it.

For the first five minutes or so everything was going fine; however, Janet sensed something was wrong as soon as Jenny adopted a careless posture whilst sitting in her chair; she also started to fidget quite nervously with one of her jacket buttons as if something was plaguing her mind.

It was Jenny's fidgeting that gave Janet the clue she needed to suggest they stepped into the garden together.

'Strolling might give us the appetite we need for dinner,' was the excuse she made. But in reality, it had dawned on Janet that it had been in the garden when Jenny had emptied out her heart to her on a previous occasion and she felt it likely that a similar result might be achieved by such a walk this time.

And so, locking Jenny's arm in her own, Janet led her from the house and they strolled together along the path in the direction of the netted koi pond, as they had on many occasions walked the distance.

The late afternoon was bright enough with some watery sunshine filtering the leafless branches of the old elms that bordered the rear garden. And although the recent fall of snow was still evident in shaded parts, the air was a little less than cool rather than cold - they had each coated and scarved themselves in order to deter any freshness that may unsettle them, anyway. And so they walked slowly, just sauntering in shared content.

Too short a time had passed for Jenny to feel disconnected from this, her familiar home, and although some major path repairs had been carried out, nothing new altered the pleasure she now felt with this congenial place. Only the health of the aging housekeeper clouded her mind a little.

'How are you keeping, Janet; are you really as hale and hearty as you said you were?'

'Jennifer, I am just fine and all the better for seeing you my dear. Though I have to say that the missing of you both was more intense than I expected it to be, but now that you're both back with us again... well, I realise you're not really so far away after all.

'Jennifer, it isn't my wellbeing that is the issue at this moment in time, is it my dear? Do I not sense a wee problem you are not yet wishing to share with me? You know you have never been able to hide your problems from me in the past, young lady, not for very long, anyway.'

The lilt in the aging, Scottish woman's voice was akin to a melody in Jenny's ears - a Burn's air - the like of which she would never tire of hearing, and she suddenly realised, without having to take a great deal of thought, how much of the missing pain she also had endured since she had abandoned this homely place and abandoned these homely people.

'It really is so good to be with you again Janet, even though it was but a short time since I was last here' said Jenny, plainly ignoring the first request. 'I really must make an effort to visit you more often and now that everything is going so swimmingly at Hyde Hall, I promise I'll do just that. But in any case, you would be more than welcome to come to Dorset you know and stay with us awhile; after all, life is fast becoming dull now that mother has left us, and is in desperate need of being perked up a little.' As both ladies stole a casual glance from each other, grins of familiarity settled on their faces.

'Well Jennifer, I might surprise you one of these fine days and do just that. Meanwhile, won't you confide in me? You never know my dear; I might be able to help.'

Jenny pulled her old friend's withering arm closer to her and began to narrate the Jane Howe episode in unabridged frankness, leaving nothing to conjecture, nothing half hidden to be wheedled out by gentle persuasion; nothing was withheld, even the frankness of her own desires were there for Janet to consider.

"Ah... so now we have it. Now we have the real reason for your visit; you poor wee thing." Janet's thoughts had been concise, but concerned for all that; and after Jenny had completed the candid description of Jane's visit, Janet deliberately brought their stroll to an end.

They sat awhile, next to the old koi pond, as they had before sat there when Jenny sought advice. And the nervous anticipation that burdened Jenny's mind became even more troubled by the lack of knowing what her friend might say.

Janet, after searching her own mind, as if exploring the cold depths of the koi pond for some aquatic nymph to appear and to supply her with some form of magical inspiration, turned to her ward again with a loving but unhurried way about her. And taking Jenny's hand in her own she reflected on the issue carefully.

'Well my dear, it seems to me that your senses have been tampered with; they have been wilfully rearranged for you, quite as if Jane is wanting to redirect your own way of thinking so that it is more attuned to hers; that is why all of this confusion is being felt. She has planted illusions in your mind, Jennifer, the like of which can be most disturbing, I'm quite sure of that.

'I take it there is still no young man in your life, am I not right Jennifer?' she asked, as Jenny vehemently shook her head. 'Well then, don't you think that it is about time there was?' The question remained ignored. 'You see, Jennifer,' the old lady went on, 'we all of us have a need for affection in our lives, intense or no, and you, dear child, have had none, excepting of course, that which your dear aunt, Jacob and we have shown you; all of which, I might add, came far too late in your young life.

'Frankly, my dear, you should have been receiving parental love ever since the day you were born, but, being deprived of that relationship you now seem to be reaching out for the love you never had - unwittingly, I'm sure. But it is now with a degree of desperation you are seeking comfort from this surrogate union; any sort of relationship would have done it seems to me, for you are feeling the need to claim it for yourself with arms wide open.

'Oh, I know your father loved you, but he never displayed that love, not until it was far too late, and it seems to me that Jane is in a similar situation herself and is trying to hand you the loving affection she handed your dear father at the highest peak of their affair.

'An intense affection it would have been, no doubt of that, and one she had fashioned deeply for him within her own heart. And so this confusion has been built up and has presented itself to you both in this distorted form, a distorted form that is unacceptable to the two of you, if the truth of the matter be known, for I am sure you would both prefer it to be a bona fide relationship that is accepted by everyone.

'It seems to me neither of you would wish to admit its abnormality, not yet, not even to yourselves maybe; almost certainly for fear of loosing it. But this new love affair, romance, call it what you will, which you both now consider to be quite genuine, even though nothing has been said just yet to make it so, is proving to be quite difficult for you to handle, or you wouldn't be here relating it to me now. But sooner or later, Jennifer, you will both have to face reality, hopefully, before you are so deeply involved that it would be too difficult for you to escape. If you do face reality, then all of the sexual feelings, you tell me you have discovered, will very soon be seen as being totally unnatural and unreal and eventually they will disappear completely.

'This relationship could easily become an addiction to you, my dear, as addictive as any drug might be, and once you have been truly initiated you might easily find life to be intolerable.

'You see, God made woman to be man's complete sexual companion, surely you must appreciate that my dear. I made that discovery for myself a long time ago when I became infatuated with a friend... maybe that is why I never married; though I had the opportunity.

'So, my advise to you, Jennifer, such as it is, is to not divorce yourself from Jane's society but rather encourage it, only please make sure that it is *you* who tightly hold the reins, *you* are to be in sole control of the situation Jennifer, not Jane. And soon, hopefully, you will both arrive at the same conclusion - that there is real merit in true friendship, and that it is well worth the having.

'If you neglect doing what I say, Jennifer, my worry is that tender feelings might soon be damaged - valuable lives might, in next to no time, be shattered, especially if someone else comes along for either of you; someone with whom you feel the need to enter a committed and a more socially accepted relationship, a relationship more fitting in every way - a monogamous, man and woman relationship.

'In the meanwhile try to build a healthy friendship with Jane, my dear, one unwavering in purpose; fashion Jane into the realisation that you are a person worth having as a friend, and then hopefully all these sexual fantasies, for in truth, that is all they are, will disappear from both your minds.'

Quite frankly, Janet had communicated Jenny's own opinion of the situation almost word for word, but more intricately woven and without the so called 'friendship' get out clause, and she felt more at ease with herself now, and was glad she had sought the wisdom of someone whom she knew to be the embodiment of trust and one who would never betray her confidence no matter how attractive the proposal might be.

'And is there any news of that good for nothing Barnabas Bell who worked here at the Old House? Only you told me, if you recall how he had goaded you with his move to Dorset. Have you seen or heard anything of that contemptible young man yet? Or were all his threats brought to nothing and his intentions proven to be quite harmless?'

Almost immediately the name Bell had entered the Scottish housekeeper's thoughts it prompted alarm bells to sound in her mind. And so she reflected deeply for awhile but without exposing her opinion and before Jenny had had chance to make her own reply.

"I am somehow convinced that the fear of that imbecile Bell has had a lasting affect on you, Jennifer, my girl and without you

340

realising it. This may well have a bearing on your present predicament in not finding a man for yourself. The hideous thought of him touching you, in that sickly manner of his, when you were still a child… must have remained in your mind over the years, and could easily have done more damage to your wee psyche than you or anyone else could possibly imagine and the intense revulsion of his improper suggestions may have set your mind firmly against a healthy relationship with any man or men; who knows what damage that imbecile may have caused you at such a tender age?"

Jenny began to fidget with her button once again in an uncomfortable manner as she became aware that Janet was deep in thought.

'Oh yes Janet,' she said, as soon as she could see Janet's contemplations were at an end, 'Bell has joined a band of gypsy people, the leader of whom we saw at the cathedral that searing hot afternoon, if you remember; when you instructed me to follow him to give him my help. But he wasn't the helpless victim I thought him to be; apparently he had raced from the far side of Lincoln City that day and was shattered beyond belief by the effort, but, not wishing for me to see him in such a state of debilitation, he left promptly without saying too much.

'It is that very same group of gypsies that is now situated on the far side of the forest I was telling you and Uncle Hamish about earlier. Bell must have learned in some way that their destination was intended for Dorset and him knowing where I originated from joined them in the sure and certain hope of getting ahead of me. Apparently he has now left them, and for good, I hope, but I have the leader's assurance that should the ogre return then the caravans will be on their way once again.

'Anyhow, I haven't seen that obnoxious creature since and have no wish to see him either. I tell you, Janet, I experience attacks of the shivers just thinking about that insufferable creature.'

Janet smiled.

'You know, Jennifer, when I think back, I consider I should have handled his dismissal more appropriately. Had I not been so robust in the action I took in his leaving your uncle's employment, then you wouldn't have had those awful problems. Yes, maybe I ought to have exercised more Christian charity and explained to him the error of his ways at the time, rather than being so determined in punishing him. We live and learn but ne'er the wiser grow, Jennifer my dear - we live and learn.'

***

On the penultimate morning of their return to Dorset, Jenny took the two boys on a trip to Lincoln City so they might purchase certain mementos of their visit that the two of them considered to be so necessary.

They had walked just halfway up the steep hill that leads to the cathedral when Jenny stopped to examine a fascinating suit in a fascinating shop widow, displaying a fascinating price. Both Jacob and Fredrick, noticing that a delay was imminent, crossed the narrow, grey bricked road and began to enter a shop stocked with dubious commodities especially designed for boy like curiosity.

Jacob called out to his mother indicating the shop that had caught their interest and she turned her head briefly to note where they had gone.

Twisting her head this way and that she studied the elegant suit with the utmost consideration. She walked past the shop a few paces before she turned to approach the window from the opposite direction in order to benefit from a different view of the garment.

She had almost come to a decision.

'Can't make your mind up, eh Miss Kent?'

The voice, not unlike the voice of death, filled her with an intense fear that terrorised the whole of her nervous system, sending shock waves of dread up and down her spine. These discharges, having a long lasting and far reaching effect upon the whole of her lovely body, shook her from the roots of her hair to the tips of her toes and caused goose pimples to invade the total area of her skin and for her stomach muscles to be cramped with such an intense loathing that it made her gag. Her scalp and the back of her neck were affected most of all, and in-between, her teeth were set on edge and were tightly clenched despite the noiseless chatter occurring at the insufferable sound.

Jenny was desperate to pull herself together and to summon up energies, courage and strengths beyond her ability in order to control her feelings.

But it wasn't to be.

And so, in the certain knowledge that her body had now been deserted by the responses that should have attended her in her time of need, she refused to acknowledge the questioner's enquiry and walked ten paces up the hill instead.

Upon the accomplishment of the numbered paces, she felt scrawny, perspiring, dirty fingers gripping her shoulder in crazed desperation to gain her attention.

'Not ignoring an old friend, I should hope, Miss Kent. Not after all my willing attentions to your every need and service?'

At last, with a modicum of success in the gathering of her wits, she stopped and turned; not completely but sufficient to see the expected creature who craved her attention.

But the forceful Barnabas Bell, not wishing to be only half attended to, walked in front of her to face Jenny in her misery.

'Why, Mr Bell,' answered Jenny. Her body was still shaking with fear, so she used no other phrase.

'Hello Miss Kent, it's nice to see you once again. Not moved back to Lincolnshire already have you?'

'No Mr Bell, just visiting.'

'Ah, like me then,' he said, as a nervous twitching in his jaw muscles betrayed the excitement already set within his brain. 'I'm just a visiting as well. Now ain't that a coincidence? If only I'd known you was a coming this way, well, you might have given me a ride in your lovely yellow motorcar; still, perhaps you'll be good enough to offer an old friend a lift back to Dorset, when you go.'

Jenny ignored the request without consideration. And so the monster decided to enlarge upon the events that caused his sojourn in the city.

'Yes, I'm staying with my young brother William who lives in mother's old house along with our old aunt. You've probably met him already Miss Kent; he's got my old job at The Old House. I do hope you won't get him the sack, not like what you got me. Never will forget that Miss Kent, not in all my days I won't.

'Oh, by the way, you may be interested to know I've changed my job. Yes, I'm in service once again and working as a handyman for a Lord Melchamp; don't know if you know of the gentleman at all Miss Kent?'

As of old, his voice was menacing and the left eye performed its usual rituals thereby indicating the arousal of his feelings of desire.

'Well this won't do Mr Bell, I have shopping to attend to.'

'Not leaving an old friend quite so soon, are you Miss Kent. I thought how nice it would be if we took a little stroll together... you know, just the two of us - like what we always used to do.'

'You must have a vivid imagination Mr Bell, for I don't ever remember strolling with you.'

'Don't you Miss Kent? Don't you really? Why, bless me yes. Many are the times we strolled together, you and me. Got up to all sorts of intimacies... we did. Now you think back... you'll get there in the end... you see if you don't.'

Just then, Jacob and Fredrick came out of the shop with a bag apiece in their hands, and seeing Jenny talking to the same man they had seen at the gypsy encampment they hurried across the road to be by her side.

Jenny was still in a state of jumpy nervousness and fear - both at the same time it seems. Learning of Bell's new appointment and his brother's presence at The Old House were disturbing pieces of information that didn't sit well with her; and Fredrick, noticing her agitation, placed himself between Jenny and her adversary and looking straight into B. Bell's eyes and in a forthright way he said:

'We've met before haven't we? Didn't I see you at the gypsy camp not so long ago?'

'My, what an observant young man you are to be sure, and handsome with it,' he replied, trying to brazen his way out of the situation by using false compliments. 'Yes, you're quite right young man. But not anymore I don't... no I have moved on since then.

'Miss Kent and me, we were just talking over old times and bringing back all of the happy memories we both share. Ain't that right Miss Kent?' Barnabas Bell was on the defensive and it wasn't sexual excitement that was causing his left eye to wander about its socket now, for beads of sweat began to appear on his forehead and to trickle slowly down his angled face and patches of dampness were seen beneath his coatless arms.

With her son and Fredrick standing to support her, Jenny at last availed herself of the power her usual self assuredness was used to; though the fear that this man implanted in her mind was still evident.

'No Mr Bell that most certainly was not what we were talking about. You, in your usual threatening manner were attempting to cast indecent aspersions on my name by saying that we had had a close relationship in the past. This, as you well know Bell, is both erroneous and evil. You are a most despicable man from hell and will stop at nothing in order to terrorise me as much as you possibly can; am I not right? There you are, Bell, I have at long last managed to involve witnesses in my accusation... so deny it if you can.'

Barnabas Bell didn't wait to deny the accusation, instead, in his eagerness to rid himself of this trying situation, he made a very hasty retreat by way of the downward path of the steep hill - glancing but once over his shoulder as he vanished from view.

When Jenny and the two boys were comfortably seated in the Lotus Elan, she thanked Fredrick for his part and the two of them for their presence in what she could only describe as 'a most unfortunate encounter' and she explained to the both of them what had hitherto gone on in her younger days regarding B. Bell. She also warned them, in no uncertain terms, of the danger that surrounded this hateful creature and for the two of them to be on their guard at all times.

Even though Jenny now felt secure in the allies she had formed: both of them had supported and comforted her so efficiently, she still felt extreme uneasiness at the thought of the unforeseen problems that lay ahead, since nothing had changed - not really.

Remembering the familiar young lad carrying the heavy suitcases after their arrival, Jenny questioned in her mind how yet another Bell could have found employment within the sanctuary of her uncle's service. And upon their arrival back at The Old House Jenny approached Janet and enquired if the aging housekeeper was aware of the young lad's identity.

'Oh yes, indeed Jennifer, I am fully aware who the young lad is. But you see, my dear, it is better by far to keep ones enemies as near as possible for one can never tell, not exactly, what snippet of intelligence might be forthcoming at their own expense.'

CHAPTER TEN

Inspired words of fond farewell, no matter how well chosen and deeply felt are never the most pleasing of verbal skills to use; and idle promises, stimulated by a moment's consideration, despite meaningful intent, are rarely attended to.

And so it was with Jenny on the cloudless morning of their departure from Lincoln's county.

The goodbyes each exchanged alongside promises to meet with each other a few weeks hence were well hoped for but without intention. But by so doing, they did, for the most part, adequately conceal all regrets the dismal parting stirred inside and so they fearlessly faced the sad farewells by feigning feelings of good cheer.

Jenny had said nothing about the previous day's unfortunate encounter with her nemesis in Lincoln City for she felt she had burdened her loved ones far too much already with this ongoing and undesirable saga.

And so she opted for quietness to persist rather than saying too much and in the end was relieved to have chosen that course, because by so doing she had encouraged a more relaxed attitude of mind to be established rather than anxious feelings that needs must be hidden.

Jacob, noticing his mother's reluctance in bringing her meeting with Bell to the fore, was a little perplexed at first and wondered why. In the end he said nothing and buried the matter in the folds of his active mind.

The sun had deserted the skies by the time they regained the lower reaches of Dorset and relentless rain had gathered in its stead. Although the deeply embedded sadness that the leaving of Brenton had promoted still crowded their minds, they each attempted happier faces to hide their mental gloom.

Fred Worth had been sheltering from the torrential rain neath his Dutch barn's tall roof for a good fifteen minutes when suddenly his thoughts were distracted by the purring of Jenny's car.

After hearing it in the distance, then upon seeing the motor as it careered the paddock area, Fred stepped out from his shelter with lively, lengthened strides and a welcoming smile.

The yellow car trailed deep channels in the yard's sludge ridden surface quite up to its wheel's steel rims: so deep was the quagmire in places; but they filled again as soon as the car had past and were hardly seen at all when it slowed to a standstill on the slightly firmer ground.

Fred pulled the waterproof cover, which was about his shoulders, over his head as he moved directly to that side of the car where his son was sitting and despite the torrential rain, both father and son devotedly embraced as they greeted one another.

This display of affection did not pass unnoticed by Jenny and she looked on in astonishment: not realising, of course, that farmers and farmer's sons were also capable of displaying the same affection as she herself - that they too had feelings akin to hers.

'Had a good time, have you son?' asked the farmer, almost in a whisper as he shared the long grey-green waterproof groundsheet with his boy. And after Jacob had passed the particular suitcase over to his friend, Fred bent down to smile at Jenny.

'Thanks Miss Kent... thanks for everything.'

'No trouble at all Fred; my pleasure,' she returned.

While father and son ran for the shelter of their modest white farmhouse with stooped liveliness, Jenny turned the car round to slowly exit the paddock area, and each offered a friendly wave to the other, as they moved away; Jenny and Jacob from the car and farmer and son from the back porch of the house.

'Curious that Fredrick never mentions his mother when he's in our company, Jacob.'

'That's because he hasn't one; Fredrick told me only yesterday, she died soon after he was born.'

***

The following few days saw Jenny attentively working at estate business; almost eighteen hours in every one of them or so it seemed. The problems had become so heaped up since she'd been away that all thoughts of the brief visit to Brenton, and all that that had brought about, soon disappeared.

She had met with Alf Abrams on two relatively brief occasions since her return, but on neither one had there been a mention of the gypsy encampment topside the broad leafed forest, even though Jenny had wanted the subject raised; but, certain reservations on her part had prevented her from bringing the matter forward.

Despite all this, on the second occasion Jenny furtively ferreted out a hoard of information about Chambers Farm and the Worth family who lived there; thereby gathering more knowledge to add to that which she had previously garnered.

All of this petty gossip about the farm, about its owner's activities and about its owner's family history, seemed endless. But it was a subject on which Alf Abrams seemed well versed; and with him having all of this information and idle gossip at his fingertips and he being more than willing to divulge this knowledge to his employer, well, it seemed churlish, to Jenny's way of thinking, not to take advantage of his willingness to share.

'I don't wish to seem overly inquisitive or demean myself with unconfirmed gossip, Alf, but to me it is most important to be aware of the ambitions of all my tenant farmers and keep up to date with any looming problems that may plague their minds from time to time, and it seems to me you are the only source I can turn to.'

Jenny spoke the sentence regarding her tenants in complete sincerity as she sipped tea with her pleasant and most obliging farm manager - although, it might be observed, she seemed content to hold back all enquiries regarding her other tenants' private lives which Alf Abrams was not slow to notice. But he gladly persisted with the subject of Chambers Farm thereby encouraging his employer's inquisitiveness without so much as a hint of censure entering his mind.

'Strangely enough, I knew Fred's father pretty well and much better than I know Fred,' said Alf. 'I used to work with the old man when I was still a kid and before Fred was born, when times were a lot harder than they are today.

'Mucking out stables and then carting and heaping that same rotting muck onto the fields and spreading it over the entire acreage with a four tined muck fork was hard work for a youngster I can tell you, Miss Kent.

'Then, come the summer, old man Fred Worth, he would have his fields of corn cut by a couple of horses dragging a binder behind them and with a horseman on the back controlling their every move... himself more often than not. Then old Diddy, he was a tinker type bloke who used to help out occasionally, and I would stand all the sheaves of corn in stooks for it to dry. Then we carted it all away later and stacked it ready for threshing.

'You know, I can still remember Diddy and me cutting a whole field of kale by means of a billhook apiece and a bottle of cold tea with which to quench our thirst, now that will tell you what times were like.

'Although, he was older than me by twenty years or more, old man Fred Worth, he taught me almost all he could teach me in the time I was with him and he added to that knowledge right up until the time I went to the agricultural college.

'By the time Fred junior came along I was engaged in my first managerial job, so I didn't really get to know him all that well, not as well as I did his father, anyway, and not as well as I should have liked.

'But what I have since learned about Fred is that he is a most excellent farmer; like me, he had a pretty good teacher I suppose. He has brought that farm of his bang up to date with new, modern machinery, and new ideas in farming efficiency and the like, so that he pretty well runs the place single handed these days, well, with the help of a couple of casual hands.

'I expect his son Fredrick will eventually be taken on to follow in his father's footsteps. He'll more than likely go to the same agricultural college I went to and be able to build even more on his father's ideas and hard work.'

Jenny smiled as a thought sped through her mind.

'It seems that the whole of the Worth family, since time immemorial, have been called Fredrick or Fred; must be a family name I suppose.'

'That's right, Miss; I expect there's been a Fred Worth working these parts since Adam. Names always run in the families of ordinary country folk; leastways they always did.'

'Alf, what happened to Fred's wife? Jacob tells me she died when Fredrick was quite young.'

'Don't know what happened there, Miss Kent. It seems she died in childbirth or soon after, that's as much as I know. Apparently Fred doesn't say too much about it, leastways not that I know off; he seems to be a quiet, modest and private sort of chap and tends to keep all personal matters like that to himself; though he dotes on that son of his enormously... anyone will tell you that.'

'Yes Alf, I noticed the other day as we were returning from the Lincolnshire trip how fond they were of each other, and moreover, they were not ashamed to outwardly express it, which to me was uplifting and a wonderful thing to have done... especially these days. Probably due to the fact that no female resides with them any longer, so they are more or less left to their own devises.'

'Don't know about that Miss Kent, you see, the old mother, she still lives there with them, and looks after them, as best she can.

'Well Miss Kent, thank you for the chat and the tea so if there is nothing else to keep me here; I shall be on my way, if that's alright with you... I'll see myself out.'

After repossessing his smart flat cap he had placed on the

stone floor earlier and offering a quick farewell, he left his employer's presence quietly but in a state of measured reflection.

"Hmm, now there's a funny thing," he thought to himself as he crossed the hallway toward the front door, *"there are a good few other tenants that are offshoots of the Hyde Hall estate, so I wonder why it was that Fred Worth was singled out for attention."* And although Alf Abrams was the most loyal of servants, he was still human with human curiosities; but he kept his thoughts to himself and shared them with not a soul.

***

Spring had all but passed before Jenny heard from Jane Howe again. She had deliberately refrained from making the first move as her ordeal with her father's lover had left her with a disturbed mind, and to quite an extent. But in any event she didn't wish to show Jane she was overly enthusiastic in pursuing any relationship at the moment, if at any time all.

Janet Nun's remarks and remembered advice had been thoroughly etched in Jenny's mind and so she would exercise a great deal of caution before approaching Jane in the future, no matter how vital Jane may have considered their relationship to be, or indeed, how eager she may be in creating a liaison with Jenny in the times ahead.

Actually, since Jenny's return from Lincolnshire Jane had scarcely entered her mind at all, that is why it came as a considerable surprise when she heard the lethargic voice of Jane sigh her relief at finding Jenny at home - at last - and in such a way that Jenny felt quite piqued. It all happened rather suddenly, and after she had been inconvenienced in answering the telephone in the first place.

The occasion arose when Agnes had called to her mistress from one of the half open front windows just as Jenny was walking from her car toward the house. By so doing, Agnes exhibited no propriety in her behaviour whatsoever and so Jenny felt compelled to hasten her stride to avoid any further awkwardness.

Agnes' summoning failed to impress the Mistress of Hyde Hall: she feeling that it would have been more fitting and a little more courteous had Agnes waited a moment or two longer, thereby allowing Jenny the right to enter the portal of her home quietly, instead of shouting her name from the rooftops.

But the temporary housekeeper, anxious to appear efficient, called out that a telephone call from no less a person than Miss Jane

Howe awaited her mistress's attention, and in a knowing kind of way at that. Agnes beamed and was filled with childish curiosity as she completed the message and closed the window in an eager manner.

Jenny stated she would take the phone call in the privacy of her study and idle curiosity crossed her face as she opened the door.

'Hello Jane, I'm sorry to have kept you waiting. Just wandered in from taking my son to school,' said Jenny, sounding rather breathless. 'How are you, anyway? It's been quite a while since we last spoke and I was beginning to think you had eloped or something equally exciting.'

'No Jenny, nothing like that. Actually I did try to make contact with you a while ago but apparently you were in Lincolnshire at the time. I have also tried on a couple of other occasions but unfortunately you were unavailable. You seem to be somewhat elusive these days Jenny; I do hope I haven't upset you in any way.'

'Yes well, since my return from Lincolnshire I have found myself caught up in all sorts; what with keeping tabs on matters here and other mundane chores, it's been a hectic time for me, I can tell you.

'Anyway, why have you called this morning Jane? Not in any bother with the law I hope,' said Jenny, hoping to lighten the mood a little and with ultimate success it seems, for the two ladies eventually chuckled at the idea.

'Jenny, I wondered if you would be free to dine with me on Saturday. I know it's short notice but I haven't yet been able to repay your hospitality and so I thought that now was as good a time as any to do it.'

'Jane, I should love to have had dinner with you but unfortunately Saturday is quite out of the question.

'You see I am holding a cocktail party here at Hyde Hall expressly for my tenants and their wives, just so that we can be better acquainted, that's all. Obviously I have never met with all of them; some yes, but not all.' At this point Jenny stretched the truth a little by adding: 'of course I would have invited you along as well but I thought you would be bored silly with everyone going on about their farming problems, so that in the end you might easily have felt left out of it... to a certain extent, anyway; some other time perhaps... if that's agreeable to you.'

'Oh no Jenny, I should love to come. It would be good for me to meet new people and it will be something pleasant to look forward to... for a change.'

Jane's directness took Jenny completely on the hop thus

quashing all sensible reasoning and debate and it placed her in a corner from which there seemed to be no escape. Jenny was quite unsure how to react for the moment, and so she bit into her bottom lip quite firmly as the feeling of being forced into submission totally overawed her.

Jenny had certainly not expected the extremely vague invite to have been exploited in this way, and it certainly had not been intended as a literal invitation; however, Jane had taken it to be such, and so the questionable request for Jane's attendance had to stay, there was no going back, not now.

Of course, Jenny had arranged the cocktail party in order to acquaint herself with the wives as well as her tenant farmers; after her conversation with Alf Abrams had stimulated the idea. She also hoped that by doing this she would be able to extend her tiny list of friends and acquaintances.

She also felt the need to socialise with everyone associated with the Hyde Hall estate in order to cement business relations and to pre-empt any pertinent problems that may have been in the offing.

But mainly, of course, for Jenny to be introduced as being the recent owner of Hyde Hall and all that that entailed. This to her mind was very important; but it had to be done with a certain amount of diplomacy…

Fred Worth was of minor consequence as far as the party was concerned, or so Jenny told herself; she was already fairly well acquainted with this particular tenant anyway. But because of his warmth and obvious ability as a farmer, she did in the end feel she needed to get better acquainted with the man, but she had emphasised to herself that it had nothing to do with the fact that he displayed a manly figure and rugged good looks.

Jenny had employed outside caterers to provide for the Saturday evening social gathering, which seemed to have an adverse effect on Agnes' feelings; for not only did the acting housekeeper feel she had been firmly sidelined, but she felt it obligatory to mention this grievance to Jenny - and in such a way as to show her disrespect - tactlessness being more prominent with Agnes than diplomacy, it seems.

The objection was placed shortly after lunch on the same day as the party; although Agnes had been made aware of Jenny's plans well before this time.

'I do hope you didn't think me to be incapable of organising such a small party as this Miss Kent,' said she, abandoning the title she had used for her employer throughout her working life. 'I've organised many parties like this one in the past and much bigger ones than this as well... for your mother and for your father too... and without complaint from either one of them.

'I won't deny that being ignored in this way hasn't upset me, cause it has... upset me a whole lot it has, and shook me to my very foundations too... and to such an extent that I doubt I shall ever get over it,' she said, as her face flushed with her excessive sensitivity.

'Agnes, why have you left registering your protest for so long even until the last minute?'

'Because I have had time to think... that's why.'

'Be assured Agnes, I had no intentions of upsetting you in this way. I just felt that I would be giving you too little notice, and that, to my way of thinking, would have been quite unfair and most inappropriate. Believe me Agnes, when I say, I was thinking of your inconvenience and not your incompetence in the hiring of outside caterers. After all, it most certainly would have been one expense less for me to cope with had I given the matter more consideration. And so I can only apologise to you and bear it in mind for any future functions of this sort.'

The stand-in housekeeper hadn't seemed all that impressed with the explanation on offer or the apology either for that matter and so she walked away from her employer in a state of dire distress - even before being properly dismissed.

Jenny wasn't exactly overcome with grief but a certain amount of anguish did reach out to her.

"I really do have to improve my staffing skills; obviously I am sadly lacking in that department. My only hope now is that she doesn't hand in her notice thereby leaving me stuck completely and in a helpless situation for this evening," she thought.

Jenny felt most discouraged and somewhat gloomy at this disastrous conclusion.

And well she may have felt that way, for a mere half an hour had past before Jenny was unceremoniously handed a letter of resignation hastily scrawled by Agnes, together with the assurance that she would not be available to attend the cocktail party as a server as Jenny had hoped.

Not only was Jenny furious with the outcome of the trivial misunderstanding but she was beside herself with not knowing who to turn to for the help she now needed.

A notion came to her from out of the blue.

'Jane, this is Jennifer Kent. Look I have been let down rather badly by my housekeeper at the last minute. It seems she is no longer available to help with overseeing the cocktail party with me this evening as I had hoped. I know it is a blessed nuisance, but I wondered if you would be prepared to step into the breach, as it were. I am well aware that it is a complete imposition on my part, Jane, but I know of no other to whom I might turn at such short notice.'

Jane was bowled over by the idea.

'Jenny, please relax. It most certainly is not an imposition at all and I shall be delighted to help you in any way I possibly can, you must know that. What time would you like me to be with you, will six o'clock be early enough?'

Jane had arrived an hour before the party was to due to commence and looking more like the guest of honour than a stand in for the housekeeper - no matter how temporary that position was deemed to be.

Jane was then briefed by Jenny as to her expected duties.

'All that is really needed, Jane, is for you to mingle. Chatting with all and sundry and seeing that the guests are happily cared for will be more than useful. Please make sure everyone has sufficient to eat and drink and that everything runs as smoothly as possible. It shouldn't be too difficult as both Jacob and his friend Fredrick will be on hand to fetch and carry for you and of course the catering staff will see to everything else.

'Please endeavour to steer clear of all gossip though, as all that sort of nonsense will almost certainly be on tap. Enjoy yourself as much as possible is all I ask.

'I, for my part, will be taking an interest in my tenants and their wives as well. Any worries and or concerns they may have regarding their tenancy will be brought to my notice... I have little doubt of that; after all, that is partly the object of the exercise anyway. So good luck and have a nice time.'

The guests began arriving at seven thirty and everything was going smoothly with Jane providing the exact catalyst required in making the evening a total success. She hovered about the large drawing room with grace and charm; and abandoning her customarily tentative voice she chatted with almost everyone she set her eyes on; moving from couple to couple effortlessly and with a manner of complete self-assurance.

Jane, it seemed, was quite a hit and was causing comments of good opinion from all who spoke with her - especially those of the male gender.

Jenny too, was not lacking in receiving rewarding observations regarding her generosity and affability, but it was not until she was engaged in a particularly close conversation with one of her tenants that she was made aware of the fact.

Hectorial Chambers, *"strange name,"* thought Jenny, had been completely engrossed in conversation with Jenny for a considerable fifteen minutes, as his small, old-fashioned wife looked on in a way that displayed her appalling inhibitions. And not only were her inhibitions on show but she also gave the distinct impression of being overawed by an overbearing husband who was quite unmistakable in his intentions. And no matter how bravely she faced the situation it was apparent she was being affected by his verbal interaction with Jenny - and more than she enjoyed.

Her husband it seems had a problem with his verbal exchanges, meaning of course that he was unable to prevent himself from talking in a tedious way. This was one difficulty the meek little lady had seemingly not gotten used to over the years and so her husband's behaviour still rankled with her.

Jenny, spotting Mrs Chamber's dilemma, did her level best to incorporate the inhibited lady into the conversation but without too much success; for as soon as Jenny focussed a single word in the lady's direction her husband would pounce on it like a Jack Russell terrier, taking over once again to redirect the humourless conversation to his own self. And so, his uncontrolled manner in the handling of dialogue with this particularly beautiful host bore all the traits of unadulterated flirtatiousness.

'Miss Kent I should like you to know how much your little effort is appreciated by us all: your having brought about a gathering of this nature, I mean,' said he, attempting to take his hostess' hand in his own without any success at all. 'It is something that your father never did and in fact neither has any other of the local landowners attempted to provide such a feast, as far as I'm aware. But to me it bears all the hallmarks of sincerity and is most welcome, most welcome indeed. You are to be applauded Miss Kent.'

Jenny coloured appropriately and thanked her guest for his kind words; although the irrepressible farmer, ignoring the expressed gratitude and her eagerness to move on, reclaimed Jenny's attention.

'I suppose you are well aware of the fact that Chambers Farm once belonged to my ancestors, hence its name. It was bought by your forebear, Sir Alistair Kent, way back in the nineteenth century due to poor economic farming on my family's part, I'm afraid; or a non existent harvest; not sure which. But either way it meant we were unable to continue working the place.

'After purchasing from my family your forebear then leased

the farm to the Worth family and it has been with them ever since; while the poor old Chambers species of the human race went on to take a tenancy on the much smaller farm I now serve, namely Rookery Farm' he said, jovially, as if his family's failure was something to have been proud of.

'No, Mr Chambers, I had no idea, no idea at all. So the Worth family name doesn't have the history attached to it that I assumed had stood for centuries.'

'Oh yes, they are indeed an ancient family in these parts Miss Kent, there's no doubting that and dating from way back in time too; they have farmed several pieces of land hereabouts for centuries, but as I say Chambers Farm was only leased to the Worth family relatively recently; well, recently as far as farming terms go.'

'Well now, I find that all very fascinating Mr Chambers, but what I am more concerned about is the present day and if my existing tenants are making reasonable profits out of their farms, only if they are not then I consider it my duty to assist them all I can,' said Jenny, feeling more than a little bored with this particular conversation and was wondering where it was all leading to - if indeed there was any point to it at all.

'Oh, do come-along, Miss Kent, I'm sure you will find no need for feelings of despondency in that regard. I can't imagine any of your tenants being in need of your assistance, be it financial or advisory, as I'm sure they are all doing rather nicely for themselves; I mean to say, have you ever come across a poor farmer? In the long-ago yes... but not these days.'

Jenny was pleased to bring the conversation to a fairly abrupt halt and to move on to the next of her tenants.

And so the evening tediously progressed; boring at times and enlightening at others with each tenant speaking highly of the hostess and of the pleasant evening they had all so enjoyed together and when the time for parting came it was the wives who were seen to be driving their husbands home with the exception of Fred Worth who had purposefully refrained from all alcoholic beverages.

As already alluded to above, during the course of the evening Jenny had made it her business to chat to each and every one of her tenant farmers - but to the exclusion of Fred Worth it seems. Jenny had purposely saved him to last, she thinking that at least Fred would provide a semblance of interesting conversation. But she was quite surprised to find that the man was rather reticent on the subject he held most dear. She had approached the farmer as he was being served a glass of cordial by one of the catering staff.

'I was glad you could make our little soirée Fred, I only hope you have enjoyed it as much as I have in giving it.'

'Yes Miss Kent, it's been good to meet up with the rest of the local farming community, only it's not often an opportunity like this come along.'

'And do you have any problems with your tenancy arrangements that you would like to discuss with me or are you happy with the way Daddy left matters?'

'Oh, I didn't think that was the reason for the party, if I'd known that then I should have given the matter some thought.'

'Well no, of course the real reason is for me to get to know everyone a little more intimately and for everyone to be able to put a face to the new Mistress of Hyde Hall; only I haven't had the opportunity to meet everyone before this evening. But since we know each other quite well already, Fred, I wondered if anything bothered you regarding your tenancy that was all.'

A startling pause occurred before Fred answered.

'No Miss Kent everything is just fine, no problems at all.'

With that, and much to Jenny's dismay, he turned his back on his hostess and headed towards the door.

Needless to say, the lovely Mistress of Hyde Hall searched in vain to find a reason for this obscure and rather rude departure but ended up being none the wiser.

At the end of it all and with the safe exodus of all the guests and with the caterers eventually clearing everything away and clearing themselves away too, Jenny went to the kitchen to put the kettle on only to find Agnes sitting alone in the corner looking rather despondent and tearful.

'Agnes, you're still hear or have you returned? I thought you had left me before the revelry began.'

'No Miss Jenny, I mean, yes I did leave, but when I reached home... well... before I reached home actually, I began to feel terrible about the way I had left you. I've been with your family for over forty years and I have never before come even close to handing in my notice, so happy have I always been with your family. And so I am now wondering if you will take me back, in my old position, if you please, as I don't seem to be up to a more responsible job.'

Jenny walked over to her head parlour maid and took her hands in her own with a smile of extreme relief.

'Of course you can have your old job back Agnes; if you hadn't returned tonight then I had made my mind up to approach you tomorrow. So let's say no more about the ghastly matter, OK?'

'Thank you Miss Jenny, thank you for your kindness in being so understanding, and I'm so sorry for being so silly and over sensitive; it won't happen again.'

Jenny was about to put Agnes further at her ease when Jane entered the kitchen and not noticing immediately that Jenny was engaged in conversation she spoke as she opened the door.

'Well I must be off now Jenny... oh sorry, I didn't realise that I was interrupting, shall I come back later?'

'No Jane that's quite alright; Agnes and I were about finished anyway.' Then turning to Agnes she added: 'I'll see you in the morning then Agnes, so try not to worry.'

Agnes turned to make her exit but as she did so a smile brightened her face as she looked directly at Jane.

'It's nice to make your acquaintance Miss Howe.'

Jenny was delighted with Agnes' boldness as she now considered all illicit rumours to be scotched for ever.

CHAPTER ELEVEN

It was the following morning when Jenny, still in a confused state of mind, stopped off at Chamber's Farm hoping that Fred Worth might cast a little light on the rude behaviour he had unpredictably exhibited the previous evening.

Worrying thoughts had entered Jenny's mind as soon as Fred had left her drinks party and they had remained with her for most of the night, thereby causing an unjustifiable bout of restlessness to wreck her slumber.

Naturally, she had been afraid that something dreadful had taken hold of her tenant farmer's mind and in such a way that it had caused some sort of irritation to install itself there - if that was the case, then she had no idea what the cause could possibly have been.

Since being mistress of Hyde Hall, or rather since Alf Abram's example had been set in her mind, Jenny had felt the need to deal with all problems as soon as they arose and not allow them to drag on ad infinitum as had been her wont in former years.

She felt that same need bothering her last night.

"My sleep is far too important to be played around with or abandoned in this fashion,' she had thought, *"so, the sooner I get this problem sorted the better I shall like it."*

Fred was seen to be crossing the badly drained yard on his way to the Dutch barn when Jenny's bright yellow Lotus arrived. And not unlike the car's previous experience with the paddock cum yard's slimy surface, it soon discovered the ground to be still steeped in the same thick layer of mud it had then.

Bearing this in mind Jenny manoeuvred her motor closer to the backdoor of the ancient farmhouse where she knew the ground would be a little firmer.

Fred Worth stopped and turned as soon as he realised someone was calling this morning; and without so much as a wave of his hand to greet his visitor, he remained motionless as if paralysed. He stayed in this static mode for quite some time - even his breathing seemed to be adversely affected - his feet and legs certainly were.

Maybe it was because Jenny was still seated behind the car's driving wheel without stirring or soliciting his attention that was causing his unwillingness to shift himself along or maybe some intrusive thought had entered his mind that had no business in being there; who knows? But whichever it was it was noticeable that something was wrong, even to the most careless observer.

Minutes passed like hours before Fred even considered moving himself. Slowly he shuffled his feet about in a disorderly fashion as though he was unsure how he should proceed. And then, after a few more minutes of bad manners being displayed, he walked the distance to Jenny's car - but taking his time as though he was filled with dread.

When he finally arrived a cynical smile broadened his stubbly face in a way that hinted at insincerity; though, suffice it to say, it did emphasise the striking appearance of his features.

'I expect you are waiting for an explanation for my hasty departure last night, Miss Kent,' said he, bending down and speaking as soon as Jenny had wound the window fully down but without taking too much rational thought, for the courtesy of a greeting had not thus far left his lips.

'Well, you see, I can't be doing with pomposity in any way shape or form and you saying last night as how you wanted everyone in the room to get to know the face of the Mistress of Hyde Hall, well it fair made my hackles rise. So, not wanting you to witness any criticism on my part, I took it in my head to leave the party there and then, afore my mouth had a chance to spout any ill-mannered words that might upset you.

'So, you want everyone to bow down to you, do you Miss Kent? Well I can tell you this for nothing, although you have been mighty kind to my son, we neither of us bows down to no one, let alone to anyone that's been born with a silver spoon sticking out of their mouths like what you have... but who are no better than the rest of us put together.

'I thought all that sort of nonsense was dead and buried alongside your father, Miss Kent, but it seems I was sadly mistaken, as I now see it ain't dead at all... it's still alive and kicking ain't it? There, I've had my say, and now you know what it was all about don't you? And how I felt about what you said. So I'll bid you good day Miss Kent and with no tugging of my forelock either.'

Jenny was instantly appalled. Never in the whole of her life had she been accused of such behaviour; for she too had abhorred such undignified conduct in others. Why, even as a small child she remembered how her own father's approval of subservience from his fellowman had filled her with disgust - so she would never have it in mind to emulate him, not in that way, no matter what. And by the same token she would never hope to have heard such offensive accusations emerging from the mouths of others either.

'Look, Fred I know you are a busy man with a lot on your

plate at the moment but do you think you could spare a moment to make me a nice cup of tea, I'm quite parched after listening to your childish prattle?'

***

After Jenny and Fred Worth had settled themselves over an acceptable pot of tea and Jenny had taken Fred to task for his unwarranted comments regarding her attitude toward him the previous evening: seemingly to the rest of her guests as well; and Jenny had taken the trouble to explain to Fred his despicable lack of understanding and Fred had expressed sincere remorse for his reaction a moment or so ago, a new relationship began to blossom forth. Not altogether an intimate relationship, it should be pointed out; far too early in the day for such a connection as that to untangle itself. But one appropriate enough for acquaintances, with a reasonable amount in common, to appreciate a meaningful connection between good friends and with sufficient sparks about it to stir interesting thoughts in both their minds; and for those thoughts to be mulled over in quieter, more responsive moments - if indeed such future moments allowed.

That aside, another problem loomed in Jenny's mind as she left her newly formed friend and his farm that morning. A problem that reduced the importance of the feelings she had felt for this noteworthy farmer to mere nothingness - no matter how appealing those feelings may have been at the time. And one that could not be solved by refined words of reconciliation either or any other expressions of atonement for that matter; since action with fixed purpose was now deemed necessary to settle a much more important problem.

Because of her former temporary housekeeper's decision to quit her post and for she to resume a lesser position within the Kent household once again, Jenny felt the need to seek the services of a butler or housekeeper to oversee the day-to-day running of Hyde Hall in an efficient way. Someone with whom Jenny could build a satisfactory connection was needed, someone who was able to convey confidence, was reliable and not given to tantrums at the drop of a hat - as was seen in Agnes's appalling conduct from time to time.

As soon as she reached her home Jenny went to her study and telephoned all the employment agencies in the local directory - as she had in the past explored all of those particular avenues; but without too much success being forthcoming, well, none at all, in actual fact.

She was replacing the warm receiver after the final agency had yet again proved to be a frustration, when a bright and fortuitous brainwave entered her busy mind.

'Could I speak with Mr Tooke, please,' she asked the receptionist at the official offices of the Colin Tooke Empire; without there being too much hope filling her mind: *"but a casual call like this out of the blue might easily work,"* she thought, to herself.

A lengthy pause caused Jenny to wonder if she was being a little presumptuous in soliciting the estate's legal mind with this somewhat mundane appeal; but then again, why not, for wasn't she paying for advise when she needed it; be it mundane or otherwise?

'Hello Miss Kent,' said the familiar voice of Colin Tooke. 'How may I be of assistance to you on this lovely, sunny morning?'

'I'm in a bit of a fix Mr Tooke and I'm seeking some helpful advice. You see I am investigating the possibility of employing the services of a butler or housekeeper, don't mind which, but after speaking with a multitude of employment agencies I find I'm stuck, as no such creature exists in these parts these days; or so it would appear, and I wondered if you could come up with any solutions that would end my dilemma.'

'Life is full of wonderful coincidences, Miss Kent, or so it would appear. I have a lady who has dealt with the everyday running of my house since my lady wife died over two years ago and it seems she is unhappy at the moment; not with me you understand, but with there being insufficient variables to occupy her time here. And so she is looking for an alternative position; one that will provide her with a challenge… or so she says.

'She is attending an interview at this very moment with your mother at the Melchamp residence. If you would like me to send her to you this afternoon then I shall be most pleased to do so. You see, Miss Kent, I would much prefer her to be securely established in your service than that of your mother's, if you understand my meaning - you have my assurance on that.'

After settling a trivial debate, regarding a suitable time to bring about such an interview, the brief exchange was brought to an abrupt close, most amicably, in so far as Jenny was concerned.

Barely a minute passed, after Jenny had replaced the receiver, when an unexpected caller arrived.

Alf Abrams was looking more than a little tense when he stepped into Jenny's study that morning; he even failed to wait for the customary niceties to be performed before wading in with what was concerning his worried mind.

'Miss Kent, I fear I may have done you a disservice. I truly meant to have kept an eye on those gypsies who you kindly let stay on the estate, but what with one thing and another it completely slipped my mind; and it wasn't until I took a stroll that way earlier this morning that I discovered they had disappeared, up sticks and gone they have, the lot of them and without a trace, or a word from anyone.

'Now I have no idea when they left the place, as I said, I haven't been round that way for some considerable time; but I should have thought they might have found enough common decency to let one of us know that they were leaving the place, just so I could satisfy myself they had left everywhere clean and tidy. But I must say nobody has approached me; I don't expect you have heard a word from that direction either, have you Miss Kent?'

Jenny was troubled at receiving this information and a feeling of being rather let down by the father of her son overcame her mind and to such an extent that she felt herself becoming rather fidgety. She stood up and walked the room to relieve the tension that was building up inside.

'No I haven't heard from any of them, Alf, and like you I am extremely disappointed, especially with their so called spokesman; as it was he to whom I gave leave for their stay in the first place. But there, why should we be surprised, for I assume they failed to notify anyone when they first turned up. In any case, nothing has been said to me prior to your report Alf and as I have just said, I am disappointed to say the least... with every one of them.

'On the other hand, maybe something has occurred that has prevented their contacting us, but for the life of me I can't imagine what that could possibly be.

'I don't suppose there is any quick way we might be able find out, is there Alf?' she asked, and then realising the improbability of such a question being answered with any degree of certainty, she answered it herself - in the negative.

The meeting was short lived but it left Jenny feeling extremely worried and the case for not knowing what had happened at the camp was growing steadily stronger by the minute and caused all her feelings of disappointment to linger.

Jenny once again employed the telephone's services in an effort to assure herself that nothing untoward had happened to Tom.

Three calls to as many local hospitals found Jenny

continuing in a condition of anguish and confusion as her investigation had gathered little in way of a level-headed explanation.

And so, with negative answers from everyone she had spoken to filling her mind, Jenny concluded that all must be well with her erstwhile friend and that a severe bout of bad manners was all the gypsies were afflicted with.

***

As arranged with Colin Tooke, Mary Pumphrey arrived for her interview promptly at three thirty that afternoon.

Although Miss Pumphrey seemed the embodiment of austerity, she was seen to be an attractive lady in her late forties, and one who possessed an intellect capable of generating interest in an extraordinary way.

According to the facts she presented to Jenny, Miss Pumphrey had spent the greater part of her working life in the service of the upper classes.

'I commenced my career as a trainee nursery maid at the tender age of sixteen, madam, and then broadened my experience by becoming a trainee lady's maid two years later,' she said, in a forthright manner. 'Both of these posts were achieved in a very large house in the centre of Kensington and I felt I had progressed as far as I was able by that time. But with extremely hard work and stubbornness I succeeded to the role of a fully fledged lady's maid by the age of twenty four, and within the same household at that.

'Several years passed before I eventually gained an important housekeeper position… not by some academic acclaim, you understand, but by reason of competence, coupled with good fortune.'

Mary Pumphrey continued in this manner for quite a while; revealing to her interviewer the long history of her employment without interruption.

It would appear she had served two such households over a period of thirty or so years prior to her service with the Colin Tooke household, without criticism and from whom glowing references of recommendation had been supplied. These were now presented to Jenny.

Jenny studied the letters carefully and exhibited her fitting approval.

It became apparent that Mary Pumphrey was now seeking a

move to a more inspirational position, within the household of a reputable family - if that were possible. One where she not only held the right of opinion, but also one with a promising future coupled with security.

During the interview it became apparent that the post on offer at the Melchamp's quiet residence was there for the taking for Miss Pumphrey, but she, being a more cautious woman these days, had decided to delay her decision until she had exhausted all other possibilities. Besides, she might easily be exchanging one office of boredom for another if she had accepted the post straight away; she was in no great hurry anyway as she had promised herself to 'get it right' this time.

Jenny, equal in her determination to also 'get it right' had delayed her decision even though her immediate evaluation of the woman, who had been so composedly seated before her, was most favourable.

Four days later, Jenny's anticipated telephone call to the Colin Tooke household was pre-empted by Mary Pumphrey's own call, anxiously seeking a final decision from Jenny and was delighted to have been told that the interview had been a complete success for her.

And so, after three more trying days had elapsed, for Jenny, the new housekeeper arrived at Hyde Hall.

It was a Saturday morning, which meant she had a day and a half in which to accustom herself to her new situation before her duties were thrust upon her. But it would be a gentle thrusting, if there be such a thing, for Jenny sat down with Mary Pumphrey and went over the boundaries of her duties yet again before her formal introduction to the household staff was made.

Everything seemed satisfactory, in so far as the rest of the staff were concerned, for they all appeared pleased at having an immediate personage to whom they might turn - when the need arose.

All of them, that is, with the exception of Agnes. Agnes appeared rather hesitant in coming forward at the introductory meeting and withheld her words of greeting without just cause.

Jenny was furious at what she considered to be a very public insult being offered to the newly appointed housekeeper and insisted that she should report to her study at once.

'That is quite alright Miss Kent,' said the practiced housekeeper, forcefully, so that all could hear. 'Please be good enough to leave the matter with me, I shall deal with the situation in my own way.'

Endeavouring to disguise her own severe façade, Jenny smiled calmly and left her housekeeper to her own extremely unorthodox procedure: she feeling assured that her choice in this particular housekeeper had been the right one and that self-confidence abounded above all else - with which she was more than satisfied.

***

In the latish morning, following the introductory meeting between Mary Pumphrey and the house staff, a relentless droning was heard from the front door of Hyde Hall; the persistent din was promptly answered by Agnes as she was passing through the great hall.

After taking the breathless visitor's name she left him standing in the doorway and set off to seek her mistress.

'There's an old man at the door, Miss Jenny, asking for you by name and who would like to have a quiet word with you... if it's at all convenient, that is. He don't look none to clean to me, Miss Jenny, so do you want to see him or not?'

'Does the gentleman have a name, Agnes, or am I supposed to read your mind?'

'Oh, sorry Miss Jenny, he says his name is Noah.'

'Please be good enough to show the gentleman into the library, Agnes... tell him I will receive him there in a couple of minutes.

'Oh, by the way Agnes, can I take it that all is well between Miss Pumphrey and yourself; only I found your attitude rather disturbing yesterday. Also, in future please leave the housekeeper to welcome any guest; after all, I do consider that to be one of her duties. '

After a hurried 'yes miss, sorry miss', Agnes scurried away to see to her mistresses bidding with an expression of humiliation firmly settled on her face.

As soon as the head parlour-maid had disappeared a state of uncertainty filled Jenny's mind for she failed to recall anyone by the name of Noah. And then, as she rose from her desk to attend the library the name took on a semblance of meaning as she recalled her final chat with Tom.

She found a gentleman with a mass of snowy white hair, so presumed to be Noah, waiting in the library, with a desolate look about him.

'Good morning… you must be Noah. We haven't met before but I'm sure we know of each other through Mr Hawk, is that not so?' said Jenny.

'Yes ma'am, I surely do - know of you I mean. I do hope I ain't disturbed your day at all ma'am but there has been some terrible goings-on at the site ma'am. Someone snuck into the camp at dead of night… a couple of nights ago it were… and plunged a knife deep into Tom's chest.

'We didn't find poor old Tom till the followin' mornin' so we had no idea what had been happenin' and 'cause we didn't want to get involved with the police or anythin' we all set to and left… straight away you might say. But poor old Tom, well he's in a bit of a state and I don't know what to do about it. So I thought of comin' to you for your advice.'

'Sit down Noah and allow me to pour you a brandy, you look as though you might need it.' So saying, Jenny went over to the cabinet and poured the man a drink.

'When did all this take place, Noah, and where is Tom now?'

'It took place a couple of nights ago, as I said, ma'am. Tom, he mutters about he's bein' alright, but me, well, I'm not so sure… the wound… well, it looks pretty fierce to me and I think somethin' ought to be done 'cause he keeps driftin' in and out of consciousness.

'But you see ma'am, we don't have no truck with the law or doctors and the like; we always take care of our own and leave the good Lord to keep us well. But I'm afeared ma'am, afeared that Tom might not make it if somethin' ain't done pretty soon.'

'Where did you say Tom is?'

'I didn't ma'am, but we're camped about five miles further on… up the north road that's leavin' the village. I walked, ran and tried to hitch a ride here after I took it in my head to get some help. All the others, they think I'm fussin' over nowt; but me… well, I knows different. Can you offer me any advice ma'am or should I let things ride and stay as they are… and for Tom to take his chances?'

'No! Take me to him Noah; I shall decide what to do when we get there.'

Jenny rang immediately for Mary Pumphrey. After she had explained she would be absent from the Hall for quite a while Jenny took Noah by the arm and led him to her car.

The journey was as brief as Jenny could make it. A mere ten minute interval saw them climbing the steps of Tom's van.

They found him lying on his bed in a state of semi-consciousness with a fever causing intermittent attacks of shivering to plague his body and continuous perspiration to saturate his bed.

The instant Jenny removed the makeshift dressing she saw what was needed, it was obvious!

'Bathe Toms head, chest and limbs. Keep him as cool as possible... I'm going to fetch a doctor,' she ordered, as Noah looked on nervously.

'No good in doin' that ma'am. Doctors... well; they don't have any truck with the likes of us travellers on account we don't have a fixed address.'

'Well an ambulance then, I shall telephone for an ambulance, surely an ambulance crew will see to Tom.'

With no further delay she ran back to the road where she had carelessly parked her car.

Hurriedly, Jenny entered her motor and drove to the nearest public telephone kiosk - half mile away - feeling worried and panic-stricken.

She was so shaky that she mishandled the dialling apparatus three times before she managed to contact the emergency services.

After speaking to the necessary department, debates arose regarding the ins and outs regarding the procedure for the treatment of uninsured travellers.

'Any action required for the treatment of gypsies has to be sanctioned by the necessary authority,' said a stern voice, at the other end, in a condescending way, 'and that will take some considerable time.'

Jenny was furious, both with the off-hand advice she was being given and by the attitude being displayed. It wasn't until Jenny had promised to pay for all the help so vital to Tom that she was assured an ambulance would be on the scene as soon as possible.

Jenny then hurried back to be by her friend's side and waited there for a further one and half hours.

Eventually an ambulance arrived.

After seeing Tom safely on board, Jenny entered her motor and followed the cream vehicle to the hospital where she was allowed to sit by his side until he attained awareness.

She learned from a passing nurse that the weapon used in attacking Tom had narrowly missed his heart but had punctured the upper lobe of his right lung thereby causing it to partially collapse.

Tom's face was drained with a bluish-grey tinge about it that disturbed Jenny. His breathing was laboured and his general condition was debilitated as a result of the trauma.

'Who did this to you Tom?' she asked, after he had gained a slight response. 'Have you any idea at all… who the vicious brute could have been?'

Tom failed to answer Jenny in any way save for the rolling of his eyes and as those same weary eyes fought in there attempt to focus he drifted into oblivion once more.

For the remainder of the day Tom was completely unaware who it was sitting by his side or, indeed, where he was resting; it would take a further full day for him to come to terms with that.

In the meantime Jenny repeatedly plied him with all the chatter she could summon and she endeavoured to make him aware of his surroundings and who was holding his hand; and for all the time she constantly explored his face for the slightest sign of improvement.

But who was to blame for this cowardly attack and how it came about was still a mystery to her.

Quite early on the second day, Tom began to regain a conscious state, and when at last he did, the first word that drifted from his exhausted mouth was: 'Jenny'.

Jenny spent the following days by her friend's side feeding him all the health giving nourishment he needed to help him through this deplorable situation.

Gradually, over a slow period of five long days, but still enduring pain and every other symptom associated with such a sick lung, Tom was adjudged to be fit enough to be released to the wilds of England's open roads again.

'Far too soon,' Jenny had exclaimed; but as her protest was being ignored she resigned herself to the hospital's decision; for there was little else left for her to argue.

It had been during the forth of the five day period of Tom's infirmity that the hospital authorities saw fit to report the incident to the police. And so, Tom, feeling more alert by this time, was visited by two uniformed police officers - on just the one occasion - to follow up the hospital's report, was the only reason Jenny could justify their presence; for nothing was resolved.

Only an unreasonable and insignificant amount of time was afforded the patient and an indifferent attitude was largely shown throughout the whole of the officers' visit.

Jenny was appalled.

She registered her total dismay in no uncertain terms, but without result.

Whilst listening to a brief exchange between one of the

officers and Tom, Jenny learned that after checking the camp was settled for the night and finding everything to be in order and as it should have been, Tom started to climb the steps of his own vardo to retire.

'Suddenly I sensed a movement... behind me... it was more a feeling than any thing else.

'I turned round quickly and the feeling became a reality; someone was there. It was then that the intruder struck me and I felt a deep burning pain in my chest. I was unable to do anything to help myself as my legs gave way beneath me at once and my eyesight became blurred. I crawled to my bed and waited; not able to call for help.'

Nothing, but nothing, relating to anything like that of a cowardly attempt of murder was ever voiced by the police, even the attack itself wasn't accepted as being a realistic incident; it was played down as if for some unknown reason the whole episode had been a charade - an event that had been fabricated from beginning to end.

The police were adamant that even if the attack was factual and not of spurious nature it would have been the direct result of an argument between Tom and one of his friends; even though Tom had stated that this had not been the case.

'I have no way of telling who my attacker was,' said Tom, rather weakly. 'I've thought about nothing else since I've been lying here. The sky was far too dark to see clearly at that time of night; and in any case... I have always lived in close harmony with all my family and have never been at enmity or had bad feelings with any of them... not in the whole of my life.'

The police weren't so sure about that - they were still insisting that their version of events was much more likely. They persisted in stating that crimes of this nature are always perpetrated by someone close to home.

'So how do you explain the fact that none of the dogs were heard to bark when this supposed intruder broke in? They all seemed pretty lively to us when we visited there an hour or so ago.'

The constable gave an insolent smile to convey his feelings of superiority but he didn't overstress the point. Besides they had more important issues to contend with that day - rather than waste their time with irresponsible vagrants.

Jenny looked on in bewilderment, not knowing what to accept as true.

The two policemen had, however, promised to look into the

matter - in the fullness of time, but with Tom being fully aware of the local authority's feelings toward travellers and their way of life, he would expect nothing more to be carried out or for the incident to be concluded to his own satisfaction.

Of course, the weapon was never found, even though each caravan had been briefly searched. And so it was assumed the attacker had secreted the knife where it couldn't be located that easily; not that a proper search of the immediate location or its adjacent area had been made by the police - a scant glance about the place - yes that was all it was.

It was Tom who was the criminal here; it was he who was considered to be an inconsequential undesirable of no fixed address; one who failed to comply with all of the bureaucratic demands society required; and so no more would be heard from the local authorities again, not regarding this particular incident, anyway.

'Well I am certainly not allowing you to return to your campsite... definitely not yet. You are coming home with me, Tom Hawke, so that I can look after you properly... for a few more days at least and I want no arguments from your direction either.'

Tom merely smiled at the order and failed miserably in his attempt at offering a firm protest.

Instead he gave in, reluctantly, but was rather thankful to have found himself securely settled in a comfortable bed at the big house by mid morning of the sixth day.

The first couple of days at Hyde Hall were not too bad for Tom. He had found it easy to be in Jacob's company and the two of them soon became closely attached; with the young lad spending as much time with his gypsy friend as his school lessons would allow. But even that was to be short lived.

'It ain't any use, Miss Jenny,' said Tom, in the early morning of the third day of his sojourn at the house, 'I can't stay here any longer under your roof. Me being such a blessed burden and an embarrassment to you... well it isn't right. So if you have no objections I shall be on my way, tomorrow, if that would suit you.'

Tom had stayed with Jenny too short a time as far as Jenny was concerned and she was saddened to learn of his eagerness to move on. But she dismissed the subject with a hasty, 'we'll see,' although she knew deep down he'd soon be gone; there would be no stopping him.

***

An hour later a gentle tapping was heard on the door of Bramble Bush Cottage.

After Jane Howe had answered the summoning call, she was taken aback to find Jenny standing alone in the doorway, with a somewhat drained look on her face.

'Jenny, what a wonderful surprise,' said Jane, and then, after she had registered her friend's unhappy state, she extended her welcome. 'Please come in my dear and allow me to get you a restorative; you look as though you could certainly do with one.'

'Jane, I'm terribly sorry for invading your privacy, unannounced, like this,' said Jenny, after she had entered the small sitting room, 'but I need some advice and you are about the only person I can turn to. Of course, I could easily have telephoned you but I suspect my calls are being monitored in some way by my mother via one of the staff, so I thought a quick visit to be much the safest way, besides the fresh air is a boon to me at the moment... I do hope you don't mind.'

'Jenny, of course I don't mind... you silly goose, it's a pleasure to see you... here, drink this,' said Jane, as she offered her friend a small brandy. Then, seating herself on the tiny settee, she said, 'come, Jenny, sit by me and tell me all.'

Jenny hesitantly seated herself beside her friend and commenced to unburden herself of all that had happened to Tom.

'My goodness, Jenny, what an awful thing to have happened to the poor man, is there anything I can do to help you?' Jenny shook her head as Jane continued. 'So Tom feels the need to leave you before he is, in your opinion, really in a fit state to do so and you are beside yourself in not knowing how to go about tempting him to stay, is that it?'

'Yes, Jane, that is precisely it. His wound still looks inflamed to me even though he's had his stitches removed, and I fear that if he isn't looked after properly... well, anything might happen. Doctors at the hospital aren't all that sympathetic you see; I mean he's only had a couple of doses of antibiotics as far as I know. And the police are worse than useless. Look Jane, Tom's attacker didn't finish what he set out to do, so who's to say he won't try again... and be more successful next time?'

Hearing this, Jane took Jenny's hand in her own and at the same time placed a comforting arm around her friend's shoulders as a wave of jealousy, brought about by Jenny's obvious feelings for the gypsy, engulfed her mind.

'Look Jenny would it be a help if I came and stayed with you for a few days and together we might be able to plant some sense into his silly mind... at least my being there will enable you to continue with the day to day running of the estate and look after Jacob properly at the same time. And I will be on hand ready to do whatever's necessary... what do you think?'

'I don't know Jane. Is that really such a good idea? Only the last thing I need right now is for people to start talking about me... you remember what happened when your sister stayed with you and all the flak you took from that little episode.'

'What is more important, Jenny, the health and safety of your friend or the idle tittle-tattle of gossipers, who have little else to do with their time?'

Jenny pondered the idea for quite a while.

'Thank you, Jane, maybe that's not such a bad idea after all,' she said, at last.

'Just give me a couple of minutes to throw a few things into a case then you can take me back to Hyde Hall with you.'

The two ladies rose from the settee simultaneously and as Jane placed her arms around Jenny, she said:

'Please Jenny, don't look so worried, everything will turn out OK' then she kissed her friend's forehead. This action sent alarm bells ringing in Jenny's mind and as Jane went to pack a few things feelings of regret overtook the mistress of Hyde Hall. But it was too late - the agreement had already been struck.

CHAPTER TWELVE

Within two hours of the yellow sports car leaving Hyde Hall it was seen to be returning; this time with Jane Howe seated by Jenny's side.

The ten or so mile drive had been pleasant enough, with the two ladies maintaining meaningful conversation throughout; that is, until they reached the big house.

Although the day was exceptionally bright, with the sun's rays shimmering down to accentuate the mansions splendour, the sensation possessing Jenny's mind at this point in time was anything but bright.

As soon as she was set to exit the car; even before that, in fact, an unexpected case of the jitters overtook her, causing far-reaching feelings of anxiety to swamp her usually placid mind and a redness to flush her cheeks.

It was all too obvious that something was disturbing the lady of Hyde Hall at the moment for she found herself staring out of the car's window in an extremely agitated fashion - and while the ladies were still silently seated, at that.

Jenny began to fidget intensely as she waited for a few more seconds to elapse but without a single word of explanation passing her lips.

It seems as though her greatest need at the moment was to enter her home as quickly as possible - scarcely being noticed would have been good - completely hidden from view, even better.

Jane, sensing that something was wrong, found no need to look in Jenny's direction to asses the agitation that loitered there, for Jenny's bout of the fidgets said it all.

It would appear Jane's intuitions were rather acute these days in so far as Jenny was concerned - or so she prided herself; and so she withheld her opinions and kept her eyes focused directly ahead, before and after they'd left the car.

No words were exchanged by either lady as they crossed the gravelled forecourt with Jenny, rather rudely, stepping out in front of Jane by at least a yard or two.

This embarrassing silence, it seems, was the direct result of some illogical frustration being felt by Jenny, for her usually concealed emotions were unmistakable at this instant. Even so, Jane was still none the wiser as to what the cause might be.

Maybe it was Jane, herself, being embarrassingly present

that was the reason of Jenny's plight; Jane had held her own suspicion that Jenny was reluctant to be seen in her company these days, anyway: most probably brought about by some sort of insecurity stemming from their previous encounter - she had no idea.

But whatever it was, Jane soon found herself being burdened with a similar lack of ease; and as they halved the distance to the portico this lack of ease suddenly intensified to a state of complete embarrassment as her suspicions, regarding Jenny's reluctance to be seen in her company, became exaggerated in her mind, which didn't sit at all well with Jane Howe.

But it wasn't Jane's presence that was responsible for the difficulty Jenny was experiencing at this moment in time, no, not at all; but the curtain movement and the figure staring out of one of the upstairs windows certainly had caused Jenny's blush to continue; and as they approached the Hall's entrance her questioning eyes were constantly focused in the direction of her home's upper region, scouring each and every window within her sight.

Jenny refused all words of welcome to Jane as they hastened through the wide open doorway where the new housekeeper was seen to have just arrived. And although Mary Pumphrey was heard to offer a cordial greeting to both ladies as they passed her by, the greeting was ignored by Jenny, in so as far as one could tell; for no word of gratitude was heard.

Even so, Jane did advance a nod of her head and a smile of sorts in the housekeeper's direction, despite the fact that Jenny's words of hospitality were missing.

All that aside, they did enter the great hall without further embarrassment whence the drawing room was gained in very short time.

As soon as the couple reached the drawing room, Jenny, still ignoring her friend and still with a significant amount of bile attending her features, summoned her housekeeper.

While they waited Jenny allowed her outrage to show even more; for quite some time in fact, so that in the end her blushing cheeks gave way to paleness, which was plainly caused by her rising temper taking control.

Even at this point no words of explanation were offered for Jenny's exhibition of instability or indeed her lack of hospitality and correctness; it was as if Jane should have known of the problem already, or at least read Jenny's mind in order to become aware.

It was a few minutes before the housekeeper was able to attend the summoning call by which time Jenny had managed to take on a slightly calmer air.

But why her earlier observation of a window peeper should cause Jenny such irrational behaviour was anyone's guess; after all no calamity had been caused to anyone because of it and nothing unpleasant had arisen.

But Jenny, showing her customary concern for other people's feelings, failed to see it that way.

"That sort of conduct is most rude and extremely intrusive. One should always respect the privacy of others and exercise all sensitivity needed in avoiding their embarrassment," would have been Jenny's advice to anyone so preoccupied with scrutinizing other people.

It now seemed essential for Jenny to examine the situation in her own mind - a little more closely, and a certain member of her staff, with a multitude of shortcomings attributed to them, was not excused.

Without there being a shred of evidence to support her theory, Jenny duly concluded that an amount of dubious goings-on had been set up by Margaret, before she'd left Hyde Hall, but in collusion with this particular member of staff. Consequently, the previously mentioned surveillance of Jenny's movements, organised by her own mother and which the unfamiliar female voice had disclosed to Jenny over the telephone, was, at this moment, uppermost in her mind.

Anyway, after Jenny had allowed her musings to fade she began to feel easier in herself and to such an extent that she was able to regain her composure almost unnoticed.

'Miss Pumphrey,' said Jenny, when the housekeeper had at last presented herself, 'this is Miss Jane Howe, a friend of the family. She will be staying with us for a few days; and so, if you would be so good as to have one of the guestrooms made ready for her, that will be lovely.

'I can have no idea who, without guessing of course, but someone had the audacity to scrutinise our arrival from one of the upper windows… unashamedly standing there and examining our every move, quite as if we had no business in being here at all and not giving a hoot who should see them. Would it be too much to ask you to initiate some tentative enquiry on my behalf?'

"Aha, at last the mysterious mind-disturber is now to be revealed," thought Jane, and at the same time she was clearly seen to be so relieved by this disclosure that her own agitation became settled immediately.

'Yes of course; a room will be prepared at once Miss Kent.'

'As far as the matter regarding the irregularity you observed upon your arrival is concerned, Miss Kent; I have already offered a brief word of warning to the guilty person involved... the moment I made my discovery in fact; and, I might add, it was to a member of staff who should have known better. I passed the particular room as I came down to greet you and in time to catch the individual red handed. Up till now I have had no further opportunity to add to the comments I have already made, but I will berate that person in a forthright manner as soon as I am able; and so I shall expect no additional problems from that direction. Any further indiscretions of that sort, and from the person in question, will be forcefully dealt with, I can assure you of that, Miss Kent.'

After hearing this reply Jenny felt even more relieved, and, not unlike Jane, she also relaxed her body and its extremities totally and presented a smile of appreciation to her housekeeper for her proficiency.

'May I offer either of you refreshment or will that be all Miss Kent.'

'No, that will be all, thank you... Miss Pumphrey.'

Mary Pumphrey walked unhurriedly towards the door and then as if some snippet of awareness was concerning her mind she turned and walked slowly back again to face her mistress.

'Miss Kent, I can have no way of knowing if I am justified in bringing the matter to your attention or whether you are already aware, but your houseguest left Hyde Hall in a taxi soon after you left us earlier this morning. Master Jacob, I hasten to add, left with the gentleman. I assumed that to be in order Miss Kent.'

Jenny was dumbfounded; but she skilfully masked her amazement with a smile.

'Yes Miss Pumphrey, that was quite in order; but thank you for bringing it to my attention.'

After Mary Pumphrey had finally left the room Jenny turned to face Jane with a look of rage clouding her face. The look, of course, was intended to discourage Jane from making any unsavoury comments she may have had in mind to utter. And although Jane failed to respond with even the faintest of expressions, Jenny was prompt in replying to the unspoken criticism:

'Don't say it Jane, I am already aware how stupid I was to have left Tom on his own, knowing full well that his intention was to leave this place and at the first opportunity possible, but at least I know where he has gone and where I can find him.'

***

A mere three minutes saw the yellow Lotus Elan speeding along the same five mile stretch of road it had travelled twelve or so days earlier, when Noah had been its passenger. And its driver was showing similar feelings of concern now as had harassed her then.

The motor screeched to a standstill as soon as it reached its destination.

A group of horses drawing an equivalent number of caravans were seen to be leaving the overgrown field, which, of course, came as no surprise to Jenny.

The leading caravan appeared to be undertaking a difficult manoeuvre over some hazardous ruts that had been deeply worn in the field's entrance. These deep ruts, it seems, had been brought about by the continuous use of weighty farm vehicles over the years and were now beleaguering the leading caravan; thereby causing it to be in an unstable situation.

Atop this particular vardo and with a fistful of reins sat Tom Hawke with a look of caution on his face that expressed the intricacy of the exercise he was attempting to perform.

Jacob was seated by his side.

Jenny quickly exited her car, slammed the door firmly behind her and strode over to the caravan - now motionless - and with a severe look emblazoning her lovely face she asked forcefully:

'Where in blazers do you think you're going Tom Hawke and with my son as well? That wound of yours affected your head and confused your way of thinking, has it?'

Jenny, it would appear, had found some anger left over from her earlier difficulty that the morning had brought about - and she wasn't slow in using it.

The two men in her life, father and son, looked down at Jenny with widish grins spreading their faces, as impish looks were exchanged between the two of them - almost immaturely.

'It's OK Mother. Tom felt the need to be on the road again... rather than lounging about in bed at home.

'But, I have managed to convince him to return to the estate and stay much closer to the house where we can keep an eye on things... from a distance... that's all.

'Before I forget, he has said I can stay with him sometimes... I hope that's alright as well,' called out Jacob, as his grin widened still further.

Jenny failed to answer her son; she not wishing to add to the fury she had already discharged. Instead she turned and smiled inwardly to herself; then went back to her car.

Jane had heard all that had been said and claimed Jenny's hand the moment her friend seated herself behind the steering wheel.

'That sounds like the perfect solution to all your worries Jenny. What a wonderfully clever boy you have for a son.'

'Yes, not bad for one so young... I suppose.'

A moment of hesitancy and disappointment crossed Jane's face as she made the flattering remark.

'I don't expect you will need me to stay at Hyde Hall now that your problems have been sorted for you or will my immediate leaving provide you with an even bigger embarrassment than my staying?'

'Yes Jane, stay tonight at least; let's gives all those silly gossip mongers their money's worth, shall we?'

***

It took the gypsy procession a further one and a half hours to arrive back at the Hyde Hall estate and a further hour for them to settle and build a huge campfire for themselves.

During the final hour Jacob had run excitedly to the house to check on his mother's frame of mind and to ensure himself that all was well with her. He found her in the drawing room sipping tea with Jane.

Since Jenny had made no reply to the final part of Jacob's conversation with her earlier, he was a mite concerned and he felt he may have upset his mother in some small way. But the moment he came face to face with Jenny the look on his young face expressed his love in such a way that she was almost reduced to tears.

'I'm sorry if my scheme took you by surprise Mother and has upset you in any way, but as you left here this morning without saying where you were going or how long you would be away, and as Tom said he was leaving anyway, I took the initiative and did what I thought was right and what Uncle Hamish would have told me to do, had he been here.

'Am I forgiven? They'll only be staying a couple of weeks anyway, and then they'll all be gone again so you don't have to worry that much. And as I have suggested they stay much closer to the house this time... well, any would-be attacker will have to think twice if he knows he can be seen from here.'

'Jacob' you did perfectly well, my darling… and to tell you the truth… I am really proud of you. Will you go to Tom now and ask him to come and see me once he is settled; I am of the opinion he may be interested in what I have to say to him.'

Jacob smiled widely in anticipation but left without saying another word.

***

Jenny and Jane were still seated in the drawing room an hour later when Mary Pumphrey appeared at the door seeking Jenny's attention.

'Your erstwhile houseguest has arrived, Miss Kent, asking for a meeting with you. I have shown him into the library; I hope that meets with your approval.'

'Yes, thank you, Miss Pumphrey, just tell him I shall be with him in a couple of minutes, will you?'

Mary Pumphrey left as Jenny turned to Jane.

'I don't feel I can hold out any longer, Jane. Tom has to know of his being Jacob's father sometime and so it is my intention to see to it now; that way he will feel more responsible toward Jacob when and if he visits or stays with him. I shall tell Jacob later, after I have assessed Tom's reaction; but I shall say nothing to Jacob if Tom's response isn't that good.'

'Ok Jenny, I'm sure you know what's best. I wonder you haven't said something before this time though; I know I would have done; I should have thought that you owed him that much,' said Jane, with a somewhat cynical tone to her voice that was both deliberate and insolently annoying.

Jenny responded unexpectedly.

'Yes well, you're not a mother are you Jane, so you couldn't be expected to have the sensitive feelings of motherhood.'

Jane made no reply but smiled inwardly at the slight but seemingly unfortunate situation she had purposely created; she knew how she would handle it from now on and it wasn't at this moment and it wasn't here.

Jenny found Tom in the library standing and looking out of the closed window.

'Tom, please come and sit by me, I have a matter of great importance to tell you and I am not at all sure how you will react to it.'

'It surely can't be that bad, Miss Jenny, or I would have

detected any problem between us before this time.'

'Tom,' said Jenny, as she clasped the gypsy's hand to smooth it soothingly, 'I really don't know how I should start my confession to you because it is a very personal and private one and strange in the extreme.

'You remember the night of that terrible storm, the night when you sheltered me in your caravan. It was truly an awful night, wasn't it, but one that turned out to be the most important and wonderful night of my life.'

'Yes, Miss Jenny, how could I ever forget a wild night like that? But it was your own silly fault, I told you so at the time... if my memory serves me right; you should never have followed me like you did, you must have realised that as well as me.'

'Yes, I know all that. But Tom, when I went to sleep on your bed, you held me so very close that I felt more secure than I had ever felt before and as I closed my eyes I immediately fell asleep and I had no... '

'No need for you to say anymore Miss Jenny, for I know exactly what happened as we lay sleeping together that night as well as you... and I know too that Jacob is my very own. Why, it's like looking into my own eyes when I look into his; and the feelings we share between the two of us are so intense it's as if we are joined together, so obvious is our love for one another.

'I told Jacob earlier this morning. All of my theories about his conception came out... that we are father and son; and I explained all about the wonderful night you describe so well; and I can tell you here and now, Miss Jenny, he couldn't be happier.'

Jenny was caught in an immediate dilemma by this revelation and her extreme annoyance was seen in the expression of her staring eyes. She was confused; and her own mother's personality seemed to take over her vocal chords at this moment.

'What? Do you mean to tell me you have divulged your suspicions to my son without first consulting me? Have you no propriety at all? That is not the way to handle a matter of such delicacy... you surely ought to have known better than that Tom Hawke; you ought to be ashamed of yourself. Any explanation, if one is needed, would be my responsibility not yours. How could you have taken this upon yourself and dealt with it as badly as this... and without taking my own opinion into account either?'

Jenny was both livid and disappointed with Tom, for although she had yearned for her long held secret to be out in the open there were ways of achieving it and this wasn't one of them; she felt she, the mother, should have been the one doing the disclosing - not he the father.

Although she knew deep down she was being unreasonable, as unreasonable as her mother would have been over a matter with far fewer implications involved than this, but she felt it right for her point of view to persist.

It was as if Jenny had allowed her anger to spill over from the earlier problems of the day - yet again - and to be added to those particular difficulties in an unseemly way; but it was done now and it was fruitless to go over the thing again. All the same, she had no intentions in allowing any admissions of defeat to show through - she was adamant about that.

But as her anger began to subside it was replaced by pangs of remorse - more or less straight away, in fact; but not wishing for her regrets to come to the surface just yet, she remained silent, all the time wondering how she could retrieve the situation without losing sight of her own principles - or her demands.

Bearing this in mind, Jenny failed to allow her expressions to alter a jot or for her to budge from the stance she had already adopted, not straightaway. And so she churned over, in her mind, how best she could allow a more contrite attitude to be shown to Tom - a change of heart even - that would be acceptable to her gypsy man; with minimal discredit to her would do.

But she had cogitated in vain, for nothing sprang to mind that didn't show her disapproval of what Tom had done without her foolishness alone to exist.

Tom had looked dumfounded for all the time Jenny was criticising him, though he didn't allow his eyes to stray from hers for a second, and he deliberately held his peace till she was done.

Then, when all was quiet once again he said:

'I'm very sorry if I have overstepped the mark Miss Jenny; I seem to have become caught up in the moment of it all. Of course I told our son not to say a word to you; not for the minute and that you would tell him yourself in your own way and in your own time... but not before you were good and ready; but I did say he wouldn't have to wait that long as I had already sensed what was on your mind and all you have just told me. I'm only sorry for upsetting you Miss Jenny... that's all. I didn't mean to hurt you in any way, please believe me when I tell you that, but I felt Jacob had to know sooner or later and that it would be better coming from me; after all, that way he would know I weren't ashamed of him and had no wish to shirk my duty towards him... not in any way at all.'

Jenny flung her arms around the neck of her gypsy man and held him near, kissed his hands and face and then more passionately, his mouth.

'Steady on Miss Jenny my chest is still painful you know and I don't want any more damage doing to it... now do I....'

***

Jenny wasn't at all sorry to have the day over and done, although her heart was gladdened to have shared all with Tom at last.

Dinner had been strained, with Jane hardly saying a word as she waited patiently for the outcome of Jenny's meeting with Tom to be shared with her, and was rather disappointed to have received nothing. Jenny had asked Tom to stay for dinner but she knew what his answer would be... even before she'd asked.

Jenny decided the day had been filled with more than she could take and so immediately dinner was over and she had finished the final sips of her brandy she discourteously asked to be excused and went to bed.

Jenny felt sadly alone as she stared up at the ceiling of her bedroom; she knowing that Tom was no more than a few hundred yards away, but for all the good it did them both, the distance might easily have been a hundred miles.

She considered quietly, too, what her life would be like with her gypsy man being around the place for most of the time, and with him hindering her daily routine for the whole of that while. And she smiled, inwardly, at such a vision of the future ever being possible, for she knew that no one would be able to possess him - not completely - not in the hopes of tying him down to a more subdued way of living at any rate - no, not even the mother of his son would be able to do that.

A gentle tapping on the door interrupted Jenny's aimless thoughts and so she got up from her bed to open the door to find Jane standing there clad in a sparsely cut chiffon nightdress with an open negligee hiding nothing but revealing everything Jane wanted to be revealed.

Her posture was one of presumptuousness; waiting to be of service - or so she assumed - as if, by some strange decree, she should be invited in at once without a second thought being considered and for her to be warmly welcomed with open arms.

'Oh, hello Jane, what can I do for you?' said Jenny, not budging in the slightest.

Jane was taken aback by Jenny's negative reception, this wasn't the reaction she had anticipated or indeed had hoped for.

But ignoring the unwanted response she entered the bedroom anyway and closed the door firmly behind her with the kick of her heel, thereby making Jenny feel as out of her depth as she looked.

After Jane had pushed her way into the room she attempted to take Jenny in her arms, but, because of Jenny's reluctance, the move was inelegantly made. Eventually Jane's persistence took over and her action became more determined and she held Jenny as she had held her on her previous visit to Hyde Hall, when they had said their final farewells to one another.

'Jenny I just couldn't let the sun go down without telling you how sorry I am that I allowed thoughtless words of censure to escape my mouth on our arrival from seeing the gypsies; it really was an unnecessary criticism on my part... please forgive me.'

'I thought nothing of it Jane,' said Jenny, sharply, 'and so there is really no need for an apology at all.

'Please Jane, I have had a long and tiring day and I am not in the mood to be responsive to your advances. As much as I appreciate your kindness and your support I have no intentions in being a replacement for my father to you... I have to tell you that I am deeply in love with Tom and I have asked him to marry me. So you must understand from what I say, Jane, any affectionate relationship between you and me is totally wrong and out of the question.' And then, seeing Jane's despondency, Jenny panicked, as she added, 'Jane, please forgive me. Say we can still be friends, for I value your friendship more than you can imagine and much more than I can say.'

There was no immediate response from Jane after the finality of Jenny's words - only acute embarrassment existed between the two of them. Eventually Jane released Jenny from her hold and turned towards the door.

'Please Jane don't leave me like this... please say we can still be friends.'

'Yes of course Jenny, I am sure we can, but first... please allow me to deal with your rejection as best I can and in my own way.'

***

Jenny returned Jane to her home in Basham Killington the following morning - early the following morning, to be precise. Nothing was mentioned about the singularly improper and ridiculous event the previous night had so foolishly brought about - with all of that embarrassment still floating about the place how could there possibly have been.

Jenny was hoping the dust would settle quickly for all their sakes - and as for Jane - well, who knows what was going on in her head, but whatever it was Jenny didn't wish to know too much about it - or be a part of it. She had Tom in her life now, whatever that may mean. For as already stated above, it would be a hopeless task for the mother of a gypsy's child to tie the father to a life of boring normality; no matter how strong the bond that existed between them may have been.

***

It was mid July before Jane saw Jenny again. She had noticed the couple, Jenny and Jacob, on the far side of a street, just as they were entering a particular coffee shop that she knew they always frequented when they were in Bournemouth. But not wishing to promote any further embarrassment she turned her head to scrutinize the nearest shop window.

Jenny had noticed the rebuff and was about to cross the road to reassure her former friend that all in the past had been forgotten when she saw a monster in the form of Barnabas Bell as he sidled up to Jane and placed his loathsome hand on her bare shoulder.

Jenny gathered pace as she crossed the street and was in time to witness the repugnant words that issued from the hateful man's mouth.

'Ah, Miss Jane Howe, I do believe. Now, you won't know me at all, Miss Howe, but I surely know all about you, yes indeed I do... I knows all about you and the hateful sexual liberties you have taken with my intended and how you visits her room to have your wicked way with her; forcing your attentions on her in an unnatural way, like you do, and without her wanting to be near you as well.

'You see Miss Howe; there is great love between Miss Kent and me, though many a time I hid it from her. But many are the times we have done things together to show how much we love one another. She is the dearest thing in the world to me Miss Howe and I should hate for a filthy creature like you to get your hands on her... so that you come between us.'

Barney's left eye was unusually still as he made these evil insinuations.

'Now you're not the only one to try to steal my love away from me Miss Howe, no indeed not… but the other one, well, he got all what was coming to him… yes he surely did. You see I knew he had feelings for my beloved when he welcomed her to the camp. They didn't see me but I saw them alright. And so Miss Howe if you don't want to end up in hospital or the grave you must stay away from the love of my life and keep your filthy hands off of her. Do you understand me Miss Howe?'

Jane was beginning to tremble with fear as the obnoxious man continued his evil threat. But no reply broke her lips. 'I said… do you understand me, Miss Howe?' The monster repeated his demanding question more forcefully the second time. 'I hope you do, because I should hate for you to end up the same way as that dirty gypsy did. I shall surely know if you touches her again, Miss Howe, for I have my spies in Hyde Hall, and I am kept well informed of the entire goings on in that den of filth… you can be sure of that. You must listen close to me, Miss Howe, and do what I tell you, then you'll be alright… do you hear me clearly Miss Howe?'

'Yes Mr Bell'' said Jenny, as she instantly intervened on Jane's behalf, 'I'm quite sure she heard you and so did I and my son also, he heard you too; the three of us heard every word that slithered from that foul, evil mouth of yours. You don't appear to have much luck when you decide to solicit ladies in this manner do you, Mr Bell? You may remember being overheard in Lincoln as you accosted me that time; so I think you had better come with us for a friendly visit to the local police station; they will be more than glad to make your acquaintance there, Mr Bell, I'm quite sure of that.'

Barnabas Bell didn't wait around for a visit to some police station, whether it was local or far away and no matter how friendly the visit was deemed to have been - he wasn't at all interested. And so he turned round swiftly and took to his heals like the proverbial bat….

Jane was still trembling when Jenny put her arms of comfort around her and she invited her into the coffee shop she and Jacob had been about to enter.

After Jenny had explained to Jane how she had been plagued by the insufferable Bell since her early days the three of them went directly to the police station.

***

Summer was at its height and education at Jacob's place of learning had been placed on hold for the annual school summer holidays.

The gypsies were still situated fairly close to Hyde Hall but not close enough to be conspicuous and Jenny had visited Tom at every opportunity and together they had formed a bond beyond their wildest dreams, even though they had still not spent the night together as they had those stormy hours of darkness.

It was just before lunch time on this particular day and Jacob and Fredrick had returned from a seemingly exciting visit to Tom's camp; and the two boys, both looking enlivened by their visit, searched Hyde Hall for Jenny. They found her in the kitchen enjoying the company of Alf Abrams.

'Mother!' exclaimed Jacob, after acknowledging Alf Abram's presence. 'Tom is about ready to move on now and he has invited both Fredrick and me to spend a few weeks with him; he says it won't be a problem to bring us back well before school starts again and we will both be able to do our homework there. Of course we realise we have to get Fredrick's father's permission first, though Fredrick doesn't seem to think that will be a problem. What do you say Mother? Do you think it will be OK for us to go?'

'Well, as that imbecile Bell is now out of harm's way I have no worries on that score, so yes it will be great for you to spend time with your father and experience a freer way of life.'

Jenny had found no hesitation or shame in using Tom's connection with Jacob, not now that the world knew all about it; and she was relieved to use such an intimacy as this on every occasion and as often as she possibly could.

'When does Tom expect to go?'

'Tomorrow; he said for us to be at his vardo by eight in the morning so they can make an early start, if that's alright with you.'

A sleepless night preceded Jacobs's departure. Fred Worth had delivered his son at Hyde Hall's steps before the required time and Jenny and Fred had waved the two boys off; both with similar smiling faces, albeit tainted with a mite of apprehension.

As Fred moved his jeep away, Jenny was distracted by the sight of a cardboard box that had been deposited by the side of the wide doorway which she had failed to notice earlier. She stooped and opened it carefully - a little unsure of what she might find inside. And there, laying on a small piece of blanket was the prettiest Persian Blue kitten she had ever seen and on the inside of the lid was scrawled:

"Bye then young Jenny; see you again sometime; soon I hope - 'til then my love will be forever yours - Tom."

THE CONCLUSION

It was the day following Jacob's departure with his father that Jenny was delivered the sad news of the death of Janet Nunn, her fond Uncle's housekeeper. Jenny had no sooner entered her cluttered study when the black telephone on her desk relayed the news to her.

After quickly packing a few clothes, she hastened to Lincolnshire to be by her uncle's side and for them both, in unison, to perform all the closing necessities for the wisest of ladies whom they both so admired and loved.

No words of expressed concern are ever enough to take away the pain of such a loss as this but both Jenny and her uncle did what they could to support each other, despite their despondency.

Janet's frail body was laid to rest next to the final resting place of Jenny's Great Aunt Sarah so that, as one, they may find happiness in each other's society.

After pleading with her Uncle Hamish to spend some time at Hyde Hall so that the two of them would be able to comfort each other and mourn the passing of the most dearly loved housekeeper together, Sir Hamish, after initially dismissing the proposal, finally relented and agreed to the spending of a few days in Dorset.

Sir Hamish Kent visited Jane Howe on just the one occasion while he was in Dorset; a courtesy call was the intention of the visit, and Jane, recognising and accepting the call to be no more than that, was happy to receive her lover's brother and to be in his company for a short while. Neither of them had looked for a relationship to develop; nothing of the sort had crossed the mind of either one of them anyway.

Jane was fully aware she had lost the love of her life in the losing of Angus and no man, not even her lover's twin could possibly take his place. She had even sought, in a couple of misguided moments, the love of her lover's daughter hoping she would return her father's affection to her but that turned out to be a disaster of the greatest magnitude and she shuddered with disgust at what she considered to be her final attempt at happiness.

But all was not lost for the hapless lady, who might easily have spent the rest of her days in complete loneliness, for upon reflection she realised that although Jenny couldn't possibly be a replacement for her father the opposite was certainly available; for Jane could be a replacement for Angus to Jenny; and the more she thought about it the more the prospect of being a pseudo parent excited her.

For loneliness is oft a mournful place in which to be ensnared. It is a place where desolate people go to seek a fond connection and to gather world approval as the mother of the young. Then to nurture that loving friendship, which others deem unreal, until the falseness fades away and love alone remain.

Mary Pumphrey, in her quest to eradicate all the wrongdoings that arose, from time to time, at the big house, received word that Agnes was acting as a furtive observer for Margaret, the former mistress of Hyde Hall. Upon the fruitful investigation of these misdemeanours she dismissed Agnes on the spot thereby allowing her to seek employment at the Melchamp residence - which she was openly pleased to do and where she was welcomed with opened arms.

Barnabas Bell, for attempted murder and for other indiscretions served a lonely spell in prison where his left eye found no delight in its wanderings anymore; in fact, it seemed to be stuck for ever in the corner of its socket, and all because there were no fantasies available to release it anymore.

The intended short spell that Sir Hamish had proposed took slightly longer than was originally intended and within two full months of his stay at Hyde Hall he had built a fondness for the shapely Mary Pumphrey who was requested to change her location, yet again, in favour of employment at The Old House in Brenton which left Jenny with a huge problem to overcome.

It was late one sunny afternoon, when a caller, not wanting to be occupied by total loneliness again, caused a gentle tapping to be heard on the door of Bramble Bush Cottage:

For loneliness is oft a mournful place in which to be ensnared. It is where all manner of orphans go, no matter what their age, and so consent to a surrogate's care whilst eagerness remain.